THE RIVALS OF
Dracula

Other Pocket Essentials by Nick Rennison

Freud and Psychoanalysis
Peter Mark Roget: The Man Who Became a Book
Robin Hood: Myth, History & Culture
A Short History of Polar Exploration

THE RIVALS OF
Dracula

Stories from
The GOLDEN AGE of GOTHIC HORROR

edited and introduced by

NICK RENNISON

NO EXIT PRESS

First published in 2015 by No Exit Press,
an imprint of Oldcastle Books Ltd,
PO Box 394, Harpenden,
Herts, AL5 1XJ
Noexit.co.uk

ISBN
978-1-84344-632-3 (print)
978-1-84344-633-0 (epub)
978-1-84344-634-7 (kindle)
978-1-84344-635-4 (pdf)

2 4 6 8 10 9 7 5 3 1

Typeset by Avocet Typeset, Somerton, Somerset
in 11.25pt Bembo
Printed and bound in Denmark by Nørhaven, Denmark

Acknowledgements

Firstly, I would like to thank Ion Mills, Claire Watts, Frances Teehan, Clare Quinlivan and everybody at Oldcastle Books for their hard work and help as I was compiling this anthology. Thanks too to Elsa Mathern for the excellent cover design and to Jayne Lewis and Irene Goodacre for the copy-editing and proof-reading skills which enabled them to pick up many mistakes which would have otherwise gone uncorrected. However, my greatest thanks, as always, go to my wife Eve who is an ever-present source of love and encouragement.

CONTENTS

Introduction

In 1897, the Irish author Bram Stoker published a novel which has become the most famous of all vampire stories. The novel was, of course, *Dracula*. It is almost needless to note that Stoker did not invent the figure of the vampire. Indeed, belief in creatures which return from the grave to prey upon their living victims or which suck the blood and the life from human beings seems to have existed for millennia. The Edimmu in Sumerian mythology, the Strix in Ancient Greece and Rome, the Vetala in Hindu mythology all have attributes that link them to the vampire. Fast forward to Europe in the Middle Ages and there are plenty of stories of vampire-like creatures from England to Hungary. They continued to be recorded for several centuries and, even in the supposedly enlightened eighteenth century, reports of real-life vampires flooded out of Eastern Europe. The idea of vampirism seems to have been particularly strong in Slavic folklore and it was in Transylvania that Stoker chose to place the homeland of his own vampire.

The name 'Dracula' he took from a historical figure, Vlad III, Prince of Wallachia, born in 1431. Vlad's father had been given the honorary name of 'Dracul' (the Wallachian word for 'dragon') and Vlad was described as 'Dracula' or 'son of the dragon'. Schooled in the brutal politics of Eastern Europe in the mediaeval era, Vlad Dracula was renowned for the bloodthirsty punishments he inflicted on his enemies. During several spells as ruler, which finally ended with his death in battle in 1476, he gained the nickname Vlad the Impaler because of his fondness for impaling those who opposed him on wooden stakes and leaving their bodies to terrorise any others who might think of taking up arms against him. One chronicler reports seeing twenty thousand men, women and children who had suffered this punishment. After his death, Vlad Dracula rapidly became a byword for cruelty and books describing his misdeeds with alluring titles like *The Frightening and Truly Extraordinary Story of a Wicked Blood-drinking Tyrant Called Prince Dracula* were published in the Balkans and further afield. Some scholars claim that Vlad Dracula has been unjustly stigmatised. His cruelties were no worse than those of many other mediaeval rulers whose reputations have not suffered as his has done. In Romania he is seen as a significant figure in the nation's history who built a strong and independent state of Wallachia and defended it against the Turks. In the rest of the world he is fated to be remembered because, one day in the 1890s, Bram Stoker read of him in a history of Eastern Europe and decided to borrow his name for the vampiric anti-hero of a novel he was writing.

Stoker did not invent the vampire and nor was he the first writer to make use of the creature in his work. The literary vampire first makes an appearance in eighteenth-century poetry, originally in Germany and, towards the end of the century, in England. An obscure German poet, Heinrich August Ossenfelder, published 'Der Vampir' in 1748, a short poem which reflected interest at the time in a series of reports from Eastern Europe and the Balkans of vampire activity in the Austrian Empire. Ossenfelder seems to have introduced the vampire into European literature and other German poets, most notably Goethe in 'The Bride of Corinth', followed his example. In England, a vampire is a peripheral character in Robert Southey's *Thalaba the Destroyer* and Coleridge's unfinished *Christabel* can be interpreted as a vampire romance.

Romantic poets also had a role to play in the appearance of the vampire in prose fiction. In the summer of 1816, Byron and Shelley, together with Shelley's soon-to-be wife Mary, were staying at the Villa Diodati in the Swiss village of Cologny. Conversation turned frequently to the supernatural and all three began to write stories on the subject. The only one that was finished was Mary Shelley's *Frankenstein*. However, Byron did produce a fragment of a novel, which found its way into print (against the poet's wishes) in 1819. What was published does suggest that Byron intended to write a vampire story and his personal physician John Polidori, who was also present at the Villa Diodati, took inspiration from what little had been written. Polidori created his own supernatural tale which was published as *The Vampyre* in the same year. Confusingly, it first appeared under Byron's name, presumably in order to increase its commercial appeal, but Polidori soon laid claim to it and his authorship was acknowledged in later editions.

Polidori followed romantic tradition by dying young in 1821 at the age of only twenty-five but his book lived on. In the words of Christopher Frayling, in an introduction to a 1990s anthology of vampire literature, his novella is 'the first story successfully to fuse the disparate elements of vampirism into a coherent literary genre'. It was popular enough to be plagiarised in copycat stories, adapted into plays and even set to music. Heinrich Marschner's *Der Vampyr* of 1828 took one of the dramas cobbled together from Polidori's work and transformed it into an opera which is still occasionally performed today. Over the next decade and a half there were one or two noteworthy examples of vampire literature (the 1841 Russian novella *Oupyr* by Alexei Tolstoy, a distant cousin of the more famous Leo, is an interesting curiosity) but the most significant development came in the mid-1840s.

At the time, a new audience for cheap, sensationalist reading matter was developing and the so-called 'penny dreadful' had emerged to cater for it. One of the most successful of the penny dreadful serials, first published between 1845 and 1847 and eventually running to more than half a million words, was *Varney the Vampire*. Most probably written by a prolific hack author named James Malcolm Rymer (who may also have had a hand in the first story to feature the demon barber Sweeney Todd) this was what a recent writer has described as 'a rambling gore-fest' in which the vampire Sir Francis Varney regularly indulges his lust for human blood. Actually sub-titled 'The Feast of Blood', Varney's bloodsucking adventures were immensely popular with their target readership (broadly speaking, the newly literate urban working class) and introduced a number of standard ideas about fictional vampires that have survived to the present day. Varney was, for example, one of the first vampires to come equipped with fangs, the better to get at his favourite sustenance. In pursuit of one victim, he 'seizes her neck in his fang-like teeth – a gush of blood, and a hideous sucking noise follows'.

Across Europe in the decades to follow, writers produced vampire novels. Some were as lurid as the tales of Varney; others were more subtle and sophisticated. The French novelist Paul Féval, a rival of Dumas in historical fiction, wrote a trilogy (*Le Chevalier Ténèbre*, *La Vampire* and *La Ville Vampire*) which has been translated into English by the science fiction and horror writer Brian Stableford; in Germany the prolific travel writer and novelist Hans Wachenhusen published *Der Vampyr* in 1878 which is set in Bulgaria under the rule of the Ottoman Empire and features a former Orthodox priest as its villain.

In English, the best-known vampire fiction by far of this period is *Carmilla*, a novella by Sheridan Le Fanu which was serialised in a magazine in 1871 and published in a collection of short works entitled *In a Glass Darkly* the following year. Born into a Huguenot family long resident in Dublin and related on his mother's side to the playwright Sheridan, Le Fanu trained as a lawyer but soon turned to journalism and fiction. He published more than a dozen novels, including *Uncle Silas* and *The House by the Church Yard*, and became renowned for his ghost stories. *Carmilla*, with its tale of the unsettling relationship between the narrator Laura and the enigmatic title character, was not the first work of vampire fiction in which the main vampiric protagonist is female but it has become the most influential. On screen, it has provided the inspiration for a wide variety of works from

Hammer horror films to YouTube web series. And in the two decades immediately after its publication it influenced other writers, including most notably Le Fanu's fellow Irishman Bram Stoker. Names in the later novel echo the earlier book (Rheinfeldt in *Carmilla*, Renfield in *Dracula*); the lonely castle in Styria which is the setting for Le Fanu's story is pushed even further east and made even more remote when it is reimagined as Dracula's castle in Stoker's novel; the descriptions of the vampiric women in the two tales (Carmilla in the earlier work, Lucy Westenra in the later) are similar. Ideas about repressed sexual desire, implicit in *Dracula*, are, bearing in mind the constraints of the Victorian era, closer to the surface in Le Fanu's book. And, even more shockingly, the desires are lesbian.

Dracula very clearly drew on Le Fanu's earlier book but it contains the vampire who would soon overshadow all other literary vampires. Who exactly was its creator? Abraham 'Bram' Stoker was born in Dublin in 1847 and originally worked as a civil servant in the city. His first published book was the less than exciting volume, *The Duties of Clerks of Petty Sessions in Ireland*. In 1876, Stoker, a great theatre-lover, met the legendary Victorian actor Henry Irving and, two years later, he gave up his civil service career to become Irving's manager at the Lyceum Theatre in London. In London, he began to publish short stories and novels, often with a supernatural theme. His most famous novel did win praise on its first publication in May 1897. Sir Arthur Conan Doyle wrote to Stoker to say how much he had enjoyed the book calling it 'the very best story of *diablerie* which I have read for many years'. The *Daily Mail* reviewer thought it a better book than Mary Shelley's *Frankenstein*. Yet other reviewers at the time were dismissive. 'It reads at times,' one wrote, 'like a mere series of grotesquely incredible events.' The book was not a bestseller and, thanks to mistakes in registering its copyright, Stoker made little money from it. He continued to publish further fiction including *The Jewel of Seven Stars*, a story of mummies, reincarnation and ancient Egyptian curses, and

The Lair of the White Worm, a tale of ancient evil that was fated to be modernised and made into a fantastically bad but curiously enjoyable film by Ken Russell in the 1980s. When Stoker died in London on 20 April 1912 he was not a rich man and Dracula had not yet become the archetypal figure of sinister power and allure which we know today. It was the twentieth-century adaptations, revisions, sequels and re-tellings of his story, most notably those on film, which were to turn the Count into legend.

So famous has Dracula become that it is all too easy to believe that he was the only fictional vampire of his day. Nothing could be further from the truth. There was something about the figure of the vampire that appealed to the imaginations of late Victorian and Edwardian readers as much as it does, in different ways, to so many people today. This anthology attempts to reflect the diversity of vampire stories that flourished in the two decades before and the two decades after the publication of Stoker's iconic tale. The authors range from writers like EF Benson and MR James who are rightly renowned for the literary qualities of their supernatural fiction to those like the Askews, husband and wife, and the Prichards (aka the Herons), mother and son, who have been more or less forgotten. The Askews and the Prichards, like other writers such as Richard Marsh whose work features in the anthology, made their livings by producing stories for the vast number of weekly and monthly magazines that proliferated in the period. They were not literary stylists and they were often obliged to pour out fiction at such a rate that quantity became as important as quality but they aimed always to write exciting and readable narratives and they mostly succeeded. What can be termed 'weird' fiction was a very important part of the entertainment served up by the story magazines and the vampires took their places alongside the ghosts, ghouls and supernatural creatures of all kinds which populated their pages.

These vampires reflect a variety of turn-of-the-century anxieties and interests. Readers will notice just how many of them are voracious women who prey on initially unsuspecting men. Whether traditional vampires like Hume Nisbet's vampire maid or homicidal maniacs like Mary Brooker in Richard Marsh's 'The Mask' or psychic vampires like Mrs Tierce in Phil Robinson's 'Medusa', the female of the species is often deadlier than the male. It's not too much of an imaginative leap to link this preponderance of she-vampires with the rise of the 'New Woman', the self-assertive feminist of the 1880s and 1890s, and the concerns about sexuality and the relationship between the sexes that she aroused. The classic vampire story is wary of the foreign as well as the feminine. In *Carmilla*, the title character who threatens the English heroine Laura comes from the backwaters of the Austro-Hungarian Empire; in *Dracula*, emphasis is laid upon the distance from the safety of home that Jonathan Harker has travelled to reach the Count's castle and the Count's arrival at Whitby marks a terrible intrusion of violent otherness into the ordered society of late Victorian England.

Perhaps more than anything, however, the stories selected in *The Rivals of Dracula* show an awareness of the power of history. In tale after tale of the fifteen in the book, the past is not past. Like the undead Dracula it returns to trouble people in the present. Both the narrator of HB Marriott Watson's 'The Stone Chamber' and his friend Warrington are frighteningly influenced by the violent events that took place nearly two centuries earlier in the room of its title. In Mary Cholmondeley's 'Let Loose', the remote Yorkshire village of Wet Waste-on-the-Wolds seems trapped in the past and the evil spirit of an extinct family is accidentally released to prey once more on the villagers. MR James's stories are permeated by his ambivalent fascination with history and 'Count Magnus' shows the dangers of prying too insistently into its nooks and corners.

The stories I have included in *The Rivals of Dracula* reveal a wide variety of vampires at work. There is an undead Icelander who fights with one of the heroes of the sagas ('Grettir at Thorhall-stead'); there is a vampiric spirit which takes over the physical form of an ancient mummy ('Aylmer Vance and the

Vampire'); there is a murdered Italian girl who returns to feed upon the blood of the man she once loved ('For the Blood is the Life'); there is even a tree which sucks the life from those who rest in its branches ('The Sumach'). These rivals are, more often than not, very different from the bloodsucking Count of Stoker's novel and very different one from another. The stories in which they appear all, however, remain well worth reading.

Aylmer Vance and the Vampire

Alice Askew (1874–1917) and Claude Askew (1865–1917)

The son of a clergyman, Claude Askew was at school at Eton and then travelled on the Continent as a young man. He married Alice Leake, the daughter of an army colonel, in 1900 and they were soon earning their living with their pens. Their first successes were with newspaper serials but they rapidly moved on to hardcover fiction. The Askews were astonishingly prolific and published nearly ninety books in a dozen years (nine novels appeared under their names in 1913 alone) but almost all of them have been forgotten and are long out of print. Their one venture into the realm of the supernatural consisted of eight stories which appeared in an obscure magazine named The Weekly Tale-Teller *in 1914. These featured an intrepid psychic detective named Aylmer Vance and his Watson-like sidekick Dexter. Vance and Dexter face an assortment of supernatural beings in their adventures, including, in the one printed below, a vampire. During the First World War, both Askews travelled to Serbia to work with a field hospital attached to the Serbian army and to write about the country which was one of Britain's allies in the war. In 1917, they both died when the Italian steamer on which they were making their way to Corfu to join Serbian soldiers in exile was torpedoed by a German submarine and sank.*

Aylmer Vance had rooms in Dover Street, Piccadilly, and now that I had decided to follow in his footsteps and to accept him as my instructor in matters psychic, I found it convenient to lodge in the same house. Aylmer and I quickly became close friends, and he showed me how to develop that faculty of clairvoyance which I had possessed without being aware of it. And I may say at once that this particular faculty of mine proved of service on several important occasions.

At the same time I made myself useful to Vance in other ways, not the least of which was that of acting as recorder of his many strange adventures. For himself, he never cared much about publicity, and it was some time before I could persuade him, in the interests of science, to allow me to give any detailed account of his experiences to the world.

The incidents which I will now narrate occurred very soon after we had taken up our residence together, and while I was still, so to speak, a novice.

It was about ten o'clock in the morning that a visitor was announced. He sent up a card which bore upon it the name of Paul Davenant.

The name was familiar to me, and I wondered if this could be the same Mr Davenant who was so well known for his polo playing and for his success as an amateur rider, especially over the hurdles? He was a young man of wealth and position, and I recollected that he had married, about a year ago, a girl who was reckoned the greatest beauty of the season. All the illustrated papers had given their portraits at the time, and I remember thinking what a remarkably handsome couple they made.

Mr Davenant was ushered in, and at first I was uncertain as to whether this could be the individual whom I had in mind, so wan and pale and ill did he appear. A finely built, upstanding man at the time of his marriage, he had now acquired a languid droop of the shoulders and a shuffling gait, while his face, especially about the lips, was bloodless to an alarming degree.

And yet it was the same man, for behind all this I could recognise the shadow of the good looks that had once distinguished Paul Davenant.

He took the chair which Aylmer offered him – after the usual preliminary civilities had been exchanged – and then glanced doubtfully in my direction. 'I wish to consult you privately, Mr Vance,' he said. 'The matter is of considerable importance to myself, and, if I may say so, of a somewhat delicate nature.'

Of course I rose immediately to withdraw from the room, but Vance laid his hand upon my arm.

'If the matter is connected with research in my particular line, Mr Davenant,' he said, 'if there is any investigation you wish me to take up on your behalf, I shall be glad if you will include Mr Dexter in your confidence. Mr Dexter assists me in my work. But, of course...'

'Oh, no,' interrupted the other, 'if that is the case, pray let Mr Dexter remain. I think,' he added, glancing at me with a friendly smile, 'that you are an Oxford man, are you not, Mr Dexter? It was before my time, but I have heard of your name in connection with the river. You rowed at Henley, unless I am very much mistaken.'

I admitted the fact, with a pleasurable sensation of pride. I was very keen upon rowing in those days, and a man's prowess at school and college always remain dear to his heart. After this we quickly became on friendly terms, and Paul Davenant proceeded to take Aylmer and myself into his confidence.

He began by calling attention to his personal appearance. 'You would hardly recognise me for the same man I was a year ago,' he said. 'I've been losing flesh steadily for the last six months. I came up from Scotland about a week ago, to consult a London doctor. I've seen two – in fact, they've held a sort of consultation over me – but the result, I may say, is far from satisfactory. They don't seem to know what is really the matter with me.'

'Anaemia – heart,' suggested Vance. He was scrutinising his visitor keenly, and yet without any particular appearance of doing so. 'I believe it not infrequently happens that you athletes overdo yourselves – put too much strain upon the heart...'

'My heart is quite sound,' responded Davenant. 'Physically it is in perfect condition. The trouble seems to be that it hasn't enough blood to pump into my veins. The doctors wanted to know if I had met with an accident involving a great loss of blood – but I haven't. I've had no accident at all, and as for anaemia, well, I don't seem to show the ordinary symptoms of it. The inexplicable thing is that I've lost blood without knowing it, and apparently this has been going on for some time, for I have been getting steadily worse. It was almost imperceptible at first – not a sudden collapse, you understand, but a gradual failure of health.'

'I wonder,' remarked Vance slowly, 'what induced you to consult me? For you know, of course, the direction in which I pursue my investigations. May I ask if you have reason to consider that your state of health is due to some cause which we may describe as super-physical?'

A slight colour came to Davenant's white cheeks.

'There are curious circumstances,' he said in a low and earnest tone of voice. 'I've been turning them over in my mind, trying to see light through them. I daresay it's all the sheerest folly – and I must tell you that I'm not in the least a superstitious sort of man. I don't mean to say that I'm absolutely incredulous, but I've never given thought to such things – I've led too active a life. But, as I have said, there are curious circumstances about my case, and that is why I decided upon consulting you.'

'Will you tell me everything without reserve?' said Vance. I could see that he was interested.

He was sitting up in his chair, his feet supported on a stool, his elbows on his knees, his chin in his hands – a favourite attitude of his. 'Have you,' he suggested, slowly, 'any mark upon your body, anything that you might associate, however remotely, with your present weakness and ill-health?'

'It's a curious thing that you should ask me that question,' returned Davenant, 'because I have got a curious mark, a sort of scar, that I can't account for. But I showed it to the doctors, and they assured me that it could have nothing whatever to do with my condition. In any case, if it had, it was something altogether outside their experience. I think they imagined it to be nothing more than a birthmark, a sort of mole, for they asked me if I'd had it all my life. But that I can swear I haven't. I only noticed it for the first time about six months ago, when my health began to fail. But you can see for yourself.'

He loosened his collar and bared his throat. Vance rose and made a careful scrutiny of the suspicious mark. It was situated a very little to the left of the central line, just above the clavicle, and, as Vance pointed out, directly over the big vessels of the throat. My friend called to me so that I might examine it, too. Whatever the opinion of the doctors may have been, Aylmer was obviously deeply interested. And yet there was very little to show. The skin was quite intact, and there was no sign of inflammation. There were two red marks, about an inch apart, each of which was inclined to be crescent in shape. They were more visible than they might otherwise have been owing to the peculiar whiteness of Davenant's skin.

'It can't be anything of importance,' said Davenant, with a slightly uneasy laugh. 'I'm inclined to think the marks are dying away.'

'Have you ever noticed them more inflamed than they are at present?' inquired Vance. 'If so, was it at any special time?'

Davenant reflected. 'Yes,' he replied slowly, 'there have been times, usually, I think perhaps invariably, when I wake up in the morning, that I've noticed them larger and more angry looking. And I've felt a slight sensation of pain – a tingling – oh, very slight, and I've never worried about it. Only now you suggest it to my mind, I believe that those same mornings I have felt particularly tired and done up – a sensation of lassitude absolutely unusual to me. And once, Mr Vance, I remember quite distinctly that there was a stain of blood close to the mark. I didn't think anything of it at the time, and just wiped it away.'

'I see.' Aylmer Vance resumed his seat and invited his visitor to do the same. 'And now,' he resumed, 'you said, Mr Davenant, that there are certain peculiar circumstances you wish to acquaint me with. Will you do so?'

And so Davenant readjusted his collar and proceeded to tell his story. I will tell it as far as I can, without any reference to the occasional interruptions of Vance and myself.

Paul Davenant, as I have said, was a man of wealth and position, and so, in every sense of the word, he was a suitable husband for Miss Jessica MacThane, the young lady who eventually became his wife. Before coming to the incidents attending his loss of health, he had a great deal to recount about Miss MacThane and her family history.

She was of Scottish descent, and although she had certain characteristic features of her race, she was not really Scotch in appearance. Hers was the beauty of the far South rather than that of the Highlands from which she had her origin. Names are not always suited to their owners, and Miss MacThane's was peculiarly inappropriate. She had, in fact, been christened Jessica in a sort of pathetic effort to counteract her obvious departure from normal type. There was a reason for this which we were soon to learn.

Miss MacThane was especially remarkable for her wonderful red hair, hair such as one hardly ever sees outside of Italy – not the Celtic red – and it was so long that it reached to her feet, and it had an extraordinary gloss upon it so that it seemed almost to have individual life of its own.

Then she had just the complexion that one would expect with such hair, the purest ivory white, and not in the least marred by freckles, as is so often the case with red-haired girls. Her beauty was derived from an ancestress who had been brought to Scotland from some foreign shore – no one knew exactly whence.

Davenant fell in love with her almost at once and he had every reason to believe, in spite of her many admirers, that his love was returned. At this time he knew very little about her personal history. He was aware only that she was very wealthy in her own right, an orphan, and the last representative of a race that had once been famous in the annals of history – or rather infamous, for the MacThanes had distinguished themselves more by cruelty and lust of blood than by deeds of chivalry. A clan of turbulent robbers in the past, they had helped to add many a blood-stained page to the history of their country.

Jessica had lived with her father, who owned a house in London, until his death when she was about fifteen years of age. Her mother had died in Scotland when Jessica was still a tiny child. Mr MacThane had been so affected by his wife's death that, with his little daughter, he had abandoned his Scotch estate altogether – or so it was believed – leaving it to the management of a bailiff – though, indeed, there was but little work for the bailiff to do, since there were practically no tenants left. Blackwick Castle had borne for many years a most unenviable reputation.

After the death of her father, Miss MacThane had gone to live with a certain Mrs Meredith, who was a connection of her mother's – on her father's side she had not a single relation left.

Jessica was absolutely the last of a clan once so extensive that intermarriage had been a tradition of the family, but for which the last two hundred years had been gradually dwindling to extinction.

Mrs Meredith took Jessica into Society – which would never have been her privilege had Mr MacThane lived, for he was a moody, self-absorbed man, and prematurely old – one who seemed worn down by the weight of a great grief.

Well, I have said that Paul Davenant quickly fell in love with Jessica, and it was not long before he proposed for her hand. To his great surprise, for he had good reason to believe that she cared for him, he met with a refusal; nor would she give any explanation, though she burst into a flood of pitiful tears.

Bewildered and bitterly disappointed, he consulted Mrs Meredith, with whom he happened to be on friendly terms, and from her he learnt that Jessica had already had several proposals, all from quite desirable men, but that one after another had been rejected.

Paul consoled himself with the reflection that perhaps Jessica did not love them, whereas he was quite sure that she cared for himself. Under these circumstances he determined to try again.

He did so, and with better result. Jessica admitted her love, but at the same time she repeated that she would not marry him. Love and marriage were not for her. Then, to his utter amazement, she declared that she had been born under a curse – a curse which, sooner or later was bound to show itself in her, and which, moreover, must react cruelly, perhaps fatally, upon anyone with whom she linked her life. How could she allow a man she loved to take such a risk? Above all, since the evil was hereditary, there was one point upon which she had quite made up her mind: no child should ever call her mother – she must be the last of her race indeed.

Of course, Davenant was amazed and inclined to think that Jessica had got some absurd idea into her head which a little reasoning on his part would dispel. There was only one other possible explanation. Was it lunacy she was afraid of? But Jessica shook her head. She did not know of any lunacy in her family. The ill was deeper, more subtle than that. And then she told him all that she knew.

The curse – she made use of that word for want of a better – was attached to the ancient race from which she had her origin. Her father had suffered from it, and his father and grandfather before him. All three had taken to themselves young wives who had died mysteriously, of some wasting disease, within a few years. Had they observed the ancient family tradition of intermarriage this might possibly not have happened, but in their case, since the family was so near extinction, this had not been possible.

For the curse – or whatever it was – did not kill those who bore the name of MacThane. It only rendered them a danger to others. It was as if they absorbed from the blood-soaked walls of their fatal castle a deadly taint which reacted terribly upon those with whom they were brought into contact, especially their nearest and dearest.

'Do you know what my father said we have it in us to become?' said Jessica with a shudder.

'He used the word vampires. Paul, think of it – vampires – preying upon the life blood of others.' And then, when Davenant was inclined to laugh, she checked him. 'No,' she cried out, 'it is not impossible. Think. We are a decadent race. From the earliest times our history has been marked by bloodshed and cruelty. The walls of Blackwick Castle are impregnated with evil – every stone could tell its tale, of violence, pain, lust, and murder. What can one expect of those who have spent their lifetime between its walls?'

'But you have not done so,' exclaimed Paul. 'You have been spared that, Jessica. You were taken away after your mother died, and you have no recollection of Blackwick Castle, none at all. And you need never set foot in it again.'

'I'm afraid the evil is in my blood,' she replied sadly, 'although I am unconscious of it now. And as for not returning to Blackwick – I'm not sure I can help myself. At least, that is what my father warned me of. He said there is something there, some compelling force that will call me to it in spite of myself. But, oh, I don't know – I don't know, and that is what makes it so difficult. If I could only believe that all this is nothing but an idle superstition, I might be happy again, for I have it in me to enjoy life, and I'm young, very young, but my father told me these things when he was on his deathbed.' She added the last words in a low, awe-stricken tone.

Paul pressed her to tell him all that she knew, and eventually she revealed another fragment of family history which seemed to have some bearing upon the case. It dealt with her own astonishing likeness to that ancestress of a couple of hundred years ago, whose existence seemed to have presaged the gradual downfall of the clan of the MacThanes.

A certain Robert MacThane, departing from the traditions of his family, which demanded that he should not marry outside his clan, brought home a wife from foreign shores, a woman of wonderful beauty, who was possessed of glowing masses of red hair and a complexion of ivory whiteness – such as had more or less distinguished since then every female of the race born in the direct line.

It was not long before this woman came to be regarded in the neighbourhood as a witch. Queer stories were circulated abroad as to her doings, and the reputation of Blackwick Castle became worse than ever before.

And then one day she disappeared. Robert MacThane had been absent upon some business for twenty-four hours, and it was upon his return that he found her gone. The neighbourhood was searched, but without avail, and then Robert, who was a violent man and who had adored his foreign wife, called together certain of his tenants whom he suspected, rightly or wrongly, of foul play, and had them murdered in cold blood. Murder was easy in those days, yet such an outcry was raised that Robert had to take flight, leaving his two children in the care of their nurse, and for a long while Blackwick Castle was without a master.

But its evil reputation persisted. It was said that Zaida, the witch, though dead, still made her presence felt. Many children of the tenantry and young people of the neighbourhood sickened and died – possibly of quite natural causes; but this did not prevent a mantle of terror settling upon the countryside, for it was said that Zaida had been seen – a pale woman clad in white – flitting about the cottages at night, and where she passed sickness and death were sure to supervene.

And from that time the fortune of the family gradually declined. Heir succeeded heir, but no sooner was he installed at Blackwick Castle than his nature, whatever it may previously have been, seemed to undergo a change. It was as if he absorbed into himself all the weight of evil that had stained his family name – as if he did, indeed, become a vampire, bringing blight upon any not directly connected with his own house. And so, by degrees, Blackwick was deserted of its tenantry. The land around it was left uncultivated – the farms stood empty. This had persisted to the present day, for the superstitious peasantry still told their tales of the mysterious white woman who hovered about the neighbourhood, and whose appearance betokened death – and possibly worse than death.

And yet it seemed that the last representatives of the MacThanes could not desert their ancestral home. Riches they had, sufficient to live happily upon elsewhere, but, drawn by some power they could not contend against, they had preferred to spend their lives in the solitude of the now half-ruined castle, shunned by their neighbours, feared and execrated by the few tenants that still clung to their soil.

So it had been with Jessica's grandfather and great-grandfather. Each of them had married a young wife, and in each case their love story had been all too brief. The vampire spirit was still abroad, expressing itself – or so it seemed – through the living representatives of bygone generations of evil, and young blood had been demanded as the sacrifice.

And to them had succeeded Jessica's father. He had not profited by their example, but had followed directly in their footsteps. And the same fate had befallen the wife whom he passionately adored. She had died of pernicious anaemia – so the doctors said – but he had regarded himself as her murderer.

But, unlike his predecessors, he had torn himself away from Blackwick – and this for the sake of his child. Unknown to her, however, he had returned year after year, for there were times when the passionate longing for the gloomy, mysterious halls and corridors of the old castle, for the wild stretches of moorland, and the dark pinewoods, would come upon him too strongly to be resisted. And so he knew that for his daughter, as for himself, there was no escape, and he warned her, when the relief of death was at last granted to him, of what her fate must be.

This was the tale that Jessica told the man who wished to make her his wife, and he made light of it, as such a man would, regarding it all as foolish superstition, the delusion of a mind overwrought. And at last – perhaps it was not very difficult, for she loved him with all her heart and soul – he succeeded in inducing Jessica to think as he did, to banish morbid ideas, as he called them, from her brain, and to consent to marry him at an early date.

'I'll take any risk you like,' he declared. 'I'll even go and live at Blackwick if you should desire it. To think of you, my lovely Jessica, a vampire! Why, I never heard such nonsense in my life.'

'Father said I'm very like Zaida, the witch,' she protested, but he silenced her with a kiss.

And so they were married and spent their honeymoon abroad, and in the autumn Paul accepted an invitation to a house party in Scotland for the grouse shooting, a sport to which he was absolutely devoted, and Jessica agreed with him that there was no reason why he should forgo his pleasure.

Perhaps it was an unwise thing to do, to venture to Scotland, but by this time the young couple, more deeply in love with each other than ever, had got quite over their fears. Jessica was redolent with health and spirits, and more than once she declared that if they should be anywhere in the neighbourhood of Blackwick she would like to see the old castle out of curiosity, and just to show how absolutely she had got over the foolish terrors that used to assail her.

This seemed to Paul to be quite a wise plan, and so one day, since they were actually staying at no great distance, they motored over to Blackwick, and finding the bailiff, got him to show them over the castle.

It was a great castellated pile, grey with age, and in places falling into ruin. It stood on a steep hillside, with the rock of which it seemed to form part, and on one side of it there was a precipitous drop to a mountain stream a hundred feet below. The robber MacThanes of the old days could not have desired a better stronghold.

At the back, climbing up the mountainside were dark pinewoods, from which, here and there, rugged crags protruded, and these were fantastically shaped, some like gigantic and misshapen human forms, which stood up as if they mounted guard over the castle and the narrow gorge, by which alone it could be approached.

This gorge was always full of weird, uncanny sounds. It might have been a storehouse for the wind, which, even on calm days, rushed up and down as if seeking an escape, and it moaned among the pines and whistled in the crags and shouted derisive laughter as it was tossed from side to side of the rocky heights. It was like the plaint of lost souls – that is the expression Davenant made use of – the plaint of lost souls.

The road, little more than a track now, passed through this gorge, and then, after skirting a small but deep lake, which hardly knew the light of the sun so shut in was it by overhanging trees, climbed the hill to the castle.

And the castle! Davenant used but a few words to describe it, yet somehow I could see the gloomy edifice in my mind's eye, and something of the lurking horror that it contained communicated itself to my brain. Perhaps my clairvoyant sense assisted me, for when he spoke of them I seemed already acquainted with the great stone halls, the long corridors, gloomy and cold even on the brightest and warmest of days, the dark, oak-panelled rooms, and the broad central staircase up which one of the early MacThanes had once led a dozen men on horseback in pursuit of a stag which had taken refuge within the precincts of the castle. There was the keep, too, its walls so thick that the ravages of time had made no impression upon them, and beneath the keep were dungeons which could tell terrible tales of ancient wrong and lingering pain.

Well, Mr and Mrs Davenant visited as much as the bailiff could show them of this ill-omened edifice, and Paul, for his part, thought pleasantly of his own Derbyshire home, the fine Georgian mansion, replete with every modern comfort, where he proposed to settle with his wife. And so he received something of a shock when, as they drove away, she slipped her hand into his and whispered:

'Paul, you promised, didn't you, that you would refuse me nothing?'

She had been strangely silent till she spoke those words. Paul, slightly apprehensive, assured her that she only had to ask – but the speech did not come from his heart, for he guessed vaguely what she desired.

She wanted to go and live 'at the castle – oh, only for a little while, for she was sure she would soon tire of it. But the bailiff had told her that there were papers, documents, which she ought to examine, since the property was now hers – and, besides, she was interested in this home of her ancestors, and wanted to explore it more thoroughly. Oh, no, she wasn't in the least influenced by the old superstition – that wasn't the attraction – she had quite got over those silly ideas. Paul had cured her, and since he himself was so convinced that they were without foundation he ought not to mind granting her her whim.

This was a plausible argument, not easy to controvert. In the end Paul yielded, though it was not without a struggle. He suggested amendments. Let him at least have the place done up for her – that would take time; or let them postpone their visit till next year – in the summer – not move in just as the winter was upon them.

But Jessica did not want to delay longer than she could help, and she hated the idea of redecoration. Why, it would spoil the illusion of the old place, and, besides, it would be a waste of money since she only wished to remain there for a week or two. The Derbyshire house was not quite ready yet; they must allow time for the paper to dry on the walls.

And so, a week later, when their stay with their friends was concluded, they went to Blackwick, the bailiff having engaged a few raw servants and generally made things as comfortable for them as possible. Paul was worried and apprehensive, but he could not admit this to his wife after having so loudly proclaimed his theories on the subject of superstition.

They had been married three months at this time – nine had passed since then, and they had never left Blackwick for more than a few hours – till now Paul had come to London – alone.

'Over and over again,' he declared, 'my wife has begged me to go. With tears in her eyes, almost upon her knees, she has entreated me to leave her, but I have steadily refused unless she will accompany me. But that is the trouble, Mr Vance, she cannot; there is something, some mysterious horror, that holds her there as surely as if she were bound with fetters. It holds her more strongly even than it held her father – we found out that he used to spend six months at least of every year at Blackwick – months when he pretended that he was travelling abroad. You see the spell – or whatever the accursed thing may be – never really relaxed its grip of him.'

'Did you never attempt to take your wife away?' asked Vance.

'Yes, several times; but it was hopeless. She would become so ill as soon as we were beyond the limit of the estate that I invariably had to take her back. Once we got as far as Dorekirk – that is the nearest town, you know – and I thought I should be successful if only I could get through the night. But she escaped me; she climbed out of a window – she meant to go back on foot, at night, all those long miles. Then I have had doctors down; but it is I who wanted the doctors, not she. They have ordered me away, but I have refused to obey them till now.'

'Is your wife changed at all – physically?' interrupted Vance.

Davenant reflected. 'Changed,' he said, 'yes, but so subtly that I hardly know how to describe it. She is more beautiful than ever – and yet it isn't the same beauty, if you can understand me. I have spoken of her white complexion, well, one is more than ever conscious of it now, because her lips have become so red – they are almost like a splash of blood upon her face. And the upper one has a peculiar curve that I don't think it had before, and when she laughs she doesn't smile...'

'Do you know what I mean? Then her hair – it has lost its wonderful gloss. Of course, I know she is fretting about me; but that is so peculiar, too, for at times, as I have told you, she will implore me to go and leave her, and then perhaps only a few minutes later, she will wreathe her arms round my neck and say she cannot live without me. And I feel that there is a struggle going on within her, that she is only yielding slowly to the horrible influence – whatever it is – that she is herself when she begs me to go, but when she entreats me to stay- and it is then that her fascination is most intense – oh, I can't help remembering what she told me before we were married, and that word' – he lowered his voice – 'the word "vampire"…'

He passed his hand over his brow that was wet with perspiration. 'But that's absurd, ridiculous,' he muttered; 'these fantastic beliefs have been exploded years ago. We live in the twentieth century.'

A pause ensued, then Vance said quietly, 'Mr Davenant, since you have taken me into your confidence, since you have found doctors of no avail, will you let me try to help you? I think I may be of some use – if it is not already too late. Should you agree, Mr Dexter and I will accompany you, as you have suggested, to Blackwick Castle as early as possible – by tonight's mail North. Under ordinary circumstances I should tell you as you value your life, not to return….'

Davenant shook his head. 'That is advice which I should never take,' he declared. 'I had already decided, under any circumstances, to travel North tonight. I am glad that you both will accompany me.'

And so it was decided. We settled to meet at the station, and presently Paul Davenant took his departure. Any other details that remained to be told he would put us in possession of during the course of the journey.

'A curious and most interesting case,' remarked Vance when we were alone. 'What do you make of it, Dexter?'

'I suppose,' I replied cautiously, 'that there is such a thing as vampirism even in these days of advanced civilization? I can understand the evil influence that a very old person may have upon a young one if they happen to be in constant intercourse – the worn-out tissue sapping healthy vitality for their own support. And there are certain people – I could think of several myself – who seem to depress one and undermine one's energies, quite unconsciously, of course, but one feels somehow that

32

vitality has passed from oneself to them. And in this case, when the force is centuries old, expressing itself, in some mysterious way, through Davenant's wife, is it not feasible to believe that he may be physically affected by it, even though the whole thing is sheerly mental?'

'You think, then,' demanded Vance, 'that it is sheerly mental? Tell me, if that is so, how do you account for the marks on Davenant's throat?'

This was a question to which I found no reply, and though I pressed him for his views, Vance would not commit himself further just then.

Of our long journey to Scotland I need say nothing. We did not reach Blackwick Castle till late in the afternoon of the following day. The place was just as I had conceived it – as I have already described it. And a sense of gloom settled upon me as our car jolted us over the rough road that led through the Gorge of the Winds – a gloom that deepened when we penetrated into the vast cold hall of the castle.

Mrs Davenant, who had been informed by telegram of our arrival, received us cordially. She knew nothing of our actual mission, regarding us merely as friends of her husband's. She was most solicitous on his behalf, but there was something strained about her tone, and it made me feel vaguely uneasy. The impression that I got was that the woman was impelled to everything that she said or did by some force outside herself – but, of course, this was a conclusion that the circumstances I was aware of might easily have conduced to. In every other aspect she was charming, and she had an extraordinary fascination of appearance and manner that made me readily understand the force of a remark made by Davenant during our journey.

'I want to live for Jessica's sake. Get her away from Blackwick, Vance, and I feel that all will be well. I'd go through hell to have her restored to me – as she was.'

And now that I had seen Mrs Davenant I realised what he meant by those last words. Her fascination was stronger than ever, but it was not a natural fascination – not that of a normal woman, such as she had been. It was the fascination of a Circe, of a witch, of an enchantress – and as such was irresistible.

We had a strong proof of the evil within her soon after our arrival. It was a test that Vance had quietly prepared. Davenant had mentioned that no flowers grew at Blackwick, and Vance declared that we must take some with us as a present for the lady of the house. He purchased a bouquet of pure white roses at the little town where we left the train, for the motorcar had been sent to meet us. Soon after our arrival he presented these to Mrs Davenant. She took them it seemed to me nervously, and hardly had her hand touched them before they fell to pieces, in a shower of crumpled petals, to the floor.

'We must act at once,' said Vance to me when we were descending to dinner that night. 'There must be no delay.'

'What are you afraid of?' I whispered.

'Davenant has been absent a week,' he replied grimly. 'He is stronger than when he went away, but not strong enough to survive the loss of more blood. He must be protected. There is danger tonight.'

'You mean from his wife?' I shuddered at the ghastliness of the suggestion.

'That is what time will show.' Vance turned to me and added a few words with intense earnestness. 'Mrs Davenant, Dexter, is at present hovering between two conditions. The evil thing has not yet completely mastered her – you remember what Davenant said, how she would beg him to go away and the next moment entreat him to stay? She has made a struggle, but she is gradually succumbing, and this last week, spent here alone, has strengthened the evil. And that is what I have got to fight, Dexter – it is to be a contest of will, a contest that will go on silently till one or the other obtains the mastery. If you watch, you may see. Should a change show itself in Mrs Davenant you will know that I have won.'

Thus I knew the direction in which my friend proposed to act.

It was to be a war of his will against the mysterious power that had laid its curse upon the house of MacThane. Mrs Davenant must be released from the fatal charm that held her.

And I, knowing what was going on, was able to watch and understand. I realised that the silent contest had begun even while we ate dinner. Mrs Davenant ate practically nothing and seemed ill at ease; she fidgeted in her chair, talked a great deal, and laughed – it was the laugh without a smile, as Davenant had described it. And as soon as she was able to she withdrew.

Later, as we sat in the drawing room, I could feel the clash of wills. The air in the room felt electric and heavy, charged with tremendous but invisible forces. And outside, round the castle, the wind whistled and shrieked and moaned – it was as if all the dead and gone MacThanes, a grim army, had collected to fight the battle of their race.

And all this while we four in the drawing room were sitting and talking the ordinary commonplaces of after-dinner conversation! That was the extraordinary part of it – Paul Davenant suspected nothing, and I, who knew, had to play my part. But I hardly took my eyes from Jessica's face. When would the change come, or was it, indeed, too late!

At last Davenant rose and remarked that he was tired and would go to bed. There was no need for Jessica to hurry. He would sleep that night in his dressing room and did not want to be disturbed.

And it was at that moment, as his lips met hers in a goodnight kiss, as she wreathed her enchantress arms about him, careless of our presence, her eyes gleaming hungrily, that the change came.

It came with a fierce and threatening shriek of wind, and a rattling of the casement, as if the horde of ghosts without was about to break in upon us. A long, quivering sigh escaped from Jessica's lips, her arms fell from her husband's shoulders, and she drew back, swaying a little from side to side.

'Paul,' she cried, and somehow the whole timbre of her voice was changed, 'what a wretch I've been to bring you back to

Blackwick, ill as you are! But we'll go away, dear; yes, I'll go, too. Oh, will you take me away – take me away tomorrow?' She spoke with an intense earnestness – unconscious all the time of what had been happening to her. Long shudders were convulsing her frame. 'I don't know why I've wanted to stay here,' she kept repeating. 'I hate the place, really – it's evil… evil.'

Having heard these words I exulted, for surely Vance's success was assured. But I was to learn that the danger was not yet past.

Husband and wife separated, each going to their own room. I noticed the grateful, if mystified glance that Davenant threw at Vance, vaguely aware, as he must have been, that my friend was somehow responsible for what had happened. It was settled that plans for departure were to be discussed on the morrow.

'I have succeeded,' Vance said hurriedly, when we were alone, 'but the change may be transitory. I must keep watch tonight. Go you to bed, Dexter, there is nothing that you can do.'

I obeyed – though I would sooner have kept watch, too – watch against a danger of which I had no understanding. I went to my room, a gloomy and sparsely furnished apartment, but I knew that it was quite impossible for me to think of sleeping. And so, dressed as I was, I went and sat by the open window, for now the wind that had raged round the castle had died down to a low moaning in the pine trees – a whimpering of time-worn agony.

And it was as I sat thus that I became aware of a white figure that stole out from the castle by a door that I could not see, and, with hands clasped, ran swiftly across the terrace to the wood. I had but a momentary glance, but I felt convinced that the figure was that of Jessica Davenant.

And instinctively I knew that some great danger was imminent. It was, I think, the suggestion of despair conveyed by those clasped hands. At any rate, I did not hesitate. My window was some height from the ground, but the wall below was ivy-clad and afforded good foothold. The descent was quite easy. I achieved it, and was just in time to take up the pursuit in the right direction, which was into the thickness of the wood that clung to the slope of the hill.

I shall never forget that wild chase. There was just sufficient room to enable me to follow the rough path, which, luckily, since I had now lost sight of my quarry, was the only possible way that she could have taken; there were no intersecting tracks, and the wood was too thick on either side to permit of deviation.

And the wood seemed full of dreadful sounds – moaning and wailing and hideous laughter. The wind, of course, and the screaming of night birds – once I felt the fluttering of wings in close proximity to my face. But I could not rid myself of the thought that I, in my turn, was being pursued, that the forces of hell were combined against me.

The path came to an abrupt end on the border of the sombre lake that I have already mentioned. And now I realised that I was indeed only just in time, for before me, plunging knee deep in the water, I recognised the white-clad figure of the woman I had been pursuing. Hearing my footsteps, she turned her head, and then threw up her arms and screamed. Her red hair fell in heavy masses about her shoulders, and her face, as I saw it in that moment, was hardly human for the agony of remorse that it depicted.

'Go!' she screamed. 'For God's sake let me die!'

But I was by her side almost as she spoke. She struggled with me – sought vainly to tear herself from my clasp – implored me, with panting breath, to let her drown.

'It's the only way to save him!' she gasped. 'Don't you understand that I am a thing accursed? For it is I – I – who have sapped his life blood! I know it now, the truth has been revealed to me tonight! I am a vampire, without hope in this world or the next, so for his sake – for the sake of his unborn child – let me die – let me die!' Was ever so terrible an appeal made? Yet I – what could I do? Gently I overcame her resistance and drew her back to shore. By the time I reached it she was lying a dead weight upon my arm. I laid her down upon a mossy bank, and, kneeling by her side, gazed intently into her face.

And then I knew that I had done well. For the face I looked upon was not that of Jessica the vampire, as I had seen it that afternoon, it was the face of Jessica, the woman whom Paul Davenant had loved.

And later Aylmer Vance had his tale to tell.

'I waited', he said, 'until I knew that Davenant was asleep, and then I stole into his room to watch by his bedside. And presently she came, as I guessed she would, the vampire, the accursed thing that has preyed upon the souls of her kin, making them like to herself when they too have passed into Shadowland, and gathering sustenance for her horrid task from the blood of those who are alien to her race. Paul's body and Jessica's soul – it is for one and the other, Dexter, that we have fought.'

'You mean,' I hesitated, 'Zaida the witch?'

'Even so,' he agreed. 'Hers is the evil spirit that has fallen like a blight upon the house of MacThane. But now I think she may be exorcised for ever.'

'Tell me.'

'She came to Paul Davenant last night, as she must have done before, in the guise of his wife. You know that Jessica bears a strong resemblance to her ancestress. He opened his arms, but she was foiled of her prey, for I had taken my precautions; I had placed that upon Davenant's breast while he slept which robbed the vampire of her power of ill. She sped wailing from the room – a shadow – she who a minute before had looked at him with Jessica's eyes and spoken to him with Jessica's voice. Her red lips were Jessica's lips, and they were close to his when his eyes were opened and he saw her as she was – a hideous phantom of the corruption of the ages. And so the spell was removed, and she fled away to the place whence she had come...'

He paused. 'And now?' I inquired.

'Blackwick Castle must be razed to the ground,' he replied. 'That is the only way. Every stone of it, every brick, must be ground to powder and burnt with fire, for therein is the cause of all the evil. Davenant has consented.'

'And Mrs Davenant?'

'I think,' Vance answered cautiously, 'that all may be well with her. The curse will be removed with the destruction of the castle. She has not – thanks to you – perished under its influence. She was less guilty than she imagined – herself preyed upon rather than preying. But can't you understand her remorse when she realised, as she was bound to realise, the part she had played? And the knowledge of the child to come – its fatal inheritance…'

'I understand.' I muttered with a shudder. And then, under my breath, I whispered, 'Thank God!'

The Room in the Tower

EF Benson (1867–1940)

The son of a nineteenth-century Archbishop of Canterbury, Benson was a prolific writer in many genres. His best-known works are the Mapp and Lucia novels, tart satires of snobbery and social-climbing in the fictional seaside town of Tilling, a place not entirely dissimilar to Rye in Sussex where Benson lived for many years. Their popularity has been increased by two TV series based on them, one made in the 1980s and one shown on the BBC in 2014. However, he also wrote many other novels as well as biographies of Queen Victoria and Sir Francis Drake, a book on figure skating (as a young man he represented England at the sport), and memoirs of his deeply strange but widely talented family. He was a fine writer of what he called 'spook stories', tales of the supernatural which were collected in a variety of volumes, including Visible and Invisible, Spook Stories *and* More Spook Stories. *Two of these stories are about vampires. 'Mrs Amworth', memorable in that the bloodsucker of the title is a plump and seemingly jolly widow living in retirement in a picturesque Sussex village, was published outside the period covered by this anthology. Benson's other vampire story, 'The Room in the Tower', is a compelling account of a nightmare metamorphosing into an all too horrible reality.*

It is probable that everybody who is at all a constant dreamer has had at least one experience of an event or a sequence of circumstances which have come to his mind in sleep being subsequently realised in the material world. But, in my opinion, so far from this being a strange thing, it would be far odder if this fulfilment did not occasionally happen, since our dreams are, as a rule, concerned with people whom we know and places with which we are familiar, such as might very naturally occur in the awake and daylit world. True, these dreams are often broken into by some absurd and fantastic incident, which puts them out of court in regard to their subsequent fulfilment, but on the mere calculation of chances, it does not appear in the least unlikely that a dream imagined by anyone who dreams constantly should occasionally come true. Not long ago, for instance, I experienced such a fulfilment of a dream which seems to me in no way remarkable and to have no kind of psychical significance. The manner of it was as follows.

A certain friend of mine, living abroad, is amiable enough to write to me about once in a fortnight. Thus, when fourteen days or thereabouts have elapsed since I last heard from him, my mind, probably, either consciously or subconsciously, is expectant of a letter from him. One night last week I dreamed that as I was going upstairs to dress for dinner I heard, as I often heard, the sound of the postman's knock on my front door, and diverted my direction downstairs instead. There, among other correspondence, was a letter from him. Thereafter the fantastic entered, for on opening it I found inside the ace of diamonds, and scribbled across it in his well-known handwriting, 'I am sending you this for safe custody, as you know it is running an unreasonable risk to keep aces in Italy.' The next evening I was just preparing to go upstairs to dress when I heard the postman's knock, and did precisely as I had done in my dream. There, among other letters, was one from my friend. Only it did not contain the ace of diamonds. Had it done so, I should have attached more weight to the matter, which, as it stands, seems to me a perfectly ordinary coincidence. No doubt I consciously or subconsciously expected a letter from him, and this suggested to me my dream. Similarly, the fact that my friend had not written to me for a fortnight suggested to him that he should do so. But occasionally it is not so easy to find such an explanation, and for the following story I can find no explanation at all. It came out of the dark, and into the dark it has gone again.

All my life I have been a habitual dreamer: the nights are few, that is to say, when I do not find on awaking in the morning that some mental experience has been mine, and sometimes, all night long, apparently, a series of the most dazzling adventures befall me. Almost without exception these adventures are pleasant, though often merely trivial. It is of an exception that I am going to speak.

It was when I was about sixteen that a certain dream first came to me, and this is how it befell. It opened with my being set down at the door of a big red-brick house, where, I understood, I was going to stay. The servant who opened the door told me that tea was being served in the garden, and led me through a low dark-panelled hall, with a large open fireplace, on to a cheerful green lawn set round with flower beds. There were grouped about the tea table a small party of people, but they were all strangers to me except one, who was a schoolfellow called Jack Stone, clearly the son of the house, and he introduced me to his mother and father and a couple of sisters. I was, I remember, somewhat astonished to find myself here, for the boy in question was scarcely known to me, and I rather disliked what I knew of him; moreover, he had left school nearly a year before. The afternoon was very hot, and an intolerable oppression reigned. On the far side of the lawn ran a red-brick wall, with an iron gate in its centre, outside which stood a walnut tree. We sat in the shadow of the house opposite a row of long windows, inside which I could see a table with cloth laid, glimmering with glass and silver. This garden front of the house was very long, and at one end of it stood a tower of three stories, which looked to me much older than the rest of the building.

Before long, Mrs Stone, who, like the rest of the party, had sat in absolute silence, said to me, 'Jack will show you your room: I have given you the room in the tower.'

Quite inexplicably my heart sank at her words. I felt as if I had known that I should have the room in the tower, and that it contained something dreadful and significant. Jack instantly got up, and I understood that I had to follow him. In silence we passed through the hall, and mounted a great oak staircase with many corners, and arrived at a small landing with two doors set in it. He pushed one of these open for me to enter, and without coming in himself, closed it after me. Then I knew that my conjecture had been right: there was something awful in the room, and with the terror of nightmare growing swiftly and enveloping me, I awoke in a spasm of terror.

Now that dream or variations on it occurred to me intermittently for fifteen years. Most often it came in exactly this form, the arrival, the tea laid out on the lawn, the deadly silence succeeded by that one deadly sentence, the mounting with Jack Stone up to the room in the tower where horror dwelt, and it always came to a close in the nightmare of terror at that which was in the room, though I never saw what it was. At other times I experienced variations on this same theme. Occasionally, for instance, we would be sitting at dinner in the dining room, into the windows of which I had looked on the first night when the dream of this house visited me, but wherever we were, there was the same silence, the same sense of dreadful oppression and foreboding. And the silence I knew would always be broken by Mrs Stone saying to me, 'Jack will show you your room: I have given you the room in the tower.' Upon which (this was invariable) I had to follow him up the oak staircase with many corners, and enter the place that I dreaded more and more each time that I visited it in sleep. Or, again, I would find myself playing cards still in silence in a drawing room lit with immense chandeliers that gave a blinding illumination. What the game was I have no idea; what I remember, with a sense of miserable anticipation, was that soon Mrs Stone would get up and say to me, 'Jack will show you your room: I have given you the room in the tower.' This drawing room where we played cards was next to the dining room, and, as I have said, was always brilliantly illuminated, whereas the rest of the house was full of dusk and shadows. And yet, how often, in spite of those bouquets of lights, have I not pored over the cards that were dealt me, scarcely able for some reason to see them. Their designs, too, were strange: there were no red suits, but all were black, and among them there were certain cards which were black all over. I hated and dreaded those.

As this dream continued to recur, I got to know the greater part of the house. There was a smoking room beyond the drawing room, at the end of a passage with a green baize door. It was always very dark there, and as often as I went there I passed somebody whom I could not see in the doorway coming out. Curious developments, too, took place in the characters that peopled the dream as might happen to living persons. Mrs Stone, for instance, who, when I first saw her, had been black-haired, became grey, and instead of rising briskly, as she had done at first when she said, 'Jack will show you your room: I have given you the room in the tower,' got up very feebly, as if the strength was leaving her limbs. Jack also grew up, and became a rather ill-looking young man, with a brown moustache, while one of the sisters ceased to appear, and I understood she was married.

Then it so happened that I was not visited by this dream for six months or more, and I began to hope, in such inexplicable dread did I hold it, that it had passed away for good. But one night after this interval I again found myself being shown out onto the lawn for tea, and Mrs Stone was not there, while the others were all dressed in black. At once I guessed the reason, and my heart leaped at the thought that perhaps this time I should not have to sleep in the room in the tower, and though we usually all sat in silence, on this occasion the sense of relief made me talk and laugh as I had never yet done. But even then matters were not altogether comfortable, for no one else spoke, but they all looked secretly at each other. And soon the foolish stream of my talk ran dry, and gradually an apprehension worse than anything I had previously known gained on me as the light slowly faded.

Suddenly a voice which I knew well broke the stillness, the voice of Mrs Stone, saying, 'Jack will show you your room: I have given you the room in the tower.' It seemed to come from near the gate in the red-brick wall that bounded the lawn, and looking up, I saw that the grass outside was sown thick with gravestones. A curious greyish light shone from them, and I could read the lettering on the grave nearest me, and it was, 'In evil memory of Julia Stone'. And as usual Jack got up, and again I followed him through the hall and up the staircase with many corners. On this occasion it was darker than usual, and when I passed into the room in the tower I could only just see the furniture, the position of which was already familiar to me. Also there was a dreadful odour of decay in the room, and I woke screaming.

The dream, with such variations and developments as I have mentioned, went on at intervals for fifteen years. Sometimes I would dream it two or three nights in succession; once, as I have said, there was an intermission of six months, but taking a reasonable average, I should say that I dreamed it quite as often as once in a month. It had, as is plain, something of nightmare about it, since it always ended in the same appalling terror, which so far from getting less, seemed to me to gather fresh fear every time that I experienced it. There was, too, a strange and dreadful consistency about it. The characters in it, as I have mentioned, got regularly older, death and marriage visited this silent family, and I never in the dream, after Mrs Stone had died, set eyes on her again. But it was always her voice that told me that the room in the tower was prepared for me, and whether we had tea out on the lawn, or the scene was laid in one of the rooms overlooking it, I could always see her gravestone standing just outside the iron gate. It was the same, too, with the married daughter; usually she was not present, but once or twice she returned again, in company with a man, whom I took to be her husband. He, too, like the rest of them, was always silent. But, owing to the constant repetition of the dream, I had ceased to attach, in my waking hours, any significance to it. I never met Jack Stone again during all those years, nor did I ever see a house that resembled this dark house of my dream. And then something happened.

I had been in London in this year, up till the end of the July, and during the first week in August went down to stay with a friend in a house he had taken for the summer months, in the Ashdown Forest district of Sussex. I left London early, for John Clinton was to meet me at Forest Row Station, and we were going to spend the day golfing, and go to his house in the evening. He had his motor with him, and we set off, about five of the afternoon, after a thoroughly delightful day, for the drive, the distance being some ten miles. As it was still so early we did not have tea at the club house, but waited till we should get home. As we drove, the weather, which up till then had been, though hot, deliciously fresh, seemed to me to alter in quality, and become very stagnant and oppressive, and I felt that indefinable sense of ominous apprehension that I am accustomed to before thunder. John, however, did not share my views, attributing my loss of lightness to the fact that I had lost both my matches. Events proved, however, that I was right, though I do not think that the thunderstorm that broke that night was the sole cause of my depression.

Our way lay through deep high-banked lanes, and before we had gone very far I fell asleep, and was only awakened by the stopping of the motor. And with a sudden thrill, partly of fear but chiefly of curiosity, I found myself standing in the doorway of my house of dream. We went, I half wondering whether or not I was dreaming still, through a low oak-panelled hall, and out onto the lawn, where tea was laid in the shadow of the house. It was set in flower beds, a red-brick wall, with a gate in it, bounded one side, and out beyond that was a space of rough grass with a walnut tree. The facade of the house was very long, and at one end stood a three-storied tower, markedly older than the rest.

Here for the moment all resemblance to the repeated dream ceased. There was no silent and somehow terrible family, but a large assembly of exceedingly cheerful persons, all of whom were known to me. And in spite of the horror with which the dream itself had always filled me, I felt nothing of it now that the scene of it was thus reproduced before me. But I felt intensest curiosity as to what was going to happen.

Tea pursued its cheerful course, and before long Mrs Clinton got up. And at that moment I think I knew what she was going to say. She spoke to me, and what she said was:

'Jack will show you your room: I have given you the room in the tower.'

At that, for half a second, the horror of the dream took hold of me again. But it quickly passed, and again I felt nothing more than the most intense curiosity. It was not very long before it was amply satisfied.

John turned to me.

'Right up at the top of the house,' he said, 'but I think you'll be comfortable. We're absolutely full up. Would you like to go and see it now? By Jove, I believe that you are right, and that we are going to have a thunderstorm. How dark it has become.'

I got up and followed him. We passed through the hall, and up the perfectly familiar staircase. Then he opened the door, and I went in. And at that moment sheer unreasoning terror again possessed me. I did not know what I feared: I simply feared. Then like a sudden recollection, when one remembers a name which has long escaped the memory, I knew what I feared. I feared Mrs Stone, whose grave with the sinister inscription, 'In evil memory', I had so often seen in my dream, just beyond the lawn which lay below my window. And then once more the fear passed so completely that I wondered what there was to fear, and I found myself, sober and quiet and sane, in the room in the tower, the name of which I had so often heard in my dream, and the scene of which was so familiar.

I looked around it with a certain sense of proprietorship, and found that nothing had been changed from the dreaming nights in which I knew it so well. Just to the left of the door was the bed, lengthways along the wall, with the head of it in the angle. In a line with it was the fireplace and a small bookcase; opposite the door the outer wall was pierced by two lattice-paned windows, between which stood the dressing table, while ranged along the fourth wall was the washing stand and a big cupboard. My luggage had already been unpacked, for the furniture of dressing and undressing lay orderly on the washstand and toilet table, while my dinner clothes were spread out on the coverlet of the bed. And then, with a sudden start of unexplained dismay, I saw that there were two rather conspicuous objects which I had not seen before in my dreams: one a life-sized oil painting of Mrs Stone, the other a black-and-white sketch of Jack Stone, representing him as he had appeared to me only a week before in the last of the series of these repeated dreams, a rather secret and evil-looking man of about thirty. His picture hung between the windows, looking straight across the room to the other portrait, which hung at the side of the bed. At that I looked next, and as I looked I felt once more the horror of nightmare seize me.

It represented Mrs Stone as I had seen her last in my dreams: old and withered and white-haired. But in spite of the evident feebleness of body, a dreadful exuberance and vitality shone through the envelope of flesh, an exuberance wholly malign, a vitality that foamed and frothed with unimaginable evil. Evil beamed from the narrow, leering eyes; it laughed in the demon-like mouth. The whole face was instinct with some secret and appalling mirth; the hands, clasped together on the knee, seemed shaking with suppressed and nameless glee. Then I saw also that it was signed in the left-hand bottom corner, and wondering who the artist could be, I looked more closely, and read the inscription, 'Julia Stone by Julia Stone'.

There came a tap at the door, and John Clinton entered.

'Got everything you want?' he asked.

'Rather more than I want,' said I, pointing to the picture.

He laughed.

'Hard-featured old lady,' he said. 'By herself, too, I remember. Anyhow she can't have flattered herself much.'

'But don't you see?' said I. 'It's scarcely a human face at all. It's the face of some witch, of some devil.'

He looked at it more closely.

'Yes; it isn't very pleasant,' he said. 'Scarcely a bedside manner, eh? Yes; I can imagine getting the nightmare if I went to sleep with that close by my bed. I'll have it taken down if you like.'

'I really wish you would,' I said. He rang the bell, and with the help of a servant we detached the picture and carried it out onto the landing, and put it with its face to the wall.

'By Jove, the old lady is a weight,' said John, mopping his forehead. 'I wonder if she had something on her mind.'

The extraordinary weight of the picture had struck me too. I was about to reply, when I caught sight of my own hand. There was blood on it, in considerable quantities, covering the whole palm.

'I've cut myself somehow,' said I.

John gave a little startled exclamation.

'Why, I have too,' he said.

Simultaneously the footman took out his handkerchief and wiped his hand with it. I saw that there was blood also on his handkerchief.

John and I went back into the tower room and washed the blood off; but neither on his hand nor on mine was there the slightest trace of a scratch or cut. It seemed to me that, having ascertained this, we both, by a sort of tacit consent, did not allude to it again. Something in my case had dimly occurred to me that I did not wish to think about. It was but a conjecture, but I fancied that I knew the same thing had occurred to him.

The heat and oppression of the air, for the storm we had expected was still undischarged, increased very much after dinner, and for some time most of the party, among whom were John Clinton and myself, sat outside on the path bounding the lawn, where we had had tea. The night was absolutely dark, and no twinkle of star or moon ray could penetrate the pall of cloud that overset the sky. By degrees our assembly thinned, the women went up to bed, men dispersed to the smoking or billiard room, and by eleven o'clock my host and I were the only two left. All the evening I thought that he had something on his mind, and as soon as we were alone he spoke.

'The man who helped us with the picture had blood on his hand, too, did you notice?' he said.

'I asked him just now if he had cut himself, and he said he supposed he had, but that he could find no mark of it. Now where did that blood come from?'

By dint of telling myself that I was not going to think about it, I had succeeded in not doing so, and I did not want, especially just at bedtime, to be reminded of it.

'I don't know,' said I, 'and I don't really care so long as the picture of Mrs Stone is not by my bed.'

He got up.

'But it's odd,' he said. 'Ha! Now you'll see another odd thing.'

A dog of his, an Irish terrier by breed, had come out of the house as we talked. The door behind us into the hall was open, and a bright oblong of light shone across the lawn to the iron gate which led on to the rough grass outside, where the walnut tree stood. I saw that the dog had all his hackles up, bristling with rage and fright; his lips were curled back from his teeth, as if he was ready to spring at something, and he was growling to himself. He took not the slightest notice of his master or me, but stiffly and tensely walked across the grass to the iron gate. There he stood for a moment, looking through the bars and still growling. Then of a sudden his courage seemed to desert him: he gave one long howl, and scuttled back to the house with a curious crouching sort of movement.

'He does that half-a-dozen times a day.' said John. 'He sees something which he both hates and fears.'

I walked to the gate and looked over it. Something was moving on the grass outside, and soon a sound which I could not instantly identify came to my ears. Then I remembered what it was: it was the purring of a cat. I lit a match, and saw the purrer, a big blue Persian, walking round and round in a little circle just outside the gate, stepping high and ecstatically, with tail carried aloft like a banner. Its eyes were bright and shining, and every now and then it put its head down and sniffed at the grass.

I laughed.

'The end of that mystery, I am afraid,' I said. 'Here's a large cat having Walpurgis night all alone.'

'Yes, that's Darius,' said John. 'He spends half the day and all night there. But that's not the end of the dog mystery, for Toby and he are the best of friends, but the beginning of the cat mystery. What's the cat doing there? And why is Darius pleased, while Toby is terror-stricken?'

At that moment I remembered the rather horrible detail of my dreams when I saw through the gate, just where the cat was now, the white tombstone with the sinister inscription. But before I could answer the rain began, as suddenly and heavily as if a tap had been turned on, and simultaneously the big cat squeezed through the bars of the gate, and came leaping across the lawn to the house for shelter. Then it sat in the doorway, looking out eagerly into the dark. It spat and struck at John with its paw, as he pushed it in, in order to close the door.

Somehow, with the portrait of Julia Stone in the passage outside, the room in the tower had absolutely no alarm for me, and as I went to bed, feeling very sleepy and heavy, I had nothing more than interest for the curious incident about our bleeding hands, and the conduct of the cat and dog. The last thing I looked at before I put out my light was the square empty space by my bed where the portrait had been. Here the paper was of its original full tint of dark red: over the rest of the walls it had faded. Then I blew out my candle and instantly fell asleep.

My awaking was equally instantaneous, and I sat bolt upright in bed under the impression that some bright light had been flashed in my face, though it was now absolutely pitch dark. I knew exactly where I was, in the room which I had dreaded in dreams, but no horror that I ever felt when asleep approached the fear that now invaded and froze my brain. Immediately after a peal of thunder crackled just above the house, but the probability that it was only a flash of lightning which awoke me gave no reassurance to my galloping heart. Something I knew was in the room with me, and instinctively I put out my right hand, which was nearest the wall, to keep it away. And my hand touched the edge of a picture frame hanging close to me.

I sprang out of bed, upsetting the small table that stood by it, and I heard my watch, candle, and matches clatter onto the floor. But for the moment there was no need of light, for a blinding flash leaped out of the clouds, and showed me that by my bed again hung the picture of Mrs Stone. And instantly the room went into blackness again. But in that flash I saw another thing also, namely a figure that leaned over the end of my bed, watching me. It was dressed in some close-clinging white garment, spotted and stained with mould, and the face was that of the portrait.

Overhead the thunder cracked and roared, and when it ceased and the deathly stillness succeeded, I heard the rustle of movement coming nearer me, and, more horrible yet, perceived an odour of corruption and decay. And then a hand was laid on the side of my neck, and close beside my ear I heard quick-taken, eager breathing. Yet I knew that this thing, though it could be perceived by touch, by smell, by eye and by ear, was still not of this earth, but something that had passed out of the body and had power to make itself manifest. Then a voice, already familiar to me, spoke.

'I knew you would come to the room in the tower,' it said. 'I have been long waiting for you. At last you have come. Tonight I shall feast; before long we will feast together.'

And the quick breathing came closer to me; I could feel it on my neck.

At that the terror, which I think had paralysed me for the moment, gave way to the wild instinct of self-preservation. I hit wildly with both arms, kicking out at the same moment, and heard a little animal-squeal, and something soft dropped with a thud beside me. I took a couple of steps forward, nearly tripping up over whatever it was that lay there, and by the merest good luck found the handle of the door. In another second I ran out on the landing, and had banged the door behind me. Almost at the same moment I heard a door open somewhere below, and John Clinton, candle in hand, came running upstairs.

'What is it?' he said. 'I sleep just below you, and heard a noise as if – Good heavens, there's blood on your shoulder.'

I stood there, so he told me afterwards, swaying from side to side, white as a sheet, with the mark on my shoulder as if a hand covered with blood had been laid there.

'It's in there,' I said, pointing. 'She, you know. The portrait is in there, too, hanging up on the place we took it from.'

At that he laughed.

'My dear fellow, this is mere nightmare,' he said.

He pushed by me, and opened the door, I standing there simply inert with terror, unable to stop him, unable to move.

'Phew! What an awful smell,' he said.

Then there was silence; he had passed out of my sight behind the open door. Next moment he came out again, as white as myself, and instantly shut it.

'Yes, the portrait's there,' he said, 'and on the floor is a thing – a thing spotted with earth, like what they bury people in. Come away, quick, come away.'

How I got downstairs I hardly know. An awful shuddering and nausea of the spirit rather than of the flesh had seized me, and more than once he had to place my feet upon the steps, while every now and then he cast glances of terror and apprehension up the stairs. But in time we came to his dressing room on the floor below, and there I told him what I have here described.

The sequel can be made short; indeed, some of my readers have perhaps already guessed what it was, if they remember that inexplicable affair of the churchyard at West Fawley, some eight years ago, where an attempt was made three times to bury the body of a certain woman who had committed suicide. On each occasion the coffin was found in the course of a few days again protruding from the ground. After the third attempt, in order that the thing should not be talked about, the body was buried elsewhere in unconsecrated ground. Where it was buried was just outside the iron gate of the garden belonging to the house where this woman had lived. She had committed suicide in a room at the top of the tower in that house. Her name was Julia Stone.

Subsequently the body was again secretly dug up, and the coffin was found to be full of blood.

Let Loose

Mary Cholmondeley (1859–1925)

Born in Shropshire, the daughter of a vicar and his wife, Mary Cholmondeley was obliged for much of her early adult life to balance her desire to write with family responsibilities that were thrust upon her by her mother's chronic illness. Her first novel was published in 1885 but it was only after she moved to London in 1896, following her mother's death, that she was able fully to spread her literary wings. Her greatest success as a writer was the novel Red Pottage, *published in 1899, which was a bestseller in both Britain and America and was later made into a silent film. A story of two women in* fin-de siècle *England who both, in their different ways, battle against the restraints society places on them, it was controversial at the time and was even denounced as immoral from the pulpit of a London church. Her other novels included* The Danvers Jewels *and* Diana Tempest, *recently reprinted by an American publisher. Cholmondeley (the name is actually pronounced 'Chumley') also wrote a sizeable number of short stories for the monthly magazines which proliferated in the late Victorian and Edwardian eras. 'Let Loose' was one of these, first appearing in* Temple Bar *in 1890 before its reprinting in a collection of Cholmondeley's short stories published a dozen years later. With its narrative of an architect who visits a remote Yorkshire church and accidentally releases an undead spirit that may not be a bloodsucker but is definitely vampiric, the story is reminiscent of MR James's fiction.*

> The dead abide with us! Though stark and cold
> Earth seems to grip them, they are with us still.

Some years ago I took up architecture, and made a tour through Holland, studying the buildings of that interesting country. I was not then aware that it is not enough to take up art. Art must take you up, too. I never doubted but that my passing enthusiasm for her would be returned. When I discovered that she was a stern mistress, who did not immediately respond to my attentions, I naturally transferred them to another shrine. There are other things in the world besides art. I am now a landscape gardener.

But at the time of which I write I was engaged in a violent flirtation with architecture. I had one companion on this expedition, who has since become one of the leading architects of the day. He was a thin, determined-looking man with a screwed-up face and heavy jaw, slow of speech, and absorbed in his work to a degree which I quickly found tiresome. He was possessed of a certain quiet power of overcoming obstacles which I have rarely seen equalled. He has since become my brother-in-law, so I ought to know; for my parents did not like him much and opposed the marriage, and my sister did not like him at all, and refused him over and over again; but, nevertheless, he eventually married her.

I have thought since that one of his reasons for choosing me as his travelling companion on this occasion was because he was getting up steam for what he subsequently termed 'an alliance with my family', but the idea never entered my head at the time. A more careless man as to dress I have rarely met, and yet, in all the heat of July in Holland, I noticed that he never appeared without a high, starched collar, which had not even fashion to commend it at that time.

I often chaffed him about his splendid collars, and asked him why he wore them, but without eliciting any response. One evening, as we were walking back to our lodgings in Middeburg, I attacked him for about the thirtieth time on the subject.

'Why on earth do you wear them?' I said.

'You have, I believe, asked me that question many times,' he replied, in his slow, precise utterance; 'but always on occasions when I was occupied. I am now at leisure, and I will tell you.'

And he did.

I have put down what he said, as nearly in his own words as I can remember them.

Ten years ago, I was asked to read a paper on English Frescoes at the Institute of British Architects. I was determined to make the paper as good as I could, down to the slightest details, and I consulted many books on the subject, and studied every fresco I could find. My father, who had been an architect, had left me, at his death, all his papers and notebooks on the subject of architecture. I searched them diligently, and found in one of them a slight unfinished sketch of nearly fifty years ago that specially interested me. Underneath was noted, in his clear, small hand – Frescoed east wall of crypt. Parish Church. Wet Waste-on-the-Wolds, Yorkshire (via Pickering).

The sketch had such a fascination for me that I decided to go there and see the fresco for myself. I had only a very vague idea as to where Wet Waste-on-the-Wolds was, but I was ambitious for the success of my paper; it was hot in London, and I set off on my long journey not without a certain degree of pleasure, with my dog Brian, a large nondescript brindled creature, as my only companion.

I reached Pickering, in Yorkshire, in the course of the afternoon, and then began a series of experiments on local lines which ended, after several hours, in my finding myself deposited at a little out-of-the-world station within nine or ten miles of Wet Waste. As no conveyance of any kind was to be had, I shouldered my portmanteau, and set out on a long white road that stretched away into the distance over the bare, treeless wold. I must have walked for several hours, over a waste of moorland patched with heather, when a doctor passed me, and gave me a lift to within a mile of my destination. The mile was a long one, and it was quite dark by the time I saw the feeble glimmer of lights in front of me, and found that I had reached Wet Waste. I had considerable difficulty in getting anyone to take me in; but at last I persuaded the owner of the public house to give me a bed, and, quite tired out, I got into it as soon as possible, for fear he should change his mind, and fell asleep to the sound of a little stream below my window.

I was up early next morning, and inquired directly after breakfast the way to the clergyman's house, which I found was close at hand. At Wet Waste everything was close at hand. The whole village seemed composed of a straggling row of one-storeyed grey stone houses, the same colour as the stone walls that separated the few fields enclosed from the surrounding waste, and as the little bridges over the beck that ran down one side of the grey wide street. Everything was grey.

The church, the low tower of which I could see at a little distance, seemed to have been built of the same stone; so was the parsonage when I came up to it, accompanied on my way by a mob of rough, uncouth children, who eyed me and Brian with half-defiant curiosity.

The clergyman was at home, and after a short delay I was admitted. Leaving Brian in charge of my drawing materials, I followed the servant into a low panelled room, in which, at a latticed window, a very old man was sitting. The morning light fell on his white head bent low over a litter of papers and books.

'Mr er...?' he said, looking up slowly, with one finger keeping his place in a book.

'Blake.'

'Blake,' he repeated after me, and was silent.

I told him that I was an architect; that I had come to study a fresco in the crypt of his church, and asked for the keys.

'The crypt,' he said, pushing up his spectacles and peering hard at me. 'The crypt has been closed for thirty years. Ever since...' and he stopped short.

'I should be much obliged for the keys,' I said again.

He shook his head.

'No,' he said. 'No one goes in there now.'

'It is a pity,' I remarked, 'for I have come a long way with that one object'; and I told him about the paper I had been asked to read, and the trouble I was taking with it.

He became interested. 'Ah!' he said, laying down his pen, and removing his finger from the page before him, 'I can understand that. I also was young once, and fired with ambition. The lines have fallen to me in somewhat lonely places, and for forty years I have held the cure of souls in this place, where, truly, I have seen but little of the world, though I myself may be not unknown in the paths of literature. Possibly you may have read a pamphlet, written by myself, on the Syrian version of the Three Authentic Epistles of Ignatius?'

'Sir,' I said, 'I am ashamed to confess that I have not time to read even the most celebrated books. My one object in life is my art. *Ars longa, vita brevis*, you know.'

'You are right, my son,' said the old man, evidently disappointed, but looking at me kindly. 'There are diversities of gifts, and if the Lord has entrusted you with a talent, look to it. Lay it not up in a napkin.'

I said I would not do so if he would lend me the keys of the crypt. He seemed startled by my recurrence to the subject and looked undecided.

'Why not?' he murmured to himself. 'The youth appears a good youth. And superstition! What is it but distrust in God!'

He got up slowly, and taking a large bunch of keys out of his pocket, opened with one of them an oak cupboard in the corner of the room.

'They should be here,' he muttered, peering in; 'but the dust of many years deceives the eye. See, my son, if among these parchments there be two keys; one of iron and very large, and the other steel, and of a long thin appearance.'

I went eagerly to help him, and presently found in a back drawer two keys tied together, which he recognised at once.

'Those are they,' he said. 'The long one opens the first door at the bottom of the steps which go down against the outside wall of the church hard by the sword graven in the wall. The second opens (but it is hard of opening and of shutting) the iron door within the passage leading to the crypt itself. My son, is it necessary to your treatise that you should enter this crypt?'

I replied that it was absolutely necessary.

'Then take them,' he said, 'and in the evening you will bring them to me again.'

I said I might want to go several days running, and asked if he would not allow me to keep them till I had finished my work; but on that point he was firm.

'Likewise,' he added, 'be careful that you lock the first door at the foot of the steps before you unlock the second, and lock the second also while you are within. Furthermore, when you come out, lock the iron inner door as well as the wooden one.'

I promised I would do so, and, after thanking him, hurried away, delighted at my success in obtaining the keys. Finding Brian and my sketching materials waiting for me in the porch, I eluded the vigilance of my escort of children by taking the narrow private path between the parsonage and the church which was close at hand, standing in a quadrangle of ancient yews.

The church itself was interesting, and I noticed that it must have arisen out of the ruins of a previous building, judging from the number of fragments of stone caps and arches, bearing traces of very early carving, now built into the walls. There were incised crosses, too, in some places, and one especially caught my attention, being flanked by a large sword. It was in trying to get a nearer look at this that I stumbled, and, looking down, saw at my feet a flight of narrow stone steps green with moss and mildew. Evidently this was the entrance to the crypt. I at once descended the steps, taking care of my footing, for they were damp and slippery in the extreme.

Brian accompanied me, as nothing would induce him to remain behind. By the time I had reached the bottom of the stairs, I found myself almost in darkness, and I had to strike a light before I could find the keyhole and the proper key to fit into it. The door, which was of wood, opened inwards fairly easily, although an accumulation of mould and rubbish on the ground outside showed it had not been used for many years. Having got through it, which was not altogether an easy matter, as nothing would induce it to open more than about eighteen inches, I carefully locked it behind me, although I should have preferred to leave it open, as there is to some minds an unpleasant feeling in being locked in anywhere, in case of a sudden exit seeming advisable.

I kept my candle alight with some difficulty, and after groping my way down a low and of course exceedingly dank passage, came to another door. A toad was squatting against it, who looked as if he had been sitting there about a hundred years. As I lowered the candle to the floor, he gazed at the light with unblinking eyes, and then retreated slowly into a crevice in the wall, leaving against the door a small cavity in the dry mud which had gradually silted up round his person. I noticed that this door was of iron, and had a long bolt, which, however, was broken.

Without delay, I fitted the second key into the lock, and pushing the door open after considerable difficulty, I felt the cold breath of the crypt upon my face. I must own I experienced a momentary regret at locking the second door again as soon as I was well inside, but I felt it my duty to do so. Then, leaving the key in the lock, I seized my candle and looked round. I was standing in a low vaulted chamber with groined roof, cut out of the solid rock. It was difficult to see where the crypt ended, as further light thrown on any point only showed other rough archways or openings, cut in the rock, which had probably served at one time for family vaults.

A peculiarity of the Wet Waste crypt, which I had not noticed in other places of that description, was the tasteful arrangement of skulls and bones which were packed about four feet high on either side. The skulls were symmetrically built up to within a few inches of the top of the low archway on my left, and the shin bones were arranged in the same manner on my right. But the fresco! I looked round for it in vain. Perceiving at the further end

of the crypt a very low and very massive archway, the entrance
to which was not filled up with bones, I passed under it, and
found myself in a second smaller chamber. Holding my candle
above my head, the first object its light fell upon was – the fresco,
and at a glance I saw that it was unique. Setting down some of
my things with a trembling hand on a rough stone shelf hard by,
which had evidently been a credence table, I examined the work
more closely. It was a reredos over what had probably been the
altar at the time the priests were proscribed. The fresco belonged
to the earliest part of the fifteenth century, and was so perfectly
preserved that I could almost trace the limits of each day's work
in the plaster, as the artist had dashed it on and smoothed it
out with his trowel. The subject was the Ascension, gloriously
treated. I can hardly describe my elation as I stood and looked
at it, and reflected that this magnificent specimen of English
fresco painting would be made known to the world by myself.
Recollecting myself at last, I opened my sketching bag, and,
lighting all the candles I had brought with me, set to work.

Brian walked about near me, and though I was not otherwise
than glad of his company in my rather lonely position, I wished
several times I had left him behind. He seemed restless, and even
the sight of so many bones appeared to exercise no soothing
effect upon him. At last, however, after repeated commands, he
lay down, watchful but motionless, on the stone floor.

I must have worked for several hours, and I was pausing to rest
my eyes and hands, when I noticed for the first time the intense
stillness that surrounded me. No sound from me reached the
outer world. The church clock which had clanged out so loud
and ponderously as I went down the steps, had not since sent the
faintest whisper of its iron tongue down to me below. All was
silent as the grave. This was the grave. Those who had come
here had indeed gone down into silence. I repeated the words to
myself, or rather they repeated themselves to me.

Gone down into silence.

I was awakened from my reverie by a faint sound. I sat still and listened. Bats occasionally frequent vaults and underground places.

The sound continued, a faint, stealthy, rather unpleasant sound. I do not know what kinds of sounds bats make, whether pleasant or otherwise. Suddenly there was a noise as of something falling, a momentary pause – and then – an almost imperceptible but distant jangle as of a key.

I had left the key in the lock after I had turned it, and I now regretted having done so. I got up, took one of the candles, and went back into the larger crypt – for though I trust I am not so effeminate as to be rendered nervous by hearing a noise for which I cannot instantly account; still, on occasions of this kind, I must honestly say I should prefer that they did not occur. As I came towards the iron door, there was another distinct (I had almost said hurried) sound. The impression on my mind was one of great haste. When I reached the door, and held the candle near the lock to take out the key, I perceived that the other one, which hung by a short string to its fellow, was vibrating slightly. I should have preferred not to find it vibrating, as there seemed no occasion for such a course; but I put them both into my pocket, and turned to go back to my work. As I turned, I saw on the ground what had occasioned the louder noise I had heard, namely, a skull which had evidently just slipped from its place on the top of one of the walls of bones, and had rolled almost to my feet. There, disclosing a few more inches of the top of an archway behind, was the place from which it had been dislodged. I stooped to pick it up, but fearing to displace any more skulls by meddling with the pile, and not liking to gather up its scattered teeth, I let it lie, and went back to my work, in which I was soon so completely absorbed that I was only roused at last by my candles beginning to burn low and go out one after another.

Then, with a sigh of regret, for I had not nearly finished, I turned to go. Poor Brian, who had never quite reconciled himself to the place, was beside himself with delight. As I opened the iron door he pushed past me, and a moment later I heard him whining and scratching, and I had almost added, beating, against the wooden one. I locked the iron door, and hurried down the passage as quickly as I could, and almost before I had got the other one ajar there seemed to be a rush past me into the open air, and Brian was bounding up the steps and out of sight. As I stopped to take out the key, I felt quite deserted and left behind. When I came out once more into the sunlight, there was a vague sensation all about me in the air of exultant freedom.

It was already late in the afternoon, and after I had sauntered back to the parsonage to give up the keys, I persuaded the people of the public house to let me join in the family meal, which was spread out in the kitchen. The inhabitants of Wet Waste were primitive people, with the frank, unabashed manner that flourishes still in lonely places, especially in the wilds of Yorkshire; but I had no idea that in these days of penny posts and cheap newspapers such entire ignorance of the outer world could have existed in any corner, however remote, of Great Britain.

When I took one of the neighbour's children on my knee – a pretty little girl with the palest aureole of flaxen hair I had ever seen – and began to draw pictures for her of the birds and beasts of other countries, I was instantly surrounded by a crowd of children, and even grown-up people, while others came to their doorways and looked on from a distance, calling to each other in the strident unknown tongue which I have since discovered goes by the name of 'Broad Yorkshire'.

The following morning, as I came out of my room, I perceived that something was amiss in the village. A buzz of voices reached me as I passed the bar, and in the next house I could hear through the open window a high-pitched wail of lamentation.

The woman who brought me my breakfast was in tears, and in answer to my questions, told me that the neighbour's child, the little girl whom I had taken on my knee the evening before, had died in the night.

I felt sorry for the general grief that the little creature's death seemed to arouse, and the uncontrolled wailing of the poor mother took my appetite away.

I hurried off early to my work, calling on my way for the keys, and with Brian for my companion descended once more into the crypt, and drew and measured with an absorption that gave me no time that day to listen for sounds real or fancied. Brian, too, on this occasion seemed quite content, and slept peacefully beside me on the stone floor. When I had worked as long as I could, I put away my books with regret that even then I had not quite finished, as I had hoped to do. It would be necessary to come again for a short time on the morrow. When I returned the keys late that afternoon, the old clergyman met me at the door, and asked me to come in and have tea with him.

'And has the work prospered?' he asked, as we sat down in the long, low room, into which I had just been ushered, and where he seemed to live entirely.

I told him it had, and showed it to him.

'You have seen the original, of course?' I said.

'Once,' he replied, gazing fixedly at it. He evidently did not care to be communicative, so I turned the conversation to the age of the church.

'All here is old,' he said. 'When I was young, forty years ago, and came here because I had no means of mine own, and was much moved to marry at that time, I felt oppressed that all was so old; and that this place was so far removed from the world, for which I had at times longings grievous to be borne; but I had chosen my lot, and with it I was forced to be content. My son, marry not in youth, for love, which truly in that season is a mighty power, turns away the heart from study, and young children break the back of ambition. Neither marry in middle life, when a woman is seen to be but a woman and her talk a weariness, so you will not be burdened with a wife in your old age.'

I had my own views on the subject of marriage, for I am of opinion that a well-chosen companion of domestic tastes and docile and devoted temperament may be of material assistance to a professional man. But, my opinions once formulated, it is not of moment to me to discuss them with others, so I changed the subject, and asked if the neighbouring villages were as antiquated as Wet Waste. 'Yes, all about here is old,' he repeated. 'The paved road leading to Dyke Fens is an ancient pack road, made even in the time of the Romans. Dyke Fens, which is very near here, a matter of but four or five miles, is likewise old, and forgotten by the world. The Reformation never reached it. It stopped here. And at Dyke Fens they still have a priest and a bell, and bow down before the saints. It is a damnable heresy, and weekly I expound it as such to my people, showing them true doctrines; and I have heard that this same priest has so far yielded himself to the Evil One that he has preached against me as withholding gospel truths from my flock; but I take no heed of it, neither of his pamphlet touching the Clementine Homilies, in which he vainly contradicts that which I have plainly set forth and proven beyond doubt, concerning the word "Asaph".'

The old man was fairly off on his favourite subject, and it was some time before I could get away. As it was, he followed me to the door, and I only escaped because the old clerk hobbled up at that moment, and claimed his attention.

The following morning I went for the keys for the third and last time. I had decided to leave early the next day. I was tired of Wet Waste, and a certain gloom seemed to my fancy to be gathering over the place. There was a sensation of trouble in the air, as if, although the day was bright and clear, a storm were coming.

This morning, to my astonishment, the keys were refused to me when I asked for them. I did not, however, take the refusal as final – I make it a rule never to take a refusal as final – and after a short delay I was shown into the room where, as usual, the clergyman was sitting, or rather, on this occasion, was walking up and down.

'My son,' he said with vehemence, 'I know wherefore you

have come, but it is of no avail. I cannot lend the keys again.'

I replied that, on the contrary, I hoped he would give them to me at once.

'It is impossible,' he repeated. 'I did wrong, exceeding wrong. I will never part with them again.'

'Why not?'.

He hesitated, and then said slowly:

'The old clerk, Abraham Kelly, died last night.' He paused, and then went on: 'The doctor has just been here to tell me of that which is a mystery to him. I do not wish the people of the place to know it, and only to me he has mentioned it, but he has discovered plainly on the throat of the old man, and also, but more faintly on the child's, marks as of strangulation. None but he has observed it, and he is at a loss how to account for it. I, alas! can account for it but in one way, but in one way!'

I did not see what all this had to do with the crypt, but to humour the old man, I asked what that way was.

'It is a long story, and, haply, to a stranger it may appear but foolishness, but I will even tell it; for I perceive that unless I furnish a reason for withholding the keys, you will not cease to entreat me for them.

'I told you at first when you inquired of me concerning the crypt, that it had been closed these thirty years, and so it was. Thirty years ago a certain Sir Roger Despard departed this life, even the Lord of the manor of Wet Waste and Dyke Fens, the last of his family, which is now, thank the Lord, extinct. He was a man of a vile life, neither fearing God nor regarding man, nor having compassion on innocence, and the Lord appeared to have given him over to the tormentors even in this world, for he suffered many things of his vices, more especially from drunkenness, in which seasons, and they were many, he was as one possessed by seven devils, being an abomination to his household and a root of bitterness to all, both high and low.

'And, at last, the cup of his iniquity being full to the brim, he came to die, and I went to exhort him on his deathbed; for I heard that terror had come upon him, and that evil imaginations encompassed him so thick on every side, that few of them that were with him could abide in his presence. But when I saw him I perceived that there was no place of repentance left for him, and he scoffed at me and my superstition, even as he lay dying, and swore there was no God and no angel, and all were damned even as he was. And the next day, towards evening, the pains of death came upon him, and he raved the more exceedingly, inasmuch as he said he was being strangled by the Evil One. Now, on his table was his hunting knife, and with his last strength he crept and laid hold upon it, no man withstanding him, and swore a great oath that if he went down to burn in hell, he would leave one of his hands behind on earth, and that it would never rest until it had drawn blood from the throat of another and strangled him, even as he himself was being strangled. And he cut off his own right hand at the wrist, and no man dared go near him to stop him, and the blood went through the floor, even down to the ceiling of the room below, and thereupon he died.

'And they called me in the night, and told me of his oath, and I counselled that no man should speak of it, and I took the dead hand, which none had ventured to touch, and I laid it beside him in his coffin; for I thought it better he should take it with him, so that he might have it, if haply some day after much tribulation he should perchance be moved to stretch forth his hands towards God. But the story got spread about, and the people were affrighted, so, when he came to be buried in the place of his fathers, he being the last of his family, and the crypt likewise full, I had it closed, and kept the keys myself, and suffered no man to enter therein any more; for truly he was a man of an evil life, and the devil is not yet wholly overcome, nor cast chained into the lake of fire. So in time the story died out, for in thirty years much is forgotten. And when you came and asked me for the keys, I was at the first minded to withhold them; but I thought it was a vain superstition, and I perceived that you do but ask a second time for what is first refused; so I let you have them, seeing it was not an idle curiosity, but a desire to improve the talent committed to you, that led you to require them.'

The old man stopped, and I remained silent, wondering what would be the best way to get them just once more.

'Surely, sir,' I said at last, 'one so cultivated and deeply read as yourself cannot be biased by an idle superstition.'

'I trust not,' he replied, 'and yet − it is a strange thing that since the crypt was opened two people have died, and the mark is plain upon the throat of the old man and visible on the young child. No blood was drawn, but the second time the grip was stronger than the first. The third time, perchance...'

'Superstition such as that,' I said with authority, 'is an entire want of faith in God. You once said so yourself.'

I took a high moral tone which is often efficacious with conscientious, humble-minded people.

He agreed, and accused himself of not having faith as a grain of mustard seed; but even when I had got him so far as that, I had a severe struggle for the keys. It was only when I finally explained to him that if any malign influence had been let loose the first day, at any rate, it was out now for good or evil, and no further going or coming of mine could make any difference, that I finally gained my point. I was young, and he was old; and, being much shaken by what had occurred, he gave way at last, and I wrested the keys from him.

I will not deny that I went down the steps that day with a vague, indefinable repugnance, which was only accentuated by the closing of the two doors behind me. I remembered then, for the first time, the faint jangling of the key and other sounds which I had noticed the first day, and how one of the skulls had fallen. I went to the place where it still lay. I have already said these walls of skulls were built up so high as to be within a few inches of the top of the low archways that led into more distant portions of the vault. The displacement of the skull in question had left a small hole just large enough for me to put my hand through. I noticed for the first time, over the archway above it, a carved coat of arms, and the name, now almost obliterated, of Despard. This, no doubt, was the Despard vault. I could not resist moving a few more skulls and looking in, holding my candle as near the aperture as I could. The vault was full. Piled high, one upon another, were old coffins, and remnants of coffins, and strewn bones. I attribute my present determination to be cremated to the painful impression produced on me by this spectacle. The coffin nearest the archway alone was intact, save for a large crack across the lid. I could not get a ray from my candle to fall on the brass plates, but I felt no doubt this was the coffin of the wicked Sir Roger. I put back the skulls, including the one which had rolled down, and carefully finished my work. I was not there much more than an hour, but I was glad to get away.

If I could have left Wet Waste at once I should have done so, for I had a totally unreasonable longing to leave the place; but I found that only one train stopped during the day at the station from which I had come, and that it would not be possible to be in time for it that day.

Accordingly I submitted to the inevitable, and wandered about with Brian for the remainder of the afternoon and until late in the evening, sketching and smoking. The day was oppressively hot, and even after the sun had set across the burnt stretches of the wolds, it seemed to grow very little cooler. Not a breath stirred. In the evening, when I was tired of loitering in the lanes, I went up to my own room, and after contemplating afresh my finished study of the fresco, I suddenly set to work to write the part of my paper bearing upon it. As a rule, I write with difficulty, but that evening words came to me with winged speed, and with them a hovering impression that I must make haste, that I was much pressed for time. I wrote and wrote, until my candles guttered out and left me trying to finish by the moonlight, which, until I endeavoured to write by it, seemed as clear as day.

I had to put away my MS, and, feeling it was too early to go to bed, for the church clock was just counting out ten, I sat down by the open window and leaned out to try and catch a breath of air. It was a night of exceptional beauty; and as I looked out my nervous haste and hurry of mind were allayed. The moon, a perfect circle, was – if so poetic an expression be permissible – as it were, sailing across a calm sky. Every detail of the little village was as clearly illuminated by its beams as if it were broad day; so, also, was the adjacent church with its primeval yews, while even the wolds beyond were dimly indicated, as if through tracing paper.

I sat a long time leaning against the windowsill. The heat was still intense. I am not, as a rule, easily elated or readily cast down; but as I sat that night in the lonely village on the moors, with Brian's head against my knee, how, or why, I know not, a great depression gradually came upon me.

My mind went back to the crypt and the countless dead who had been laid there. The sight of the goal to which all human life, and strength, and beauty, travel in the end, had not affected me at the time, but now the very air about me seemed heavy with death.

What was the good, I asked myself, of working and toiling, and grinding down my heart and youth in the mill of long and strenuous effort, seeing that in the grave folly and talent, idleness and labour lie together, and are alike forgotten? Labour seemed to stretch before me till my heart ached to think of it, to stretch before me even to the end of life, and then came, as the recompense of my labour – the grave. Even if I succeeded, if, after wearing my life threadbare with toil, I succeeded, what remained to me in the end? The grave. A little sooner, while the hands and eyes were still strong to labour, or a little later, when all power and vision had been taken from them; sooner or later only – the grave.

I do not apologise for the excessively morbid tenor of these reflections, as I hold that they were caused by the lunar effects which I have endeavoured to transcribe. The moon in its various quarterings has always exerted a marked influence on what I may call the sub-dominant, namely, the poetic side of my nature.

I roused myself at last, when the moon came to look ill upon me where I sat, and, leaving the window open, I pulled myself together and went to bed.

I fell asleep almost immediately, but I do not fancy I could have been asleep very long when I was wakened by Brian. He was growling in a low, muffled tone, as he sometimes did in his sleep, when his nose was buried in his rug. I called out to him to shut up; and as he did not do so, turned in bed to find my match box or something to throw at him. The moonlight was still in the room, and as I looked at him I saw him raise his head and evidently wake up. I admonished him, and was just on the point of falling asleep when he began to growl again in a low, savage manner that waked me most effectually. Presently he shook himself and got up, and began prowling about the room. I sat up in bed and called to him, but he paid no attention. Suddenly I saw him stop short in the moonlight; he showed his teeth, and crouched down, his eyes following something in the air. I looked at him in horror. Was he going mad? His eyes were glaring, and his head moved slightly as if he were following the rapid movements of an enemy. Then, with a furious snarl, he suddenly sprang from the ground, and rushed in great leaps across the room towards me, dashing himself against the furniture, his eyes rolling, snatching and tearing wildly in the air with his teeth. I saw he had gone mad. I leaped out of bed, and rushing at him, caught him by the throat. The moon had gone behind a cloud; but in the darkness I felt him turn upon me, felt him rise up, and his teeth close in my throat. I was being strangled. With all the strength of despair, I kept my grip of his neck, and, dragging him across the room, tried to crush in his head against the iron rail of my bedstead.

It was my only chance. I felt the blood running down my neck. I was suffocating. After one moment of frightful struggle, I beat his head against the bar and heard his skull give way. I felt him give one strong shudder, a groan, and then I fainted away.

When I came to myself I was lying on the floor, surrounded by the people of the house, my reddened hands still clutching

Brian's throat. Someone was holding a candle towards me, and the draught from the window made it flare and waver. I looked at Brian. He was stone dead.

The blood from his battered head was trickling slowly over my hands. His great jaw was fixed in something that – in the uncertain light – I could not see.

They turned the light a little.

'Oh, God!' I shrieked. 'There! Look! Look!'

'He's off his head,' said someone, and I fainted again.

I was ill for about a fortnight without regaining consciousness, a waste of time of which even now I cannot think without poignant regret. When I did recover consciousness, I found I was being carefully nursed by the old clergyman and the people of the house. I have often heard the unkindness of the world in general inveighed against, but for my part I can honestly say that I have received many more kindnesses than I have time to repay. Country people especially are remarkably attentive to strangers in illness.

I could not rest until I had seen the doctor who attended me, and had received his assurance that I should be equal to reading my paper on the appointed day. This pressing anxiety removed, I told him of what I had seen before I fainted the second time. He listened attentively, and then assured me, in a manner that was intended to be soothing, that I was suffering from an hallucination, due, no doubt, to the shock of my dog's sudden madness.

'Did you see the dog after it was dead?' I asked.

He said he did. The whole jaw was covered with blood and foam; the teeth certainly seemed convulsively fixed, but the case being evidently one of extraordinarily virulent hydrophobia, owing to the intense heat, he had had the body buried immediately.

My companion stopped speaking as we reached our lodgings, and went upstairs. Then, lighting a candle, he slowly turned down his collar.

'You see I have the marks still,' he said, 'but I have no fear of dying of hydrophobia. I am told such peculiar scars could not have been made by the teeth of a dog. If you look closely you see the pressure of the five fingers. That is the reason why I wear high collars.'

For the Blood is the Life

F Marion Crawford (1854–1909)

Crawford was an American whose novels, bestsellers in their day, have now been largely forgotten. Born in Italy where his father, an American sculptor, was working, he spent his childhood half in Europe and half in America. As a young man, he travelled to India which was the setting for his first novel Mr Isaacs, *published in 1882. The following year he settled permanently in Italy and began to produce a string of novels, including titles such as* Saracinesca, Don Orsino *and* Katharine Lauderdale, *many of them set in the country he considered his home. His own favourite amongst his novels was said to be* Khaled: A Tale of Arabia, *an oriental romance which has come to be considered a landmark in the history of fantasy fiction and was reprinted in the famous Ballantine Adult Fantasy series in the 1970s. Marion Crawford wrote a lot of 'supernatural' fiction and stories including 'The Upper Berth', about a man on board a steamship who has an unexpected companion in his cabin, 'The Screaming Skull' and 'The Dead Smile', all of which remain reasonably well known to connoisseurs of the genre. Written in 1905 but first published in a posthumous collection of stories entitled* Wandering Ghosts, *'For the Blood is the Life' is a powerful vampire story, much admired by HP Lovecraft, which is set in Crawford's beloved Italy.*

We had dined at sunset on the broad roof of the old tower, because it was cooler there during the great heat of summer. Besides, the little kitchen was built at one corner of the great square platform, which made it more convenient than if the dishes had to be carried down the steep stone steps, broken in places and everywhere worn with age. The tower was one of those built all down the west coast of Calabria by the Emperor

Charles V early in the sixteenth century, to keep off the Barbary pirates, when the unbelievers were allied with Francis I against the Emperor and the Church. They have gone to ruin, a few still stand intact, and mine is one of the largest. How it came into my possession ten years ago, and why I spend a part of each year in it, are matters which do not concern this tale. The tower stands in one of the loneliest spots in Southern Italy, at the extremity of a curving rocky promontory, which forms a small but safe natural harbour at the southern extremity of the Gulf of Policastro, and just north of Cape Scalea, the birthplace of Judas Iscariot, according to the old local legend. The tower stands alone on this hooked spur of the rock, and there is not a house to be seen within three miles of it. When I go there I take a couple of sailors, one of whom is a fair cook, and when I am away it is in charge of a gnome-like little being who was once a miner and who attached himself to me long ago.

My friend, who sometimes visits me in my summer solitude, is an artist by profession, a Scandinavian by birth, and a cosmopolitan by force of circumstances. We had dined at sunset; the sunset glow had reddened and faded again, and the evening purple steeped the vast chain of the mountains that embrace the deep gulf to eastward and rear themselves higher and higher toward the south. It was hot, and we sat at the landward corner of the platform, waiting for the night breeze to come down from the lower hills. The colour sank out of the air, there was a little interval of deep-grey twilight, and a lamp sent a yellow streak from the open door of the kitchen, where the men were getting their supper.

Then the moon rose suddenly above the crest of the promontory, flooding the platform and lighting up every little spur of rock and knoll of grass below us, down to the edge of the motionless water. My friend lighted his pipe and sat looking at a spot on the hillside. I knew that he was looking at it, and for a long time past I had wondered whether he would ever see anything there that would fix his attention. I knew that spot well. It was clear that he was interested at last, though it was a long time before he spoke. Like most painters, he trusts to his own eyesight, as a lion trusts his strength and a stag his speed, and he is always disturbed when he cannot reconcile what he sees with what he believes that he ought to see.

'It's strange,' he said. 'Do you see that little mound just on this side of the boulder?'

'Yes,' I said, and I guessed what was coming.

'It looks like a grave,' observed Holger.

'Very true. It does look like a grave.'

'Yes,' continued my friend, his eyes still fixed on the spot. 'But the strange thing is that I see the body lying on the top of it. Of course,' continued Holger, turning his head on one side as artists do, 'it must be an effect of light. In the first place, it is not a grave at all. Secondly, if it were, the body would be inside and not outside. Therefore, it's an effect of the moonlight. Don't you see it?'

'Perfectly; I always see it on moonlight nights.'

'It doesn't seem to interest you much,' said Holger.

'On the contrary, it does interest me, though I am used to it. You're not so far wrong, either. The mound is really a grave.'

'Nonsense!' cried Holger, incredulously. 'I suppose you'll tell me what I see lying on it is really a corpse!'

'No,' I answered, 'it's not. I know, because I have taken the trouble to go down and see.'

'Then what is it?' asked Holger.

'It's nothing.'

'You mean that it's an effect of light, I suppose?'

'Perhaps it is. But the inexplicable part of the matter is that it makes no difference whether the moon is rising or setting, or waxing or waning. If there's any moonlight at all, from east or west or overhead, so long as it shines on the grave you can see the outline of the body on top.'

Holger stirred up his pipe with the point of his knife, and then used his finger for a stopper. When the tobacco burned well he rose from his chair.

'If you don't mind,' he said, 'I'll go down and take a look at it.'

He left me, crossed the roof, and disappeared down the dark steps. I did not move, but sat looking down until he came out of the tower below. I heard him humming an old Danish song as he crossed the open space in the bright moonlight, going straight to the mysterious mound. When he was ten paces from it, Holger stopped short, made two steps forward, and then three or four backward, and then stopped again. I knew what that meant. He had reached the spot where the Thing ceased to be visible – where, as he would have said, the effect of light changed.

Then he went on till he reached the mound and stood upon it. I could see the Thing still, but it was no longer lying down; it was on its knees now, winding its white arms round Holger's body and looking up into his face. A cool breeze stirred my hair at that moment, as the night wind began to come down from the hills, but it felt like a breath from another world.

The Thing seemed to be trying to climb to its feet, helping itself up by Holger's body while he stood upright, quite unconscious of it and apparently looking toward the tower, which is very picturesque when the moonlight falls upon it on that side.

'Come along!' I shouted. 'Don't stay there all night!'

It seemed to me that he moved reluctantly as he stepped from the mound, or else with difficulty. That was it. The Thing's arms were still round his waist, but its feet could not leave the grave. As he came slowly forward it was drawn and lengthened like a wreath of mist, thin and white, till I saw distinctly that Holger shook himself, as a man does who feels a chill. At the same instant a little wail of pain came to me on the breeze – it might have been the cry of the small owl that lives among the rocks – and the misty presence floated swiftly back from Holger's advancing figure and lay once more at its length upon the mound.

Again I felt the cool breeze in my hair, and this time an icy thrill of dread ran down my spine. I remembered very well that I had once gone down there alone in the moonlight; that presently, being near, I had seen nothing; that, like Holger, I had gone and had stood upon the mound; and I remembered how, when I came back, sure that there was nothing there, I had felt the sudden conviction that there was something after all if I would only look behind me. I remembered the strong temptation to look back, a temptation I had resisted as unworthy of a man of sense, until, to get rid of it, I had shaken myself just as Holger did.

And now I knew that those white, misty arms had been round me too; I knew it in a flash, and I shuddered as I remembered that I had heard the night owl then too. But it had not been the night owl. It was the cry of the Thing.

I refilled my pipe and poured out a cup of strong southern wine; in less than a minute Holger was seated beside me again.

'Of course there's nothing there,' he said, 'but it's creepy, all the same. Do you know, when I was coming back I was so sure that there was something behind me that I wanted to turn round and look? It was an effort not to.'

He laughed a little, knocked the ashes out of his pipe, and poured himself out some wine. For a while neither of us spoke, and the moon rose higher, and we both looked at the Thing that lay on the mound.

'You might make a story about that,' said Holger after a long time.

'There is one,' I answered. 'If you're not sleepy, I'll tell it to you.'

'Go ahead,' said Holger, who likes stories.

★ ★ ★ ★ ★

Old Alario was dying up there in the village behind the hill. You remember him, I have no doubt. They say that he made his money by selling sham jewellery in South America, and escaped with his gains when he was found out. Like all those fellows, if they bring anything back with them, he at once set to work to enlarge his house, and as there are no masons here, he sent all the way to Paola for two workmen. They were a rough-looking pair of scoundrels – a Neapolitan who had lost one eye and a Sicilian with an old scar half an inch deep across his left cheek. I often saw them, for on Sundays they used to come down here and fish off the rocks. When Alario caught the fever that killed him the masons were still at work. As he had agreed that part of their pay should be their board and lodging, he made them sleep in the house. His wife was dead, and he had an only son called Angelo, who was a much better sort than himself. Angelo was to marry the daughter of the richest man in the village, and, strange to say, though the marriage was arranged by their parents, the young people were said to be in love with each other.

For that matter, the whole village was in love with Angelo, and among the rest a wild, good-looking creature called Cristina, who was more like a gipsy than any girl I ever saw about here. She had very red lips and very black eyes, she was built like a greyhound, and had the tongue of the devil. But Angelo did not care a straw for her. He was rather a simple-minded fellow, quite different from his old scoundrel of a father, and under what I should call normal circumstances I really believe that he would never have looked at any girl except the nice plump little creature, with a fat dowry, whom his father meant him to marry. But things turned up which were neither normal nor natural.

On the other hand, a very handsome young shepherd from the hills above Maratea was in love with Cristina, who seems to have been quite indifferent to him. Cristina had no regular means of subsistence, but she was a good girl and willing to do any work or go on errands to any distance for the sake of a loaf of bread or a mess of beans, and permission to sleep under cover. She was especially glad when she could get something to do about the house of Angelo's father. There is no doctor in the village, and when the neighbours saw that old Alario was dying they sent Cristina to Scalea to fetch one. That was late in the afternoon, and if they had waited so long, it was because the dying miser refused to allow any such extravagance while he was able to speak. But while Cristina was gone matters grew rapidly worse, the priest was brought to the bedside, and when he had done what he could he gave it as his opinion to the bystanders that the old man was dead, and left the house.

You know these people. They have a physical horror of death. Until the priest spoke, the room had been full of people. The words were hardly out of his mouth before it was empty. It was night now. They hurried down the dark steps and out into the street.

Angelo, as I have said, was away, Cristina had not come back – the simple woman-servant who had nursed the sick man fled with the rest, and the body was left alone in the flickering light of the earthen oil lamp.

Five minutes later two men looked in cautiously and crept forward toward the bed. They were the one-eyed Neapolitan mason and his Sicilian companion. They knew what they wanted. In a moment they had dragged from under the bed a small but heavy iron-bound box, and long before anyone thought of coming back to the dead man they had left the house and the village under cover of the darkness. It was easy enough, for Alario's house is the last toward the gorge which leads down here, and the thieves merely went out by the back door, got over the stone wall, and had nothing to risk after that except the possibility of meeting some belated countryman, which was very small indeed, since few of the people use that path. They had a mattock and shovel, and they made their way here without accident.

I am telling you this story as it must have happened, for, of course, there were no witnesses to this part of it. The men brought the box down by the gorge, intending to bury it until they should be able to come back and take it away in a boat. They must have been clever enough to guess that some of the money would be in paper notes, for they would otherwise have buried it on the beach in the wet sand, where it would have been much safer. But the paper would have rotted if they had been obliged to leave it there long, so they dug their hole down there, close to that boulder. Yes, just where the mound is now.

Cristina did not find the doctor in Scalea, for he had been sent for from a place up the valley, halfway to San Domenico. If she had found him, he would have come on his mule by the upper road, which is smoother but much longer. But Cristina took the short cut by the rocks, which passes about fifty feet above the mound, and goes round that corner. The men were digging when she passed, and she heard them at work. It would not have been like her to go by without finding out what the noise was, for she was never afraid of anything in her life, and, besides, the fishermen sometimes come ashore here at night to get a stone for an anchor or to gather sticks to make a little fire. The night was dark, and Cristina probably came close to the two men before she could see what they were doing. She knew them, of course, and they knew her, and understood instantly that they were in her power. There was only one thing to be done for their safety, and they did it. They knocked her on the head, they dug the hole deep, and they buried her quickly with the iron-bound chest. They must have understood that their only chance of escaping suspicion lay in getting back to the village before their absence was noticed, for they returned immediately, and were found half an hour later gossiping quietly with the man who was making Alario's coffin. He was a crony of theirs, and had been working at the repairs in the old man's house. So far as I have been able to make out, the only persons who were supposed to know where Alario kept his treasure were Angelo and the one woman-servant I have mentioned. Angelo was away; it was the woman who discovered the theft.

It is easy enough to understand why no one else knew where the money was. The old man kept his door locked and the key in his pocket when he was out, and did not let the woman enter to clean the place unless he was there himself. The whole village knew that he had money somewhere, however, and the masons had probably discovered the whereabouts of the chest by climbing in at the window in his absence. If the old man had not been delirious until he lost consciousness, he would have been in frightful agony of mind for his riches. The faithful woman-servant forgot their existence only for a few moments when she fled with the rest, overcome by the horror of death. Twenty minutes had not passed before she returned with the two hideous old hags who are always called in to prepare the dead for burial. Even then she had not at first the courage to go near the bed with them, but she made a pretence of dropping something, went down on her knees as if to find it, and looked under the bedstead. The walls of the room were newly whitewashed down to the floor, and she saw at a glance that the chest was gone. It had been there in the afternoon, it had therefore been stolen in the short interval since she had left the room.

There are no carabineers stationed in the village; there is not so much as a municipal watchman, for there is no municipality. There never was such a place, I believe. Scalea is supposed to look after it in some mysterious way, and it takes a couple of hours to get anybody from there. As the old woman had lived in the village all her life, it did not even occur to her to apply to any civil authority for help. She simply set up a howl and ran through the village in the dark, screaming out that her dead master's house had been robbed. Many of the people looked out, but at first no one seemed inclined to help her. Most of them, judging her by themselves, whispered to each other that she had probably stolen the money herself. The first man to move was the father of the girl whom Angelo was to marry; having collected his household, all of whom felt a personal interest in the wealth which was to have come into the family, he declared it to be his opinion that the chest had been stolen by the two journeyman masons who lodged in the house. He headed a search for them, which naturally began in Alario's house and ended in the carpenter's workshop, where the thieves were found discussing a measure of wine with the carpenter over the half-finished coffin, by the light of one earthen lamp filled with oil and tallow. The search party at once accused the delinquents of the crime, and threatened to lock them up in the cellar till the carabineers could be fetched from Scalea. The two men looked at each other for one moment, and then without the slightest hesitation they put out the single light, seized the unfinished coffin between them, and using it as a sort of battering ram, dashed upon their assailants in the dark. In a few moments they were beyond pursuit.

That is the end of the first part of the story. The treasure had disappeared, and as no trace of it could be found the people naturally supposed that the thieves had succeeded in carrying it off. The old man was buried, and when Angelo came back at last he had to borrow money to pay for the miserable funeral, and had some difficulty in doing so. He hardly needed to be told that in losing his inheritance he had lost his bride. In this part of the world marriages are made on strictly business principles, and if the promised cash is not forthcoming on the appointed day the bride or the bridegroom whose parents have failed to produce it may as well take themselves off, for there will be no wedding. Poor Angelo knew that well enough. His father had been possessed of hardly any land, and now that the hard cash which he had brought from South America was gone, there was nothing left but debts for the building materials that were to have been used for enlarging and improving the old house. Angelo was beggared, and the nice plump little creature who was to have been his turned up her nose at him in the most approved fashion. As for Cristina, it was several days before she was missed, for no one remembered that she had been sent to Scalea for the doctor, who had never come. She often disappeared in the same way for days together, when she could find a little work here and there at the distant farms among the hills. But when she did not come back at all, people began to wonder, and at last made up their minds that she had connived with the masons and had escaped with them.

★ ★ ★ ★ ★

I paused and emptied my glass.

'That sort of thing could not happen anywhere else,' observed Holger,
filling his everlasting pipe again. 'It is wonderful what a natural charm
there is about murder and sudden death in a romantic country like this.
Deeds that would be simply brutal and disgusting anywhere else become
dramatic and mysterious because this is Italy and we are living in a
genuine tower of Charles V built against genuine Barbary pirates.'

'There's something in that,' I admitted. Holger is the most romantic
man in the world inside of himself, but he always thinks it necessary to
explain why he feels anything.

'I suppose they found the poor girl's body with the box,' he said
presently.

'As it seems to interest you,' I answered, 'I'll tell you the rest of the
story.'

The moon had risen high by this time; the outline of the Thing on the
mound was clearer to our eyes than before.

★ ★ ★ ★ ★

The village very soon settled down to its small, dull life. No one
missed old Alario, who had been away so much on his voyages
to South America that he had never been a familiar figure in his
native place. Angelo lived in the half-finished house, and because
he had no money to pay the old woman-servant she would not
stay with him, but once in a long time she would come and wash
a shirt for him for old acquaintance's sake. Besides the house, he
had inherited a small patch of ground at some distance from the
village; he tried to cultivate it, but he had no heart in the work,
for he knew he could never pay the taxes on it and on the house,
which would certainly be confiscated by the Government, or
seized for the debt of the building material, which the man who
had supplied it refused to take back.

Angelo was very unhappy. So long as his father had been alive and rich, every girl in the village had been in love with him; but that was all changed now. It had been pleasant to be admired and courted, and invited to drink wine by fathers who had girls to marry. It was hard to be stared at coldly, and sometimes laughed at because he had been robbed of his inheritance. He cooked his miserable meals for himself, and from being sad became melancholy and morose.

At twilight, when the day's work was done, instead of hanging about in the open space before the church with young fellows of his own age, he took to wandering in lonely places on the outskirts of the village till it was quite dark. Then he slunk home and went to bed to save the expense of a light. But in those lonely twilight hours he began to have strange waking dreams. He was not always alone, for often when he sat on the stump of a tree, where the narrow path turns down the gorge, he was sure that a woman came up noiselessly over the rough stones, as if her feet were bare; and she stood under a clump of chestnut trees only half a dozen yards down the path, and beckoned to him without speaking. Though she was in the shadow he knew that her lips were red, and that when they parted a little and smiled at him she showed two small sharp teeth. He knew this at first rather than saw it, and he knew that it was Cristina, and that she was dead. Yet he was not afraid; he only wondered whether it was a dream, for he thought that if he had been awake he should have been frightened.

Besides, the dead woman had red lips, and that could only happen in a dream. Whenever he went near the gorge after sunset she was already there waiting for him, or else she very soon appeared, and he began to be sure that she came a little nearer to him every day. At first he had only been sure of her blood-red mouth, but now each feature grew distinct, and the pale face looked at him with deep and hungry eyes.

It was the eyes that grew dim. Little by little he came to know that some day the dream would not end when he turned away to go home, but would lead him down the gorge out of which the vision rose. She was nearer now when she beckoned to him. Her cheeks were not livid like those of the dead, but pale with starvation, with the furious and unappeased physical hunger of her eyes that devoured him. They feasted on his soul and cast a spell over him, and at last they were close to his own and held him. He could not tell whether her breath was as hot as fire or as cold as ice; he could not tell whether her red lips burned his or froze them, or whether her five fingers on his wrists seared scorching scars or bit his flesh like frost; he could not tell whether he was awake or asleep, whether she was alive or dead, but he knew that she loved him, she alone of all creatures, earthly or unearthly, and her spell had power over him.

When the moon rose high that night the shadow of that Thing was not alone down there upon the mound.

Angelo awoke in the cool dawn, drenched with dew and chilled through flesh, and blood, and bone. He opened his eyes to the faint grey light, and saw the stars still shining overhead. He was very weak, and his heart was beating so slowly that he was almost like a man fainting.

Slowly he turned his head on the mound, as on a pillow, but the other face was not there. Fear seized him suddenly, a fear unspeakable and unknown; he sprang to his feet and fled up the gorge, and he never looked behind him until he reached the door of the house on the outskirts of the village. Drearily he went to his work that day, and wearily the hours dragged themselves after the sun, till at last it touched the sea and sank, and the great sharp hills above Maratea turned purple against the dove-coloured eastern sky.

Angelo shouldered his heavy hoe and left the field. He felt less tired now than in the morning when he had begun to work, but he promised himself that he would go home without lingering by the gorge, and eat the best supper he could get himself, and sleep all night in his bed like a Christian man. Not again would he be tempted down the narrow way by a shadow with red lips and icy breath; not again would he dream that dream of terror and delight. He was near the village now; it was half an hour since the sun had set, and the cracked church bell sent little discordant echoes across the rocks and ravines to tell all good people that the day was done. Angelo stood still a moment where the path forked, where it led towards the village on the left, and down to the gorge on the right, where a clump of chestnut trees overhung the narrow way. He stood still a minute, lifting his battered hat from his head and gazing at the fast-fading sea westward, and his lips moved as he silently repeated the familiar evening prayer. His lips moved, but the words that followed them in his brain lost their meaning and turned into others, and ended in a name that he spoke aloud – Cristina! With the name, the tension of his will relaxed suddenly, reality went out and the dream took him again, and bore him on swiftly and surely like a man walking in his sleep, down, down, by the steep path in the gathering darkness. And as she glided beside him, Cristina whispered strange, sweet things in his ear, which somehow, if he had been awake, he knew that he could not quite have understood; but now they were the most wonderful words he had ever heard in his life. And she kissed him also, but not upon his mouth. He felt her sharp kisses upon his white throat, and he knew that her lips were red. So the wild dream sped on through twilight and darkness and moonrise, and all the glory of the summer's night. But in the chilly dawn he lay as one half dead upon the mound down there, recalling and not recalling, drained of his blood, yet strangely longing to give those red lips more. Then came the fear, the awful nameless panic, the mortal horror that guards the confines of the world we see not, neither know of as we know of other things, but which we feel when its icy chill freezes our bones and stirs our hair with the touch of a ghostly hand. Once more Angelo sprang from the mound and fled up the gorge in the breaking day, but his step was less sure this time, and he panted for breath as he ran; and when he came to the bright spring of water that rises halfway up the hillside, he dropped upon his knees and hands and plunged his whole face in and drank as he had never drunk before – for it was the thirst of the wounded man who has lain bleeding all night long upon the battlefield.

She had him fast now, and he could not escape her, but would come to her every evening at dusk until she had drained him of his last drop of blood. It was in vain that when the day was done he tried to take another turning and to go home by a path that did not lead near the gorge. It was in vain that he made promises to himself each morning at dawn when he climbed the lonely way up from the shore to the village. It was all in vain, for when the sun sank burning into the sea, and the coolness of the evening stole out as from a hiding place to delight the weary world, his feet turned toward the old way, and she was waiting for him in the shadow under the chestnut trees; and then all happened as before, and she fell to kissing his white throat even as she flitted lightly down the way, winding one arm about him. And as his blood failed, she grew more hungry and more thirsty every day, and every day when he awoke in the early dawn it was harder to rouse himself to the effort of climbing the steep path to the village; and when he went to his work his feet dragged painfully, and there was hardly strength in his arms to wield the heavy hoe. He scarcely spoke to any one now, but the people said he was 'consuming himself' for love of the girl he was to have married when he lost his inheritance; and they laughed heartily at the thought, for this is not a very romantic country. At this time, Antonio, the man who stays here to look after the tower, returned from a visit to his people, who live near Salerno. He had been away all the time since before Alario's death and knew nothing of what had happened. He has told me that he came back late in the afternoon and shut himself up in the tower to eat and sleep, for he was very tired. It was past midnight when he awoke, and when he looked out the waning moon was rising over the shoulder of the hill. He looked out toward the mound, and he saw something, and he did not sleep again that night. When he went out again in the morning it was broad daylight, and there was nothing to be seen on the mound but loose stones and driven sand. Yet he did not go very near it; he went straight up the path to the village and directly to the house of the old priest.

'I have seen an evil thing this night,' he said; 'I have seen how the dead drink the blood of the living. And the blood is the life.'

'Tell me what you have seen,' said the priest in reply.

Antonio told him everything he had seen.

'You must bring your book and your holy water tonight,' he added. 'I will be here before sunset to go down with you, and if it pleases your reverence to sup with me while we wait, I will make ready.'

'I will come,' the priest answered, 'for I have read in old books of these strange beings which are neither quick nor dead, and which lie ever fresh in their graves, stealing out in the dusk to taste life and blood.'

Antonio cannot read, but he was glad to see that the priest understood the business; for, of course, the books must have instructed him as to the best means of quieting the half-living Thing for ever.

So Antonio went away to his work, which consists largely in sitting on the shady side of the tower, when he is not perched upon a rock with a fishing line catching nothing. But on that day he went twice to look at the mound in the bright sunlight, and he searched round and round it for some hole through which the being might get in and out; but he found none. When the sun began to sink and the air was cooler in the shadows, he went up to fetch the old priest, carrying a little wicker basket with him; and in this they placed a bottle of holy water, and the basin, and sprinkler, and the stole which the priest would need; and they came down and waited in the door of the tower till it should be dark. But while the light still lingered very grey and faint, they saw something moving, just there, two figures, a man's that walked, and a woman's that flitted beside him, and while her head lay on his shoulder she kissed his throat. The priest has told me that, too, and that his teeth chattered and he grasped Antonio's arm. The vision passed and disappeared into the shadow. Then Antonio got the leathern flask of strong liquor, which he kept for great occasions, and poured such a draught as made the old man feel almost young again; and he got the lantern, and his pick and shovel, and gave the priest his stole to put on and the holy water to carry, and they went out together toward the spot where the work was to be done. Antonio says that in spite of the rum his own knees shook together, and the priest stumbled over his Latin. For when they were yet a few yards from the mound the flickering light of the lantern fell upon Angelo's white face, unconscious as if in sleep, and on his upturned throat, over which a very thin red line of blood trickled down into his collar; and the flickering light of the lantern played upon another face that looked up from the feast – upon two deep, dead eyes that saw in spite of death – upon parted lips redder than life itself – upon two gleaming teeth on which glistened a rosy drop. Then the priest, good old man, shut his eyes tight and showered holy water before him, and his cracked voice rose almost to a scream; and then Antonio, who is no coward after all, raised his pick in one hand and the lantern in the other, as he sprang forward, not knowing what the end should be; and then he swears that he heard a woman's cry, and the Thing was gone, and Angelo lay alone on the mound unconscious, with the red line on his throat and the beads of deathly sweat on his cold forehead. They lifted him, half-dead as he was, and laid him on the ground close by; then Antonio went to work, and the priest helped him, though he was old and could not do much; and they dug deep, and at last Antonio, standing in the grave, stooped down with his lantern to see what he might see.

His hair used to be dark brown, with grizzled streaks about the temples; in less than a month from that day he was as grey as a badger. He was a miner when he was young, and most of these fellows have seen ugly sights now and then, when accidents have happened, but he had never seen what he saw that night – that

Thing which is neither alive nor dead, that Thing that will abide neither above ground nor in the grave. Antonio had brought something with him which the priest had not noticed. He had made it that afternoon – a sharp stake shaped from a piece of tough old driftwood. He had it with him now, and he had his heavy pick, and he had taken the lantern down into the grave. I don't think any power on earth could make him speak of what happened then, and the old priest was too frightened to look in. He says he heard Antonio breathing like a wild beast, and moving as if he were fighting with something almost as strong as himself; and he heard an evil sound also, with blows, as of something violently driven through flesh and bone; and then the most awful sound of all – a woman's shriek, the unearthly scream of a woman neither dead nor alive, but buried deep for many days. And he, the poor old priest, could only rock himself as he knelt there in the sand, crying aloud his prayers and exorcisms to drown these dreadful sounds. Then suddenly a small iron-bound chest was thrown up and rolled over against the old man's knee, and in a moment more Antonio was beside him, his face as white as tallow in the flickering light of the lantern, shovelling the sand and pebbles into the grave with furious haste, and looking over the edge till the pit was half full; and the priest said that there was much fresh blood on Antonio's hands and on his clothes.

I had come to the end of my story. Holger finished his wine and leaned back in his chair.

'So Angelo got his own again,' he said. 'Did he marry the prim and plump young person to whom he had been betrothed?'

'No; he had been badly frightened. He went to South America, and has not been heard of since.'

'And that poor thing's body is there still, I suppose,' said Holger. 'Is it quite dead yet, I wonder?'

I wonder, too. But whether it be dead or alive, I should hardly care to see it, even in broad daylight. Antonio is as grey as a badger, and he has never been quite the same man since that night.

The Sumach

Ulric Daubeny (1888–1922)

Very little is known of Daubeny. He was born in Cheltenham, the son of a retired officer in the British army, and he trained and worked as an engineer. His interests included old musical instruments and church architecture on both of which subjects he published books. In 1919, he also published one volume of supernatural fiction entitled The Elemental *which included 'The Sumach' and other stories with titles such as 'Matheson's Mummy', 'The People of the Hidden Room' and 'The Hand of Glory'. Ulric Daubeny died at Torquay three years later, probably from tuberculosis. Perhaps surprisingly, tales of vampiric plants and trees were not uncommon in the decades covered by this anthology. Phil Robinson's story 'The Man-Eating Tree', with its self-explanatory title, was published in 1881 and, thirteen years later, HG Wells wrote a nicely tongue-in-cheek story called 'The Flowering of the Strange Orchid'. Daubeny's tale is not as cleverly done as Wells's but it's printed here as both an example of an odd sub-genre of vampire fiction and of the work of an author who deserves greater recognition than he has had.*

'How red that Sumach is!'

Irene Barton murmured something commonplace, for to her the tree brought painful recollections. Her visitor, unconscious of this fact, proceeded to elaborate.

'Do you know, Irene, that tree gives me the creeps! I can't explain, except that it is not a nice tree, not a *good* tree. For instance, why should its leaves be red in August, when they are not supposed to turn until October?'

'What queer ideas you have, May! The tree is right enough, although its significance to me is sad. Poor Spot, you know; we buried him beneath it two days ago. Come and see his grave.'

The two women left the terrace, where this conversation had been taking place, and leisurely strolled across the lawn, at the end of which, in almost startling isolation, grew the Sumach. At least, Mrs Watcombe, who evinced so great an interest in the tree, questioned whether it actually was a Sumach, for the foliage was unusual, and the branches gnarled and twisted beyond recognition. Just now, the leaves were stained with splashes of dull crimson, but rather than droop, they had a bloated appearance, as if the luxuriance of the growth were not altogether healthy.

For several moments they stood regarding the pathetic little grave, and the silence was only broken when Mrs Watcombe darted beneath the tree, and came back with something in her hand.

'Irene, look at this dead thrush. Poor little thing! Such splendid plumage, yet it hardly weighs a sugar plum!'

Mrs Barton regarded it with wrinkled brows.

'I cannot understand what happens to the birds, May – unless someone lays poison. We continually find them dead about the garden, and usually beneath, or very near, this tree.'

It is doubtful whether Mrs Watcombe listened. Her attention seemed to wander that morning, and she was studying the twisted branches of the Sumach with a thoughtful scrutiny.

'Curious that the leaves should turn at this time of year,' she murmured. 'It brings to mind poor Geraldine's illness. This tree had an extraordinary fascination for her, you know. It was quite scarlet then, yet it was only June, and it had barely finished shooting.'

'My dear May! You have red leaves on the brain this morning!' Irene retorted, uncertain whether to be irritated or amused. 'I can't think why you are so concerned about the colour. It is only the result of two days' excessive heat, for scarcely a leaf was touched, when I buried poor old Spot.'

The conversation seemed absurdly trivial, yet, Mrs Watcombe gone, Irene could not keep her mind from dwelling on her cousin's fatal illness. The news had reached them with the shock of the absolutely unexpected. Poor Geraldine, who had always been so strong, to have fallen victim to acute anaemia! It was almost unbelievable, that heart failure should have put an end to her sweet young life, after a few days' ailing. Of course, the sad event had wrought a wonderful change for Irene and her husband, giving them, in place of a cramped suburban villa, this beautiful country home, Cleeve Grange. Everything for her was filled with the delight of novelty, for she had ruled as mistress over the charmed abode for only one short week. Hilary, her husband, was yet a stranger to the more intimate of its attractions, being detained in London by the winding-up of business affairs.

Several days elapsed, for the most part given solely to the keen pleasure of arranging and re-arranging the new home. As time went by, the crimson splashes on the Sumach faded, the leaves becoming green again, though dropping as if from want of moisture. Irene noticed this when she paid her daily visits to the pathetic little dog grave, trying to induce flowers to take root upon it, but do what she might, they invariably faded. Nothing, not even grass, would grow beneath the Sumach. Only death seemed to thrive there, she mused in a fleeting moment of depression, as she searched around for more dead birds. But none had fallen since the thrush, picked up by Mrs Watcombe.

One evening, the heat inside the house becoming insupportable, Irene wandered into the garden, her steps mechanically leading her to the little grave beneath the Sumach. In the uncertain moonlight, the twisted trunk and branches of the old tree were suggestive of a rustic seat, and feeling tired, she lifted herself into the natural bower, and lolled back, joyously inhaling the cool night air. Presently she dropped asleep, and in a curiously vivid manner, dreamt of Hilary; that he had completed his business in London, and was coming home. They met at evening, near the garden gate, and Hilary spread wide his arms, and eagerly folded them about her. Swiftly the dream began to change, assuming the characteristic of a nightmare. The sky grew strangely dark, the arms fiercely masterful, while the face which bent to kiss her neck was not that of her young husband: it was leering, wicked, gnarled like the trunk of some weather-beaten tree. Chilled with horror, Irene fought long and desperately against the vision, to be at last awakened by her own frightened whimpering. Yet returning consciousness did not immediately dissipate the nightmare. In imagination she was still held rigid by brutal arms, and it was after a blind, half-waking struggle that she freed herself, and went speeding across the lawn, towards the lighted doorway.

Next morning, Mrs Watcombe called, and subjected her to a puzzled scrutiny.

'How pale you look, Irene. Do you feel ill?'

'Ill! No, only a little languid. I find this hot weather very trying.'

Mrs Watcombe studied her with care, for the pallor of Irene's face was very marked. In contrast, a vivid spot of red showed on the slender neck, an inch or so below the ear. Intuitively a hand went up, as Irene turned to her friend in explanation.

'It feels so sore. I think I must have grazed the skin last night, while sitting in the Sumach.'

'Sitting in the Sumach!' echoed Mrs Watcombe in surprise. 'How curious you should do that. Poor Geraldine used to do the same, just before she was taken ill, and yet at the last she was seized with a perfect horror of the tree. Goodness, but it is quite red again this morning!'

Irene swung round in the direction of the tree, filled with a vague repugnance. Sure enough, the leaves no longer drooped, nor were they green. They had become flecked once more with crimson, and the growth had quite regained its former vigour.

'Eugh!' she breathed, hurriedly turning towards the house. 'It reminds me of a horrid nightmare. I have rather a head this morning; let's go in and talk of something else!'

As the day advanced, the heat grew more oppressive, and night brought with it a curious stillness, the stillness which so often presages a heavy thunderstorm. No bird had offered up its evening hymn, no breeze came sufficient to stir a single leaf: everything was pervaded by the silence of expectancy.

The interval between dinner and bedtime is always a dreary one for those accustomed to companionship, and left all alone, Irene's restlessness momentarily increased. First the ceiling, then the very atmosphere seemed to weigh heavy upon her head. Although windows and doors were all flung wide, the airlessness of the house grew less and less endurable, until from sheer desperation she made her escape into the garden, where a sudden illumination of the horizon gave warning of the approaching storm. Feeling somewhat at a loss, she roamed aimlessly awhile, pausing sometimes to catch the echoes of distant thunder, until at last she found herself standing over Spot's desolate little grave. The sight struck her with a sense of utter loneliness, and tears sprang to her eyes, in poignant longing for the companionship of her faithful pet.

Moved by she knew not what, Irene swung herself into the comfortable branches of the old Sumach, and soothed by the reposeful attitude, her head soon began to nod in slumber. Afterwards it was a doubtful memory whether she actually did sleep, or whether the whole experience was not a kind of waking nightmare. Something of the previous evening's dream returned to her, but this time with added horror; for it commenced with no pleasurable vision of her husband. Instead, relentless, stick-like arms immediately closed in upon her, their vice-like grip so tight that she could scarcely breathe. Down darted the awful head, rugged and lined by every sin, darting at the fair, white neck as a wild beast on its prey. The foul lips began to eat into her skin... She struggled desperately, madly, for to her swooning senses the very branches of the tree became endowed with active life, coiling unmercifully around her, tenaciously clinging to her limbs, and tearing at her dress. Pain at last spurred her to an heroic effort, the pain of something – perhaps a twig – digging deep into her unprotected neck. With a choking cry she freed herself, and nerved by a sudden burst of thunder, ran tottering towards the shelter of the house.

Having gained the cosy lounge-hall, Irene sank into an armchair, gasping hysterically for breath. Gusts of refreshing wind came through the open windows, but although the atmosphere rapidly grew less stagnant, an hour passed before she could make sufficient effort to crawl upstairs to bed. In her room, a further shock awaited her. The bloodless, drawn face reflected in the mirror was scarcely recognisable. The eyes lacked lustre, the lips were white, the skin hung flabby on the shrunken flesh, giving it a look of premature old age. A tiny trickle of dry blood, the solitary smudge of colour, stained the chalky pallor of her neck. Taking up a hand-glass, she examined this with momentary concern. It was the old wound reopened, an angry-looking sore, almost like the bite of some small, or very sharp-toothed animal. It smarted painfully.

Mrs Watcombe, bursting into the breakfast room next morning, with suggestions of an expedition to the neighbouring town, was shocked at Irene's looks, and insisted on going at once to fetch the doctor. Mrs Watcombe fussed continually throughout the interview, and insisted on an examination of the scar upon Irene's neck. Patient and doctor regarded this as a negligible detail, but finally the latter subjected it to a slightly puzzled scrutiny, advising that it should be kept bandaged. He suggested that Irene was suffering from anaemia, and would do well to keep as quiet as possible, building up her strength with food, open windows and a general selection of pills and tonics. But despite these comforting arrangements, no one was entirely satisfied. The doctor lacked something in assurance. Irene was certain that she could not really be anaemic, while Mrs Watcombe was obsessed by inward misgivings, perfectly indefinable, yet none the less disturbing. She left the house as a woman bent under a load of care. Passing up the lane, her glance lighted on the old Sumach, more crimson now, more flourishing in its growth than she had seen it since the time of Geraldine's fatal illness.

'I loathe that horrid old tree!' she murmured, then added struck by a nameless premonition, 'Her husband ought to know. I shall wire him at once.'

Irene, womanlike, put to use her enforced idleness, by instituting a rearrangement of the box-room, the only part of her new home which yet remained unexplored. Among the odds and ends of the rubbish to be thrown away, there was a little notebook, apparently unused. In idle curiosity, Irene picked it up, and was surprised to learn, from an inscription, that her cousin Geraldine had intended to use it as a diary. A date appeared – only a few days prior to the poor girl's death – but no entries had been made, though the first two pages of the book had certainly been removed. As Irene put it down, there fluttered to the ground a torn scrap of writing. She stooped, and continued stooping, breathlessly staring at the words that had been written by her cousin's hand – *Sumach fascinates m-*

In some unaccountable manner this applied to her. It was obvious what tree was meant, the old Sumach at the end of the lawn: and it fascinated her, Irene, though not until that moment had she openly recognised the fact. Searching hurriedly through the notebook, she discovered, near the end, a heap of torn paper, evidently the first two pages of a diary. She turned the pieces in eager haste. Most of them bore no more than one short word, or portions of a longer one, but a few bigger fragments proved more enlightening, and filled with nervous apprehension, she carried the book to her escritoire, and spent the remainder of the afternoon in trying to piece together the torn-up pages.

Meanwhile, Mrs Watcombe was worrying and fretting over Irene's unexpected illness. Her pallor, her listlessness, even the curious mark upon her neck, gave cause for positive alarm, so exactly did they correspond with symptoms exhibited by her cousin Geraldine, during the few days prior to her death. She wished that the village doctor, who had attended the earlier case, would return soon from his holiday, as his locum tenens seemed sadly wanting in that authoritative decision which is so consoling to patients, relatives, and friends. Feeling, as an old friend, responsible for the welfare of Irene, she wired to Hilary, telling him of the sudden illness, and advising him to return without delay.

The urgency of the telegram alarmed him, so much so that he left London by the next train, arriving at Cleeve Grange shortly after dark.

'Where is your mistress?' was his first enquiry, as the maid met him in the hall.

'Upstairs, Sir. She complained of feeling tired, and said she would go to bed.'

He hurried to her room, only to find it empty. He called, he rang for the servants; in a moment the whole house was astir, yet nowhere was Irene to be found. Deeming it possible that she might have gone to see Mrs Watcombe, Hilary was about to follow, when that lady herself was ushered in.

'I saw the lights of your cab...' she commenced, cutting short the sentence, as she met his questioning glance.

'Where is Irene?'

'Irene? My dear Hilary, is she not here?'

'No. We can't find her anywhere. I thought she might have been with you.'

For the space of half a second, Mrs Watcombe's face presented a picture of astonishment; then the expression changed to one of dismayed concern.

'She is in that tree! I am certain of it! Hilary, we must fetch her at once!'

Completely at a loss to understand, he followed the excited woman into the garden, stumbling blindly in her wake across the lawn. The darkness was intense, and a terrific wind beat them back as if with living hands. Irene's white dress at length became discernible, dimly thrown up against the pitchy background, and obscured in places by the twists and coils of the old Sumach. Between them, they grasped the sleeping body, but the branches swung wildly in the gale, and to Hilary's confused imagination it was as if they had literally to tear it from the tree's embrace. At last they regained the shelter of the house, and laid their inanimate burden upon the sofa. She was quite unconscious, pale as death, and her face painfully contorted, as if with fear. The old wound on the neck, now bereft of bandages, had been reopened, and was wet with blood.

Hilary rushed off to fetch the doctor, while Mrs Watcombe and the servants carried Irene to her room. Several hours passed before she recovered consciousness, and during that time Hilary was gently but firmly excluded from the sickroom. Bewildered and disconsolate, he wandered restlessly about the house, until his attention was arrested by the unusual array of torn-up bits of paper on Irene's desk. He saw that she had been sorting out the pieces, and sticking them together as the sentences became complete. The work was barely finished, yet what there was to read, struck him as exceedingly strange:

The seat in the old Sumach fascinates me. I find myself going back to it unconsciously, nay, even against my will. Oh, but the nightmare visions it always brings to me! In them I seem to plumb the very depth of terror. Their memory preys upon my mind, and every day my strength grows less.
Dr H speaks of anaemia...

That was as far as Irene had proceeded. Hardly knowing why he did so, Hilary resolved to complete the task, but the chill of early morning was in the air before it was finished. Cramped and stiff, he was pushing back his chair when a footstep sounded in the doorway, and Mrs Watcombe entered.

'Irene is better,' she volunteered immediately. 'She is sleeping naturally, and Doctor Thomson says there is no longer any immediate danger. The poor child is terribly weak and bloodless.'

'May – tell me – what is the meaning of all this? Why has Irene suddenly become so ill? I can't understand it!'

Mrs Watcombe's face was preternaturally grave.

'Even the doctor admits that he is puzzled,' she answered very quietly. 'The symptoms all point to a sudden and excessive loss of blood, though in cases of anaemia...'

'God! But – not like Geraldine? I can't believe it!'

'Neither can I. Oh, Hilary, you may think me mad, but I can't help feeling that there is some unknown, some awful influence at work. Irene was perfectly well three days ago, and it was the same with Geraldine before she was taken ill. The cases are so exactly similar. Irene was trying to tell me something about a diary, but the poor girl was too exhausted to make herself properly understood.'

'Diary? Geraldine's diary, do you think? She must mean that. I have just finished piecing it together, but frankly, I can't make head or tail of it.'

Mrs Watcombe rapidly scanned the writing, then studied it again with greater care. Finally she read the second part aloud.

'Listen, Hilary! This seems to me important.'

Dr H speaks of anaemia. Pray heaven, he may be correct, for my thoughts sometimes move in a direction which foreshadows nothing short of lunacy – or so people would tell me, if I could bring myself to confide these things. I must fight alone, clinging to the knowledge that it is usual for anaemic persons to be obsessed by unhealthy fancies. If only I had not read those horribly suggestive words in Barrett...

'Barrett? What can she mean, May?'

'Wait a moment. Barrett? Barrett's *Traditions of the County*, perhaps. I have noticed a copy in the library. Let us go there; it may give the clue!'

The book was quickly found, and a marker indicated the passage to which Geraldine apparently referred.

At Cleeve, I was reminded of another of those traditions, so rapidly disappearing before the spread of education. It concerned the old belief in vampires, spirits of the evil dead, who by night, could assume a

human form, and scour the countryside in search of victims. Suspected
vampires, if caught, were buried with the mouth stuffed full of garlic,
and a stake plunged through the heart, whereby they were rendered
harmless, or, at least, confined to that one particular locality.

Some thirty years ago, an old man pointed out a tree which was
said to have grown from such a stake. So far as I can recollect, it was
an unusual variety of Sumach, and had been enclosed during a recent
extension to the garden of the old Grange ...

'Come outside,' said Mrs Watcombe, breaking a long and solemn
silence. 'I want you to see that tree.'

The sky was suffused with the blush of early dawn, and the
shrubs, flowers, even the dew upon the grass caught and reflected
something of the pink effulgence. The Sumach alone stood out,
dark and menacing. During the night, its leaves had become a
hideous, mottled purple; its growth was oily, bloated, unnaturally
vigorous, like that of some rank and poisonous weed.

Mrs Watcombe, looking from afar, spoke in frightened, husky
tones.

'See, Hilary! It was exactly like that when – when Geraldine
died!'

When evening fell, the end of the lawn was strangely bare. In
place of the old tree, there lay an enormous heap of smouldering
embers – enormous, because the Sumach had been too sodden
with dark and sticky sap, to burn without the assistance of large
quantities of other timber.

Many weeks elapsed before Irene was sufficiently recovered
to walk as far as Spot's little grave. She was surprised to find it
almost hidden in a bed of garlic.

Hilary explained that it was the only plant they could induce
to grow there.

The Vampire of Croglin Grange

Augustus Hare (1834–1903)

*Augustus Hare was a Victorian traveller, author and art lover. He was also a great eccentric. Somerset Maugham, who knew him during the last years of Hare's life, describes a visit to his country home during which the younger writer noticed that the wording of the prayers at morning worship for his servants was unfamiliar. 'I've crossed out all the passages in glorification of God,' Hare explained. 'God is certainly a gentleman and no gentleman cares to be praised to his face.' Like God, Hare was a gentleman but he was also obliged to earn money by writing. He published travel guides (*Walks in Rome, Wanderings in Spain, *etc.), a number of biographies of obscure and now forgotten aristocrats and a multi-volumed memoir entitled* The Story of My Life. *Filled with anecdotes and encounters with the great and good of Victorian England, Hare's autobiography also includes many tales of ghosts and the supernatural. 'The Vampire of Croglin Grange' he presents as a supposedly true story told to him by a friend named Captain Fisher. Readers can decide for themselves whether or not there is any truth in it but sceptics might note that bits of it bear suspicious resemblances to passages in Rymer's lurid 1840s novel* Varney the Vampire.*

Captain Fisher... told us this really extraordinary story connected with his own family:

Fisher may sound a very plebeian name, but this family is of very ancient lineage, and for many hundreds of years they have possessed a very curious old place in Cumberland, which bears the weird name of Croglin Grange. The great characteristic of the house is that never at any period of its very long existence has it been more than one story high, but it has a terrace from which large grounds sweep away towards the church in the hollow, and a fine distant view.

When, in lapse of years, the Fishers outgrew Croglin Grange in family and fortune, they were wise enough not to destroy the long-standing characteristic of the place by adding another story to the house, but they went away to the south, to reside at Thorncombe near Guildford, and they let Croglin Grange.

They were extremely fortunate in their tenants, two brothers and a sister. They heard their praises from all quarters. To their poorer neighbours they were all that is most kind and beneficent, and their neighbours of a higher class spoke of them as a most welcome addition to the little society of the neighbourhood. On their part the tenants were greatly delighted with their new residence. The arrangement of the house, which would have been a trial to many, was not so to them. In every respect Croglin Grange was exactly suited to them.

The winter was spent most happily by the new inmates of Croglin Grange, who shared in all the little social pleasures of the district, and made themselves very popular. In the following summer, there was one day which was dreadfully, annihilatingly hot. The brothers lay under the trees with their books, for it was too hot for any active occupation. The sister sat in the verandah and worked, or tried to work, for, in the intense sultriness of that summer day, work was next to impossible. They dined early, and after dinner they still sat out in the verandah, enjoying the cool air which came with evening, and they watched the sun set, and the moon rise over the belt of trees which separated the grounds from the churchyard, seeing it mount the heavens till the whole lawn was bathed in silver light, across which the long shadows from the shrubbery fell as if embossed, so vivid and distinct were they.

When they separated for the night, all retiring to their rooms on the ground floor (for, as I said, there was no upstairs in that house), the sister felt that the heat was still so great that she could not sleep, and having fastened her window, she did not close the shutters – in that very quiet place it was not necessary – and, propped against the pillows, she still watched the wonderful, the marvellous beauty of that summer night. Gradually she became aware of two lights, two lights which flickered in and out in the belt of trees which separated the lawn from the churchyard, and as her gaze became fixed upon them, she saw them emerge, fixed in a dark substance, a definite ghastly *something*, which seemed every moment to become nearer, increasing in size and substance as it approached. Every now and then it was lost for a moment in the long shadows which stretched across the lawn from the trees, and then it emerged larger than ever, and still coming on... on. As she watched it, the most uncontrollable horror seized her. She longed to get away, but the door was close to the window and the door was locked on the inside, and while she was unlocking it, she must be for an instant nearer to *it*. She longed to scream, but her voice seemed paralysed, her tongue glued to the roof of her mouth.

Suddenly, she never could explain why afterwards, the terrible object seemed to turn to one side, seemed to be going round the house, not to be coming to her at all, and immediately she jumped out of bed and rushed to the door, but as she was unlocking it, she heard scratch, scratch, scratch upon the window, and saw a hideous brown face with flaming eyes glaring in at her. She rushed back to the bed, but the creature continued to scratch, scratch, scratch upon the window. She felt a sort of mental comfort in the knowledge that the window was securely fastened on the inside. Suddenly the scratching sound ceased, and a kind of pecking sound took its place. Then, in her agony, she became aware that the creature was unpicking the lead! The noise continued, and a diamond pane of glass fell into the room. Then a long bony finger of the creature came in and turned the handle of the window, and the window opened, and the creature came in; and it came across the room, and her terror was so great that she could not scream, and it came up to the bed, and it twisted its long, bony fingers into her hair, and it dragged her head over the side of the bed, and – it bit her violently in the throat.

As it bit her, her voice was released, and she screamed with all her might and main. Her brothers rushed out of their rooms, but the door was locked on the inside. A moment was lost while they got a poker and broke it open. Then the creature had already escaped through the window, and the sister, bleeding violently from a wound in the throat, was lying unconscious over the side of the bed. One brother pursued the creature, which fled before him through the moonlight with gigantic strides, and eventually seemed to disappear over the wall into the churchyard. Then he rejoined his brother by the sister's bedside. She was dreadfully hurt and her wound was a very definite one, but she was of strong disposition, not given either to romance or superstition, and when she came to herself she said, 'What has happened is most extraordinary and I am very much hurt. It seems inexplicable, but of course there is an explanation, and we must wait for it. It will turn out that a lunatic has escaped from some asylum and found his way here.' The wound healed and she appeared to get well, but the doctor who was sent for to her would not believe that she could bear so terrible a shock so easily, and insisted that she must have change, mental and physical; so her brothers took her to Switzerland.

Being a sensible girl, when she went abroad, she threw herself at once into the interests of the country she was in. She dried plants, she made sketches, she went up mountains, and, as autumn came on, she was the person who urged that they should return to Croglin Grange. 'We have taken it,' she said, 'for seven years, and we have only been there one; and we shall always find it difficult to let a house which is only one story high, so we had better return there; lunatics do not escape every day.' As she urged it, her brothers wished nothing better, and the family returned to Cumberland. From there being no upstairs in the house, it was impossible to make any great change in their arrangements. The sister occupied the same room, but it is unnecessary to say she always closed her shutters, which, however, as in many old houses, always left one top pane of the window uncovered. The brothers moved, and occupied a room together exactly opposite that of their sister, and they always kept loaded pistols in their room.

The winter passed most peacefully and happily. In the following March the sister was suddenly awakened by a sound she remembered only too well – scratch, scratch, scratch upon the window, and looking up, she saw, climbed up to the topmost pane of the window, the same hideous brown shrivelled face, with glaring eyes, looking in at her. This time she screamed as loud as she could. Her brothers rushed out of their room with pistols, and out of the front door. The creature was already scudding away across the lawn. One of the brothers fired and hit it in the leg, but still with the other leg it continued to make way, scrambled over the wall into the churchyard, and seemed to disappear into a vault which belonged to a family long extinct.

The next day the brothers summoned all the tenants of Croglin Grange, and in their presence the vault was opened. A horrible scene revealed itself. The vault was full of coffins; they had been broken open, and their contents, horribly mangled and distorted, were scattered over the floor. One coffin alone remained intact. Of that the lid had been lifted, but still lay loose upon the coffin. They raised it, and there, brown, withered, shrivelled, mummified, but quite entire, was the same hideous figure which had looked in at the windows of Croglin Grange, with the marks of a recent pistol shot in the leg; and they did the only thing that can lay a vampire – they burnt it.

Ken's Mystery

Julian Hawthorne (1846–1934)

The son of the novelist and short-story-writer Nathaniel Hawthorne, author of The Scarlet Letter, *Julian Hawthorne has not received the attention given to his father, one of the great figures in American literature, but he published an enormous quantity of fiction, poetry, essays and journalism in the course of a long life. He was particularly skilful as a writer of supernatural and Gothic fiction. His novella* Archibald Malmaison *(1879) is a story of double personality which predates Stevenson's* Strange Case of Dr Jekyll and Mr Hyde *by seven years. His other speculative fiction includes 'Kildhurm's Oak' in which a human personality is transferred into the tree of the title, 'The Men of the Dark', a lost world story about troglodytes in an Andean cave, and 'June, 1993', in which a man of the nineteenth century is given a glimpse of the future. 'Ken's Mystery' is an intriguing story in which a cautionary tale of an encounter with a female vampire is mixed with elements drawn from Irish folklore. As the subtitle of a recent biography (*Julian Hawthorne: The Life of a Prodigal Son*) suggests, Hawthorne Jr didn't always have an easy career. He produced a lot of hack work in pursuit of quick cash and he even spent a year in jail for financial fraud. However he is an interesting writer and his best work remains very readable.*

One cool October evening – it was the last day of the month, and unusually cool for the time of year – I made up my mind to go and spend an hour or two with my friend Keningale. Keningale was an artist (as well as a musical amateur and poet), and had a very delightful studio built onto his house, in which he was wont to sit of an evening. The studio had a cavernous fireplace, designed in imitation of the old-fashioned fireplaces of Elizabethan manor houses, and in it, when the temperature

109

outdoors warranted, he would build up a cheerful fire of dry logs. It would suit me particularly well, I thought, to go and have a quiet pipe and chat in front of that fire with my friend.

I had not had such a chat for a very long time – not, in fact, since Keningale (or Ken, as his friends called him) had returned from his visit to Europe the year before. He went abroad, as he affirmed at the time, 'for purposes of study', whereat we all smiled, for Ken, so far as we knew him, was more likely to do anything else than to study. He was a young fellow of buoyant temperament, lively and social in his habits, of a brilliant and versatile mind, and possessing an income of twelve or fifteen thousand dollars a year; he could sing, play, scribble, and paint very cleverly, and some of his heads and figure-pieces were really well done, considering that he never had any regular training in art; but he was not a worker. Personally he was fine-looking, of good height and figure, active, healthy, and with a remarkably fine brow, and clear, full-gazing eye. Nobody was surprised at his going to Europe, nobody expected him to do anything there except amuse himself, and few anticipated that he would be soon again seen in New York. He was one of the sort that find Europe agree with them. Off he went, therefore; and in the course of a few months the rumour reached us that he was engaged to a handsome and wealthy New York girl whom he had met in London. This was nearly all we did hear of him until, not very long afterward, he turned up again on Fifth Avenue, to everyone's astonishment; made no satisfactory answer to those who wanted to know how he happened to tire so soon of the Old World; while, as to the reported engagement, he cut short all allusion to that in so peremptory a manner as to show that it was not a permissible topic of conversation with him. It was surmised that the lady had jilted him; but, on the other hand, she herself returned home not a great while after, and, though she had plenty of opportunities, she has never married to this day.

Be the rights of that matter what they may, it was soon remarked that Ken was no longer the careless and merry fellow he used to be; on the contrary, he appeared grave, moody, averse from general society, and habitually taciturn and undemonstrative even in the company of his most intimate friends. Evidently something had happened to him, or he had done something. What? Had he committed a murder? Or joined the Nihilists? Or was his unsuccessful love affair at the bottom of it? Some declared that the cloud was only temporary, and would soon pass away. Nevertheless, up to the period of which I am writing, it had not passed away, but had rather gathered additional gloom, and threatened to become permanent.

Meanwhile I had met him twice or thrice at the club, at the opera, or in the street, but had as yet had no opportunity of regularly renewing my acquaintance with him. We had been on a footing of more than common intimacy in the old days, and I was not disposed to think that he would refuse to renew the former relations now. But what I had heard and myself seen of his changed condition imparted a stimulating tinge of suspense or curiosity to the pleasure with which I looked forward to the prospects of this evening. His house stood at a distance of two or three miles beyond the general range of habitations in New York at this time, and as I walked briskly along in the clear twilight air I had leisure to go over in my mind all that I had known of Ken and had divined of his character. After all, had there not always been something in his nature – deep down, and held in abeyance by the activity of his animal spirits – but something strange and separate, and capable of developing under suitable conditions into – into what? As I asked myself this question I arrived at his door; and it was with a feeling of relief that I felt the next moment the cordial grasp of his hand, and his voice bidding me welcome in a tone that indicated unaffected gratification at my presence. He drew me at once into the studio, relieved me of my hat and cane, and then put his hand on my shoulder.

'I am glad to see you,' he repeated, with singular earnestness, 'glad to see you and to feel you; and tonight of all nights in the year.'

'Why tonight especially?'

'Oh, never mind. It's just as well, too, you didn't let me know beforehand you were coming; the unreadiness is all, to paraphrase the poet. Now, with you to help me, I can drink a glass of whisky and water and take a bit draw of the pipe. This would have been a grim night for me if I'd been left to myself.'

'In such a lap of luxury as this, too!' said I, looking round at the glowing fireplace, the low, luxurious chairs, and all the rich and sumptuous fittings of the room. 'I should have thought a condemned murderer might make himself comfortable here.'

'Perhaps; but that's not exactly my category at present. But have you forgotten what night this is? This is November-eve, when, as tradition asserts, the dead arise and walk about, and fairies, goblins, and spiritual beings of all kinds have more freedom and power than on any other day of the year. One can see you've never been in Ireland.'

'I wasn't aware till now that you had been there, either.'

'Yes, I have been in Ireland. Yes...' He paused, sighed, and fell into a reverie, from which, however, he soon roused himself by an effort, and went to a cabinet in a corner of the room for the liquor and tobacco. While he was thus employed I sauntered about the studio, taking note of the various beauties, grotesquenesses, and curiosities that it contained. Many things were there to repay study and arouse admiration; for Ken was a good collector, having excellent taste as well as means to back it. But, upon the whole, nothing interested me more than some studies of a female head, roughly done in oils, and, judging from the sequestered positions in which I found them, not intended by the artist for exhibition or criticism. There were three or four of these studies, all of the same face, but in different poses and costumes. In one the head was enveloped in a dark hood, overshadowing and partly concealing the features; in another she seemed to be peering duskily through a latticed casement, lit by a faint moonlight; a third showed her splendidly attired in evening costume, with jewels in her hair and ears, and sparkling on her snowy bosom. The expressions were as various as the poses; now it was demure penetration, now a subtle inviting glance, now burning passion, and again a look of elfish and elusive mockery. In whatever phase, the countenance possessed a singular and poignant fascination, not of beauty merely, though that was very striking, but of character and quality likewise.

'Did you find this model abroad?' I inquired at length. 'She has evidently inspired you, and I don't wonder at it.'

Ken, who had been mixing the punch, and had not noticed my movements, now looked up, and said: 'I didn't mean those to be seen. They don't satisfy me, and I am going to destroy them; but I couldn't rest till I'd made some attempts to reproduce... What was it you asked? Abroad? Yes – or no. They were all painted here within the last six weeks.'

'Whether they satisfy you or not, they are by far the best things of yours I have ever seen.'

'Well, let them alone, and tell me what you think of this beverage. To my thinking, it goes to the right spot. It owes its existence to your coming here. I can't drink alone, and those portraits are not company, though, for aught I know, she might have come out of the canvas tonight and sat down in that chair.' Then, seeing my inquiring look, he added, with a hasty laugh, 'It's November-eve, you know, when anything may happen, provided it's strange enough. Well, here's to ourselves.'

We each swallowed a deep draught of the smoking and aromatic liquor, and set down our glasses with approval. The punch was excellent. Ken now opened a box of cigars, and we seated ourselves before the fireplace.

'All we need now,' I remarked, after a short silence, 'is a little music. By-the-by, Ken, have you still got the banjo I gave you before you went abroad?'

He paused so long before replying that I supposed he had not heard my question. 'I have got it,' he said, at length, 'but it will never make any more music.'

'Got broken, eh? Can't it be mended? It was a fine instrument.'

'It's not broken, but it's past mending. You shall see for yourself.'

He arose as he spoke, and going to another part of the studio, opened a black oak coffer, and took out of it a long object wrapped up in a piece of faded yellow silk. He handed it to me, and when I had unwrapped it, there appeared a thing that might once have been a banjo, but had little resemblance to one now. It bore every sign of extreme age. The wood of the handle was honeycombed with the gnawings of worms, and dusty with dry-rot. The parchment head was green with mould, and hung in shrivelled tatters. The hoop, which was of solid silver, was so blackened and tarnished that it looked like dilapidated iron. The strings were gone, and most of the tuning-screws had dropped out of their decayed sockets. Altogether it had the appearance of having been made before the Flood, and been forgotten in the forecastle of Noah's Ark ever since.

'It is a curious relic, certainly,' I said. 'Where did you come across it? I had no idea that the banjo was invented so long ago as this. It certainly can't be less than two hundred years old, and may be much older than that.'

Ken smiled gloomily. 'You are quite right,' he said; 'it is at least two hundred years old, and yet it is the very same banjo that you gave me a year ago.'

'Hardly,' I returned, smiling in my turn, 'since that was made to my order with a view to presenting it to you.'

'I know that; but the two hundred years have passed since then. Yes; it is absurd and impossible, I know, but nothing is truer. That banjo, which was made last year, existed in the sixteenth century, and has been rotting ever since. Stay. Give it to me a moment, and I'll convince you. You recollect that your name and mine, with the date, were engraved on the silver hoop?'

'Yes; and there was a private mark of my own there, also.'

'Very well,' said Ken, who had been rubbing a place on the hoop with a corner of the yellow silk wrapper, 'look at that.'

I took the decrepit instrument from him, and examined the spot which he had rubbed. It was incredible, sure enough; but there were the names and the date precisely as I had caused them to be engraved; and there, moreover, was my own private mark, which I had idly made with an old etching point not more than eighteen months before. After convincing myself that there was no mistake, I laid the banjo across my knees, and stared at my friend in bewilderment. He sat smoking with a kind of grim composure, his eyes fixed upon the blazing logs.

'I'm mystified, I confess,' said I. 'Come; what is the joke? What method have you discovered of producing the decay of centuries on this unfortunate banjo in a few months? And why did you do it? I have heard of an elixir to counteract the effects of time, but your recipe seems to work the other way – to make time rush forward at two hundred times his usual rate, in one place, while he jogs on at his usual gait elsewhere. Unfold your mystery, magician. Seriously, Ken, how on earth did the thing happen?'

'I know no more about it than you do,' was his reply. 'Either you and I and all the rest of the living world are insane, or else there has been wrought a miracle as strange as any in tradition. How can I explain it? It is a common saying – a common experience, if you will – that we may, on certain trying or tremendous occasions, live years in one moment. But that's a mental experience, not a physical one, and one that applies, at all events, only to human beings, not to senseless things of wood and metal. You imagine the thing is some trick or jugglery. If it be, I don't know the secret of it. There's no chemical appliance that I ever heard of that will get a piece of solid wood into that condition in a few months, or a few years. And it wasn't done in a few years, or a few months either. A year ago today at this very hour that banjo was as sound as when it left the maker's hands, and twenty-four hours afterward – I'm telling you the simple truth – it was as you see it now.'

The gravity and earnestness with which Ken made this astounding statement were evidently not assumed. He believed every word that he uttered. I knew not what to think. Of course my friend might be insane, though he betrayed none of the ordinary symptoms of mania; but, however that might be, there was the banjo, a witness whose silent testimony there was no gainsaying. The more I meditated on the matter the more inconceivable did it appear. Two hundred years– twenty-four hours; these were the terms of the proposed equation. Ken and the banjo both affirmed that the equation had been made; all worldly knowledge and experience affirmed it to be impossible. What was the explanation? What is time? What is life? I felt myself beginning to doubt the reality of all things. And so this was the mystery which my friend had been brooding over since his return from abroad. No wonder it had changed him. More to be wondered at was that it had not changed him more.

'Can you tell me the whole story?' I demanded at length.

Ken quaffed another draught from his glass of whisky and water and rubbed his hand through his thick brown beard. 'I have never spoken to any one of it heretofore,' he said, 'and I had never meant to speak of it. But I'll try and give you some idea of what it was. You know me better than anyone else; you'll understand the thing as far as it can ever be understood, and perhaps I may be relieved of some of the oppression it has caused me. For it is rather a ghastly memory to grapple with alone, I can tell you.'

Hereupon, without further preface, Ken related the following tale. He was, I may observe in passing, a naturally fine narrator. There were deep, lingering tones in his voice, and he could strikingly enhance the comic or pathetic effect of a sentence by dwelling here and there upon some syllable. His features were equally susceptible of humorous and of solemn expressions, and his eyes were in form and hue wonderfully adapted to showing great varieties of emotion. Their mournful aspect was extremely earnest and affecting; and when Ken was giving utterance to some mysterious passage of the tale they had a doubtful, melancholy, exploring look which appealed irresistibly to the imagination. But the interest of his story was too pressing to allow of noticing these incidental embellishments at the time, though they doubtless had their influence upon me all the same.

'I left New York on an Inman Line steamer, you remember,' began Ken, 'and landed at Havre. I went the usual round of sightseeing on the Continent, and got round to London in July, at the height of the season. I had good introductions, and met any number of agreeable and famous people. Among others was a young lady, a countrywoman of my own – you know whom I mean – who interested me very much, and before her family left London she and I were engaged. We parted there for the time, because she had the Continental trip still to make, while I wanted to take the opportunity to visit the north of England and Ireland. I landed at Dublin about the 1st of October, and, zigzagging about the country, I found myself in County Cork about two weeks later.

'There is in that region some of the most lovely scenery that human eyes ever rested on, and it seems to be less known to tourists than many places of infinitely less picturesque value. A lonely region too: during my rambles I met not a single stranger like myself, and few enough natives. It seems incredible that so beautiful a country should be so deserted. After walking a dozen Irish miles you come across a group of two or three one-roomed cottages, and, like as not, one or more of those will have the roof off and the walls in ruins. The few peasants whom one sees, however, are affable and hospitable, especially when they hear you are from that terrestrial heaven whither most of their friends and relatives have gone before them. They seem simple and primitive enough at first sight, and yet they are as strange and incomprehensible a race as any in the world. They are as superstitious, as credulous of marvels, fairies, magicians, and omens, as the men whom St Patrick preached to, and at the same time they are shrewd, skeptical, sensible, and bottomless liars. Upon the whole, I met with no nation on my travels whose company I enjoyed so much, or who inspired me with so much kindliness, curiosity, and repugnance.

'At length I got to a place on the sea-coast, which I will not further specify than to say that it is not many miles from Ballymacheen, on the south shore. I have seen Venice and Naples, I have driven along the Cornice Road, I have spent a month at our own Mount Desert, and I say that all of them together are not so beautiful as this glowing, deep-hued, soft-gleaming, silvery-lighted, ancient harbour and town, with the tall hills crowding round it and the black cliffs and headlands planting their iron feet in the blue, transparent sea. It is a very old place, and has had a history which it has outlived ages since. It may once have had two or three thousand inhabitants; it has scarce five or six hundred today. Half the houses are in ruins or have disappeared; many of the remainder are standing empty. All the people are poor, most of them abjectly so; they saunter about with bare feet and uncovered heads, the women in quaint black or dark-blue cloaks, the men in such anomalous attire as only an Irishman knows how to get together, the children half naked. The only comfortable-looking people are the monks and the priests, and the soldiers in the fort. For there is a fort there, constructed on the huge ruins of one which may have done duty in the reign of Edward the Black Prince, or earlier, in whose mossy embrasures are mounted a couple of cannon, which occasionally sent a practice shot or two at the cliff on the other side of the harbour. The garrison consists of a dozen men and three or four officers and non-commissioned officers. I suppose they are relieved occasionally, but those I saw seemed to have become component parts of their surroundings.

'I put up at a wonderful little old inn, the only one in the place, and took my meals in a dining saloon fifteen feet by nine, with a portrait of George I (a print varnished to preserve it) hanging over the mantelpiece. On the second evening after dinner a young gentleman came in – the dining saloon being public property of course – and ordered some bread and cheese and a bottle of Dublin stout. We presently fell into talk; he turned out to be an officer from the fort, Lieutenant O'Connor, and a fine young specimen of the Irish soldier he was. After telling me all he knew about the town, the surrounding country, his friends, and himself, he intimated a readiness to sympathise with whatever tale I might choose to pour into his ear; and I had pleasure in trying to rival his own outspokenness. We became excellent friends; we had up a half-pint of Kinahan's whisky, and the lieutenant expressed himself in terms of high praise of my countrymen, my country, and my own particular cigars. When it became time for him to depart I accompanied him– for there was a splendid moon abroad – and bade him farewell at the fort entrance, having promised to come over the next day and make the acquaintance of the other fellows. "And mind your eye, now, going back, my dear boy," he called out, as I turned my face homeward. "Faith, 'tis a spooky place, that graveyard, and you'll as likely meet the black woman there as anywhere else!"

'The graveyard was a forlorn and barren spot on the hillside, just the hither side of the fort: thirty or forty rough headstones, few of which retained any semblance of the perpendicular, while many were so shattered and decayed as to seem nothing more than irregular natural projections from the ground. Who the black woman might be I knew not, and did not stay to inquire. I had never been subject to ghostly apprehensions, and as a matter of fact, though the path I had to follow was in places very bad going, not to mention a haphazard scramble over a ruined bridge that covered a deep-lying brook, I reached my inn without any adventure whatever.

'The next day I kept my appointment at the fort, and found no reason to regret it; and my friendly sentiments were abundantly reciprocated, thanks more especially, perhaps, to the success of my banjo, which I carried with me, and which was as novel as it was popular with those who listened to it. The chief personages in the social circle besides my friend the lieutenant were Major

Molloy, who was in command, a racy and juicy old campaigner, with a face like a sunset, and the surgeon, Dr Dudeen, a long, dry, humorous genius, with a wealth of anecdotical and traditional lore at his command that I have never seen surpassed. We had a jolly time of it, and it was the precursor of many more like it. The remains of October slipped away rapidly, and I was obliged to remember that I was a traveller in Europe, and not a resident in Ireland. The major, the surgeon, and the lieutenant all protested cordially against my proposed departure, but, as there was no help for it, they arranged a farewell dinner to take place in the fort on All-halloween.

'I wish you could have been at that dinner with me! It was the essence of Irish good-fellowship. Dr Dudeen was in great force; the major was better than the best of Lever's novels; the lieutenant was overflowing with hearty good-humour, merry chaff, and sentimental rhapsodies anent this or the other pretty girl of the neighbourhood. For my part I made the banjo ring as it had never rung before, and the others joined in the chorus with a mellow strength of lungs such as you don't often hear outside of Ireland. Among the stories that Dr Dudeen regaled us with was one about the Kern of Querin and his wife, Ethelind Fionguala – which being interpreted signifies "the white-shouldered". The lady, it appears, was originally betrothed to one O'Connor (here the lieutenant smacked his lips), but was stolen away on the wedding night by a party of vampires, who, it would seem, were at that period a prominent feature among the troubles of Ireland. But as they were bearing her along – she being unconscious – to that supper where she was not to eat but to be eaten, the young Kern of Querin, who happened to be out duck-shooting, met the party, and emptied his gun at it. The vampires fled, and the Kern carried the fair lady, still in a state of insensibility, to his house. "And by the same token, Mr Keningale," observed the doctor, knocking the ashes out of his pipe, "ye're after passing that very house on your way here. The one with the dark archway underneath it, and the big mullioned window at the corner, ye recollect, hanging over the street as I might say ..."

'"Go 'long wid the house, Dr Dudeen, dear," interrupted the lieutenant; "sure can't you see we're all dying to know what happened to sweet Miss Fionguala, God be good to her, when I was after getting her safe upstairs..."

'"Faith, then, I can tell ye that myself, Mr O'Connor," exclaimed the major, imparting a rotary motion to the remnants of whisky in his tumbler. "Tis a question to be solved on general principles, as Colonel O'Halloran said that time he was asked what he'd do if he'd been the Dook o' Wellington, and the Prussians hadn't come up in the nick o' time at Waterloo. 'Faith,' says the colonel, 'I'll tell ye...'

'"Arrah, then, major, why would ye be interruptin' the doctor, and Mr Keningale there lettin' his glass stay empty till he hears... The Lord save us! The bottle's empty!"

'In the excitement consequent upon this discovery, the thread of the doctor's story was lost; and before it could be recovered the evening had advanced so far that I felt obliged to withdraw. It took some time to make my proposition heard and comprehended; and a still longer time to put it in execution; so that it was fully midnight before I found myself standing in the cool pure air outside the fort, with the farewells of my boon companions ringing in my ears.

'Considering that it had been rather a wet evening indoors, I was in a remarkably good state of preservation, and I therefore ascribed it rather to the roughness of the road than to the smoothness of the liquor, when, after advancing a few rods, I stumbled and fell. As I picked myself up I fancied I had heard a laugh, and supposed that the lieutenant, who had accompanied me to the gate, was making merry over my mishap; but on looking round I saw that the gate was closed and no one was visible. The laugh, moreover, had seemed to be close at hand, and to be even pitched in a key that was rather feminine than masculine. Of course I must have been deceived; nobody was near me: my imagination had played me a trick, or else there was more truth than poetry in the tradition that Halloween is the carnival-time of disembodied spirits. It did not occur to me at the time that a stumble is held by the superstitious Irish to be an evil omen, and had I remembered it it would only have been to laugh at it. At all events, I was physically none the worse for my fall, and I resumed my way immediately.

'But the path was singularly difficult to find, or rather the path I was following did not seem to be the right one. I did not recognise it; I could have sworn (except I knew the contrary) that I had never seen it before. The moon had risen, though her light was as yet obscured by clouds, but neither my immediate surroundings nor the general aspect of the region appeared familiar. Dark, silent hillsides mounted up on either hand, and the road, for the most part, plunged downward, as if to conduct me into the bowels of the earth. The place was alive with strange echoes, so that at times I seemed to be walking through the midst of muttering voices and mysterious whispers, and a wild, faint sound of laughter seemed ever and anon to reverberate among the passes of the hills. Currents of colder air sighing up through narrow defiles and dark crevices touched my face as with airy fingers. A certain feeling of anxiety and insecurity began to take possession of me, though there was no definable cause for it, unless that I might be belated in getting home. With the perverse instinct of those who are lost I hastened my steps, but was impelled now and then to glance back over my shoulder, with a sensation of being pursued. But no living creature was in sight. The moon, however, had now risen higher, and the clouds that were drifting slowly across the sky flung into the naked valley dusky shadows, which occasionally assumed shapes that looked like the vague semblance of gigantic human forms.

'How long I had been hurrying onward I know not, when, with a kind of suddenness, I found myself approaching a graveyard. It was situated on the spur of a hill, and there was no fence around it, nor anything to protect it from the incursions of passers-by. There was something in the general appearance of this spot that made me half fancy I had seen it before; and I should have taken it to be the same that I had often noticed on my way to the fort, but that the latter was only a few hundred yards distant therefrom, whereas I must have traversed several miles at least. As I drew near, moreover, I observed that the headstones did not appear so ancient and decayed as those of the other. But what chiefly attracted my attention was the figure that was leaning or half sitting upon one of the largest of the upright slabs near the road. It was a female figure draped in black, and a closer inspection — for I was soon within a few yards of her — showed that she wore the calla, or long hooded cloak, the most common as well as the most ancient garment of Irish women, and doubtless of Spanish origin.

'I was a trifle startled by this apparition, so unexpected as it was, and so strange did it seem that any human creature should be at that hour of the night in so desolate and sinister a place. Involuntarily I paused as I came opposite her, and gazed at her intently. But the moonlight fell behind her, and the deep hood of her cloak so completely shadowed her face that I was unable to discern anything but the sparkle of a pair of eyes, which appeared to be returning my gaze with much vivacity.

'"You seem to be at home here," I said, at length. "Can you tell me where I am?"

'Hereupon the mysterious personage broke into a light laugh, which, though in itself musical and agreeable, was of a timbre and intonation that caused my heart to beat rather faster than my late pedestrian exertions warranted; for it was the identical laugh (or so my imagination persuaded me) that had echoed in my ears as I arose from my tumble an hour or two ago. For the rest, it was the laugh of a young woman, and presumably of a pretty one; and yet it had a wild, airy, mocking quality, that seemed hardly human at all, or not, at any rate, characteristic of a being of affections and limitations like unto ours. But this impression of mine was fostered, no doubt, by the unusual and uncanny circumstances of the occasion.

'"Sure, sir," said she, "you're at the grave of Ethelind Fionguala."

'As she spoke she rose to her feet, and pointed to the inscription on the stone. I bent forward, and was able, without much difficulty, to decipher the name, and a date which indicated that the occupant of the grave must have entered the disembodied state between two and three centuries ago.

'"And who are you?" was my next question.

'"I'm called Elsie," she replied. "But where would your honour be going November-eve?'

.'I mentioned my destination, and asked her whether she could direct me thither.

'"Indeed, then, 'tis there I'm going myself," Elsie replied; "and if your honour'll follow me, and play me a tune on the pretty instrument, 'tisn't long we'll be on the road."

'She pointed to the banjo which I carried wrapped up under my arm. How she knew that it was a musical instrument I could not imagine; possibly, I thought, she may have seen me playing on it as I strolled about the environs of the town. Be that as it may, I offered no opposition to the bargain, and further intimated that I would reward her more substantially on our arrival. At that she laughed again, and made a peculiar gesture with her hand above her head. I uncovered my banjo, swept my fingers across the strings, and struck into a fantastic dance-measure, to the music of which we proceeded along the path, Elsie slightly in advance, her feet keeping time to the airy measure. In fact, she trod so lightly, with an elastic, undulating movement, that with a little more it seemed as if she might float onward like a spirit. The extreme whiteness of her feet attracted my eye, and I was surprised to find that instead of being bare, as I had supposed, these were incased in white satin slippers quaintly embroidered with gold thread.

'"Elsie," said I, lengthening my steps so as to come up with her, "where do you live, and what do you do for a living?"

' "Sure, I live by myself," she answered; "and if you'd be after knowing how, you must come and see for yourself."

' "Are you in the habit of walking over the hills at night in shoes like that?"

' "And why would I not?" she asked, in her turn. "And where did your honour get the pretty gold ring on your finger?"

'The ring, which was of no great intrinsic value, had struck my eye in an old curiosity shop in Cork. It was an antique of very old-fashioned design, and might have belonged (as the vender assured me was the case) to one of the early kings or queens of Ireland.

' "Do you like it?" said I.

' "Will your honour be after making a present of it to Elsie?" she returned, with an insinuating tone and turn of the head.

' "Maybe I will, Elsie, on one condition. I am an artist; I make pictures of people. If you will promise to come to my studio and let me paint your portrait, I'll give you the ring, and some money besides."

' "And will you give me the ring now?" said Elsie.

' "Yes, if you'll promise."

' "And will you play the music to me?" she continued.

' "As much as you like."

' "But maybe I'll not be handsome enough for ye," said she, with a glance of her eyes beneath the dark hood.

' "I'll take the risk of that," I answered, laughing, "though, all the same, I don't mind taking a peep beforehand to remember you by." So saying, I put forth a hand to draw back the concealing hood. But Elsie eluded me, I scarce know how, and laughed a third time, with the same airy, mocking cadence.

' "Give me the ring first, and then you shall see me," she said, coaxingly.

' "Stretch out your hand, then," returned I, removing the ring from my finger. "When we are better acquainted, Elsie, you won't be so suspicious."

'She held out a slender, delicate hand, on the forefinger of which I slipped the ring. As I did so, the folds of her cloak fell a little apart, affording me a glimpse of a white shoulder and of a dress that seemed in that deceptive semi-darkness to be wrought of rich and costly material; and I caught, too, or so I fancied, the frosty sparkle of precious stones.

'"Arrah, mind where ye tread!" said Elsie, in a sudden, sharp tone.

'I looked round, and became aware for the first time that we were standing near the middle of a ruined bridge which spanned a rapid stream that flowed at a considerable depth below. The parapet of the bridge on one side was broken down, and I must have been, in fact, in imminent danger of stepping over into empty air. I made my way cautiously across the decaying structure; but, when I turned to assist Elsie, she was nowhere to be seen.

'What had become of the girl? I called, but no answer came. I gazed about on every side, but no trace of her was visible. Unless she had plunged into the narrow abyss at my feet, there was no place where she could have concealed herself – none at least that I could discover. She had vanished, nevertheless; and since her disappearance must have been premeditated, I finally came to the conclusion that it was useless to attempt to find her. She would present herself again in her own good time, or not at all. She had given me the slip very cleverly, and I must make the best of it. The adventure was perhaps worth the ring.

'On resuming my way, I was not a little relieved to find that I once more knew where I was. The bridge that I had just crossed was none other than the one I mentioned some time back; I was within a mile of the town, and my way lay clear before me. The moon, moreover, had now quite dispersed the clouds, and shone down with exquisite brilliance. Whatever her other failings, Elsie had been a trustworthy guide; she had brought me out of the depth of elf-land into the material world again. It had been a singular adventure, certainly; and I mused over it with a sense of mysterious pleasure as I sauntered along, humming snatches of airs, and accompanying myself on the strings. Hark! What light step was that behind me? It sounded like Elsie's; but no, Elsie was not there. The same impression or hallucination, however, recurred several times before I reached the outskirts of the town – the tread of an airy foot behind or beside my own. The fancy did not make me nervous; on the contrary, I was pleased with the notion of being thus haunted, and gave myself up to a romantic and genial vein of reverie.

'After passing one or two roofless and moss-grown cottages, I entered the narrow and rambling street which leads through the town. This street a short distance down widens a little, as if to afford the wayfarer space to observe a remarkable old house that stands on the northern side. The house was built of stone, and in a noble style of architecture; it reminded me somewhat of certain palaces of the old Italian nobility that I had seen on the Continent, and it may very probably have been built by one of the Italian or Spanish immigrants of the sixteenth or seventeenth century. The moulding of the projecting windows and arched doorway was richly carved, and upon the front of the building was an escutcheon wrought in high relief, though I could not make out the purport of the device. The moonlight falling upon this picturesque pile enhanced all its beauties, and at the same time made it seem like a vision that might dissolve away when the light ceased to shine. I must often have seen the house before, and yet I retained no definite recollection of it; I had never until now examined it with my eyes open, so to speak. Leaning against the wall on the opposite side of the street, I contemplated it for a long while at my leisure. The window at the corner was really a very fine and massive affair. It projected over the pavement below, throwing a heavy shadow aslant; the frames of the diamond-paned lattices were heavily mullioned. How often in past ages had that lattice been pushed open by some fair hand, revealing to a lover waiting beneath in the moonlight the charming countenance of his high-born mistress! Those were brave days. They had passed away long since. The great house had stood empty for who could tell how many years; only bats and vermin were its inhabitants. Where now were those who had built it? And who were they? Probably the very name of them was forgotten.

'As I continued to stare upward, however, a conjecture presented itself to my mind which rapidly ripened into a conviction. Was not this the house that Dr Dudeen had described that very evening as having been formerly the abode of the Kern of Querin and his mysterious bride? There was the projecting window, the arched doorway. Yes, beyond a doubt this was the very house. I emitted a low exclamation of renewed interest and pleasure, and my speculations took a still more imaginative, but also a more definite turn.

'What had been the fate of that lovely lady after the Kern had brought her home insensible in his arms? Did she recover, and were they married and made happy ever after; or had the sequel been a tragic one? I remembered to have read that the victims of vampires generally became vampires themselves. Then my thoughts went back to that grave on the hillside. Surely that was unconsecrated ground. Why had they buried her there? Ethelind of the white shoulder! Ah! Why had not I lived in those days; or why might not some magic cause them to live again for me? Then would I seek this street at midnight, and standing here beneath her window, I would lightly touch the strings of my bandore until the casement opened cautiously and she looked down. A sweet vision indeed! And what prevented my realizing it? Only a matter of a couple of centuries or so. And was time, then, at which poets and philosophers sneer, so rigid and real a matter that a little faith and imagination might not overcome it? At all events, I had my banjo, the bandore's legitimate and lineal descendant, and the memory of Fionguala should have the love-ditty.

'Hereupon, having retuned the instrument, I launched forth into an old Spanish love-song, which I had met with in some mouldy library during my travels, and had set to music of my own. I sang low, for the deserted street re-echoed the lightest sound, and what I sang must reach only my lady's ears. The words were warm with the fire of the ancient Spanish chivalry, and I threw into their expression all the passion of the lovers of romance. Surely Fionguala, the white-shouldered, would hear, and awaken from her sleep of centuries, and come to the latticed casement and look down! Hist! See yonder! What light – what shadow is that that seems to flit from room to room within the abandoned house, and now approaches the mullioned window? Are my eyes dazzled by the play of the moonlight, or does the casement move – does it open? Nay, this is no delusion; there is no error of the senses here. There is simply a woman, young, beautiful, and richly attired, bending forward from the window, and silently beckoning me to approach.

'Too much amazed to be conscious of amazement, I advanced until I stood directly beneath the casement, and the lady's face, as she stooped toward me, was not more than twice a man's height from my own. She smiled and kissed her fingertips; something white fluttered in her hand, then fell through the air to the ground at my feet. The next moment she had withdrawn, and I heard the lattice close. I picked up what she had let fall; it was a delicate lace handkerchief, tied to the handle of an elaborately wrought bronze key. It was evidently the key of the house, and invited me to enter. I loosened it from the handkerchief, which bore a faint, delicious perfume, like the aroma of flowers in an ancient garden, and turned to the arched doorway. I felt no misgiving, and scarcely any sense of strangeness. All was as I had wished it to be, and as it should be; the mediaeval age was alive once more, and as for myself, I almost felt the velvet cloak hanging from my shoulder and the long rapier dangling at my belt. Standing in front of the door I thrust the key into the lock, turned it, and felt the bolt yield. The next instant the door was opened, apparently from within; I stepped across the threshold, the door closed again, and I was alone in the house, and in darkness.

'Not alone, however! As I extended my hand to grope my way it was met by another hand, soft, slender, and cold, which insinuated itself gently into mine and drew me forward. Forward I went, nothing loath; the darkness was impenetrable, but I could hear the light rustle of a dress close to me, and the same delicious perfume that had emanated from the handkerchief enriched the air that I breathed, while the little hand that clasped and was clasped by my own alternately tightened and half relaxed the hold of its soft cold fingers. In this manner, and treading lightly, we traversed what I presumed to be a long, irregular passageway, and ascended a staircase. Then another corridor, until finally we paused, a door opened, emitting a flood of soft light, into which we entered, still hand in hand. The darkness and the doubt were at an end.

'The room was of imposing dimensions, and was furnished and decorated in a style of antique splendour. The walls were draped with mellow hues of tapestry; clusters of candles burned in polished silver sconces, and were reflected and multiplied in tall mirrors placed in the four corners of the room. The heavy beams of the dark oaken ceiling crossed each other in squares, and were laboriously carved; the curtains and the drapery of the chairs were of heavy-figured damask. At one end of the room was a broad ottoman, and in front of it a table, on which was set forth, in massive silver dishes, a sumptuous repast, with wines in crystal beakers. At the side was a vast and deep fireplace, with space enough on the broad hearth to burn whole trunks of trees. No fire, however, was there, but only a great heap of dead embers; and the room, for all its magnificence, was cold – cold as a tomb, or as my lady's hand – and it sent a subtle chill creeping to my heart.

'But my lady! How fair she was! I gave but a passing glance at the room; my eyes and my thoughts were all for her. She was dressed in white, like a bride; diamonds sparkled in her dark hair and on her snowy bosom; her lovely face and slender lips were pale, and all the paler for the dusky glow of her eyes. She gazed at me with a strange, elusive smile; and yet there was, in her aspect and bearing, something familiar in the midst of strangeness, like the burden of a song heard long ago and recalled among other conditions and surroundings. It seemed to me that something in me recognised her and knew her, had known her always. She was the woman of whom I had dreamed, whom I had beheld in visions, whose voice and face had haunted me from boyhood up. Whether we had ever met before, as human beings meet, I knew not; perhaps I had been blindly seeking her all over the world, and she had been awaiting me in this splendid room, sitting by those dead embers until all the warmth had gone out of her blood, only to be restored by the heat with which my love might supply her.

' "I thought you had forgotten me," she said, nodding as if in answer to my thought. "The night was so late – our one night of the year! How my heart rejoiced when I heard your dear voice singing the song I know so well! Kiss me – my lips are cold!"

'Cold indeed they were – cold as the lips of death. But the warmth of my own seemed to revive them. They were now tinged with a faint colour, and in her cheeks also appeared a delicate shade of pink. She drew fuller breath, as one who recovers from a long lethargy. Was it my life that was feeding her? I was ready to give her all. She drew me to the table and pointed to the viands and the wine.

' "Eat and drink," she said. "You have travelled far, and you need food."

' "Will you eat and drink with me?" said I, pouring out the wine.

' "You are the only nourishment I want," was her answer. "This wine is thin and cold. Give me wine as red as your blood and as warm, and I will drain a goblet to the dregs."

'At these words, I know not why, a slight shiver passed through me. She seemed to gain vitality and strength at every instant, but the chill of the great room struck into me more and more.

'She broke into a fantastic flow of spirits, clapping her hands, and dancing about me like a child. Who was she? And was I myself, or was she mocking me when she implied that we had belonged to each other of old? At length she stood still before me, crossing her hands over her breast. I saw upon the forefinger of her right hand the gleam of an antique ring.

'"Where did you get that ring?" I demanded.

'She shook her head and laughed. "Have you been faithful?" she asked. "It is my ring; it is the ring that unites us; it is the ring you gave me when you loved me first. It is the ring of the Kern – the fairy ring, and I am your Ethelind – Ethelind Fionguala."

'"So be it," I said, casting aside all doubt and fear, and yielding myself wholly to the spell of her inscrutable eyes and wooing lips. "You are mine, and I am yours, and let us be happy while the hours last."

'"You are mine, and I am yours," she repeated, nodding her head with an elfish smile. "Come and sit beside me, and sing that sweet song again that you sang to me so long ago. Ah, now I shall live a hundred years."

'We seated ourselves on the ottoman, and while she nestled luxuriously among the cushions, I took my banjo and sang to her. The song and the music resounded through the lofty room, and came back in throbbing echoes. And before me as I sang I saw the face and form of Ethelind Fionguala, in her jewelled bridal dress, gazing at me with burning eyes. She was pale no longer, but ruddy and warm, and life was like a flame within her. It was I who had become cold and bloodless, yet with the last life that was in me I would have sung to her of love that can never die. But at length my eyes grew dim, the room seemed to darken, the form of Ethelind alternately brightened and waxed indistinct, like the last flickerings of a fire; I swayed toward her, and felt myself lapsing into unconsciousness, with my head resting on her white shoulder.'

Here Keningale paused a few moments in his story, flung a fresh log upon the fire, and then continued:

'I awoke, I know not how long afterward. I was in a vast,

empty room in a ruined building. Rotten shreds of drapery depended from the walls, and heavy festoons of spiders' webs grey with dust covered the windows, which were destitute of glass or sash; they had been boarded up with rough planks which had themselves become rotten with age, and admitted through their holes and crevices pallid rays of light and chilly draughts of air. A bat, disturbed by these rays or by my own movement, detached himself from his hold on a remnant of mouldy tapestry near me, and after circling dizzily around my head, wheeled the flickering noiselessness of his flight into a darker corner. As I arose unsteadily from the heap of miscellaneous rubbish on which I had been lying, something which had been resting across my knees fell to the floor with a rattle. I picked it up, and found it to be my banjo – as you see it now.

'Well, that is all I have to tell. My health was seriously impaired; all the blood seemed to have been drawn out of my veins; I was pale and haggard, and the chill – Ah, that chill,' murmured Keningale, drawing nearer to the fire, and spreading out his hands to catch the warmth – 'I shall never get over it; I shall carry it to my grave.'

The Story of Baelbrow

E and H Heron
(pseudonyms of Kate Prichard [1851–1935]
and Hesketh Prichard [1876–1922])

Hesketh Prichard led an extraordinarily adventurous life as an explorer and big-game hunter, travelling the world from Patagonia to Newfoundland and from Haiti to Norway. He was also a first-class cricketer and a brilliant marksman. During the First World War he was in charge of training snipers for the Western Front. Somehow, amidst all this other activity, he managed to find time to write fiction, often in collaboration with his mother Kate. Of the fiction Hesketh Prichard wrote on his own, the most interesting features 'November Joe', a Canadian backwoodsman and amateur detective who appears in a number of stories. Working with Kate, he produced tales of a Zorro-like figure named Don Q and, in the 1920s, one of them was turned into a Hollywood film starring Douglas Fairbanks. The Flaxman Low stories, which were the Prichards' first major successes were about an occult detective, and predate William Hope Hodgson's better-known Carnacki stories by almost a decade. They were originally published in Pearson's Magazine *in 1898 and 1899 and were later collected in book form. In the twelve stories, Flaxman Low investigates all kinds of psychic phenomena including a spirit which attacks travellers on a lonely road ('The Story of the Moor Road') and a ghost with a peculiarly unnerving laugh ('The Story of Medhans Lea'). In 'The Story of Baelbrow', arguably the best of Low's adventures, the Prichards' psychic Sherlock faces a dangerous combination of vampire and ancient mummy.*

It is a matter for regret that so many of Mr Flaxman Low's reminiscences should deal with the darker episodes of his career. Yet this is almost unavoidable, as the more purely scientific and less strongly marked cases would not, perhaps, contain the same elements of interest for the general public however valuable and instructive they might be to the expert student. It has also been considered better to choose the completer cases, those that ended in something like satisfactory proof, rather than the many instances where the thread broke abruptly amongst surmisings, which it was never possible to subject to convincing tests.

North of a low-lying strip of promontory Bael Ness thrusts a blunt nose into the sea. On the ness, backed by pinewoods, stands a square, comfortable stone mansion, known to the countryside as Baelbrow. It has faced the east winds for close upon three hundred years, and during the whole period has been the home of the Swaffam family, who were never in any wise put out of conceit of their ancestral dwelling by the fact that it had always been haunted. Indeed, the Swaffams were proud of the Baelbrow Ghost, which enjoyed a wide notoriety, and no one dreamt of complaining of its behaviour until Professor Jungvort, of Nuremburg, laid information against it, and sent an urgent appeal for help to Mr Flaxman Low.

The Professor, who was well acquainted with Mr Low, detailed the circumstances of his tenancy of Baelbrow, and the unpleasant events that had followed thereupon.

It appeared that Mr Swaffam, senior, who spent a large portion of his time abroad, had offered to lend his house to the Professor for the summer season. When the Jungvorts arrived at Baelbrow, they were charmed with the place. The prospect, though not very varied, was at least extensive, and the air exhilarating. Also the Professor's daughter enjoyed frequent visits from her betrothed – Harold Swaffam – and the Professor was delightfully employed in overhauling the Swaffam library.

The Jungvorts had been duly told of the ghost, which lent distinction to the old house, but never in any way interfered with the comfort of the inmates. For some time they found this description to be strictly true, but with the beginning of October came a change. Up to this time and as far back as the Swaffam annals reached, the ghost had been a shadow, a rustle, a passing sigh – nothing definite or troublesome. But early in October strange things began to occur, and the terror culminated when a housemaid was found dead in a corridor three weeks later. Upon this the Professor felt that it was time to send for Flaxman Low.

Mr Low arrived upon a chilly evening when the house was already beginning to blur in the purple twilight, and the resinous scent of the pines came sweetly on the land breeze. Jungvort welcomed him in the spacious, firelit hall. He was a stout German with a quantity of white hair, round eyes emphasised by spectacles, and a kindly, dreamy face. His life-study was philology, and his two relaxations: chess and the smoking of a big Bismarck-bowled meerschaum.

'Now, Professor,' said Mr Low when they had settled themselves in the smoking room, 'how did it all begin?'

'I will tell you,' replied Jungvort, thrusting out his chin, and tapping his broad chest, and speaking as if an unwarrantable liberty had been taken with him. 'First of all, it has shown itself to me!'

Mr Flaxman Low smiled and assured him that nothing could be more satisfactory.

'But not at all satisfactory!' exclaimed the Professor, 'I was sitting here alone, it might have been midnight – when I hear something come creeping like a little dog with its nails, tick-tick, upon the oak flooring of the hall. I whistle, for I think it is the little "Rags" of my daughter, and afterwards opened the door, and I saw' – he hesitated and looked hard at Low through his spectacles, 'something that was just disappearing into the passage which connects the two wings of the house. It was a figure, not unlike the human figure, but narrow and straight. I fancied I saw a bunch of black hair, and a flutter of something detached, which may have been a handkerchief. I was overcome by a feeling of repulsion. I heard a few, clicking steps, then it stopped, as I thought, at the Museum door. Come, I will show you the spot.'

The Professor conducted Mr Low into the hall. The main staircase, dark and massive, yawned above them, and directly behind it ran the passage referred to by the Professor. It was over twenty feet long, and about midway led past a deep arch containing a door reached by two steps. Jungvort explained that this door formed the entrance to a large room called the Museum, in which Mr Swaffam senior, who was something of a dilettante, stored the various curios he picked up during his excursions abroad. The Professor went on to say that he immediately followed the figure, which he believed had gone into the museum, but he found nothing there except the cases containing Swaffam's treasures.

'I mentioned my experience to no one. I concluded that I had seen the ghost. But two days after, one of the female servants coming through the passage in the dark, declared that a man leapt out at her from the embrasure of the Museum door, but she released herself and ran screaming into the servants' hall. We at once made a search but found nothing to substantiate her story.

'I took no notice of this, though it coincided pretty well with my own experience. The week after, my daughter Lena came down late one night for a book. As she was about to cross the hall, something leapt upon her from behind. Women are of little use in serious investigations – she fainted! Since then she has been ill and the doctor says "run down".' Here the Professor spread out his hands. 'So she leaves for a change tomorrow. Since then other members of the household have been attacked in much the same manner, with always the same result, they faint and are weak and useless when they recover.

'But, last Wednesday, the affair became a tragedy. By that time the servants had refused to come through the passage except in a crowd of three or four – most of them preferring to go round by the terrace to reach this part of the house. But one maid, named Eliza Freeman, said she was not afraid of the Baelbrow Ghost, and undertook to put out the lights in the hall one night. When she had done, and was returning through the passage past the Museum door, she appears to have been attacked, or at any rate frightened. In the grey of the morning they found her lying beside the steps dead. There was a little blood upon her sleeve but no mark upon her body except a small raised pustule under the ear. The doctor said the girl was extraordinarily anaemic, and that she probably died from fright, her heart being weak. I was surprised at this, for she had always seemed to be a particularly strong and active young woman.'

'Can I see Miss Jungvort tomorrow before she goes?' asked Low, as the Professor signified he had nothing more to tell.

The Professor was rather unwilling that his daughter should be questioned, but he at last gave his permission, and next morning Low had a short talk with the girl before she left the house. He found her a very pretty girl, though listless and startlingly pale, and with a frightened stare in her light brown eyes. Mr Low asked if she could describe her assailant.

'No,' she answered, 'I could not see him, for he was behind me. I only saw a dark, bony hand, with shining nails, and a bandaged arm pass just under my eyes before I fainted.'

'Bandaged arm? I have heard nothing of this.'

'Tut-tut, mere fancy!' put in the Professor impatiently.

'I saw the bandages on the arm,' repeated the girl, turning her head wearily away, 'and I smelt the antiseptics it was dressed with.'

'You have hurt your neck,' remarked Mr Low, who noticed a small circular patch of pink under her ear.

She flushed and paled, raising her hand to her neck with a nervous jerk, as she said in a low voice:

'It has almost killed me. Before he touched me, I knew he was there! I felt it!'

When they left her the Professor apologised for the unreliability of her evidence, and pointed out the discrepancy between her statement and his own.

'She says she sees nothing but an arm, yet I tell you it had no arms! Preposterous! Conceive a wounded man entering this house to frighten the young women! I do not know what to make of it! Is it a man, or is it the Baelbrow Ghost?'

During the afternoon when Mr Low and the Professor returned from a stroll on the shore, they found a dark-browed young man with a bull neck, and strongly marked features, standing sullenly before the hall fire. The Professor presented him to Mr Low as Harold Swaffam. Swaffam seemed to be about thirty, but was already known as a far-seeing and successful member of the Stock Exchange.

'I am pleased to meet you, Mr Low,' he began, with a keen glance, 'though you don't look sufficiently high-strung for one of your profession.'

Mr Low merely bowed.

'Come, you don't defend your craft against my insinuations?' went on Swaffam. 'And so you have come to rout out our poor old ghost from Baelbrow? You forget that he is an heirloom, a family possession! What's this about his having turned rabid, eh, Professor?' he ended, wheeling round upon Jungvort in his brusque way.

The Professor told the story over again. It was plain that he stood rather in awe of his prospective son-in-law.

'I heard much the same from Lena, whom I met at the station,' said Swaffam. 'It is my opinion that the women in this house are suffering from an epidemic of hysteria. You agree with me, Mr Low?'

'Possibly. Though hysteria could hardly account for Freeman's death.'

'I can't say as to that until I have looked further into the particulars. I have not been idle since I arrived. I have examined the Museum. No one has entered it from the outside, and there is no other way of entrance except through the passage. The flooring is laid, I happen to know, on a thick layer of concrete. And there the case for the ghost stands at present.' After a few moments of dogged reflection, he swung round on Mr Low, in a manner that seemed peculiar to him when about to address any person. 'What do you say to this plan, Mr Low? I propose to drive the Professor over to Ferryvale, to stop there for a day or two at the hotel, and I will also dispose of the servants who still remain in the house for, say, forty-eight hours. Meanwhile you and I can try to go further into the secret of the ghost's new pranks?'

Flaxman Low replied that this scheme exactly met his views. But the Professor protested against being sent away. Harold Swaffam however was a man who liked to arrange things in his own fashion, and within forty-five minutes he and Jungvort departed in the dogcart.

The evening was lowering, and Baelbrow, like all houses built in exposed situations, was extremely susceptible to the changes of the weather. Therefore, before many hours were over, the place was full of creaking noises as the screaming gale battered at the shuttered windows, and the tree branches tapped and groaned against walls.

Harold Swaffam, on his way back, was caught in the storm and drenched to the skin. It was, therefore, settled that after he had changed his clothes he should have a couple of hours' rest on the smoking-room sofa, while Mr Low kept watch in the hall.

The early part of the night passed over uneventfully. A light burned faintly in the great wainscotted hall, but the passage was dark. There was nothing to be heard but the wild moan and whistle of the wind coming in from the sea, and the squalls of rain dashing against the windows. As the hours advanced, Mr Low lit a lantern that lay at hand, and, carrying it along the passage, tried the Museum door. It yielded, and the wind came muttering through to meet him. He looked round at the shutters and behind the big cases which held Mr Swaffam's treasures, to make sure that the room contained no living occupant but himself.

Suddenly he fancied he heard a scraping noise behind him, and turned round, but discovered nothing to account for it. Finally, he laid the lantern on a bench so that its light should fall through the door into the passage, and returned again to the hall, where he put out the lamp, and then once more took up his station by the closed door of the smoking room.

A long hour passed, during which the wind continued to roar down the wide hall chimney, and the old boards creaked as if furtive footsteps were gathering from every corner of the house. But Flaxman Low heeded none of these; he was waiting for a certain sound.

After a while, he heard it – the cautious scraping of wood on wood. He leant forward to watch the Museum door. Click, click came the curious dog-like tread upon the tiled floor of the Museum till the thing, whatever it was, paused and listened behind the open door. The wind lulled at the moment, and Low listened also, but no further sound was to be heard, only slowly across the broad ray of light falling through the door grew a stealthy shadow.

Again the wind rose, and blew in heavy gusts about the house, till even the flame in the lantern flickered, but when it steadied once more, Flaxman Low saw that the silent form had passed through the door, and was now on the steps outside. He could just make out a dim shadow in the dark angle of the embrasure.

Presently, from the shapeless shadow came a sound Mr Low was not prepared to hear. The thing sniffed the air with the strong, audible inspiration of a bear, or some large animal. At the same moment, carried on the draughts of the hall, a faint, unfamiliar odour reached his nostrils. Lena Jungvort's words flashed back upon him – this, then, was the creature with the bandaged arm!

Again, as the storm shrieked and shook the windows, a darkness passed across the light. The thing had sprung out from the angle of the door, and Flaxman Low knew that it was making its way towards him through the illusive blackness of the hall. He hesitated for a second; then he opened the smoking-room door.

Harold Swaffam sat up on the sofa, dazed with sleep.

'What has happened? Has it come?'

Low told him what he had just seen. Swaffam listened half-smilingly.

'What do you make of it now?' he said.

'I must ask you to defer that question for a little,' replied Low.

'Then you mean me to suppose that you have a theory to fit all these incongruous items?'

'I have a theory, which may be modified by further knowledge,' said Low. 'Meantime, am I right in concluding from the name of this house that it was built on a barrow or burying-place?'

'You are right, though that has nothing to do with the latest freaks of our ghost,' returned Swaffam decidedly.

'I also gather that Mr Swaffam has lately sent home one of the many cases now lying in the Museum?' went on Mr Low.

'He sent one, certainly, last September.'

'And you have opened it,' asserted Low.

'Yes; though I flattered myself I had left no trace of my handiwork.'

'I have not examined the cases,' said Low. 'I inferred that you had done so from other facts.'

'Now, one thing more,' went on Swaffam, still smiling. 'Do you imagine there is any danger – I mean to men like ourselves? Hysterical women cannot be taken into serious account.'

'Certainly; the gravest danger to any person who moves about this part of the house alone after dark,' replied Low.

Harold Swaffam leant back and crossed his legs.

'To go back to the beginning of our conversation, Mr Low, may I remind you of the various conflicting particulars you will have to reconcile before you can present any decent theory to the world?'

'I am quite aware of that.'

'First of all, our original ghost was a mere misty presence, rather guessed at from vague sounds and shadows – now we have something that is tangible, and that can, as we have proof, kill with fright. Next Jungvort declares the thing was a narrow, long and distinctly armless object, while Miss Jungvort has not only seen the arm and hand of a human being, but saw them clearly enough to tell us that the nails were gleaming and the arm bandaged. She also felt its strength. Jungvort, on the other hand, maintained that it clicked along like a dog – you bear out this description with the additional information that it sniffs like a wild beast. Now what can this thing be? It is capable of being seen, smelt, and felt, yet it hides itself successfully in a room where there is no cavity or space sufficient to afford covert to a cat! You still tell me that you believe that you can explain?'

'Most certainly,' replied Flaxman Low with conviction.

'I have not the slightest intention or desire to be rude, but as a mere matter of common sense, I must express my opinion plainly. I believe the whole thing to be the result of excited imaginations, and I am about to prove it. Do you think there is any further danger tonight?'

'Very great danger tonight,' replied Low.

'Very well as I said, I am going to prove it. I will ask you to allow me to lock you up in one of the distant rooms, where I can get no help from you, and I will pass the remainder of the night walking about the passage and hall in the dark. That should give proof one way or the other.'

'You can do so if you wish, but I must at least beg to be allowed to look on. I will leave the house and watch what goes on from the window in the passage, which I saw opposite the Museum door. You cannot, in all fairness, refuse to let me be a witness.'

'I cannot, of course,' returned Swaffam. 'Still, the night is too bad to turn a dog out into, and I warn you that I shall lock you out.'

'That will not matter. Lend me a macintosh, and leave the lantern lit in the Museum, where I placed it.'

Swaffam agreed to this. Mr Low gives a graphic account of what followed. He left the house and was duly locked out, and after groping his way round the house, found himself at length outside the window of the passage, which was almost opposite to the door of the Museum. The door was still ajar and a thin band of light cut out into the gloom. Further down the hall gaped black and void. Low, sheltering himself as well as he could from the rain, waited for Swaffam's appearance. Was the terrible yellow watcher balancing itself upon its lean legs in the dim corner opposite, ready to spring out with its deadly strength upon the passer-by?

Presently Low heard a door bang inside the house, and the next moment Swaffam appeared with a candle in his hand, an isolated spread of weak rays against the vast darkness behind. He advanced steadily down the passage, his dark face grim and set, and as he came Mr Low experienced that tingling sensation, which is so often the forerunner of some strange experience. Swaffam passed on towards the other end of the passage. There was a quick vibration of the Museum door as a lean shape with a shrunken head leapt out into the passage after him. Then all together came a hoarse shout, the noise of a fall and utter darkness.

In an instant, Mr Low had broken the glass, opened the window, and swung himself into the passage. There he lit a match and as it flared he saw by its dim light a picture painted for a second upon the obscurity beyond.

Swaffam's big figure lay with outstretched arms, face downwards, and as Low looked a crouching shape extricated itself from the fallen man, raising a narrow vicious head from his shoulder.

The match spluttered feebly and went out, and Low heard a flying step click on the boards, before he could find the candle Swaffam had dropped. Lighting it, he stooped over Swaffam and turned him on his back. The man's strong colour had gone, and the wax-white face looked whiter still against the blackness of hair and brows, and upon his neck under the ear, was a little raised pustule from which a thin line of blood was streaked up to the angle of his cheekbone.

Some instinctive feeling prompted Low to glance up at this

moment. Half extended from the Museum doorway were a face and bony neck – a high-nosed, dull-eyed, malignant face, the eye-sockets hollow, and the darkened teeth showing. Low plunged his hand into his pocket, and a shot rang out in the echoing passageway and hall. The wind sighed through the broken panes, a ribbon of stuff fluttered along the polished flooring, and that was all, as Flaxman Low half dragged, half carried Swaffam into the smoking room.

It was some time before Swaffam recovered consciousness. He listened to Low's story of how he had found him with a red angry gleam in his sombre eyes.

'The ghost has scored off me,' he said with an odd, sullen laugh, 'but now I fancy it's my turn! But before we adjourn to the Museum to examine the place, I will ask you to let me hear your notion of things. You have been right in saying there was real danger. For myself I can only tell you that I felt something spring upon me, and I knew no more. Had this not happened I am afraid I should never have asked you a second time what your idea of the matter might be,' he ended with a sort of sulky frankness.

'There are two main indications,' replied Low. 'This strip of yellow bandage, which I have just now picked up from the passage floor, and the mark on your neck.'

'What's that you say?' Swaffam rose quickly and examined his neck in a small glass beside the mantelshelf.

'Connect those two, and I think I shall leave you to work it out for yourself,' said Low.

'Pray let us have your theory in full,' requested Swaffam shortly.

'Very well,' answered Low good-humouredly – he thought Swaffam's annoyance natural under the circumstances – 'The long, narrow figure which seemed to the Professor to be armless is developed on the next occasion. For Miss Jungvort sees a bandaged arm and a dark hand with gleaming – which means, of course, gilded – nails. The clicking sound of the footstep coincides with these particulars, for we know that sandals made of strips of leather are not uncommon in company with gilt nails and bandages. Old and dry leather would naturally click upon your polished floors.'

'Bravo, Mr Low! So you mean to say that this house is haunted by a mummy!'

'That is my idea, and all I have seen confirms me in my opinion.'

'To do you justice, you held this theory before tonight – before, in fact, you had seen anything for yourself. You gathered that my father had sent home a mummy, and you went on to conclude that I had opened the case.'

'Yes. I imagine you took off most of, or rather all, the outer bandages, thus leaving the limbs free, wrapped only in the inner bandages which were swathed round each separate limb. I fancy this mummy was preserved by the Theban method with aromatic spices which left the skin olive-coloured, dry and flexible, like tanned leather, the features remaining distinct, and the hair, teeth and eyebrows perfect.'

'So far, good,' said Swaffam. 'But now, how about the intermittent vitality? The pustule on the neck of those whom it attacks? And where is our old Baelbrow ghost to come in?'

Swaffam tried to speak in a rallying tone, but his excitement and lowering temper were visible enough, in spite of the attempts he made to suppress them.

'To begin at the beginning,' said Flaxman Low, 'everybody who, in a rational and honest manner, investigates the phenomena of spiritism will, sooner or later, meet in them some perplexing element, which is not to be explained by any of the ordinary theories. For reasons into which I need not now enter, this present case appears to me to be one of these. I am led to believe that the ghost which has for so many years given dim and vague manifestations of its existence in this house is a vampire.'

Swaffam threw back his head with an incredulous gesture.

'We no longer live in the middle ages, Mr Low! And besides

how could a vampire come here?' he said scoffingly.

'It is held by some authorities on these subjects that under certain conditions a vampire may be self-created. You tell me that this house is built upon an ancient barrow, in fact, on a spot where we might naturally expect to find such an elemental psychic germ. In those dead human systems were contained all the seeds for good and evil. The power which causes these psychic seeds or germs to grow is thought, and from being long dwelt on and indulged, a thought might finally gain a mysterious vitality, which could go on increasing more and more by attracting to itself suitable and appropriate elements from its environment. For a long period this germ remained a helpless intelligence, awaiting the opportunity to assume some material form, by means of which to carry out its desires. The invisible is the real; the material only subserves its manifestation. The impalpable reality already existed, when you provided for it a physical medium for action by unwrapping the mummy's form. Now, we can only judge of the nature of the germ by its manifestation through matter. Here we have every indication of a vampire intelligence touching into life and energy the dead human frame. Hence the mark on the neck of its victims, and their bloodless and anaemic condition. For a vampire, as you know, sucks blood.'

Swaffam rose, and took up the lamp.

'Now, for proof,' he said bluntly. 'Wait a second, Mr Low. You say you fired at this appearance?' And he took up the pistol which Low had laid down on the table.

'Yes, I aimed at a small portion of its foot which I saw on the step.'

Without more words, and with the pistol still in his hand, Swaffam led the way to the Museum.

The wind howled round the house, and the darkness, which precedes the dawn, lay upon the world, when the two men looked upon one of the strangest sights it has ever been given to men to shudder at.

Half in and half out of an oblong wooden box in a corner of

the great room, lay a lean shape in its rotten yellow bandages, the scraggy neck surmounted by a mop of frizzled hair. The toe strap of a sandal and a portion of the right foot had been shot away.

Swaffam, with a working face, gazed down at it, then seizing it by its tearing bandages, he flung it into the box, where it fell into life-like posture, its wide, moist-lipped mouth gaping up at them.

For a moment Swaffam stood over the thing; then with a curse he raised the revolver and shot into the grinning face again and again with a deliberate vindictiveness. Finally he rammed the thing down into the box, and clubbing the weapon, smashed the head into fragments with a vicious energy that coloured the whole horrible scene with a suggestion of murder done.

Then, turning to Low, he said:

'Help me to fasten the cover on it.'

'Are you going to bury it?'

'No, we must rid the earth of it,' he answered savagely. 'I'll put it into the old canoe and burn it.'

The rain had ceased when in the daybreak they carried the old canoe down to the shore. In it they placed the mummy case with its ghastly occupant, and piled faggots about it. The sail was raised and the pile lighted, and Low and Swaffam watched it creep out on the ebb-tide, at first a twinkling spark, then a flare of waving fire, until far out to sea the history of that dead thing ended 3000 years after the priests of Amen had laid it to rest in its appointed pyramid.

Count Magnus

MR James (1862–1936)

Montague Rhodes James was the greatest English writer of ghost stories of his era and many of his tales ('Oh, Whistle and I'll Come to You, My Lad', 'The Treasure of Abbot Thomas', 'A Warning to the Curious') have found new and appreciative audiences through television and radio adaptations. First and foremost James was a scholar. He was Provost of King's College, Cambridge from 1905 to 1918 and of Eton from 1918 until his death. He was also director of the Fitzwilliam Museum in Cambridge for fifteen years. His primary scholarly interest was in mediaeval manuscripts – an interest reflected in the plots and protagonists of many of his stories – and some of the work he produced on them is still of value to scholars today. His ghost stories began as entertainments to be read out to friends and were later collected in volumes such as Ghost Stories of an Antiquary *(1904) and* More Ghost Stories of an Antiquary *(1911). A handful of James's tales could arguably be classified as vampire stories. 'An Episode of Cathedral History', which is an exemplary title for a James story, has appeared in anthologies as such in the past. 'Count Magnus', about a travel writer on a journey in Sweden who unleashes something awful from an ancient mausoleum, may not concern itself with blood and bloodsucking but the terrible count and his monstrous companion undoubtedly feed on the life of their victim.*

By what means the papers out of which I have made a connected story came into my hands is the last point which the reader will learn from these pages. But it is necessary to prefix to my extracts from them a statement of the form in which I possess them.

They consist, then, partly of a series of collections for a book of travels, such a volume as was a common product of the forties and fifties. Horace Marryat's *Journal of a Residence in Jutland and the Danish Isles* is a fair specimen of the class to which I allude. These books usually treated of some unknown district on the Continent. They were illustrated with woodcuts or steel plates. They gave details of hotel accommodation and of means of communication, such as we now expect to find in any well-regulated guidebook, and they dealt largely in reported conversations with intelligent foreigners, racy innkeepers, and garrulous peasants. In a word, they were chatty.

Begun with the idea of furnishing material for such a book, my papers as they progressed assumed the character of a record of one single personal experience, and this record was continued up to the very eve, almost, of its termination.

The writer was a Mr Wraxall. For my knowledge of him I have to depend entirely on the evidence his writings afford, and from these I deduce that he was a man past middle age, possessed of some private means, and very much alone in the world. He had, it seems, no settled abode in England, but was a denizen of hotels and boarding houses. It is probable that he entertained the idea of settling down at some future time which never came; and I think it also likely that the Pantechnicon fire in the early seventies must have destroyed a great deal that would have thrown light on his antecedents, for he refers once or twice to property of his that was warehoused at that establishment.

It is further apparent that Mr Wraxall had published a book, and that it treated of a holiday he had once taken in Brittany. More than this I cannot say about his work, because a diligent search in bibliographical works has convinced me that it must have appeared either anonymously or under a pseudonym.

As to his character, it is not difficult to form some superficial opinion. He must have been an intelligent and cultivated man. It seems that he was near being a Fellow of his college at Oxford – Brasenose, as I judge from the Calendar. His besetting fault was pretty clearly that of over-inquisitiveness, possibly a good fault in a traveller, certainly a fault for which this traveller paid dearly enough in the end.

On what proved to be his last expedition, he was plotting another book. Scandinavia, a region not widely known to Englishmen forty years ago, had struck him as an interesting field. He must have alighted on some old books of Swedish history or memoirs, and the idea had struck him that there was room for a book descriptive of travel in Sweden, interspersed with episodes from the history of some of the great Swedish families. He procured letters of introduction, therefore, to some persons of quality in Sweden, and set out thither in the early summer of 1863.

Of his travels in the North there is no need to speak, nor of his residence of some weeks in Stockholm. I need only mention that some *savant* resident there put him on the track of an important collection of family papers belonging to the proprietors of an ancient manor house in Vestergothland, and obtained for him permission to examine them.

The manor house, or *herrgard*, in question is to be called Råbäck (pronounced something like Roebeck), though that is not its name. It is one of the best buildings of its kind in all the country, and the picture of it in Dahlenberg's *Suecia antiqua et moderna*, engraved in 1694, shows it very much as the tourist may see it today. It was built soon after 1600, and is, roughly speaking, very much like an English house of that period in respect of material – red-brick with stone facings – and style. The man who built it was a scion of the great house of De la Gardie, and his descendants possess it still. De la Gardie is the name by which I will designate them when mention of them becomes necessary.

They received Mr Wraxall with great kindness and courtesy, and pressed him to stay in the house as long as his researches lasted. But, preferring to be independent, and mistrusting his powers of conversing in Swedish, he settled himself at the village inn, which turned out quite sufficiently comfortable, at any rate during the summer months. This arrangement would entail a short walk daily to and from the manor house of something under a mile. The house itself stood in a park, and was protected – we should say grown up – with large old timber. Near it you found the walled garden, and then entered a close wood fringing one of the small lakes with which the whole country is pitted. Then came the wall of the demesne, and you climbed a steep knoll – a knob of rock lightly covered with soil – and on the top of this stood the church, fenced in with tall dark trees. It was a curious building to English eyes. The nave and aisles were low, and filled with pews and galleries. In the western gallery stood the handsome old organ, gaily painted, and with silver pipes. The ceiling was flat, and had been adorned by a seventeenth-century artist with a strange and hideous 'Last Judgement', full of lurid flames, falling cities, burning ships, crying souls, and brown and smiling demons. Handsome brass coronae hung from the roof; the pulpit was like a doll's house covered with little painted wooden cherubs and saints; a stand with three hourglasses was hinged to the preacher's desk. Such sights as these may be seen in many a church in Sweden now, but what distinguished this one was an addition to the original building. At the eastern end of the north aisle the builder of the manor house had erected a mausoleum for himself and his family. It was a largish eight-sided building, lighted by a series of oval windows, and it had a domed roof, topped by a kind of pumpkin-shaped object rising into a spire, a form in which Swedish architects greatly delighted. The roof was of copper externally, and was painted black, while the walls, in common with those of the church, were staringly white. To this mausoleum there was no access from the church. It had a portal and steps of its own on the northern side.

Past the churchyard the path to the village goes, and not more than three or four minutes bring you to the inn door.

On the first day of his stay at Råbäck Mr Wraxall found the church door open, and made these notes of the interior which I have epitomised. Into the mausoleum, however, he could not make his way. He could by looking through the keyhole just descry that there were fine marble effigies and sarcophagi of copper, and a wealth of armorial ornament, which made him very anxious to spend some time in investigation.

The papers he had come to examine at the manor house proved to be of just the kind he wanted for his book. There were family correspondence, journals, and account books of the earliest owners of the estate, very carefully kept and clearly written, full of amusing and picturesque detail. The first De la Gardie appeared in them as a strong and capable man. Shortly after the building of the mansion there had been a period of distress in the district, and the peasants had risen and attacked several châteaux and done some damage. The owner of Råbäck took a leading part in suppressing trouble, and there was reference to executions of ringleaders and severe punishments inflicted with no sparing hand.

The portrait of this Magnus de la Gardie was one of the best in the house, and Mr Wraxall studied it with no little interest after his day's work. He gives no detailed description of it, but I gather that the face impressed him rather by its power than by its beauty or goodness; in fact, he writes that Count Magnus was an almost phenomenally ugly man.

On this day Mr Wraxall took his supper with the family, and walked back in the late but still bright evening.

'I must remember,' he writes, 'to ask the sexton if he can let me into the mausoleum at the church. He evidently has access to it himself, for I saw him tonight standing on the steps, and, as I thought, locking or unlocking the door.'

I find that early on the following day Mr Wraxall had some conversation with his landlord. His setting it down at such length as he does surprised me at first; but I soon realised that the papers I was reading were, at least in their beginning, the materials for the book he was meditating, and that it was to have been one of those quasi-journalistic productions which admit of the introduction of an admixture of conversational matter.

His object, he says, was to find out whether any traditions of Count Magnus de la Gardie lingered on in the scenes of that gentleman's activity, and whether the popular estimate of him were favourable or not. He found that the Count was decidedly not a favourite. If his tenants came late to their work on the days which they owed to him as Lord of the Manor, they were set on the wooden horse, or flogged and branded in the manor-house yard. One or two cases there were of men who had occupied lands which encroached on the lord's domain, and whose houses had been mysteriously burnt on a winter's night, with the whole family inside. But what seemed to dwell on the innkeeper's mind most – for he returned to the subject more than once – was that the Count had been on the Black Pilgrimage, and had brought something or someone back with him.

You will naturally inquire, as Mr Wraxall did, what the Black Pilgrimage may have been. But your curiosity on the point must remain unsatisfied for the time being, just as his did. The landlord was evidently unwilling to give a full answer, or indeed any answer, on the point, and, being called out for a moment, trotted out with obvious alacrity, only putting his head in at the door a few minutes afterwards to say that he was called away to Skara, and should not be back till evening.

So Mr Wraxall had to go unsatisfied to his day's work at the manor house. The papers on which he was just then engaged soon put his thoughts into another channel, for he had to occupy himself with glancing over the correspondence between Sophia Albertina in Stockholm and her married cousin Ulrica Leonora at Råbäck in the years 1705–10. The letters were of exceptional interest from the light they threw upon the culture of that period in Sweden, as anyone can testify who has read the full edition of them in the publications of the Swedish Historical Manuscripts Commission.

In the afternoon he had done with these, and after returning the boxes in which they were kept to their places on the shelf, he proceeded, very naturally, to take down some of the volumes nearest to them, in order to determine which of them had best be his principal subject of investigation next day. The shelf he had hit upon was occupied mostly by a collection of account books in the writing of the first Count Magnus. But one among them was not an account book, but a book of alchemical and other tracts in another sixteenth-century hand. Not being very familiar with alchemical literature, Mr Wraxall spends much space which he might have spared in setting out the names and beginnings of the various treatises: The book of the Phoenix, book of the Thirty Words, book of the Toad, book of Miriam, Turba philosophorum, and so forth; and then he announces with a good deal of circumstance his delight at finding, on a leaf originally left blank near the middle of the book, some writing of Count Magnus himself headed 'Liber nigrae peregrinationis'. It is true that only a few lines were written, but there was quite enough to show that the landlord had that morning been referring to a belief at least as old as the time of Count Magnus, and probably shared by him. This is the English of what was written:

'If any man desires to obtain a long life, if he would obtain a faithful messenger and see the blood of his enemies, it is necessary that he should first go into the city of Chorazin, and there salute the prince...' Here there was an erasure of one word, not very thoroughly done, so that Mr Wraxall felt pretty sure that he was right in reading it as *aeris* ('of the air'). But there was no more of the text copied, only a line in Latin: *Quaere reliqua hujus materiei inter secretiora.* (Seek the rest of this matter among the more private things.)

It could not be denied that this threw a rather lurid light upon the tastes and beliefs of the Count; but to Mr Wraxall, separated from him by nearly three centuries, the thought that he might have added to his general forcefulness alchemy, and to alchemy something like magic, only made him a more picturesque figure, and when, after a rather prolonged contemplation of his picture in the hall, Mr Wraxall set out on his homeward way, his mind was full of the thought of Count Magnus. He had no eyes for his surroundings, no perception of the evening scents of the woods or the evening light on the lake; and when all of a sudden he pulled up short, he was astonished to find himself already at the gate of the churchyard, and within a few minutes of his dinner. His eyes fell on the mausoleum.

'Ah,' he said, 'Count Magnus, there you are. I should dearly like to see you.'

'Like many solitary men,' he writes, 'I have a habit of talking to myself aloud; and, unlike some of the Greek and Latin particles, I do not expect an answer. Certainly, and perhaps fortunately in this case, there was neither voice nor any that regarded: only the woman who, I suppose, was cleaning up the church, dropped some metallic object on the floor, whose clang startled me. Count Magnus, I think, sleeps sound enough.'

That same evening the landlord of the inn, who had heard Mr Wraxall say that he wished to see the clerk or deacon (as he would be called in Sweden) of the parish, introduced him to that official in the inn parlour. A visit to the De la Gardie tomb-house was soon arranged for the next day, and a little general conversation ensued.

Mr Wraxall, remembering that one function of Scandinavian deacons is to teach candidates for Confirmation, thought he would refresh his own memory on a Biblical point.

'Can you tell me,' he said, 'anything about Chorazin?'

The deacon seemed startled, but readily reminded him how that village had once been denounced.

'To be sure,' said Mr Wraxall; 'it is, I suppose, quite a ruin now?'

'So I expect,' replied the deacon. 'I have heard some of our old priests say that Antichrist is to be born there; and there are tales...'

'Ah! What tales are those?' Mr Wraxall put in.

'Tales, I was going to say, which I have forgotten,' said the deacon; and soon after that he said goodnight.

The landlord was now alone, and at Mr Wraxall's mercy; and that inquirer was not inclined to spare him.

'Herr Nielsen,' he said, 'I have found out something about the Black Pilgrimage. You may as well tell me what you know. What did the Count bring back with him?'

Swedes are habitually slow, perhaps, in answering, or perhaps the landlord was an exception. I am not sure; but Mr Wraxall notes that the landlord spent at least one minute in looking at him before he said anything at all. Then he came close up to his guest, and with a good deal of effort he spoke:

'Mr Wraxall, I can tell you this one little tale, and no more – not any more. You must not ask anything when I have done. In my grandfather's time – that is, ninety-two years ago – there were two men who said: "The Count is dead; we do not care for him. We will go tonight and have a free hunt in his wood" – the long wood on the hill that you have seen behind Råbäck. Well, those that heard them say this, they said: "No, do not go; we are sure you will meet with persons walking who should not be walking. They should be resting, not walking." These men laughed. There were no forest men to keep the wood, because no one wished to live there. The family were not here at the house. These men could do what they wished.

'Very well, they go to the wood that night. My grandfather was sitting here in this room. It was the summer, and a light night. With the window open, he could see out to the wood, and hear.

'So he sat there, and two or three men with him, and they listened. At first they hear nothing at all; then they hear someone – you know how far away it is – they hear someone scream, just as if the most inside part of his soul was twisted out of him. All of them in the room caught hold of each other, and they sat so for three-quarters of an hour. Then they hear someone else, only about three hundred ells off. They hear him laugh out loud: it was not one of those two men that laughed, and, indeed, they have all of them said that it was not any man at all. After that they hear a great door shut.

'Then, when it was just light with the sun, they all went to the priest. They said to him:

' "Father, put on your gown and your ruff, and come to bury these men, Anders Bjornsen and Hans Thorbjorn." '

'You understand that they were sure these men were dead. So they went to the wood – my grandfather never forgot this. He said they were all like so many dead men themselves. The priest, too, he was in a white fear. He said when they came to him:

' "I heard one cry in the night, and I heard one laugh afterwards. If I cannot forget that, I shall not be able to sleep again." '

'So they went to the wood, and they found these men on the edge of the wood. Hans Thorbjorn was standing with his back against a tree, and all the time he was pushing with his hands – pushing something away from him which was not there. So he was not dead. And they led him away, and took him to the house at Nykjoping, and he died before the winter; but he went on pushing with his hands. Also Anders Bjornsen was there; but he was dead. And I tell you this about Anders Bjornsen, that he was once a beautiful man, but now his face was not there, because the flesh of it was sucked away off the bones. You understand that? My grandfather did not forget that. And they laid him on the bier which they brought, and they put a cloth over his head, and the priest walked before; and they began to sing the psalm for the dead as well as they could. So, as they were singing the end of the first verse, one fell down, who was carrying the head of the bier, and the others looked back, and they saw that the cloth had fallen off, and the eyes of Anders Bjornsen were looking up, because there was nothing to close over them. And this they could not bear. Therefore the priest laid the cloth upon him, and sent for a spade, and they buried him in that place.'

The next day Mr Wraxall records that the deacon called for him soon after his breakfast, and took him to the church and mausoleum. He noticed that the key of the latter was hung on a nail just by the pulpit, and it occurred to him that, as the church door seemed to be left unlocked as a rule, it would not be difficult for him to pay a second and more private visit to the monuments if there proved to be more of interest among them than could be digested at first. The building, when he entered it, he found not unimposing. The monuments, mostly large erections of the seventeenth and eighteenth centuries, were dignified if luxuriant, and the epitaphs and heraldry were copious. The central space of the domed room was occupied by three copper sarcophagi, covered with finely engraved ornament. Two of them had, as is commonly the case in Denmark and Sweden, a large metal crucifix on the lid. The third, that of Count Magnus, as it appeared, had, instead of that, a full-length effigy engraved upon it, and round the edge were several bands of similar ornament representing various scenes. One was a battle, with cannon belching out smoke, and walled towns, and troops of pikemen. Another showed an execution. In a third, among trees, was a man running at full speed, with flying hair and outstretched hands. After him followed a strange form; it would be hard to say whether the artist had intended it for a man, and was unable to give the requisite similitude, or whether it was intentionally made as monstrous as it looked. In view of the skill with which the rest of the drawing was done, Mr Wraxall felt inclined to adopt the latter idea. The figure was unduly short, and was for the most part muffled in a hooded garment which swept the ground. The only part of the form which projected from that shelter was not shaped like any hand or arm. Mr Wraxall compares it to the tentacle of a devil-fish, and continues: 'On seeing this, I said to myself, "This, then, which is evidently an allegorical representation of some kind – a fiend pursuing a hunted soul – may be the origin of the story of Count Magnus and his mysterious companion. Let us see how the huntsman is pictured: doubtless it will be a demon blowing his horn."' But, as it turned out, there was no such sensational figure, only the semblance of a cloaked man on a hillock, who stood leaning on a stick, and watching the hunt with an interest which the engraver had tried to express in his attitude.

Mr Wraxall noted the finely worked and massive steel padlocks – three in number – which secured the sarcophagus. One of them, he saw, was detached, and lay on the pavement. And then, unwilling to delay the deacon longer or to waste his own working time, he made his way onward to the manor house.

'It is curious,' he notes, 'how, on retracing a familiar path, one's thoughts engross one to the absolute exclusion of surrounding objects. Tonight, for the second time, I had entirely failed to notice where I was going (I had planned a private visit to the tomb-house to copy the epitaphs), when I suddenly, as it were, awoke to consciousness, and found myself (as before) turning in at the churchyard gate, and, I believe, singing or chanting some such words as, "Are you awake, Count Magnus? Are you asleep, Count Magnus?" and then something more which I have failed to recollect. It seemed to me that I must have been behaving in this nonsensical way for some time.'

He found the key of the mausoleum where he had expected to find it, and copied the greater part of what he wanted; in fact, he stayed until the light began to fail him.

'I must have been wrong,' he writes, 'in saying that one of the padlocks of my Count's sarcophagus was unfastened; I see tonight that two are loose. I picked both up, and laid them carefully on the window ledge, after trying unsuccessfully to close them. The remaining one is still firm, and, though I take it to be a spring lock, I cannot guess how it is opened. Had I succeeded in undoing it, I am almost afraid I should have taken the liberty of opening the sarcophagus. It is strange, the interest I feel in the personality of this, I fear, somewhat ferocious and grim old noble.'

The day following was, as it turned out, the last of Mr Wraxall's stay at Råbäck. He received letters connected with certain investments which made it desirable that he should return to England; his work among the papers was practically done, and travelling was slow. He decided, therefore, to make his farewells, put some finishing touches to his notes, and be off.

These finishing touches and farewells, as it turned out, took more time than he had expected. The hospitable family insisted on his staying to dine with them – they dined at three – and it was verging on half past six before he was outside the iron gates of Råbäck. He dwelt on every step of his walk by the lake, determined to saturate himself, now that he trod it for the last time, in the sentiment of the place and hour. And when he reached the summit of the churchyard knoll, he lingered for many minutes, gazing at the limitless prospect of woods near and distant, all dark beneath a sky of liquid green. When at last he turned to go, the thought struck him that surely he must bid farewell to Count Magnus as well as the rest of the De la Gardies. The church was but twenty yards away, and he knew where the key of the mausoleum hung. It was not long before he was standing over the great copper coffin, and, as usual, talking to himself aloud: 'You may have been a bit of a rascal in your time, Magnus,' he was saying, 'but for all that I should like to see you, or, rather…'

'Just at that instant,' he says, 'I felt a blow on my foot. Hastily enough I drew it back, and something fell on the pavement with a clash. It was the third, the last of the three padlocks which had fastened the sarcophagus. I stooped to pick·it up, and – Heaven is my witness that I am writing only the bare truth – before I had raised myself there was a sound of metal hinges creaking, and I distinctly saw the lid shifting upwards. I may have behaved like a coward, but I could not for my life stay for one moment. I was outside that dreadful building in less time than I can write – almost as quickly as I could have said – the words; and what frightens me yet more, I could not turn the key in the lock. As I sit here in my room noting these facts, I ask myself (it was not twenty minutes ago) whether that noise of creaking metal continued, and I cannot tell whether it did or not. I only know that there was something more than I have written that alarmed me, but whether it was sound or sight I am not able to remember. What is this that I have done?'

★ ★ ★ ★ ★

Poor Mr Wraxall! He set out on his journey to England on the next day, as he had planned, and he reached England in safety; and yet, as I gather from his changed hand and inconsequent jottings, a broken man. One of the several small notebooks that have come to me with his papers gives, not₊a key to, but a kind of inkling of, his experiences. Much of his journey was made by canal boat, and I find not less than six painful attempts to enumerate and describe his fellow passengers. The entries are of this kind:

24. Pastor of village in Skane. Usual black coat and soft black hat.
25. Commercial traveller from Stockholm going to Trollhättan. Black cloak, brown hat.
26. Man in long black cloak, broad-leafed hat, very old-fashioned.

This entry is lined out, and a note added: 'Perhaps identical with No. 13. Have not yet seen his face.' On referring to No. 13, I find that he is a Roman priest in a cassock.

The net result of the reckoning is always the same. Twenty-eight people appear in the enumeration, one being always a man in a long black cloak and broad hat, and another a 'short figure in dark cloak and hood'. On the other hand, it is always noted that only twenty-six passengers appear at meals, and that the man in the cloak is perhaps absent, and the short figure is certainly absent.

On reaching England, it appears that Mr Wraxall landed at Harwich, and that he resolved at once to put himself out of the reach of some person or persons whom he never specifies, but whom he had evidently come to regard as his pursuers. Accordingly he took a vehicle – it was a closed fly – not trusting the railway and drove across country to the village of Belchamp St Paul. It was about nine o'clock on a moonlight August night when he neared the place. He was sitting forward, and looking out of the window at the fields and thickets – there was little else to be seen – racing past him. Suddenly he came to a crossroad. At the corner two figures were standing motionless; both were in dark cloaks; the taller one wore a hat, the shorter a hood. He had no time to see their faces, nor did they make any motion that he could discern. Yet the horse shied violently and broke into a gallop, and Mr Wraxall sank back into his seat in something like desperation. He had seen them before.

Arrived at Belchamp St Paul, he was fortunate enough to find a decent furnished lodging, and for the next twenty-four hours he lived, comparatively speaking, in peace. His last notes were written on this day. They are too disjointed and ejaculatory to be given here in full, but the substance of them is clear enough. He is expecting a visit from his pursuers – how or when he knows not – and his constant cry is 'What has he done?' and 'Is there no hope?' Doctors, he knows, would call him mad, policemen would laugh at him. The parson is away. What can he do but lock his door and cry to God?

People still remember last year at Belchamp St Paul how a strange gentleman came one evening in August years back; and how the next morning but one he was found dead, and there was an inquest; and the jury that viewed the body fainted, seven of 'em did, and none of 'em wouldn't speak to what they see, and the verdict was visitation of God; and how the people as kep' the 'ouse moved out that same week, and went away from that part. But they do not, I think, know that any glimmer of light has ever been thrown, or could be thrown, on the mystery. It so happened that last year the little house came into my hands as part of a legacy. It had stood empty since 1863, and there seemed no prospect of letting it; so I had it pulled down, and the papers of which I have given you an abstract were found in a forgotten cupboard under the window in the best bedroom.

Marsyas in Flanders

Vernon Lee (1856–1935)

Vernon Lee was the pseudonym of a remarkable woman named Violet Paget. She was born in Boulogne to British parents and lived most of her life on the continent, particularly in Florence. She probably decided, rightly, that Italy would be more tolerant of her sexuality and the way she chose to live her life than Victorian Britain would have been. Paget was a lesbian and feminist who dressed in male attire and made little secret of her emotional and sexual attraction to other women. She published works on a wide range of subjects, from aesthetics and Italian renaissance art to her travels around Europe but she is remembered today for her stories of ghosts and haunting. A few years before her death, she was described by one critic as 'the greatest of modern exponents of the supernatural in fiction' and her reputation as a true original of the genre has lasted to the present day. Hauntings, *a volume of four fantastic tales, was first published in 1890 and 'Prince Alberic and the Snake Lady', which appeared in* The Yellow Book, *house magazine of English* fin-de-siècle *decadence, in 1896, is an unusual and compelling fairy tale for adult readers. 'Marsyas in Flanders' dates from 1900 and was reprinted in a volume entitled* For Maurice: Five Unlikely Stories *in 1927. A kind of perverted legend, which mixes elements of Ancient Greek mythology with Christian beliefs, it moves elegantly from the late nineteenth century to the mediaeval era and back. Is the being in the story a true vampire? Perhaps not but it is only by driving an iron stake through its heart that it is brought to rest.*

I

'You are right. This is not the original crucifix at all. Another one has been put instead. *Il y a eu substitution,*' and the little old

Antiquary of Dunes nodded mysteriously, fixing his ghostseer's eyes upon mine.

He said it in a scarce audible whisper. For it happened to be the vigil of the Feast of the Crucifix, and the once famous church was full of semi-clerical persons decorating it for the morrow, and of old ladies in strange caps, clattering about with pails and brooms. The Antiquary had brought me there the very moment of my arrival, lest the crowd of faithful should prevent his showing me everything next morning.

The famous crucifix was exhibited behind rows and rows of unlit candles and surrounded by strings of paper flowers and coloured muslin and garlands of sweet resinous maritime pine; and two lighted chandeliers illumined it.

'There has been an exchange,' he repeated, looking round that no one might hear him. '*Il y a eu substitution.*'

For I had remarked, as anyone would have done, at the first glance, that the crucifix had every appearance of French work of the thirteenth century, boldly realistic, whereas the crucifix of the legend, which was a work of St Luke, which had hung for centuries in the Holy Sepulchre at Jerusalem and been miraculously cast ashore at Dunes in 1195, would surely have been a more or less Byzantine image, like its miraculous companion of Lucca.

'But why should there have been a substitution?' I inquired innocently.

'Hush, hush,' answered the Antiquary, frowning, 'not here... later, later...'

He took me all over the church, once so famous for pilgrimages; but from which, even like the sea which has left it in a salt marsh beneath the cliffs, the tide of devotion has receded for centuries. It is a very dignified little church, of charmingly restrained and shapely Gothic, built of a delicate pale stone, which the sea damp has picked out, in bases and capitals and carved foliation, with stains of a lovely bright green. The Antiquary showed me where the transept and belfry had been left unfinished when the miracles had diminished in the fourteenth century. And he took me up to the curious warder's chamber, a large room up some steps in the triforium; with a fireplace and stone seats for the men who guarded the precious crucifix day and night. There had even been beehives in the window, he told me, and he remembered seeing them still as a child.

'Was it usual, here in Flanders, to have a guardroom in churches containing important relics?' I asked, for I could not remember having seen anything similar before.

'By no means,' he answered, looking round to make sure we were alone, 'but it was necessary here. You have never heard in what the chief miracles of this church consisted?'

'No,' I whispered back, gradually infected by his mysteriousness, 'unless you allude to the legend that the figure of the Saviour broke all the crosses until the right one was cast up by the sea?'

He shook his head but did not answer, and descended the steep stairs into the nave, while I lingered a moment looking down into it from the warder's chamber. I have never had so curious an impression of a church. The chandeliers on either side of the crucifix swirled slowly round, making great pools of light which were broken by the shadows of the clustered columns, and among the pews of the nave moved the flicker of the sacristan's lamp. The place was full of the scent of resinous pine branches, evoking dunes and mountainsides; and from the busy groups below rose a subdued chatter of women's voices, and a splash of water and clatter of pattens. It vaguely suggested preparations for a witches' sabbath.

'What sort of miracles did they have in this church?' I asked, when we had passed into the dusky square, 'and what did you mean about their having exchanged the crucifix – about a substitution?'

It seemed quite dark outside. The church rose black, a vague lopsided mass of buttresses and high-pitched roofs, against the watery, moonlit sky; the big trees of the churchyard behind wavering about in the seawind; and the windows shone yellow, like flaming portals, in the darkness.

'Please remark the bold effect of the gargoyles,' said the Antiquary pointing upwards.

They jutted out, vague wild beasts, from the roofline; and, what was positively frightening, you saw the moonlight, yellow and blue through the open jaws of some of them. A gust swept through the trees, making the weathercock clatter and groan.

'Why, those gargoyle wolves seem positively to howl,' I exclaimed.

The old Antiquary chuckled. 'Aha,' he answered, 'did I not tell you that this church has witnessed things like no other church in Christendom? And it still remembers them! There – have you ever known such a wild, savage church before?'

And as he spoke there suddenly mingled with the sough of the wind and the groans of the weathervane, a shrill quavering sound as of pipers inside.

'The organist trying his *vox humana* for tomorrow,' remarked the Antiquary.

II

Next day I bought one of the printed histories of the miraculous crucifix which they were hawking all round the church; and next day also, my friend the Antiquary was good enough to tell me all that he knew of the matter. Between my two informants, the following may be said to be the true story.

In the autumn of 1195, after a night of frightful storm, a boat was found cast upon the shore of Dunes, which was at that time a fishing village at the mouth of the Nys, and exactly opposite a terrible sunken reef.

The boat was broken and upset; and close to it, on the sand and bent grass, lay a stone figure of the crucified Saviour, without its cross and, as seems probable, also without its arms, which had been made of separate blocks. A variety of persons immediately came forward to claim it; the little church of Dunes, on whose glebe it was found; the Barons of Croy, who had the right of jetsam on that coast, and also the great Abbey of St Loup of Arras, as possessing the spiritual overlordship of the place. But a holy man who lived close by in the cliffs, had a vision which settled the dispute. St Luke in person appeared and told him that he was the original maker of the figure; that it had been one of three which had hung round the Holy Sepulchre of Jerusalem; that three knights, a Norman, a Tuscan, and a man of Arras, had with the permission of Heaven stolen them from the Infidels and placed them on unmanned boats, that one of the images had been cast upon the Norman coast near Salenelles; that the second had run aground not far from the city of Lucca, in Italy, and that this third was the one which had been embarked by the knight from Artois. As regarded its final resting place, the hermit, on the authority of St Luke, recommended that the statue should be left to decide the matter itself. Accordingly the crucified figure was solemnly cast back into the sea. The very next day it was found once more in the same spot, among the sand and bent grass at the mouth of the Nys. It was therefore deposited in the little church of Dunes; and very soon indeed the flocks of pious persons who brought it offerings from all parts made it necessary and possible to rebuild the church thus sanctified by its presence.

The Holy Effigy of Dunes – *Sacra Dunarum Effigies* as it was called – did not work the ordinary sort of miracles. But its fame spread far and wide by the unexampled wonders which became the constant accompaniment of its existence. The Effigy, as above mentioned, had been discovered without the cross to which it had evidently been fastened, nor had any researches or any subsequent storms brought the missing blocks to light, despite the many prayers which were offered for the purpose. After some time therefore, and a deal of discussion, it was decided that a new cross should be provided for the Effigy to hang upon. And certain skilful stonemasons of Arras were called to Dunes for this purpose. But behold! The very day after the cross had been solemnly erected in the church, an unheard of and terrifying fact was discovered. The Effigy, which had been hanging perfectly straight the previous evening, had shifted its position, and was bent violently to the right, as if in an effort to break loose.

This was attested not merely by hundreds of laymen, but by the priests of the place, who notified the fact in a document, existing in the episcopal archives of Arras until 1790, to the Abbot of St Loup their spiritual overlord.

This was the beginning of a series of mysterious occurrences which spread the fame of the marvellous crucifix all over Christendom. The Effigy did not remain in the position into which it had miraculously worked itself: it was found, at intervals of time, shifted in some other manner upon its cross, and always as if it had gone through violent contortions. And one day, about ten years after it had been cast up by the sea, the priests of the church and the burghers of Dunes discovered the Effigy hanging in its original outstretched, symmetrical attitude, but O wonder! with the cross, broken in three pieces, lying on the steps of its chapel.

Certain persons, who lived in the end of the town nearest the church, reported to have been roused in the middle of the night by what they had taken for a violent clap of thunder, but which was doubtless the crash of the Cross falling down, or perhaps, who knows? the noise with which the terrible Effigy had broken loose and spurned the alien cross from it. For that was the secret: the Effigy, made by a saint and come to Dunes by miracle, had evidently found some trace of unholiness in the stone to which it had been fastened. Such was the ready explanation afforded by the Prior of the church, in answer to an angry summons of the Abbot of St Loup, who expressed his disapproval of such unusual miracles. Indeed, it was discovered that the piece of marble had not been cleaned from sinful human touch with the necessary rites before the figure was fastened on; a most grave, though excusable oversight. So a new cross was ordered, although it was noticed that much time was lost about it; and the consecration took place only some years later.

Meanwhile the Prior had built the warder's chamber, with the fireplace and recess, and obtained permission from the Pope himself that a clerk in orders should watch day and night, on the score that so wonderful a relic might be stolen. For the relic had by this time entirely cut out all similar crucifixes, and the village of Dunes, through the concourse of pilgrims, had rapidly grown into a town, the property of the now fabulously wealthy Priory of the Holy Cross.

The Abbots of St Loup, however, looked upon the matter with an unfavourable eye. Although nominally remaining their vassals, the Priors of Dunes had contrived to obtain gradually from the Pope privileges which rendered them virtually independent, and in particular, immunities which sent to the treasury of St Loup only a small proportion of the tribute money brought by the pilgrims. Abbot Walterius in particular, showed himself actively hostile. He accused the Prior of Dunes of having employed his warders to trump up stories of strange movements and sounds on the part of the still crossless Effigy, and of suggesting, to the ignorant, changes in its attitude which were more credulously believed in now that there was no longer the straight line of the cross by which to verify. So finally the new cross was made, and consecrated, and on Holy Cross Day of the year, the Effigy was fastened to it in the presence of an immense concourse of clergy and laity. The Effigy, it was now supposed, would be satisfied, and no unusual occurrences would increase or perhaps fatally compromise its reputation for sanctity.

These expectations were violently dispelled. In November, 1293, after a year of strange rumours concerning the Effigy, the figure was again discovered to have moved, and continued moving, or rather (judging from the position on the cross) writhing; and on Christmas Eve of the same year, the cross was a second time thrown down and dashed in pieces. The priest on duty was, at the same time, found, it was thought, dead, in his warder's chamber. Another cross was made and this time privately consecrated and put in place, and a hole in the roof made a pretext to close the church for a while, and to perform the rites of purification necessary after its pollution by workmen. Indeed, it was remarked that on this occasion the Prior of Dunes took as much trouble to diminish and if possible to hide away the miracles, as his predecessor had done his best to blazon the preceding ones abroad. The priest who had been on duty on the eventful Christmas Eve disappeared mysteriously, and it was thought by many persons that he had gone mad and was confined in the Prior's prison, for fear of the revelations he might make. For by this time, and not without some encouragement from the Abbots at Arras, extraordinary stories had begun to circulate about the goings-on in the church of Dunes. This church, be it remembered, stood a little above the town, isolated and surrounded by big trees. It was surrounded by the precincts of the Priory and, save on the water side, by high walls. Nevertheless, persons there were who affirmed that, the wind having been in that direction, they had heard strange noises come from the church of nights. During storms, particularly, sounds had been heard which were variously described as howls, groans, and the music of rustic dancing. A master mariner affirmed that one Halloween, as his boat approached the mouth of the Nys, he had seen the church of Dunes brilliantly lit up, its immense windows flaming. But he was suspected of being drunk and of having exaggerated the effect of the small light shining from the warder's chamber. The interest of the townsfolk of Dunes coincided with that of the Priory, since they prospered greatly by the pilgrimages, so these tales were promptly hushed up. Yet they undoubtedly reached the ear of the Abbot of St Loup. And at last there came an event which brought them all back to the surface.

For, on the Vigil of All Saints, 1299, the church was struck by lightning. The new warder was found dead in the middle of the nave, the cross broken in two; and oh, horror! the Effigy was missing. The indescribable fear which overcame everyone was merely increased by the discovery of the Effigy lying behind the high altar, in an attitude of frightful convulsion, and, it was whispered, blackened by lightning.

This was the end of the strange doings at Dunes.

An ecclesiastical council was held at Arras, and the church shut once more for nearly a year. It was opened this time and re-consecrated by the Abbot of St Loup, whom the Prior of Holy Cross served humbly at Mass. A new chapel had been built, and in it the miraculous crucifix was displayed, dressed in more splendid brocade and gems than usual, and its head nearly hidden by one of the most gorgeous crowns ever seen before; a gift, it was said, of the Duke of Burgundy.

All this new splendour, and the presence of the great Abbot himself, was presently explained to the faithful, when the Prior came forward to announce that a last and greatest miracle had now taken place. The original cross, on which the figure had hung in the Church of the Holy Sepulchre, and for which the Effigy had spurned all others made by less holy hands, had been cast on the shore of Dunes, on the very spot where, a hundred years before, the figure of the Saviour had been discovered in the sands. 'This,' said the Prior, 'was the explanation of the terrible occurrences which had filled all hearts with anguish. The Holy Effigy was now satisfied, it would rest in peace and its miraculous powers would be engaged only in granting the prayers of the faithful.' One half of the forecast came true: from that day forward the Effigy never shifted its position, but from that day forward also, no considerable miracle was ever registered; the devotion of Dunes diminished, other relics threw the Sacred Effigy into the shade; and the pilgrimages dwindling to mere local gatherings, the church was never brought to completion.

What had happened? No one ever knew, guessed, or perhaps even asked. But, when in 1790 the Archiepiscopal palace of Arras was sacked, a certain notary of the neighbourhood bought a large portion of the archives at the price of waste paper, either from historical curiosity, or expecting to obtain thereby facts which might gratify his aversion to the clergy. These documents lay unexamined for many years, till my friend the Antiquary bought them. Among them taken helter skelter from the Archbishop's palace, were sundry papers referring to the suppressed Abbey of St. Loup of Arras, and among these latter, a series of notes concerning the affairs of the church of Dunes; they were, so far as their fragmentary nature explained, the minutes of an inquest made in 1309, and contained the deposition of sundry witnesses. To understand their meaning it is necessary to remember that this was the time when witch trials had begun, and when the proceedings against the Templars had set the fashion of inquests which could help the finances of the country while furthering the interests of religion.

What appears to have happened is that after the catastrophe of the Vigil of All Saints, October, 1299, the Prior, Urbain de Luc, found himself suddenly threatened with a charge of sacrilege and witchcraft, of obtaining miracles of the Effigy by devilish means, and of converting his church into a chapel of the Evil One.

Instead of appealing to high ecclesiastical tribunals, as the privileges obtained from the Holy See would have warranted, Prior Urbain guessed that this charge came originally from the wrathful Abbot of St Loup, and, dropping all his pretensions in order to save himself, he threw himself upon the mercy of the Abbot whom he had hitherto flouted. The Abbot appears to have been satisfied by his submission, and the matter to have dropped after a few legal preliminaries, of which the notes found among the archiepiscopal archives of Arras represented a portion. Some of these notes my friend the Antiquary kindly allowed me to translate from the Latin, and I give them here, leaving the reader to make what he can of them.

'Item. The Abbot expresses himself satisfied that His Reverence the Prior has had no personal knowledge of or dealings with the Evil One (Diabolus). Nevertheless, the gravity of the charge requires ...' – here the page is torn.

'Hugues Jacquot, Simon le Couvreur, Pierre Denis, burghers of Dunes, being interrogated, witness:

'That the noises from the Church of the Holy Cross always happened on nights of bad storms, and foreboded shipwrecks on the coast; and were very various, such as terrible rattling, groans, howls as of wolves, and occasional flute playing. A certain Jehan, who has twice been branded and flogged for lighting fires on the coast and otherwise causing ships to wreck at the mouth of the Nys, being promised immunity, after two or three slight pulls on the rack, witnesses as follows: That the band of wreckers to which he belongs always knew when a dangerous storm was brewing, on account of the noises which issued from the church of Dunes. Witness has often climbed the walls and prowled round in the churchyard, waiting to hear such noises. He was not unfamiliar with the howlings and roarings mentioned by the previous witnesses. He has heard tell by a countryman who passed in the night that the howling was such that the countryman thought himself pursued by a pack of wolves, although it is well known that no wolf has been seen in these parts for thirty years. But the witness himself is of the opinion that the most singular of all the noises, and the one which always accompanied or foretold the worst storms, was a noise of flutes and pipes (quod vulgo dicuntur flustes et musettes) so sweet that the King of France could not have sweeter at his Court. Being interrogated whether he had ever seen anything the witness answers: 'That he has seen the church brightly lit up from the sands; but on approaching found all dark, save the light from the warder's chamber. That once, by moonlight, the piping and fluting and howling being uncommonly loud, he thought he had seen wolves, and a human figure on the roof, but that he ran away from fear, and cannot be sure.'

'Item. His Lordship the Abbot desires the Right Reverend Prior to answer truly, placing his hand on the Gospels, whether or not he had himself heard such noises.

'The Right Reverend Prior denies ever having heard anything similar. But, being threatened with further proceedings (the rack?) acknowledges that he had frequently been told of these noises by the Warder on duty.

'Query: Whether the Right Reverend Prior was ever told anything else by the Warder?

'Answer: Yes; but under the seal of confession. The last Warder, moreover, the one killed by lightning, had been a reprobate priest, having committed the greatest crimes and obliged to take asylum, whom the Prior had kept there on account of the difficulty of finding a man sufficiently courageous for the office.

'Query: Whether the Prior has ever questioned previous Warders?

'Answer: That the Warders were bound to reveal only in confession whatever they had heard; that the Prior's predecessors had kept the seal of confession inviolate, and that though unworthy, the Prior himself desired to do alike.

'Query: What had become of the Warder who had been found in a swoon after the occurrences of Halloween?

'Answer: That the Prior does not know. The Warder was crazy. The Prior believes he was secluded for that reason.

A disagreeable surprise had been, apparently, arranged for Prior Urbain de Luc. For the next entry states that:

'Item. By order of His Magnificence the Lord Abbot, certain servants of the Lord Abbot aforesaid introduce Robert Baudouin, priest, once Warder in the Church of the Holy Cross, who has been kept ten years in prison by His Reverence the Prior, as being of unsound mind. Witness manifests great terror on finding himself in the presence of their Lordships, and particularly of His Reverence the Prior. And refuses to speak, hiding his face in his hands and uttering shrieks. Being comforted with kind words by those present, nay even most graciously by My Lord the Abbot himself, etiam threatened with the rack if he continue obdurate, this witness deposes as follows, not without much lamentation, shrieking and senseless jabber after the manner of mad men.

'Query: Can he remember what happened on the Vigil of All Saints, in the church of Dunes, before he swooned on the floor of the church?

'Answer: He cannot. It would be sin to speak of such things before great spiritual Lords. Moreover he is but an ignorant man, and also mad. Moreover his hunger is great.

'Being given white bread from the Lord Abbot's own table, witness is again cross-questioned.

'Query: What can he remember of the events of the Vigil of All Saints?

'Answer: Thinks he was not always mad. Thinks he has not always been in prison. Thinks he once went in a boat on sea, etc.

'Query: Does witness think he has ever been in the church of Dunes?

'Answer: Cannot remember. But is sure that he was not always in prison.

'Query: Has witness ever heard anything like that? (My Lord the Abbot having secretly ordered that a certain fool in his service, an excellent musician, should suddenly play the pipes behind the Arras.)

'At which sound witness began to tremble and sob and fall on his knees, and catch hold of the robe even of My Lord the Abbot, hiding his head therein.

'Query: Wherefore does he feel such terror, being in the fatherly presence of so clement a prince as the Lord Abbot?

'Answer: That witness cannot stand that piping any longer. That it freezes his blood. That he has told the Prior many times that he will not remain any longer in the warder's chamber. That he is afraid for his life. That he dare not make the sign of the Cross nor say his prayers for fear of the Great Wild Man. That the Great Wild Man took the Cross and broke it in two and played at quoits with it in the nave. That all the wolves trooped down from the roof howling, and danced on their hind legs while the Great Wild Man played the pipes on the high altar. That witness had surrounded himself with a hedge of little crosses, made of broken rye straw, to keep off the Great Wild Man from the warder's chamber. Ah – ah – ah! He is piping again! The wolves are howling! He is raising the tempest.

'Item: That no further information can be extracted from witness, who falls on the floor like one possessed and has to be removed from the presence of His Lordship the Abbot and His Reverence the Prior.

III

Here the minutes of the inquest break off. Did those great spiritual dignitaries ever get to learn more about the terrible doings in the church of Dunes? Did they ever guess at their cause?

'For there was a cause,' said the Antiquary, folding his spectacles after reading me these notes, 'or more strictly the cause still exists. And you will understand, though those learned priests of six centuries ago could not.'

And rising, he fetched a key from a shelf and preceded me into the yard of his house, situated on the Nys, a mile below Dunes.

Between the low steadings one saw the salt marsh, lilac with sea lavender, the Island of Birds, a great sandbank at the mouth of the Nys, where every kind of sea fowl gathers; and beyond, the angry white-crested sea under an angry orange afterglow. On the other side, inland, and appearing above the farm roofs, stood the church of Dunes, its pointed belfry and jagged outlines of gables and buttresses and gargoyles and wind-warped pines black against the easterly sky of ominous livid red.

'I told you,' said the Antiquary, stopping with the key in the lock of a big outhouse, 'that there had been a substitution; that the crucifix at present at Dunes is not the one miraculously cast up by the storm of 1195. I believe the present one may be identified as a life-size statue, for which a receipt exists in the archives of Arras, furnished to the Abbot of St Loup by Estienne Le Mas and Guillaume Pernel, stonemasons, in the year 1299, that is to say the year of the inquest and of the cessation of all supernatural occurrences at Dunes. As to the original Effigy, you shall see it and understand everything.'

The Antiquary opened the door of a sloping, vaulted passage, lit a lantern and led the way. It was evidently the cellar of some mediaeval building, and a scent of wine, of damp wood, and of fir branches from innumerable stacked up faggots, filled the darkness among thickset columns.

'Here,' said the Antiquary, raising his lantern, 'he was buried

THE RIVALS OF DRACULA

beneath this vault and they had run an iron stake through his middle, like a vampire, to prevent his rising.'

The Effigy was erect against the dark wall, surrounded by brushwood. It was more than life-size, nude, the arms broken off at the shoulders, the head, with stubbly beard and clotted hair, drawn up with an effort, the face contracted with agony; the muscles dragged as of one hanging crucified, the feet bound together with a rope. The figure was familiar to me in various galleries. I came forward to examine the ear: it was leaf-shaped.

'Ah, you have understood the whole mystery,' said the Antiquary.

'I have understood,' I answered, not knowing how far his thought really went, 'that this supposed statue of Christ is an antique satyr, a Marsyas awaiting his punishment.'

The Antiquary nodded. 'Exactly,' he said drily, 'that is the whole explanation. Only I think the Abbot and the Prior were not so wrong to drive the iron stake through him when they removed him from the church.'

The Mask

Richard Marsh (1857–1915)

Born Richard Bernard Heldmann, Richard Marsh began his career as a writer (under his own name) of stories for boys' magazines and worked for GA Henty's magazine Union Jack. *After a quarrel with Henty and five years of literary silence he reinvented himself under the pseudonym by which he is remembered and began pumping out fiction in the crime and supernatural genres. Like many writers of the period he was astonishingly productive, averaging three full novels a year, not to mention dozens of short stories. His greatest success as Richard Marsh came with* The Beetle, *a novel published first as a serial in* Answers *magazine and then in book form in 1897, the same year* Dracula *first appeared in bookshops. Indeed, initially, Marsh's over-the-top tale of a shape-shifting devotee of ancient Egyptian gods seeking revenge in the fog-shrouded streets of late Victorian London was a greater commercial success than Stoker's work. Over the years, however,* Dracula *established its classic status and* The Beetle *faded into oblivion, although a silent film version of the story was released in 1919. Marsh continued to produce books with titles like* The House of Mystery *(1898),* The Goddess: A Demon *(1900) and* The Magnetic Girl *(1903) until his death from heart disease in 1915. His grandson was Robert Aickman, a much-admired writer of horror stories in the second half of the twentieth century. 'The Mask' was first published in the* Gentleman's Magazine *of December 1892 and was later reprinted in Marsh's 1900 collection entitled* Marvels and Mysteries. *Unashamedly lurid and implausible, the story is full of repetitions of phraseology which suggest that Marsh may have been getting paid for it by the word. It is, however, oddly memorable. Its villainess isn't a vampire in the undead sense but she certainly has a taste for blood.*

I WHAT HAPPENED IN THE TRAIN

'Wigmakers have brought their art to such perfection that it is difficult to detect false hair from real. Why should not the same skill be shown in the manufacture of a mask? Our faces, in one sense, are nothing but masks. Why should not the imitation be as good as the reality? Why, for instance, should not this face of mine, as you see it, be nothing but a mask, a something which I can take off and on?'

She laid her two hands softly against her cheeks. There was a ring of laughter in her voice.

'Such a mask would not only be, in the highest sense, a work of art, but it would also be a thing of beauty – a joy for ever.'

'You think that I am beautiful?'

I could not doubt it with her velvet skin just tinted with the bloom of health, her little dimpled chin, her ripe red lips, her flashing teeth, her great, inscrutable dark eyes, her wealth of hair which gleamed in the sunlight. I told her so.

'So you think that I am beautiful? How odd – how very odd!'

I could not tell if she was in jest or earnest. Her lips were parted by a smile. But it did not seem to me that it was laughter which was in her eyes.

'And you have only seen me, for the first time, a few hours ago?'

'Such has been my ill-fortune.'

She rose. She stood for a moment looking down at me.

'And you think there is nothing in my theory about a mask?'

'On the contrary, I think there is a great deal in any theory you may advance.'

A waiter brought me a card on a salver.

'Gentleman wishes to see you, sir.'

I glanced at the card. On it was printed, 'George Davis, Scotland Yard'. As I was looking at the piece of pasteboard she passed behind me.

'Perhaps I shall see you again, when we will continue our discussion about a mask.'

I rose and bowed. She went from the verandah down the steps into the garden. I turned to the waiter. 'Who is that lady?'

'I don't know her name, sir. She came in last night. She has a private sitting room at No. 22.' He hesitated. Then he added, 'I'm not sure, sir, but I think the lady's name is Jaynes – Mrs Jaynes.'

'Where is Mr Davis? Show him into my room.'

I went to my room and awaited him. Mr Davis proved to be a short, spare man, with iron-grey whiskers and a quiet, unassuming manner.

'You had my telegram, Mr Davis?'

'We had, sir.'

'I believe you are not unacquainted with my name?'

'Know it very well, sir.'

'The circumstances of my case are so peculiar, Mr Davis, that, instead of going to the local police, I thought it better to at once place myself in communication with headquarters.' Mr Davis bowed. 'I came down yesterday afternoon by the express from Paddington. I was alone in a first-class carriage. At Swindon a young gentleman got in. He seemed to me to be about twenty-three or four years of age, and unmistakably a gentleman. We had some conversation together. At Bath he offered me a drink out of his flask. It was getting evening then. I have been hard at it for the last few weeks. I was tired. I suppose I fell asleep. In my sleep I dreamed.'

'You dreamed?'

'I dreamed that I was being robbed.' The detective smiled. 'As you surmise, I woke up to find that my dream was real. But the curious part of the matter is that I am unable to tell you where my dream ended, and where my wakefulness began. I dreamed that something was leaning over me, rifling my person – some hideous, gasping thing which, in its eagerness, kept emitting short cries which were of the nature of barks. Although I say I dreamed this, I am not at all sure I did not actually see it taking place. The purse was drawn from my trousers pocket; something was taken out of it. I distinctly heard the chink of money, and then the purse was returned to where it was before. My watch and chain were taken, the studs out of my shirt, the links out of my wristbands. My pocket book was treated as my purse had been – something was taken out of it and the book returned. My keys were taken. My dressing bag was taken from the rack, opened, and articles were taken out of it, though I could not see what articles they were. The bag was replaced on the rack, the keys in my pocket.'

'Didn't you see the face of the person who did all this?'

'That was the curious part of it. I tried to, but I failed. It seemed to me that the face was hidden by a veil.'

'The thing was simple enough. We shall have to look for your young gentleman friend.'

'Wait till I have finished. The thing – I say the thing because, in my dream, I was strongly, nay, horribly under the impression that I was at the mercy of some sort of animal, some creature of the ape or monkey tribe.'

'There, certainly, you dreamed.'

'You think so? Still, wait a moment. The thing, whatever it was, when it had robbed me, opened my shirt at the breast, and, deliberately tearing my skin with what seemed to me to be talons, put its mouth to the wound, and, gathering my flesh between its teeth, bit me to the bone. Here is sufficient evidence to prove that then, at least, I did not dream.'

Unbuttoning my shirt I showed Mr Davis the open cicatrice.

'The pain was so intense that it awoke me. I sprang to my feet. I saw the thing.'

'You saw it?'

'I saw it. It was crouching at the other end of the carriage. The door was open. I saw it for an instant as it leaped into the night.'

'At what rate do you suppose the train was travelling?'

'The carriage blinds were drawn. The train had just left Newton Abbot. The creature must have been biting me when the train was actually drawn up at the platform. It leaped out of the carriage as the train was restarting.'

'And did you see the face?'

'I did. It was the face of a devil.'

'Excuse me, Mr Fountain, but you're not trying on me the plot of your next novel – just to see how it goes?'

'I wish I were, my lad, but I am not. It was the face of a devil – so hideous a face that the only detail I was able to grasp was that it had a pair of eyes which gleamed at me like burning coals.'

'Where was the young gentleman?'

'He had disappeared.'

'Precisely. And I suppose you did not only dream you had been robbed?'

'I had been robbed of everything which was of the slightest value, except eighteen shillings. Exactly that sum had been left in my purse.'

'Now perhaps you will give me a description of the young gentleman and his flask.'

'I swear it was not he who robbed me.'

'The possibility is that he was disguised. To my eye it seems unreasonable to suppose that he should have removed his disguise while engaged in the very act of robbing you. Anyhow, you give me his description, and I shouldn't be surprised if I was able to lay my finger on him on the spot.'

I described him – the well-knit young man, with his merry eyes, his slight moustache, his graceful manners.

'If he was a thief, then I am no judge of character. There was something about him which, to my eyes, marked him as emphatically a gentleman.'

The detective only smiled,

'The first thing I shall have to do will be to telegraph all over the country a list of the stolen property. Then I may possibly treat myself to a little private think. Your story is rather a curious one, Mr Fountain. And then later in the day I may want to say a word or two with you again. I shall find you here?'

I said that he would. When he had gone I sat down and wrote a letter. When I had finished the letter I went along the corridor towards the front door of the hotel. As I was going I saw in front of me a figure – the figure of a man. He was standing still, and his back was turned my way. But something about him struck me with such a sudden force of recognition that, stopping short, I stared. I suppose I must, unconsciously, have uttered some sort of exclamation, because the instant I stopped short, with a quick movement, he wheeled right round. We faced each other.

'You!' I exclaimed.

I hurried forward with a cry of recognition. He advanced, as I thought, to greet me. But he had only taken a step or two in my direction when he turned into a room upon his right, and, shutting the door behind him, disappeared.

'The man in the train!' I told myself.

If I had had any doubt upon the subject his sudden disappearance would have cleared my doubt away. If he was anxious to avoid a meeting with me, all the more reason why I should seek an interview with him. I went to the door of the room which he had entered and, without the slightest hesitation, I turned the handle. The room was empty – there could be no doubt of that. It was an ordinary hotel sitting room, own brother to the one which I occupied myself, and, as I saw at a glance, contained no article of furniture behind which a person could be concealed. But at the other side of the room was another door.

'My gentleman,' I said, 'has gone through that.'

Crossing the room again I turned the handle. This time without result – the door was locked. I rapped against the panels. Instantly someone addressed me from within.

'Who's that?'

The voice, to my surprise, and also somewhat to my discomfiture, was a woman's.

'Excuse me, but might I say one word to the gentleman who has just entered the room?'

'What's that? Who are you?'

'I'm the gentleman who came down with him in the train.'

'What?'

The door opened. A woman appeared – the lady whom the waiter had said he believed was a Mrs Jaynes, and who had advanced that curious story about a mask being made to imitate the human face. She had a dressing jacket on, and her glorious hair was flowing loose over her shoulders. I was so surprised to see her that for a moment I was tongue-tied. The surprise seemed to be mutual, for, with a pretty air of bewilderment, stepping back into the room she partially closed the door.

'I thought it was the waiter. May I ask, sir, what it is you want?'

'I beg ten thousand pardons; but might I just have one word with your husband?'

'With whom, sir?'

'Your husband.'

'My husband?'

Again throwing the door wide open she stood and stared at me.

'I refer, madam, to the gentleman whom I just saw enter the room.'

'I don't know if you intend an impertinence, sir, or merely a jest.'

Her lip curled, her eyes flashed – it was plain she was offended.

'I just saw, madam, in the corridor a gentleman with whom I travelled yesterday from London. I advanced to meet him. As I did so he turned into your sitting room. When I followed him I found it empty, so I took it for granted he had come in here.'

'You are mistaken, sir. I know no gentleman in the hotel. As for my husband, my husband has been dead three years.'

I could not contradict her, yet it was certain I had seen the stranger turn into the outer room. I told her so.

'If any man entered my sitting room – which was an unwarrantable liberty to take – he must be in it now. Except yourself, no one has come near my bedroom. I have had the door locked, and, as you see, I have been dressing. Are you sure you have not been dreaming?'

If I had been dreaming I had been dreaming with my eyes open; and yet, if I had seen the man enter the room – and I could have sworn I had – where was he now? She offered, with scathing irony, to let me examine her own apartment. Indeed, she opened the door so wide that I could see all over it from where I stood. It was plain enough that, with the exception of herself, it had no occupant.

And yet, I asked myself, as I retreated with my tail a little between my legs, how could I have been mistaken? The only hypothesis I could hit upon was, that my thoughts had been so deeply engaged upon the matter that they had made me the victim of hallucination. Perhaps my nervous system had temporarily been disorganised by my misadventures of the day before. And yet – and this was the final conclusion to which I came upon the matter – if I had not seen my fellow passenger standing in front of me, a creature of flesh and blood, I would never trust the evidence of my eyes again. The most ardent ghostseer never saw a ghost in the middle of the day.

I went for a walk towards Babbicombe. My nerves might be a little out of order – though not to the extent of seeing things which were non-existent, and it was quite possible that fresh air and exercise might do them good. I lunched at Babbicombe, spending the afternoon, as the weather was so fine, upon the seashore, in company with my thoughts, my pipe, and a book.

But as the day wore on a sea mist stole over the land, and as I returned Torquaywards it was already growing dusk. I went back by way of the seafront. As I was passing Hesketh Crescent I stood for a moment looking out into the gloom which was gathering over the sea. As I looked I heard, or I thought that I heard, a sound just behind me. As I heard it the blood seemed to run cold in my veins, and I had to clutch at the coping of the seawall to prevent my knees from giving way under me. It was the sound which I had heard in my dream in the train, and which had seemed to come from the creature which was robbing me: the cry or bark of some wild beast. It came once, one short, quick, gasping bark, then all was still. I looked round, fearing to see I know not what. Nothing was in sight. Yet, although nothing could be seen, I felt that there was something there. But, as the silence continued, I began to laugh at myself beneath my breath. I had not supposed that I was such a coward as to be frightened at less than a shadow! Moving away from the wall, I was about to resume my walk, when it came again – the choking, breathless bark so close to me that I seemed to feel the warm breath upon my cheek. Looking swiftly round, I saw, almost touching mine, the face of the creature which I had seen, but only for an instant, in the train.

II MARY BROOKER

'Are you ill?'

'I am a little tired.'

'You look as though you had seen a ghost. I am sure you are not well.'

I did not feel well. I felt as though I had seen a ghost, and something worse than a ghost! I had found my way back to the hotel – how, I scarcely knew. The first person I met was Mrs Jaynes. She was in the garden, which ran all round the building. My appearance seemed to occasion her anxiety.

'I am sure you are not well! Do sit down! Let me get you something to drink.'

'Thanks; I will go to my own room. I have not been very well lately. A little upsets me.'

She seemed reluctant to let me go. Her solicitude was flattering; though if there had been a little less of it I should have been equally content. She even offered me her arm. That I laughingly declined. I was not quite in such a piteous plight as to be in need of that. At last I escaped her. As I entered my sitting room someone rose to greet me. It was Mr Davis.

'Mr Fountain, are you not well?'

My appearance seemed to strike him as it had struck the lady.

'I have had a shock. Will you ring the bell and order me some brandy?'

'A shock?' He looked at me curiously. 'What sort of a shock?'

'I will tell you when you have ordered the brandy. I really am in need of something to revive me. I fancy my nervous system must be altogether out of order.'

He rang the bell. I sank into an easy chair, really grateful for the support which it afforded me. Although he sat still I was conscious that his eyes were on me all the time. When the waiter had brought the brandy Mr Davis gave rein to his curiosity.

'I hope that nothing serious has happened.'

'It depends upon what you call serious.' I paused to allow the spirit to take effect. It did me good. 'You remember what I told you about the strange sound which was uttered by the creature which robbed me in the train? I have heard that sound again.'

'Indeed!' He observed me attentively. I had thought he would be sceptical; he was not. 'Can you describe the sound?'

'It is difficult to describe, though when it is once heard it is impossible not to recognise it when it is heard again.' I shuddered as I thought of it. 'It is like the cry of some wild beast when in a state of frenzy – just a short, jerky, half-strangled yelp.'

'May I ask what were the circumstances under which you heard it?'

'I was looking at the sea in front of Hesketh Crescent. I heard it close behind me, not once, but twice; and the second time I – I saw the face which I saw in the train.'

I took another drink of brandy. I fancy that Mr Davis saw how even the mere recollection affected me.

'Do you think that your assailant could by any possibility have been a woman?'

'A woman!'

'Was the face you saw anything like that?'

He produced from his pocket a pocket book, and from the pocket book a photograph. He handed it to me. I regarded it intently. It was not a good photograph, but it was a strange one.

The more I looked at it the more it grew upon me that there was a likeness – a dim and fugitive likeness, but still a likeness, to the face which had glared at me only half an hour before.

'But surely this is not a woman?'

'Tell me, first of all, if you trace in it any resemblance.'

'I do, and I don't. In the portrait the face, as I know it, is grossly flattered; and yet in the portrait it is sufficiently hideous.'

Mr Davis stood up. He seemed a little excited.

'I believe I have hit it!'

'You have hit it?'

'The portrait which you hold in your hand is the portrait of a criminal lunatic who escaped last week from Broadmoor.'

'A criminal lunatic!'

As I looked at the portrait I perceived that it was the face of a lunatic.

'The woman – for it is a woman – is a perfect devil – as artful as she is wicked. She was there during Her Majesty's pleasure for a murder which was attended with details of horrible cruelty. She was more than suspected of having had a hand in other crimes. Since that portrait was taken she has deliberately burnt her face with a red-hot poker, disfiguring herself almost beyond recognition.'

'There is another circumstance which I should mention, Mr Davis. Do you know that this morning I saw the young gentleman too?'

The detective stared.

'What young gentleman?'

'The young fellow who got into the train at Swindon, and who offered me his flask.'

'You saw him! Where?'

'Here, in the hotel.'

'The devil you did! And you spoke to him?'

'I tried to.'

'And he hooked it?'

'That is the odd part of the thing. You will say there is

something odd about everything I tell you; and I must confess there is. When you left me this morning I wrote a letter; when I had written it I left the room. As I was going along the corridor I saw, in front of me, the young man who was with me in the train.'

'You are sure it was he?'

'Certain. When first I saw him he had his back to me. I suppose he heard me coming. Anyhow, he turned, and we were face to face. The recognition, I believe, was mutual, because as I advanced...'

'He cut his lucky?'

'He turned into a room upon his right.'

'Of course you followed him?'

'I did. I made no bones about it. I was not three seconds after him, but when I entered, the room was empty.'

'Empty!'

'It was an ordinary sitting room like this, but on the other side of it there was a door. I tried that door. It was locked. I rapped with my knuckles. A woman answered.'

'A woman?'

'A woman. She not only answered, she came out.'

'Was she anything like that portrait?'

I laughed. The idea of instituting any comparison between the horror in the portrait and that vision of health and loveliness was too ludicrous.

'She was a lady who is stopping in the hotel, with whom I already had had some conversation, and who is about as unlike that portrait as anything could possibly be – a Mrs Jaynes.'

'Jaynes? A Mrs Jaynes?' The detective bit his fingernails. He seemed to be turning something over in his mind. 'And did you see the man?'

'That is where the oddness of the thing comes in. She declared that there was no man.'

'What do you mean?'

'She declared that no one had been near her bedroom while

191

she had been in it. That there was no one in it at that particular moment is beyond a doubt, because she opened the door to let me see. I am inclined to think, upon reflection, that, after all, the man may have been concealed in the outer room, that I overlooked him in my haste, and that he made good his escape while I was knocking at the lady's door.'

'But if he had a finger in the pie, that knocks the other theory upon the head.' He nodded towards the portrait which I still was holding in my hand. 'A man like that would scarcely have such a pal as Mary Brooker.'

'I confess, Mr Davis, that the whole affair is a mystery to me. I suppose that your theory is that the flask out of which I drank was drugged?'

'I should say upon the face of it that there can't be two doubts about that.' The detective stood reflecting. 'I should like to have a look at this Mrs Jaynes. I will have a look at her. I'll go down to the office here, and I think it's just possible that I may be treated to a peep at her room.'

When he had gone I was haunted by the thought of that criminal lunatic, who was at least so far sane that she had been able to make good her escape from Broadmoor. It was only when Mr Davis had left me that I discovered that he had left the portrait behind him. I looked at it. What a face it was!

'Think,' I said to myself, 'of being left at the mercy of such a woman as that!'

The words had scarcely left my lips when, without any warning, the door of my room opened, and, just as I was taking it for granted that it was Mr Davis come back for the portrait, in walked the young man with whom I had travelled in the train! He was dressed exactly as he had been yesterday, and wore the same indefinable but unmistakable something which denotes good breeding.

'Excuse me,' he observed, as he stood with the handle of the door in one hand and his hat in the other, 'but I believe you are the gentleman with whom I travelled yesterday from Swindon?'

In my surprise I was for a moment tongue-tied. 'I do not think I have made a mistake.'

'No,' I said, or rather stammered, 'you have not made a mistake.'

'It is only by a fortunate accident that I have just learnt that you are staying in the hotel. Pardon my intrusion, but when I changed carriages at Excter I left behind me a cigar case.'

'A cigar case?'

'Did you notice it? I thought it might have caught your eye. It was a present to me, and one I greatly valued. It matched this flask.'

Coming a step or two towards me he held out a flask – the identical flask from which I had drunk! I stared alternately at him and at his flask.

'I was not aware that you changed carriages at Exeter.'

'I wondered if you noticed it. I fancy you were asleep.'

'A singular thing happened to me before I reached my journey's end – a singular and a disagreeable thing.'

'How do you mean?'

'I was robbed.'

'Robbed?'

'Did you notice anybody get into the carriage when you, as you say, got out?'

'Not that I am aware of. You know it was pretty dark. Why, good gracious! Is it possible that after all it wasn't my imagination?'

'What wasn't your imagination?'

He came closer to me – so close that he touched my sleeve with his gloved hand.

'Do you know why I left the carriage when I did? I left it because I was bothered by the thought that there was someone in it besides us two.'

'Someone in it besides us two?'

'Someone underneath the seat. I was dozing off as you were doing. More than once I woke up under the impression that someone was twitching my legs beneath the seat; pinching them – even pricking them.'

'Did you not look to see if anyone was there?'

'You will laugh at me, but – I suppose I was silly – something restrained me. I preferred to make a bolt of it, and become the victim of my own imagination.'

'You left me to become the victim of something besides your imagination, if what you say is correct.'

All at once the stranger made a dart at the table. I suppose he had seen the portrait lying there, because, without any sort of ceremony, he picked it up and stared at it. As I observed him, commenting inwardly about the fellow's coolness, I distinctly saw a shudder pass all over him. Possibly it was a shudder of aversion, because, when he had stared his fill, he turned to me and asked –

'Who, may I ask, is this hideous-looking creature?'

'That is a criminal lunatic who has escaped from Broadmoor – one Mary Brooker.'

'Mary Brooker! Mary Brooker! Mary Brooker's face will haunt me for many a day.'

He laid the portrait down hesitatingly, as if it had for him some dreadful fascination which made him reluctant to let it go. Wholly at a loss what to say or do, whether to detain the man or to permit him to depart, I turned away and moved across the room. The instant I did so I heard behind me the sharp, frenzied yelp which I had heard in the train, and which I had heard again when I had been looking at the sea in front of Hesketh Crescent. I turned as on a pivot. The young man was staring at me.

'Did you hear that?' he said.

'Hear it! Of course I heard it.'

'Good God!' He was shuddering so that it seemed to me that he could scarcely stand. 'Do you know that it was that sound, coming from underneath the seat in the carriage, which made me make a bolt of it? I – I'm afraid you must excuse me. There

– there's my card. I'm staying at the Royal. I will perhaps look you up again tomorrow.'

Before I had recovered my presence of mind sufficiently to interfere he had moved to the door and was out of the room. As he went out Mr Davis entered; they must have brushed each other as they passed.

'I forgot the portrait of that Brooker woman,' Mr Davis began.

'Why didn't you stop him?' I exclaimed.

'Stop whom?'

'Didn't you see him – the man who just went out?'

'Why should I stop him? Isn't he a friend of yours?'

'He's the man who travelled in the carriage with me from Swindon.'

Davis was out of the room like a flash of lightning. When he returned he returned alone.

'Where is he?' I demanded.

'That's what I should like to know.' Mr Davis wiped his brow. 'He must have travelled at the rate of about sixty miles an hour – he's nowhere to be seen. Whatever made you let him go?'

'He has left his card.' I took it up. It was inscribed "George Etherege, Coliseum Club". 'He says he is staying at the Royal Hotel. I don't believe he had anything to do with the robbery. He came to me in the most natural manner possible to inquire for a cigar case which he left behind him in the carriage. He says that while I was sleeping he changed carriages at Exeter because he suspected that someone was underneath the seat.'

'Did he, indeed?'

'He says that he did not look to see if anybody was actually there because – well, something restrained him.'

'I should like to have a little conversation with that young gentleman.'

'I believe he speaks the truth, for this reason. While he was talking there came the sound which I have described to you before.'

'The sort of bark?'

'The sort of bark. There was nothing to show from whence it came. I declare to you that it seemed to me that it came out of space. I never saw a man so frightened as he was. As he stood trembling, just where you are standing now, he stammered out that it was because he had heard that sound come from underneath the seat in the carriage that he had decided that discretion was the better part of valour, and, instead of gratifying his curiosity, had chosen to retreat.'

III THE SECRET OF THE MASK

Table d'hôte had commenced when I sat down. My right-hand neighbour was Mrs Jaynes. She asked me if I still suffered any ill effects from my fatigue.

'I suppose,' she said, when I assured her that all ill effects had passed away, 'that you have not thought anything of what I said to you this morning – about my theory of the mask?'

I confessed that I had not.

'You should. It is a subject which is a crotchet of mine, and to which I have devoted many years – many curious years of my life.'

'I own that, personally, I do not see exactly where the interest comes in.'

'No? Do me a favour. Come to my sitting room after dinner, and I will show you where the interest comes in.'

'How do you mean?'

'Come and see.'

She amused me. I went and saw. Dinner being finished, her proceedings, when together we entered her apartment – that apartment which in the morning I thought I had seen entered by my fellow passenger – took me a little by surprise.

'Now I am going to make you my confidant – you, an entire stranger – you, whom I never saw in my life before this morning. I am a judge of character, and in you I feel that I may place implicit confidence. I am going to show you all my secrets; I am going to induct you into the hidden mysteries; I am going to lay bare before you the mind of an inventor. But it doesn't follow because I have confidence in you that I have confidence in all the world besides, so, before we begin, if you please, I will lock the door.'

As she was suiting the action to the word I ventured to remonstrate.

'But, my dear madam, don't you think…'

'I think nothing. I know that I don't wish to be taken unawares, and to have published what I have devoted the better portion of my life to keeping secret.'

'But if these matters are of such a confidential nature I assure you…'

'My good sir, I lock the door.'

She did. I was sorry that I had accepted so hastily her invitation, but I yielded. The door was locked. Going to the fireplace she leaned her arm upon the mantel shelf.

'Did it ever occur to you,' she asked, 'what possibilities might be open to us if, for instance, Smith could temporarily become Jones?'

'I don't quite follow you,' I said. I did not.

'Suppose that you could at will become another person, and in the character of that other person could move about unrecognised among your friends, what lessons you might learn!'

'I suspect,' I murmured, 'that they would for the most part be lessons of a decidedly unpleasant kind.'

'Carry the idea a step further. Think of the possibilities of a dual existence. Think of living two distinct and separate lives. Think of doing as Robinson what you condemn as Brown. Think of doubling the parts and hiding within your own breast the secret of the double; think of leading a triple life; think of leading many lives in one – of being the old man and the young, the husband and the wife, the father and the son.'

'Think, in other words, of the unattainable.'

'Not unattainable!' Moving away from the mantel shelf she

raised her hand above her head with a gesture which was all at once dramatic. 'I have attained!'

'You have attained? To what?'

'To the multiple existence. It is the secret of the mask. I told myself some years ago that it ought to be possible to make a mask which should in every respect so closely resemble the human countenance that it would be difficult, if not impossible, even under the most trying conditions, to tell the false face from the real. I made experiments. I succeeded. I learnt the secret of the mask. Look at that.'

She took a leather case from her pocket. Abstracting its contents, she handed them to me. I was holding in my hand what seemed to me to be a preparation of some sort of skin – gold-beater's skin, it might have been. On one side it was curiously, and even delicately, painted. On the other side there were fastened to the skin some oddly shaped bosses or pads. The whole affair, I suppose, did not weigh half an ounce. While I was examining it Mrs Jaynes stood looking down at me.

'You hold in your hand,' she said, 'the secret of the mask. Give it to me.'

I gave it to her. With it in her hand she disappeared into the room beyond. Hardly had she vanished than the bedroom door reopened, and an old lady came out.

'My daughter begs you will excuse her.' She was a quaint old lady, about sixty years of age, with silver hair, and the corkscrew ringlets of a bygone day. 'My daughter is not very ceremonious, and is so wrapped up in what she calls her experiments that I sometimes tell her she is wanting in consideration. While she is making her preparations, perhaps you will allow me to offer you a cup of tea.'

The old lady carried a canister in her hand, which, apparently, contained tea. A tea service was standing on a little side table; a kettle was singing on the hob. The old lady began to measure out the tea into the teapot.

'We always carry our tea with us. Neither my daughter nor I

care for the tea which they give you in hotels.'

I meekly acquiesced. To tell the truth, I was a trifle bewildered. I had had no idea that Mrs Jaynes was accompanied by her mother. Had not the old lady come out of the room immediately after the young one had gone into it I should have suspected a trick – that I was being made the subject of experiment with the mysterious "mask". As it was, I was more than half inclined to ask her if she was really what she seemed to be. But I decided – as it turned out most unfortunately – to keep my own counsel and to watch the sequence of events. Pouring me out a cup of tea, the old lady seated herself on a low chair in front of the fire.

'My daughter thinks a great deal of her experiments. I hope you will not encourage her. She quite frightens me at times; she says such dreadful things.'

I sipped my tea and smiled.

'I don't think there is much cause for fear.'

'No cause for fear when she tells one that she might commit a murder; that a hundred thousand people might see her do it, and that not by any possibility could the crime be brought home to her!'

'Perhaps she exaggerates a little.'

'Do you think that she can hear?'

The old lady glanced round in the direction of the bedroom door.

'You should know better than I. Perhaps it would be as well to say nothing which you would not like her to hear.'

'But I must tell someone. It frightens me. She says it is a dream she had.'

'I don't think, if I were you, I would pay much attention to a dream.'

The old lady rose from her seat. I did not altogether like her manner. She came and stood in front of me, rubbing her hands, nervously, one over the other. She certainly seemed considerably disturbed.

'She came down yesterday from London, and she says she

dreamed that she tried one of her experiments – in the train.'

'In the train!'

'And in order that her experiment might be thorough she robbed a man.'

'She robbed a man!'

'And in her pocket I found this.'

The old lady held out my watch and chain! It was unmistakable. The watch was a hunter. I could see that my crest and monogram were engraved upon the case. I stood up. The strangest part of the affair was that when I gained my feet it seemed as though something had happened to my legs – I could not move them. Probably something in my demeanour struck the old lady as strange. She smiled at me.

'What is the matter with you? Why do you look so funny?' she exclaimed.

'That is my watch and chain.'

'Your watch and chain – yours! Then why don't you take them?'

She held them out to me in her extended palm. She was not six feet from where I stood, yet I could not reach them. My feet seemed glued to the floor.

'I – I cannot move. Something has happened to my legs.'

'Perhaps it is the tea. I will go and tell my daughter.'

Before I could say a word to stop her she was gone. I was fastened like a post to the ground. What had happened to me was more than I could say. It had all come in an instant. I felt as I had felt in the railway carriage the day before – as though I were in a dream. I looked around me. I saw the teacup on the little table at my side, I saw the flickering fire, I saw the shaded lamps; I was conscious of the presence of all these things, but I saw them as if I saw them in a dream. A sense of nausea was stealing over me – a sense of horror. I was afraid of I knew not what. I was unable to ward off or to control my fear.

I cannot say how long I stood there – certainly some minutes – helpless, struggling against the pressure which seemed to weigh upon my brain. Suddenly, without any sort of warning, the bedroom door opened, and there walked into the room the young man who, before dinner, had visited me in my own apartment, and who yesterday had travelled with me in the train. He came straight across the room, and, with the most perfect coolness, stood right in front of me. I could see that in his shirt front were my studs. When he raised his hands I could see that in his wristbands were my links. I could see that he was wearing my watch and chain. He was actually holding my watch in his hand when he addressed me.

'I have only half a minute to spare, but I wanted to speak to you about – Mary Brooker. I saw her portrait in your room – you remember? She's what is called a criminal lunatic, and she's escaped from Broadmoor. Let me see, I think it was a week today, and just about this time – no, it's now a quarter to nine; it was just after nine.' He slipped my watch into his waistcoat pocket. 'She's still at large, you know. They're on the lookout for her all over England, but she's still at large. They say she's a lunatic. There are lunatics at Broadmoor, but she's not one. She's no more a lunatic than you or I.'

He touched me lightly on the chest; such was my extreme disgust at being brought into physical contact with him that even before the slight pressure of his fingers my legs gave way under me, and I sank back into my chair.

'You're not asleep?'

'No,' I said, 'I'm not asleep.'

Even in my stupefied condition I was conscious of a desire to leap up and take him by the throat. Nothing of this, however, was portrayed upon my face, or, at any rate, he showed no sign of being struck by it.

'She's a misunderstood genius, that's what Mary Brooker is. She has her tastes and people do not understand them; she likes to kill – to kill! One of these days she means to kill herself, but in the meantime she takes pleasure in killing others.'

Seating himself on a corner of the table at my side, allowing one foot to rest upon the ground, he swung the other in the air.

'She's a bit of an actress too. She wanted to go upon the stage, but they said that she was mad. They were jealous, that's what it was. She's the finest actress in the world. Her acting would deceive the devil himself – they allowed that even at Broadmoor – but she only uses her powers for acting to gratify her taste – for killing. It was only the other day she bought this knife.'

He took, apparently out of the bosom of his vest, a long, glittering, cruel-looking knife.

'It's sharp. Feel the point – and the edge.'

He held it out towards me. I did not attempt to touch it; it is probable that I should not have succeeded even if I had attempted.

'You won't? Well, perhaps you're right. It's not much fun killing people with a knife. A knife's all very well for cutting them up afterwards, but she likes to do the actual killing with her own hands and nails. I shouldn't be surprised if, one of these days, she were to kill you – perhaps tonight. It is a long time since she killed anyone, and she is hungry. Sorry I can't stay; but this day week she escaped from Broadmoor as the clock had finished striking nine, and it only wants ten minutes, you see.'

He looked at my watch, even holding it out for me to see.

'Goodnight.'

With a careless nod he moved across the room, holding the glittering knife in his hand. When he reached the bedroom door he turned and smiled. Raising the knife he waved it towards me in the air; then he disappeared into the inner room.

I was again alone possibly for a minute or more; but this time it seemed to me that my solitude continued only for a few fleeting seconds. Perhaps the time went faster because I felt, or thought I felt, that the pressure on my brain was giving way, that I only had to make an effort of sufficient force to be myself again and free. The power of making such an effort was temporarily absent, but something within seemed to tell me that at any moment it might return. The bedroom door – that door which, even as I look back, seems to have been really and truly a door in some unpleasant dream – reopened. Mrs Jaynes came in; with rapid strides she swept across the room; she had something in her right hand, which she threw upon the table.

Well,' she cried, 'what do you think of the secret of the mask?'

'The secret of the mask?'

Although my limbs were powerless throughout it all I retained, to a certain extent, the control of my own voice.

'See here, it is such a little thing.' She picked up the two objects which she had thrown upon the table. One of them was the preparation of some sort of skin which she had shown to me before. 'These are the masks. You would not think that they were perfect representations of the human face – that masterpiece of creative art – and yet they are. All the world would be deceived by them as you have been. This is an old woman's face, this is the face of a young man.' As she held them up I could see, though still a little dimly, that the objects which she dangled before my eyes were, as she said, veritable masks. 'So perfect are they, they might have been skinned from the fronts of living creatures. They are such little things, yet I have made them with what toil! They have been the work of years, these two, and just one other. You see nothing satisfied me but perfection; I have made hundreds to make these two. People could not make out what I was doing; they thought that I was making toys; I told them that I was. They smiled at me; they thought that it was a new phase of madness. If that be so, then in madness there is more cool, enduring, unconquerable resolution than in all your sanity. I meant to conquer, and I did. Failure did not dishearten me; I went straight on. I had a purpose to fulfil; I would have fulfilled it even though I should have had first to die. Well, it is fulfilled.'

Turning, she flung the masks into the fire; they were immediately in flames. She pointed to them as they burned.

'The labour of years is soon consumed. But I should not have triumphed had I not been endowed with genius – the genius of the actor's art. I told myself that I would play certain parts –

parts which would fit the masks – and that I would be the parts I played. Not only across the footlights, not only with a certain amount of space between my audience and me, not only for the passing hour, but, if I chose, for ever and for aye. So all through the years I rehearsed these parts when I was not engaged upon the masks. That, they thought, was madness in another phase. One of the parts' – she came closer to me; her voice became shriller – 'one of the parts was that of an old woman. Have you seen her? She is in the fire.' She jerked her thumb in the direction of the fireplace. 'Her part is played – she had to see that the tea was drunk. Another of the parts was that of a young gentleman. Think of my playing the man! Absurd. For there is that about a woman which is not to be disguised. She always reveals her sex when she puts on men's clothes. You noticed it, did you not when, before dinner, he came to you; when you saw him in the corridor this morning; when yesterday he spent an hour with you in the train? I know you noticed it because of these.'

She drew out of her pocket a handful of things. There were my links, my studs, my watch and chain, and other properties of mine. Although the influence of the drug which had been administered to me in the tea was passing off, I felt, even more than ever, as though I were an actor in a dream.

'The third part which I chose to play was the part of – Mrs Jaynes!'

Clasping her hands behind her back, she posed in front of me in an attitude which was essentially dramatic.

'Look at me well. Scan all my points. Appraise me. You say that I am beautiful. I saw that you admired my hair, which flows loose upon my shoulders' – she unloosed the fastenings of her hair so that it did flow loose upon her shoulders – 'the bloom upon my cheeks, the dimple in my chin, my face in its entirety. It is the secret of the mask, my friend, the secret of the mask! You ask me why I have watched, and toiled, and schemed to make the secret mine.'

She stretched out her hand with an uncanny gesture. 'Because

I wished to gratify my taste for killing. Yesterday I might have killed you; tonight I will.'

She did something to her head and dress. There was a rustle of drapery. It was like a conjurer's change. Mrs Jaynes had gone, and instead there stood before me the creature with, as I had described it to Davis, the face of a devil – the face I had seen in the train. The transformation in its entirety was wonderful. Mrs Jaynes was a fine, stately woman with a swelling bust and in the prime of life. This was a lank, scraggy creature, with short, grey hair – fifty if a day. The change extended even to the voice. Mrs Jaynes had the soft, cultivated accents of a lady. This creature shrieked rather than spoke.

'I,' she screamed, 'am Mary Brooker. It is a week today since I won freedom. The bloodhounds are everywhere upon my track. They are drawing near. But they shall not have me till I have first of all had you.'

She came closer, crouching forward, glaring at me with a maniac's eyes. From her lips there came that hideous cry, half gasp, half yelp, which had haunted me since the day before, when I heard it in my stupor in the train.

'I scratched you yesterday. I bit you. I sucked your blood. Now I will suck it dry, for you are mine.'

She reckoned without her host. I had only sipped the tea. I had not, as I had doubtless been intended to do, emptied the cup. I was again master of myself; I was only awaiting a favourable opportunity to close. I meant to fight for life.

She came nearer to me and nearer, uttering all the time that blood-curdling sound which was so like the frenzied cry of some maddened animal. When her extended hands were all but touching me I rose up and took her by the throat. She had evidently supposed that I was still under the influence of the drug, because when I seized her she gave a shriek of astonished rage. I had taken her unawares. I had her over on her back. But I soon found that I had undertaken more than I could carry through. She had not only the face of a devil, she had the strength of one.

She flung me off as easily as though I were a child. In her turn she had me down upon my back. Her fingers closed about my neck. I could not shake her off. She was strangling me.

She would have strangled me – she nearly did. When, attracted by the creature's hideous cries, which were heard from without, they forced their way into the room, they found me lying unconscious, and, as they thought, dead, upon the floor. For days I hung between life and death. When life did come back again Mary Brooker was once more an inmate of Her Majesty's house of detention at Broadmoor.

The Vampire Maid

Hume Nisbet (1849–1923)

Born in Stirling, Hume Nisbet emigrated to Australia as a teenager and lived there for seven years before returning to Britain to work as a painter and art teacher. He began writing in the 1880s and went on to publish more than forty novels, as well as volumes of poetry, books on art and collections of short stories. He visited Australia twice more before the turn of the century and a number of his novels were inspired by his time there. The Savage Queen (1891) is shaped by prejudices of the day but is a surprisingly sympathetic tale of the last of the aboriginal peoples of Tasmania; A Bush Girl's Romance (1894) is set in Western Australia. The Land of the Hibiscus Blossom (1888) is one of the very first works of fiction to be set in Papua New Guinea. Nisbet also wrote several 'lost world' tales, including (most intriguingly) Valdmer the Viking (1893) in which eleventh-century Norsemen encounter a technologically advanced society hidden away in the Arctic. His stories of the ghostly and macabre appeared in magazines and collections throughout his career. Probably the best-known is 'The Haunted Station' which makes good use of the Australian outback which he knew well. 'The Vampire Maid' unfolds in the less remote surroundings of Westmorland. Although short and a trifle predictable, it retains a certain atmosphere and sense of dread.

It was the exact kind of abode that I had been looking after for weeks, for I was in that condition of mind when absolute renunciation of society was a necessity. I had become diffident of myself, and wearied of my kind. A strange unrest was in my blood; a barren dearth in my brains. Familiar objects and faces had grown distasteful to me. I wanted to be alone.

This is the mood which comes upon every sensitive and artistic mind when the possessor has been overworked or living too long in one groove. It is Nature's hint for him to seek pastures new; the sign that a retreat has become needful.

If he does not yield, he breaks down and becomes whimsical and hypochondriacal, as well as hypercritical. It is always a bad sign when a man becomes over-critical and censorious about his own or other people's work, for it means that he is losing the vital portions of work, freshness and enthusiasm.

Before I arrived at the dismal stage of criticism I hastily packed up my knapsack, and taking the train to Westmorland, I began my tramp in search of solitude, bracing air and romantic surroundings.

Many places I came upon during that early summer wandering that appeared to have almost the required conditions, yet some petty drawback prevented me from deciding. Sometimes it was the scenery that I did not take kindly to. At other places I took sudden antipathies to the landlady or landlord, and felt I would abhor them before a week was spent under their charge. Other places which might have suited me I could not have, as they did not want a lodger. Fate was driving me to this Cottage on the Moor, and no one can resist destiny.

One day I found myself on a wide and pathless moor near the sea. I had slept the night before at a small hamlet, but that was already eight miles in my rear, and since I had turned my back upon it I had not seen any signs of humanity; I was alone with a fair sky above me, a balmy ozone-filled wind blowing over the stony and heather-clad mounds, and nothing to disturb my meditations.

How far the moor stretched I had no knowledge; I only knew that by keeping in a straight line I would come to the ocean cliffs, then perhaps after a time arrive at some fishing village.

I had provisions in my knapsack, and being young did not fear a night under the stars. I was inhaling the delicious summer air and once more getting back the vigour and happiness I had lost; my city-dried brains were again becoming juicy.

Thus hour after hour slid past me, with the paces, until I had covered about fifteen miles since morning, when I saw before me in the distance a solitary stone-built cottage with roughly slated roof. 'I'll camp there if possible,' I said to myself as I quickened my steps towards it.

To one in search of a quiet, free life, nothing could have possibly been more suitable than this cottage. It stood on the edge of lofty cliffs, with its front door facing the moor and the back-yard wall overlooking the ocean. The sound of the dancing waves struck upon my ears like a lullaby as I drew near; how they would thunder when the autumn gales came on and the seabirds fled shrieking to the shelter of the sedges.

A small garden spread in front, surrounded by a dry-stone wall just high enough for one to lean lazily upon when inclined. This garden was a flame of colour, scarlet predominating, with those other soft shades that cultivated poppies take on in their blooming, for this was all that the garden grew.

As I approached, taking notice of this singular assortment of poppies, and the orderly cleanness of the windows, the front door opened and a woman appeared who impressed me at once favourably as she leisurely came along the pathway to the gate, and drew it back as if to welcome me.

She was of middle age, and when young must have been remarkably good-looking. She was tall and still shapely, with smooth clear skin, regular features and a calm expression that at once gave me a sensation of rest.

To my inquiries she said that she could give me both a sitting and bedroom, and invited me inside to see them. As I looked at her smooth black hair, and cool brown eyes, I felt that I would not be too particular about the accommodation. With such a landlady, I was sure to find what I was after here.

The rooms surpassed my expectation, dainty white curtains and bedding with the perfume of lavender about them, a sitting room homely yet cosy without being crowded. With a sigh of infinite relief I flung down my knapsack and clinched the bargain.

She was a widow with one daughter, whom I did not see the first day, as she was unwell and confined to her own room, but on the next day she was somewhat better, and then we met.

The fare was simple, yet it suited me exactly for the time, delicious milk and butter with home-made scones, fresh eggs and bacon; after a hearty tea I went early to bed in a condition of perfect content with my quarters.

Yet happy and tired out as I was I had by no means a comfortable night. This I put down to the strange bed. I slept certainly, but my sleep was filled with dreams so that I woke late and unrefreshed; a good walk on the moor, however, restored me, and I returned with a fine appetite for breakfast.

Certain conditions of mind, with aggravating circumstances, are required before even a young man can fall in love at first sight, as Shakespeare has shown in his *Romeo and Juliet*. In the city, where many fair faces passed me every hour, I had remained like a stoic, yet no sooner did I enter the cottage after that morning walk than I succumbed instantly before the weird charms of my landlady's daughter, Ariadne Brunnell.

She was somewhat better this morning and able to meet me at breakfast, for we had our meals together while I was their lodger. Ariadne was not beautiful in the strictly classical sense, her complexion being too lividly white and her expression too set to be quite pleasant at first sight; yet, as her mother had informed me, she had been ill for some time, which accounted for that defect. Her features were not regular, her hair and eyes seemed too black with that strangely white skin, and her lips too red for any except the decadent harmonies of an Aubrey Beardsley.

Yet my fantastic dreams of the preceding night, with my morning walk, had prepared me to be enthralled by this modern poster-like invalid.

The loneliness of the moor, with the singing of the ocean, had gripped my heart with a wistful longing. The incongruity of those flaunting and evanescent poppy flowers, dashing the giddy tints in the face of that sober heath, touched me with a shiver as

I approached the cottage, and lastly that weird embodiment of startling contrasts completed my subjugation.

She rose from her chair as her mother introduced her, and smiled while she held out her hand. I clasped that soft snowflake, and as I did so a faint thrill tingled over me and rested on my heart, stopping for the moment its beating.

This contact seemed also to have affected her as it did me; a clear flush, like a white flame, lighted up her face, so that it glowed as if an alabaster lamp had been lit; her black eyes became softer and more humid as our glances crossed, and her scarlet lips grew moist. She was a living woman now, while before she had seemed half a corpse.

She permitted her white slender hand to remain in mine longer than most people do at an introduction, and then she slowly withdrew it, still regarding me with steadfast eyes for a second or two afterwards.

Fathomless velvety eyes these were, yet before they were shifted from mine they appeared to have absorbed all my willpower and made me her abject slave. They looked like deep dark pools of clear water, yet they filled me with fire and deprived me of strength. I sank into my chair almost as languidly as I had risen from my bed that morning.

Yet I made a good breakfast, and although she hardly tasted anything, this strange girl rose much refreshed and with a slight glow of colour on her cheeks, which improved her so greatly that she appeared younger and almost beautiful.

I had come here seeking solitude, but since I had seen Ariadne it seemed as if I had come for her only. She was not very lively; indeed, thinking back, I cannot recall any spontaneous remark of hers; she answered my questions by monosyllables and left me to lead in words; yet she was insinuating and appeared to lead my thoughts in her direction and speak to me with her eyes. I cannot describe her minutely, I only know that from the first glance and touch she gave me I was bewitched and could think of nothing else.

It was a rapid, distracting, and devouring infatuation that possessed me; all day long I followed her about like a dog, every night I dreamed of that white glowing face, those steadfast black eyes, those moist scarlet lips, and each morning I rose more languid than I had been the day before. Sometimes I dreamt that she was kissing me with those red lips, while I shivered at the contact of her silky black tresses as they covered my throat; sometimes that we were floating in the air, her arms about me and her long hair enveloping us both like an inky cloud, while I lay supine and helpless.

She went with me after breakfast on that first day to the moor, and before we came back I had spoken my love and received her assent. I held her in my arms and had taken her kisses in answer to mine, nor did I think it strange that all this had happened so quickly. She was mine, or rather I was hers, without a pause. I told her it was fate that had sent me to her, for I had no doubts about my love, and she replied that I had restored her to life.

Acting upon Ariadne's advice, and also from a natural shyness, I did not inform her mother how quickly matters had progressed between us, yet although we both acted as circumspectly as possible, I had no doubt Mrs Brunnell could see how engrossed we were in each other. Lovers are not unlike ostriches in their modes of concealment. I was not afraid of asking Mrs Brunnell for her daughter, for she already showed her partiality towards me, and had bestowed upon me some confidences regarding her own position in life, and I therefore knew that, so far as social position was concerned, there could be no real objection to our marriage. They lived in this lonely spot for the sake of their health, and kept no servant because they could not get any to take service so far away from other humanity. My coming had been opportune and welcome to both mother and daughter.

For the sake of decorum, however, I resolved to delay my confession for a week or two and trust to some favourable opportunity of doing it discreetly.

Meantime Ariadne and I passed our time in a thoroughly idle

and lotus-eating style. Each night I retired to bed meditating starting work next day, each morning I rose languid from those disturbing dreams with no thought for anything outside my love. She grew stronger every day, while I appeared to be taking her place as the invalid, yet I was more frantically in love than ever, and only happy when with her. She was my lone star, my only joy – my life.

We did not go great distances, for I liked best to lie on the dry heath and watch her glowing face and intense eyes while I listened to the surging of the distant waves. It was love made me lazy, I thought, for unless a man has all he longs for beside him, he is apt to copy the domestic cat and bask in the sunshine.

I had been enchanted quickly. My disenchantment came as rapidly, although it was long before the poison left my blood.

One night, about a couple of weeks after my coming to the cottage, I had returned after a delicious moonlight walk with Ariadne. The night was warm and the moon at the full, therefore I left my bedroom window open to let in what little air there was.

I was more than usually fagged out, so that I had only strength enough to remove my boots and coat before I flung myself wearily on the coverlet and fell almost instantly asleep without tasting the nightcap draught that was constantly placed on the table, and which I had always drained thirstily.

I had a ghastly dream this night. I thought I saw a monster bat, with the face and tresses of Ariadne, fly into the open window and fasten its white teeth and scarlet lips on my arm. I tried to beat the horror away, but could not, for I seemed chained down and thralled also with drowsy delight as the beast sucked my blood with a gruesome rapture.

I looked out dreamily and saw a line of dead bodies of young men lying on the floor, each with a red mark on their arms, on the same part where the vampire was then sucking me, and I remembered having seen and wondered at such a mark on my own arm for the past fortnight. In a flash I understood the reason for my strange weakness, and at the same moment a sudden prick of pain roused me from my dreamy pleasure.

The vampire in her eagerness had bitten a little too deeply that night, unaware that I had not tasted the drugged draught. As I woke I saw her fully revealed by the midnight moon, with her black tresses flowing loosely, and with her red lips glued to my arm. With a shriek of horror I dashed her backwards, getting one last glimpse of her savage eyes, glowing white face and blood-stained red lips; then I rushed out to the night, moved on by my fear and hatred, nor did I pause in my mad flight until I had left miles between me and that accursed Cottage on the Moor.

Grettir at Thorhall-stead

Frank Norris (1870–1902)

Benjamin Franklin Norris, born in Chicago, went to Paris as a young man where he absorbed the theories of naturalist fiction espoused by novelists like Zola, and, in his short life, he became the most talented exponent of such fiction in the USA. After studying at the University of California, he published two major novels which have remained in print to the present day. McTeague *(1899), the story of a quack dentist who descends into violence and murder and ends his life in dramatic fashion, handcuffed to a corpse in the searing heat of Death Valley, was made into a classic silent movie,* Greed, *directed by Erich von Stroheim in 1924.* The Octopus *(1901) was meant to be the first in an epic trilogy about life in California but Norris died of peritonitis at the age of only thirty-two before he could finish it. The second volume,* The Pit, *was published posthumously. 'Grettir at Thorhall-stead', an untypical work by Norris, also appeared after his death, first published in* Everybody's Magazine *in 1903. Based on an episode from a mediaeval Icelandic saga, it's an interesting tale inasmuch as it presents a portrait of a vampire and its activities drawn from a very different folklore to the one in which the standard view of the creature originated. The vampire in 'Grettir at Thorhall-stead' may be undead but he is nothing like the traditional Transylvanian bloodsucker.*

I GLAMR

Thorhall the bonder had been to the great Thingvalla, or annual fair of Iceland, to engage a shepherd, and was now returning. It had been a good two-days' journey home, for his shaggy little pony, though sure footed, was slow. For the better part of three hours on the evening of the second day he had been picking

215

his way cautiously among the great boulders of black basalt that encumbered the path. At length, on the summit of a low hill, he brought the little animal to a standstill and paused a moment, looking off to the northward, a smile of satisfaction spreading over his broad, sober face. For he had just passed the white stone that marked the boundary of his own land. Below him opened the little valley named the Vale of Shadows, and in its midst, overshadowed by a single Norway pine, black, wind-distorted, was the stone farmhouse, the byre, Thorhall's home.

Only an Icelander could have found pleasure in that prospect. It was dreary beyond expression. Save only for the deformed pine, tortured and warped by its unending battle with the wintry gales, no other tree relieved the monotony of the landscape. To the west, mountains barred the horizon – volcanic mountains, gashed, cragged, basaltic, and still blackened with primeval fires. Bare of vegetation they were – sombre, solitary, empty of life. To the eastward, low, rolling sand dunes, sprinkled thinly with gorse, bore down to the sea. They shut off a view of the shore, but farther on the horizon showed itself, a bitter, inhospitable waste of grey water, blotted by fogs and murk and sudden squalls. Though the shore was invisible, it none the less asserted itself. With the rushing of the wind was mingled the prolonged, everlasting thunder of the surf, while the taint of salt, of decaying kelp, of fish, of seaweed, of all the pungent aromas of the sea, pervaded the air on every hand.

Black gulls, sharply defined against the grey sky, slanted in long tacking flights hither and thither over sea and land. The raucous bark of the seal hunting mackerel off the shore made itself occasionally heard. Otherwise there was no sign of life. Veils of fine rain, half fog, drove across the scene between ocean and mountain. The wind blew incessantly from off the sea with a steady and uninterrupted murmur.

Thorhall rode on, inclining his head against the gusts and driving wind. Soon he had come to the farmhouse. The servants led the pony to the stables and in the doorway Thorhall found his wife waiting for him. They embraced one another and – for they were pious folk – thanked God for the bonder's safe journey and speedy return. Before the roaring fire of drift that evening Thorhall told his wife of all that had passed at the Thingvalla, of the wrestling, and of the stallion fights.

'And did you find a shepherd to your liking?' asked his wife.

'Yes; a great fellow with white teeth and black hair. Rather surly, I believe, but strong as a troll. He promised to be with me by the beginning of the Winter Night. His name is Glamr.'

But the Summer passed, the sun dipped below the horizon not to reappear for six months, the Winter Night drew on, snow buried all the landscape, hurricanes sharp as boar-spears descended upon the Vale of Shadows; in their beds the dwellers in the byre heard the grind and growl of the great bergs careering onward through the ocean, and many a night the howl of hunger-driven wolves startled Thorhall from his sleep; yet Glamr did not come.

Then at length and of a sudden he appeared; and Thorhall on a certain evening, called hastily by a frightened servant, beheld the great figure of him in the midst of the kitchen floor, his eyebrows frosted yet scowling, his white teeth snapping with cold, while in a great hoarse voice, like the grumble of a bear, he called for meat and drink.

From thenceforward Glamr became a member of Thorhall's household. Yet seldom was he found in the byre. By day he was away with the sheep; by night he slept in the stables. The servants were afraid of him, though he rarely addressed them a word. He was not only feared, but disliked. This aversion was partly explained by Glamr's own peculiar disposition – gloomy, solitary, uncanny – and partly by a fact that came to light within the first month of his coming to the Vale of Shadows.

He was an unbeliever. Never did his broad bulk darken the lich-gate of the kirk; the knolling of matin- and vesper-bell put him in a season of even deeper gloom than usual. It was noticed that he could not bear to look upon a cross; the priest he abhorred as a pestilence. On holy days he kept far from home, absenting himself upon one pretext or another, withdrawing up into the chasms and gorges of the hills.

So passed the first months of the Winter.

Christmas Day came, and Christmas Night. It was bitter, bitter cold. Snow had fallen since second cockcrow the day before, and as night closed in such a gale as had not been known for years gathered from off the Northern Ocean and whirled shrieking over the Vale of Shadows. All day long Glamr was in the hills with the sheep, and even above the roaring of the wind his bell-toned voice had occasionally been heard as he called and shouted to his charges. At candle-lighting time he had not returned. The bonder and his family busked themselves to attend the Christmas Mass.

Some two hours later they were returning. The wind was going down, but even yet shreds of torn seaweed and scud of foam, swept up by the breath of the gale, drove landward across the valley. The clouds overhead were breaking up, and between their galloping courses one saw the sky, the stars glittering like hoar frost.

The bonder's party drew near the farmhouse, and the servants, going before with lanthorns and pine torches, undid the fastenings of the gate. The wind lapsed suddenly, and in the stillness between two gusts the plunge of the surf made itself heard.

Then all at once Thorhall and his wife stopped and her hand clutched quickly at his wrist.

'Hark! What was that?'

What, indeed? Was it an echo of the storm sounding hollow and faint from some thunder-split crag far off there in those hills toward which all eyes were suddenly turned; was it the cry of a wolf, the clamour of a falcon, or was it the horrid scream of human agony and fury, vibrating to a hoarse and bell-like note that sounded familiar in their ears?

'Glamr! Where is Glamr?' shouted Thorhall, as he entered the byre. But those few servants who had been left in charge of the house reported he had not yet returned.

Night passed and no Glamr; and in the morning the search party set out toward the hills. Halfway up the slope, the sheep — a few of them — were found, scattered, half buried in drifts; then a dog, dead and frozen hard as wood. From it led a track up into the higher mountains, a strange track indeed, not human certainly, yet whether of wolf or bear no one could determine. Some had started to follow when a lad who had looked behind the shoulder of a great rock raised a cry.

There was the body of Glamr. The shepherd was stretched upon his back, dead, rigid. The open eyes were glazed, the face livid; the tongue protruding from the mouth had been bitten through in the last agony. All about the snow was trampled down, and the bare bushes crushed and flattened out. Even the massive boulder near which the body had been found was moved a little from its place. A fearful struggle had been wrought out here, yet upon the body of Glamr was no trace of a wound, no mark of claw or hand. Only among his footprints was mingled that strange track that had been noticed before, and as before it led straight up toward the high part of the mountains.

The young men raised the body of the shepherd and the party moved off toward the kirk and the graveyard. Even though Glamr had shunned the Mass, the priest might be prevailed upon to bury him in consecrated ground. But soon the young men had to pause to rest. The body was unexpectedly heavy. Once again, after stopping to breathe, they raised the bier upon their shoulders. Soon another helper was summoned, then another; even Thorhall aided. Ten strong men though they were, they staggered and trembled under that unearthly weight. Even in that icy air the perspiration streamed from them. Heavier and still heavier grew the burden; it bore them to the earth. Their knees bowed out from under them, their backs bent. They were obliged to give over.

Later in the day they returned with oxen and a sledge. They repaired to the spot where the body had been left; then stared at each other with paling faces. In the snow at their feet there was the impression made by the great frame of the shepherd. But that was all; the body was gone, nor was there any footprint in the snow other than they themselves had made.

A cairn was erected over the spot, and for many a long day the strange death of the shepherd of the Vale of Shadows was the talk of the countryside. But about a month or so after the death of Glamr a strange sense of uneasiness seemed to invade the household of the byre. By degrees it took possession of first one and then another of the servants and family. No one spoke about this. It was not a thing that could be reduced to words, and for the matter of that, each one believed that he or she was the only one affected. This one thought himself sick; that one believed herself merely nervous. But nevertheless a certain perplexity, a certain disturbance of spirit was in the air.

One evening Thorhall and his wife met accidentally in the passage between the main body of the house and the dairy. They paused and looked at each other for no reason that they could imagine. Thus they stood for several seconds.

'Well,' said Thorhall at length, 'what is it?'

'Ay,' responded his wife. 'Ay, what *is* it?'

'Nothing,' he replied; and she, echoing his words, also answered 'Nothing'.

Then they laughed nervously, yet still looking fixedly into each other's eyes for all that.

'I believe,' said Thorhall the next day, 'that I am to be sick. I cannot tell... I feel no pain... no fever... and yet...'

'And I, too,' declared his wife. 'I am... no, not sick... but distressed. I... I am troubled. I cannot tell what it is. I sometimes think I am afraid.'

A week later, on a certain evening just after curfew, the whole family was aroused by a wild shriek as of someone in mortal terror. Thorhall and his wife rushed into the dairy whence the cry came and found one of the maids in a fit upon the floor. When she recovered she cried out that she had seen at one of the windows the face of Glamr.

II GRETTIR

The cold, bright Icelandic Summer shone over Thorhall's byre and the Vale of Shadows. There was no cloud in the sky. The void and lonely ocean was indigo blue. But still the prospect was barren, inhospitable. Only a few pallid flowers, hardy bluebells and buttercups, appeared here and there on the sand dunes in the hollows beneath the gorse and bracken. In the lower hills, on the far side of the valley, a tenuous skim of verdure appeared. At times a ptarmigan fluttered in and out of the crevices of these hills searching for blueberries; at times on the surfaces of the waste of dunes a sandpiper uttered its shrill and feeble piping. Always, as ever, the wind blew from off the ocean; always, as ever, the solitary pine by the farmhouse writhed and tossed its gaunt arms; always the gorse and bracken billowed and weltered under it. The sand drifted like snow, encroaching forever upon the cultivated patches around the house. Always the surf – surge on surge – boomed and thundered on the shore, casting up broken kelp and jetsam of wreck. Always, always forever and forever, the monotony remained. The bleakness, the wild, solitary stretches of sea and sky and land turned to the eye their staring emptiness. At long intervals the figure of a servant, a herdsman or at times Thorhall himself moved – a speck of black on the illimitable grey of nature – across the landscape. Ponies, shagged, half wild, their eyes hidden under tangled forelocks, sometimes wandered down upon the shore – their thick hair roughing in the wind – to snuff at the salty seaweeds. The males sometimes fought here on the shore, their hoofs thudding on the resounding beach, their screams mingling with the incessant roar of the breakers.

Once even, at Eastertide, during a gale, an empty galley drove ashore, a *snekr* with dragon prow, the broken oars dangling from the thole-pins; and in the waist of her a Viking chieftain, dead, the salt rime rusting on his helmet.

With the advent of Summer the mysterious trouble at the farmhouse in the Vale of Shadows disappeared. But the fall equinox drew on, the nights became longer; soon the daylight lasted but a few hours and the sun set before it could be said to have actually risen.

As the Winter darkness descended upon the farmhouse the trouble recommenced. During the night the tread of footsteps could be heard making the rounds of the byre. The fumbling of unseen fingers could be distinguished at the locks. The low eaves of the house were seized in the grip of strong hands and wrenched and pulled till the rafters creaked. Outhouses were plucked apart and destroyed, fences uprooted. After nightfall no one dared venture abroad.

Thorhall had engaged a new shepherd, one Thorgaut, a young man, who professed himself fearless of the haunted sheep walks and farmyard. He was as popular as Glamr had been disliked. He made love to the housemaids, helped in the butter-making and rode the children on his back. As to the Vampire, he snapped his fingers and asked only to meet him in the open.

The snow came in August, and was followed by sleet and icy rains and blotting sea-fogs. As the time went on the nightly manifestations increased. Windows were broken in; iron bars shaken and wrenched; sheep and even horses killed.

At length one night a terrible commotion broke out in the stables – the shrill squealing of the horses and the tramping and bellowing of cows, mingled with deep tones of a dreadful voice. Thorhall and his people rushed out. They found that the stable door had been riven and splintered, and they entered the stable itself across the wreckage. The cattle were goring each other, and across the stone partition between the stalls was the body of Thorgaut, the shepherd, his head upon one side, his feet on the other, and his spine snapped in twain.

★ ★ ★ ★ ★

It chanced that about this time Grettir, well known and well beloved throughout all Iceland, came into that part of the country and one eventide drew rein at Thorhall's farmhouse. This was before Grettir had been hunted from the island by the implacable Thorbjorn, called The Hook, and driven to an asylum and practical captivity upon the rock of Drangey.

He was at this time in the prime of his youth and of a noble appearance. His shoulders were broad, his arms long, his eye a bright blue and his flaxen hair braided like a Viking's. For a cloak he wore a bearskin, while as for weapons he carried nothing but a short sword.

Thorhall, as may be easily understood, welcomed the famous outlaw, but warned him of Glamr.

Grettir, however, was not to be dissuaded from remaining overnight at the byre.

'Vampire or troll, troll or vampire, here bide I till daybreak,' he declared.

Yet despite the bonder's fears the night passed quietly. No sound broke the stillness but the murmur of the distant surf, no footfall sounded around the house, no fingers came groping at the doors.

'I have never slept easier,' announced Grettir in the morning.

'Good; and Heaven be praised,' declared the bonder fervently.

They walked together toward the stables, Thorhall instructing Grettir as to the road he should follow that day. As they drew near, Grettir whistled for his horse, but no answering whicker responded.

'How is this?' he muttered, frowning.

Thorhall and the outlaw hurried into the building, and Grettir, who was in the advance, stopped stock-still in the midst of the floor and swore a great oath.

His horse lay prone in the straw of his stall, his eyeballs protruding, the foam stiff upon his lips. He was dead. Grettir approached and examined him. Between shoulder and withers, the back – as if it had been a wheat-straw – was broken.

'Never mind,' cried the bonder eagerly, 'I have another animal for you, a piebald stallion of Norway stock, just the beast for your weight. Here is your saddle. On with it. Up you go and a speedy journey to you.'

'Never!' exclaimed Grettir, his blue eyes flashing. 'Here will I stay till I meet Glamr face to face. No man did me an injury that he did not rue it. I sleep at the byre another night.'

Dark as a wolf's mouth, silent as his footfalls, the night closed down. There was no moon as yet, but the heavens were bright. Steadily as the blast of some great huntsman's horn, the wind held from the northeast. The sand skimming over the dunes and low hills near the coast was caught up and carried landward and drifted in at crevice and door-chink of the farmhouse. A young seal – lost, no doubt, from the herd that had all day been feeding in the offing – barked and barked incessantly from a rock in the breakers. In the pine tree by the house a huge night-bird, owl or hawk, stirred occasionally with a prolonged note. By and by the weather grew colder, the ground began to freeze and crack. Inside in the main hall of the house, covered by his bearskin cloak, Grettir lay wakeful and watching. He reclined in such a manner – his head pillowed on his arm – that he could see the door. At the other end of the hall the fire of drift was dying down upon the flags. On the other side of the partition, in the next room, lay the bonder, alternately dozing and waking.

The time passed heavily, slowly. From far off toward the shore could be heard the lost seal raising from time to time his hoarse, sobbing bark.

Then at length a dog howled, and an instant after the bonder spoke aloud. He had risen from his bed and stood in the door of his room.

'Hark! Did you not hear something?'

'I hear the barking of the seal,' said Grettir, 'the baying of the hound, the cry of the night-bird, and the break of the surges; nothing else.'

'No. This was a footstep. There. Listen!'

A heavy footfall sounded crunching in the snow from without

and close by. It passed around and in front of the house; and the wooden shutter of a window of the hall was plucked at and shaken. Then an outhouse was attacked – a shed where in Summer time the calves were fed. Grettir could hear the snap and rasp of splintering boards.

'It has a strong arm,' he muttered.

Once more the tread encircled the house. In a very short time it sounded again in the front of the byre.

'It has a long stride,' said Grettir.

The tread ceased. For a long moment there was silence, while the scurrying sand rattled delicately against the house like minute hailstones. Suddenly a corner eave was seized. Something tugged at it, wrenching, and the thatch gave with the long swish of rent linen.

'It has a tall figure,' said Grettir.

For nearly a quarter of an hour these different sounds continued, now distinct, now confused, now distant, now near at hand. Suddenly from overhead there came a jar and a crash, and Grettir felt the dust from the rafters descend upon his face; the Vampire was on the roof. But soon he leaped down and now the footsteps came straight to the door of the hall. The door itself was gripped with colossal strength. In the crescent-shaped openings of the upper panels a hand appeared, black against the faint outside light, groping, picking. It seized upon the edge of the board in the lower bend of the crescent and pulled. The board gave way, ripped to the very doorsill; then an arm followed the hand, reaching for one of the two iron bars with which the door was fenced. Evidently it could not find these, for the effort was soon abandoned and another panel was split and torn away. The cross-panel followed, the nails shrieking as they were drawn from out the wood. Then at last the door, shattered to its very hinges, gave way, leaving only the bars set in the stone sockets of the jamb, and against the square of grey light of the entrance stood, silhouetted, the figure of a monster. Stood but for a moment, for almost at once the bars were pulled out.

The Vampire was within the house, the light from the smouldering logs illuminating the face.

Glamr's face was livid. The pupils of the eyes were white, the hair matted and thick. The whole figure was monstrously enlarged, bulked like a *jotun*, and the vast hands, white as those of the drowned, swung heavily at his sides.

Once in the hall, he stood for a long moment looking from side to side, then moved slowly forward, reaching his great arms overhead, feeling and fumbling with the roof-beams with his fingers, and guiding himself thus from beam to beam.

Grettir, watching, alert, never moved, but lay in his place, his eyes fixed upon the monster.

But at length Glamr made out the form stretched upon the couch and came up and laid hold of a flap of the bearskin under Grettir's shoulders and tugged at it. But Grettir, bracing his feet against the foot-board of the couch, held back with all his strength. Glamr seized the flap in both hands and set his might to the pull, till the tough hide fetched away, and he staggered back, the corner of skin still in his grip. He looked at it stupidly, wondering, bewildered.

Then suddenly the bonder, listening from within his bolted door, heard the muffled crashing shock of the onset. The rafters cracked, the byre shook, the shutters rocked in their grooves, and Grettir, eyes alight, hair flying like a torch, thews rigid as iron, leaped to the attack.

Down upon the hero's arms came the numbing, crushing grip of the dead man's might. One instant of that inhuman embrace and Grettir knew that now peril of his life was toward. Never in all his days of battle and strength had such colossal might risen to match his own. Back bore the wrestlers, back, back toward the sides of the hall. Benches ironed to the wall were overturned, wrenched like paper from their fastenings. The great table crashed and splintered beneath their weight. The floor split with their tramping, and the fire was scattered upon the hearth. Now forward, now back, from side to side and from end to end of the wrecked hall drove the fight. Great of build though the fighters were, huge of bone, big of muscle, they yet leaped and writhed with the agility, the rapidity of young lambs.

But fear was not in Grettir. Never in his life had he been afraid. Only anger shook him, and fine, above-board fury, and the iron will to beat his enemy.

All at once Grettir, his arms gripped about the Vampire's middle, his head beneath the arm-pit, realised that the creature was dragging him toward the door. He fought back from this till the effort sent the blood surging in his ears, for he knew well that ill as the fight had fared within the house it must go worse without. But it was all one that he braced his feet against the broken benches, the wreck of the table, the every unevenness of the floor. The Vampire had gripped him close and dragged and clutched and heaved at his body, so that the white nails drove into his flesh, and the embrace of those arms of steel shut in the ribs till the breath gushed from the nostrils in long gasps of agony.

And now they swayed and grappled in the doorway. Grettir's back was bent like a bow, and Grettir's arms at fullest stretch strained to their sockets, till it seemed as though the very tendons must tear from off the bones. And ever the foul thing above him drew him farther and yet farther from out the entranceway of the house.

'God save you, Grettir!' cried the bonder, 'God save you, brave man and true. Never was such fight as this in all Iceland. Are you spent, Grettir?'

Muffled under the arms of his foe, the voice of Grettir shouted: 'Stand from us. I am much spent, but I fear not.'

Then with the words, feeling the half-sunk stone of the threshold beneath his feet, he bowed his knees, and with his shoulder against the Vampire's breast drove, not, as hitherto, back, but forward, and that with all the power of limb and loin.

The Vampire reeled from the attack. His shoulder crashed against the outer door-case, and with that gigantic shock the roof burst asunder. Down crushed and roared the frozen thatch, and then in that hideous ruin of splintering rafters, grinding stones and wreck of panel and beam the Vampire fell backward and prone to the ground, while Grettir toppled down upon him till his face was against the dead man's face, his eye to his dead eye, his forehead against his front, and the grey bristle of his beard between his teeth.

The moon was bright outside, and all at once, lighted by her rays, Grettir for the first time saw the Vampire's face.

Then the soul of him shrank and sank, and the fear that all his days he had not known leaped to life in his heart. Terror of that glare of the dead man's gaze caught him by the throat, till his grip relaxed, and his strength dwindled away and he crouched there motionless but for his trembling, looking, looking into those blind, white, dead eyes.

And then the Vampire began to speak:

'Eagerly hast thou striven to match thyself with me, and ill hast thou done this night. Now thou art weak with the fear and the rigour of this fight, yet never henceforth shalt thou be stronger than at this moment. Till now thou hast won much fame by great deeds, yet henceforth ill luck shall follow thee and woe and man-slayings and untoward fortune. Outlawed shalt thou be, and thy lot shall be cast in lands far from thine home. Alone shalt thou dwell, and in that loneliness, this weird I lay upon thee: Ever to see these eyes with thine eyes, till the terror of the Dark shall come upon thee and the fear of night, and the twain shall drag thee to thy death and thy undoing.'

As the voice ceased, Grettir's wits and strength returned, and suddenly seizing the hair of the creature in one hand and his short sword in the other, he hewed off the head.

But within the heart of him he knew that the Vampire had said true words, and as he stood looking down upon the great body of his enemy and saw the glazed and fish-like eyes beneath the lids, he could for one instant look ahead to the days of his life yet to be, to the ill fortune that should dog him from henceforth, and knew that at the gathering of each night's dusk the eyes of Glamr would look into his.

Thorhall came out when the fight was done, praising God for the issue, and he and Grettir together burned the body and, wrapping the ashes in a skin, buried them in a far corner of the sheep walks.

In the morning Thorhall gave Grettir the piebald horse and new clothes and set him a mile on his road. They rode through the Vale of Shadows and kissed each other farewell on the shore where the road led away toward Waterdale.

The clouds had gathered again during the dawn and the rain was falling, driven landward by the incessant wind. The seals again barked and hunted in the offing, and the rough-haired ponies once more wandered about on the beach snuffing at the kelp and seaweed.

Long time Thorhall stood on the ridge watching the figure of Grettir grow small and indistinct in the waste of north country and under the blur of the rain. Then at last he turned back to the byre.

But Grettir after these things rode on to Biarg, to his mother's house, and sat at home through the winter.

Medusa

Phil Robinson (1847–1902)

Born in India, the son of an army chaplain, Philip Stewart Robinson was educated in England at Marlborough College and then returned to his native land to work as a journalist and teacher. In his thirties he left India again to join the Daily Telegraph *in London and, for the next twenty years, he was a correspondent for that paper and others throughout the world. He reported from Afghanistan and Zululand, Egypt during the Anglo-Egyptian War of 1882 and Cuba during the Spanish-American War of 1898. In his lifetime, Robinson was admired for his tales set in India and, soon after his death, was described as a 'pioneer of Anglo-Indian literature' and someone who 'anticipated Mr Rudyard Kipling's early devotion to Indian themes'. Today, if he is remembered at all, it is for his speculative fiction which includes 'The Hunting of the Soko', a short story about a hunter in Africa coming across an enigmatic creature as much human as ape, and the self-explanatory 'The Man-Eating Tree'. 'The Last of the Vampires' might seem from its title to be an ideal candidate for inclusion in this anthology but it is actually the tale of a paleontological discovery in the Amazonian jungle. 'Medusa', which appeared in a 1902 collection of stories by Robinson and his two younger brothers entitled* Tales by Three Brothers, *features a woman who may or may not be a member of the undead but is certainly a 'psychic' vampire.*

It was on the 17th of June that the world read in its morning paper that James Westerby had died suddenly in his office at Whitehall on the preceding day. The world may still, if its memory be jogged a little, be able to remember that the cause of death was said to have been heart disease, the crisis having been accelerated by overwork. As to the sadness of the event, the newspapers of all political shades agreed.

James Westerby would have been a prominent man, even if he had not been an Under Secretary and one of the pleasantest speakers in the House of Commons. He was of the Westerbys of Oxfordshire, the last, I fear, of a fine old line. 'Hotspur' Westerby, of revolutionary fame, was one of his ancestors, and the Under Secretary prided himself not a little on his resemblance to the old hero, whom Cromwell hated so cordially. His father's place is secure in the world of letters. James Westerby promised to be worthy of his blood. Still young (he died when he was thirty-nine), he had borne himself admirably in public position; and when he died there were not wanting some who spoke of his loss as a national calamity.

To me his death was a personal sorrow. I was, and had been since his appointment, fifteen months before, his private secretary; and, previous to that again, for the twelve years since I came down from the 'Varsity we had been intimate friends, though he was some years my senior.

On the morning of that 16th day of June I was sitting at my desk as usual, between the ante-room and his private office. The last person who had been admitted to his presence was a lady, who, dressed in black and closely veiled, made at the time no distinct impression on my mind. The Under Secretary had refused admittance to some ten or twelve people that morning, but, on my handing him this lady's card, he told me to admit her. She was with him for, perhaps, half an hour. It must have been about 11 o'clock when she passed out. It was just 11.30 when I went into his office and found him dead in his chair.

Some of these facts – with many more or less imaginative details – were presented to the world by the morning papers, as already mentioned, of the 17th. But in no paper was any mention made of the veiled lady, for the altogether sufficient reason that no representative of any paper knew of the veiled lady's existence.

At about a quarter before twelve we were standing – two or three others of the higher employees of the department and myself – in my office, waiting for the arrival of the doctor. The door of the Under Secretary's private room was closed. In the excitement the doorkeeper in the ante-room had presumably deserted his post, for, seeing those to whom I was talking glance toward the outer door, I turned and found myself again confronting the veiled lady.

'Can I see Mr Westerby once more?' she asked.

'Mr Westerby, madam,' I answered, 'is dead.'

She did not reply at once, but with both hands raised her veil as if to obtain a clearer view of my face, to see if I spoke the truth. In doing so, she showed me the most beautiful face that I have ever seen, or ever expect to see. One dreams of such eyes. Perhaps Endymion looked into them. But I had never hoped to see them in a woman's face. I scarcely remember that she murmured in a low, incredulous but very musical voice, the one word…

'Dead?'

'He died, madam, suddenly, less than an hour ago.'

We had been standing, as we spoke, within earshot of the others. She now drew back to where my desk stood, in the further corner of the room, whither I followed her.

'Was any one with him after I left, can you remember?' she asked.

'No, madam, I had no occasion to go into his room for some little time after you went. When I did so, he was dead.'

It was some time before she spoke again; then…

'Excuse me,' she said, hesitatingly, 'but I hope I shall not have to appear in connection with this. You can understand how very much I should dislike' – this with the faintest smile – 'to have my name in all the newspapers. Of course, if there is an inquest, and if my evidence can be of service, I shall have to give it. But it does not seem to me that anything I can say could be of importance. He was well when I saw him – that is all.'

Then, after a pause, during which I was silent: 'If you can manage it so that my name will not be mentioned, I shall be very grateful to you,' she said. As she spoke, she drew one of her cards from a small black card case and handed it to me, adding, 'and I hope you will call and let me have the pleasure of thanking you.'

I took the card and assured her that I would do what I could in her behalf. She lowered her veil again and left the room. I read the card now with more interest than I had the former one when taking it to my chief. It said:

Mrs Walter F Tierce,
19, Grasmere Crescent, W

Mrs Tierce had hardly gone when the doctor came in, followed a moment later by a police inspector.

'Heart disease,' the doctor said. The inspector asked me a few questions and said that no inquest would be necessary.

I was hardly conscious at the time, I think, that I was telling the officer that no one had been with the Under Secretary for an hour before his death. Nor when it was over and I recognised what I had done, did my conscience disturb me much. It was a mere courtesy to a woman, such as any man would do if he had it in his power. Why should she be made to suffer because he chanced to die about the time that she happened to call upon him?

So the world next morning heard nothing of the veiled lady.

Within a month I was back in my old chambers in Lincoln's Inn trying to gather up the interrupted threads of my legal studies – a task which would, perhaps, have progressed more rapidly if it had received my entire attention. As it was, however, work had to be content to divide my thoughts somewhat unequally with another subject – Mrs Walter Tierce.

Mrs Tierce was a widow. When I called at her home immediately after the funeral, she met me with delightful cordiality.

I called frequently after my first visit, and never met any other visitor at the house. It was difficult to understand how so charming a woman could live in a fashionable quarter of London in such complete isolation. But I had no desire that it should be otherwise.

At the age of thirty-five I had settled down, more or less reconciled to the belief that I should never marry. In theory, I have always maintained that it is the duty to himself and to society of every healthy man to take to himself a wife and assume the responsibilities of a householder before he is thirty years of age. A bachelor's life is an inchoate existence; a species of half-life at best – 'like the odd half of a pair of scissors', as Benjamin Franklin said. It is as the head of a family alone, with the care of others on his shoulders, that a man arrives at the possibility of his best development. This was my loudly proclaimed belief. And still I was unmarried. If one could only wake some morning and find himself married – in his own house, with a charming and domestic wife – perhaps with children! But the necessary preliminaries to arriving at that state terrified me. The difficulty of a selection (in the face of an apparently incurable incapacity of falling seriously in love with any one individual) was appalling.

But now the picture of a home rose frequently before me, altogether pleasant to contemplate – a home in which two wonderful black eyes smiled at me across the breakfast tablecloth in the morning and were waiting to meet mine as I looked up from my reading in our library at night.

In fact, I was in love – at times. But there were also times when my condition seemed, on analysis, curiously unsatisfactory to myself, curiously contradictory. Especially was this the case immediately after being in Mrs Tierce's presence, when there was a certain reaction. On leaving her home, I never failed to ask myself wonderingly, if I really loved her as a man should love a woman before asking her to be his wife. She filled all my thoughts by day and a large share of my dreams by night. Those eyes haunted me. In her presence I was helpless – intoxicated – a blind worshipper. I longed to touch her with my hands, to stroke the fabric of her dress or any object which her hands had recently touched. My whole being ached with very tenderness to approach more nearly to her – to be in contact with her – to caress her. The physical attraction of her presence was overmastering.

Fifteen minutes after leaving her, however, I would be dimly wondering if this was really love – the love that a husband should feel for a wife. This absolute submission of my individuality to hers – would it last through days and weeks and months of constant companionship? Through all the stress of years of wedded life? And if it did not, if my individuality asserted itself, and I became critical of her, what then?

Not that her beauty was her only attraction. On the contrary, few women whom I have ever met have impressed me more distinctly with their intellectuality.

But her most charming characteristic was a certain admirable self-possession and self-control. She seemed so thoroughly to understand herself and to know what was her right relation to things around her; and this without a suspicion of masculinity or of the business air. Never for a moment was there danger of her losing either her mental or emotional equilibrium.

In fact, she was adorable. But, though there was no point of view from which she did not seem to me to be entirely the most delightful thing that I had ever seen, I never failed to experience that same misgiving immediately after quitting her presence. It was as short-lived as it was regular in its recurrence. An hour later, as I sat in my chambers alone, her eyes haunted me once more.

Though I had never spoken of my love, she must have read it in my eyes a hundred times, nor apparently was the perusal distasteful to her.

I had been back in Lincoln's Inn now five months, and was sitting in my chambers one dark mid-afternoon in December. Had I been reading, I must have lit the gas. But there was light enough to sit and dream of her; light enough to see those eyes in the shadow of my bookcase. My one clerk was away and would not return for an hour. So I dreamed uninterruptedly until a shuffling outside my office door recalled me to myself. It would have looked more businesslike in the eyes of a client to have light enough in the room to work by, and I made a movement toward the matchbox. But there was no time. A knock at the door sounded and the door itself was thrown wide open. There was an interval of some seconds and then a figure entered, moving heavily and painfully with the aid of a crutch – a man and crippled, that was all that I could see.

The figure moved laboriously halfway across the floor toward me. Then, standing on one foot, the visitor placed his crutch against the wall and allowed himself to drop heavily into a chair a few feet away from me, while I stood looking on, mutely anxious to render assistance but not knowing how to offer it.

After a short silence he spoke, simply pronouncing my name; not interrogatively, but as if to inform me that he knew to whom he was speaking and that his business was with me. I bowed in response, and with matter-of-fact business suavity asked what I could do for him.

He was silent for some moments, and as he sat fronting the window to which my back was turned, and through which came what small light there was in the office, I could see his face plainly enough. Not an old man, by any means, probably younger than myself, with features that must once have been handsome, and would be still but for the deep lines of sorrow or of pain. The figure, too, as he sat, looked full and healthy with nothing but a certain stiffness of pose to tell of its infirmity. At last he spoke, hurriedly, and in a hard, feverish-sounding voice.

'Nothing, thank you. You can do nothing for me. I have come to do something for you, instead.' I bowed acknowledgment.

'I have come to warn you,' he went on, still hurriedly and shifting uneasily in his seat, like one who has an unpleasant thing to tell and is anxious to be over with it. The strangeness of his voice and manner, and the intentness – almost the fierceness – with which he looked at me, made me uneasy in my turn. I doubted his sanity, and wished that there was more light or that my clerk was present.

'I came to warn you,' he said again, and I saw his hands moving nervously as he leaned toward me and spoke harshly and quickly. 'You are in love with her – with Mrs Tierce. No; don't deny it. I know, I know, and before heaven, if I can save you I will.'

The heaviness of his breathing told the intensity of the excitement under which he was labouring as he went on, edging further forward on his chair and reaching out his hands toward me;

'She is not a woman; she is not human. Yes, I know how beautiful she is; how helpless a man must be before her. I have known it for six years; and had I not known it I should not now be what I am. You will think me mad,' he said. 'You probably think me so now. I do not wonder at it. What else should you think when a stranger comes into your chambers and tells you that in these matter-of-fact nineteenth-century days there exist beings who are not human – who have more than human attributes, and that one of these beings is the woman whom you love?'

He was quieter now, more serious, and spoke almost argumentatively, as one who seeks only to convince, while he almost despaired of doing it.

'You are laughing at me now – or pitying me; but I call the Almighty God to witness that I speak the truth – if a God can be almighty and let her live. I tell you, sir, that to know her is death. If you do not believe me you will become worse than I am – as her husband is who died at her feet here in London – as the American is who died before her in the cafe at Nice – as heaven only knows how many more are who have crossed her path.'

Of course I had no doubt of his madness; but his earnestness – the utter strength of conviction with which he spoke – was strangely moving. That he, poor fellow, believed what he said, it was impossible to doubt.

'It is six years since I saw her first at Havre, in France. I chanced to be seated at the next table to her at Frascati's, and I knew that I loved her then. The American was with her. I followed her to Cannes, to Trouville, to Monaco, to Nice; and where she went the American went, too. There was no impropriety in their companionship, but he followed her as I did; only that he had her acquaintance and I had not. And I knew, or thought I knew, that it would be useless for me to try and win her while he was there. He evidently worshipped her, and she – for he was a handsome fellow (Reading was his name) – seemed to care for him. So I watched her from a distance, waiting and hoping; and as I have told you my turn came.

'It was in the Cafe Royal, and nobody saw it happen but herself. Suddenly she rushed out from the corner where they were sitting and called for help. Every one crowded around, and he was dead – dead in his chair, with his face upturned and his eyes fixed, staring like one suddenly terrified. They said it was heart disease. Heart disease!'

It had grown almost dark, and he drew his chair close to me. The paling light from the window just showed me the worn face and the sunken, feverish eyes.

'Then I came to know her,' he continued, after a pause. 'I hung upon her as he had done, and for three months I believed that I was the happiest man in Europe. In Venice, in Florence, in Paris, in London, I was constantly with her, day after day. She seemed to love me, and in the Bois or in Hyde Park how proud I was to be seen by her side! Then she went to stay for a month at Oxford, and I, with her permission, followed her there, and would call for her at the Mitre every morning. Under the shadow of the grey college walls and in the well-trimmed walks and gardens, it seemed that her face put on a new and holier beauty in keeping with the place. There it was that I told her that I loved her and asked her to be my wife, as we stood for a minute to rest in the cloisters of Christ Church.'

His voice was very sad. It had lost its harshness, and as he remembered – or did he only imagine? – the sweetness of those days of love-making, there was more of a soft regretfulness than of anger in his tones.

'She did not refuse me,' he said, 'nor did she explicitly accept me. But I was idiotically happy – happy for three whole days – until that afternoon in the Magdalen Walks, when in ten minutes I became, from a healthy, strong man, the wreck you see me now.'

The regretfulness was all gone, and the hard, fierce ring was in his voice again as he went on:

'It was on one of the benches in Addison's Walk, as they call it, and I pressed her for some more definite promise than she had yet given me. She did not seem to listen to me, to heed me, as she leaned back, her hands lying idly in her lap and her great, grave eyes looking out across the meadow. I grew more passionate; clasped her hands and begged for an answer. At last she turned her face towards me. I met her eyes...'

His voice broke and he stopped speaking. For a minute or more we sat in silence in the twilight, his face buried in his hands. Then he raised his head again, and in slow, unimpassioned accents, continued:

'As our eyes met, hers looked lustreless, hardly as if she saw me or was looking at me. But as I gazed into them they changed. Somewhere inside them, or behind them, a flame was lit. The pupils expanded, black and brilliant as eyes never shone before. What was it? Was it love? And leaning still closer, I gazed more intensely into the eyes that seemed now to blaze before me. And as I looked the spell came upon me. It was as though I swooned. Dimly I became aware that I was losing my power of motion, of speech, of thought. The eyes engulfed me. I was vaguely conscious that I must somehow disengage myself from the spell that was upon me; but I could not. I was powerless, and she – it was as if she fed upon my very life. I cannot phrase it otherwise. I was numb, and, though I tried to speak, could not move one muscle. Then consciousness began to leave me, and I was on the point of – God knows what – swoon or death – when the crunching of feet on the gravel path came sharply to my ears.

'Who it was that passed I do not know. I know not how long

I sat there. I remember that she rose without a word and left me. When I moved it was evening. The sun was behind the college walls, and the walk was dark. With my brain hardly awake and my lower limbs still benumbed, slowly I made my way out of the college gates and up the High Street to the Clarendon Hotel, where I was staying. Next morning I awoke what you see me now – a cripple, a paralytic for life.'

During all this narrative I had sat silent, engrossed in the madman's tale. As a piece of dramatic elocution, it was magnificent. When he finished I cast about for some commonplace remark to make, but in the state of my feelings it was not easy to find one, and it was he who again broke the silence:

'Tierce, poor fool! I warned him as I am warning you. It was two years afterward that she married him, and in two weeks more he was dead – dead in their house in Park Lane – died of heart disease! Heart disease!'

And as he said it, I could not help thinking of James Westerby.

My visitor was about to speak again when a footfall sounded on the stairs outside, the door opened, and my clerk stood in the entrance, astonished at the darkness.

'Come in, Jackson,' I called, to let him know that I was there, 'and light the gas, please.'

My visitor rose painfully, and again took his crutch.

'I have told you all that is vital to the case,' he said in the matter-of-fact voice of a client addressing his attorney, 'and you will, of course, do as you think best.'

Jackson, about to light the gas, with a burning match in his hand, held the door open for the stranger to pass out, and without another word the cripple moved laboriously away. It was not until he had gone that it occurred to me that I had not asked nor been told his name.

'Has that gentleman ever called before, Jackson?'

'I think not, sir.'

But probably I should meet him again.

And now, my thoughts reverted to her. He was mad, of

course: and his story was absurd. But as I walked home from the office, those eyes were before me, blazing with the passion which he had lit in them. What eyes they were in truth! How lovely, and how I loved them! And how easy, too, it was to imagine them dilating and engulfing one's senses until he swooned!

I had not hoped to see her again that day, having spent part of the morning in 'helping her to shop', and expecting to escort her to the theatre on the evening following. So after a solitary dinner at a restaurant, I climbed up to my chambers to dream away the evening alone.

The story which I had heard a few hours before certainly had not in any way altered my feelings towards Mrs Tierce. Indeed, I hardly thought of the story, except to pity the poor fellow who told it and to speculate upon his history. Who was he? Had he loved her and gone mad for love of her? And should I tell her of his visit? It might pain her by bringing up unpleasant memories; but on the other hand I should like to know something more of the cripple's history.

But I was restless, and my rooms seemed more than ever lonely and unhomelike that evening; so about nine o'clock, I put on my hat and overcoat and went out into the street.

It was a cold night, damp and raw, with no sign of starlight or moonlight overhead, and a heavy, misty atmosphere through which the street lights shone blurred and twinkling.

Instinctively I turned westward, and, as a matter of course, set my face towards Grasmere Crescent, not with any intention of calling at the house, but with a lover's longing to see it and to be near to her. I passed the house on the opposite side of the street. No. 19 had a large bow window in the drawing room, on the first floor, and as I approached, the blind of the narrow side window facing me being raised some few inches gave a glimpse of the brightly lighted, daintily furnished room, with which I was so familiar, within. I had hoped to catch a glimpse of her, but in the small segment of the room that was visible through the aperture, no figure was to be seen.

After passing on to the end of the street I made a circuit round some by-streets and so back to Grasmere Crescent. As I approached now from the north the house looked dark, save for a narrowest chink of light which outlined the edge of the bow window. When I had passed I turned to look back at the window of which the blind was raised; and doing so, I saw a curious thing.

It was only instantaneous; but just for that instant I saw two figures standing, herself and one of the servants, whom I recognised. They were facing one another, each, it seemed, leaning slightly forward. But even as I looked, the servant suddenly threw up her hands and fell – fell straight backward, rigidly, as if in a fit. Mrs Tierce started towards the falling girl, as if to catch her. The movement took her out of my range of vision, the projecting woodwork of the window intervening.

It all happened so suddenly that I stood for a moment bewildered and irresolute. Had I really seen it? It was more like some tableau on a stage, or the flash of a slide from a magic lantern, than a reality.

Recovering my senses, my first impulse was to cross the street and offer my services. But why? The girl had but slipped suddenly upon the polished floor, and doubtless they were laughing over it now. It would be an impertinence for me to thrust myself in with a confession of having been playing spy. So, after standing and gazing at the window for a few moments, during which I once saw Mrs Tierce pass quickly across the room and back, I moved on to my rooms.

The next morning as I sat at breakfast, a note was brought to me.

'I am very sorry,' she wrote, 'to interfere with your theatre party this evening, but a dreadful thing happened here last night. One of my servants – Mary, you know her – died very suddenly. I was talking to her, when she simply threw up her hands and fell down before me, dead. Regretting that I must ask you to excuse me, I am,

Yours cordially,
Edith Tierce'

I wished now that I had obeyed my first impulse on the preceding evening and had rung at the door to volunteer my services. I would certainly go and see her immediately after breakfast.

Fortunately my theatre party included only two other persons besides Mrs Tierce and myself, and I was on sufficiently intimate terms with John Bradstreet and his wife to have no fear of offending them. So I wrote Mrs Bradstreet a short note explaining the situation briefly, enclosing the tickets and hoping she would use the box or not, as she saw fit. Then I drove at once to Grasmere Crescent.

In her quiet, self-possessed way Mrs Tierce had already done all that was necessary, and I found that there was little excuse for thrusting my services upon her. Still I saw her frequently during the next two days, though never for any length of time and rarely to talk of things not associated immediately with the melancholy ceremony that was impending. The dead girl seemed to have had no family connections, and the funeral was conducted under Mrs Tierce's directions. I accompanied her to the church and cemetery, and left her at her own door afterwards, accepting an invitation to call again that evening.

I have spoken before of the curious self-possession, an imperturbable self-reliance, which Mrs Tierce possessed and which sat very becomingly upon her delicate grave face. Never had this quality in her seemed more admirably perfect to me than during those days when the shadow of death hung over her home.

On the evening of the day of the funeral, she was even more reposeful than usual, in a dreamy mood in which I had seen her before more than once, and in which she seemed hardly conscious of – or rather inattentive to – what passed around her. This mood of hers the cripple had recalled to me when describing the scene in the Oxford walk.

It may have been that the events and scenes of the last few days, with all their appeals to the emotions, had predisposed us both to tenderness. Certainly from the time of my entry when our greeting had been only a hand-clasp, with hardly an audible word on either side, we had spoken constrainedly, in undertones and on personal topics. Though more than once I strove desperately to be matter-of-fact, my voice in spite of myself would sink, and wherever the conversation started from, it ended in herself.

At last some chance word of hers made me broach a subject which I had never approached before, and which she rarely alluded to – her late husband. Before I was conscious of what I was doing, I had said:

'It is not, by any means, I know, your first contact with death. You have told me very little of Mr Tierce.'

'No,' she said dreamily, 'there is little to tell. We were only married a few weeks.'

And then:

'And is it not possible that you might marry again? Could you not?' and I crossed from my chair to take a seat on the sofa by her side, 'could you not – is there any hope for me?'

Instead of replying, she sat silent and inattentive, her large swimming eyes looking far into either the past or the future – I wondered which.

'Tell me,' I urged, laying my hand on one of hers, as it rested in her lap, 'tell me, is there any hope?'

She did not move, did not answer me. Again I implored her, and at last she spoke, but with seeming irrelevance.

'Did you ever hear of the Court of Love?' she asked, 'the court over which the Countess Ermengarde presided in the tenth or eleventh century?'

No, I knew nothing of the Court of Love or the Countess Ermengarde, though I have since looked them up.

'The Court decided, and the decision was affirmed by a later Court composed of half the queens and duchesses of Europe, that true love could not exist between married persons.'

'But you do not believe it? That was nine centuries ago; and how should queens and duchesses know anything of love?'

'I do not know whether I believe it or not,' she murmured, and turned her head as it lay on the cushions of the sofa, to look at me with eyes that still seemed strangely dreamy and far away.

'But you do know,' I urged impulsively, leaning forward till my face was dangerously close to hers. 'You know that you do not believe it. You know that I should always love you – that I must always love you. And if I may love you as my wife...'

She smiled faintly, charmingly, but did not answer me.

'My darling,' I whispered, 'say something! Am I to be utterly happy?'

And still she did not answer; but leaned back with the faint half-smile on her lips, and her great inscrutable eyes looking into and through mine. Then in the silence and suspense, the cripple's story came into my mind. No wonder that he should believe that he had been fascinated in some mysterious way – spellbound, benumbed – by those eyes! No wonder! And still I looked into them; and still they looked through mine. I forgot the nearness of her lips; forgot that I held her hand. I thought only of, saw only, those eyes. And still I thought only of the cripple and vaguely pitied him.

But somehow – when it began I knew not – I found that the expression of the eyes had changed. They were no longer dreamy and far away, but intensely earnest, with a passion in them that was almost hunger.

'Yes,' I thought to myself (and I must have smiled in thinking it), 'this is what he described. No wonder that they seemed to him to flame. They are not looking at my eyes now, but through, into my brain, into me. My eyes are no more than two pieces of glass in the path of her vision.' And I felt a curious, half-gratified recognition of the accuracy of the other's description. And still the eyes seemed to expand until they were many times larger than my own; till I could see nothing but them.

Have you ever, in a half-darkened room, set your face close against a mirror and looked into your own eyes and seen what terrible things they are; how the view of everything else is shut out and all your sense is drawn into the pupils confronting you? So I felt my whole being concentrating itself in – merging itself into – drowning in – her eyes. A strange feeling of intoxication possessed me; of ecstasy. I could have laughed aloud, but that it seemed as if to do it I would somehow have to summon my faculties from too far away.

At what point this strange calmness gave way to conscious fear, I do not know. I saw the pupils of her eyes expanding and contracting, as if with the regular beats of a passionate pulse behind them. I saw, or rather I was aware, that the colour flushed into her cheeks and died again, that her breath, which was warm on my face, came short and gasping. Her lips closed and parted, moist and glistening, suggesting to me somehow the craving of some animal in the presence of food which it could not reach. Her nostrils dilated, quivering, and her whole being strained with a passion which seemed carnivorous.

'It was as if she preyed upon my very life,' he had said, and I understood him now. But the memory of the cripple was fading from me. I was conscious only of myself and of her; of the terror of her fierce hunger and my own helplessness. The power of motion was gone from me; even volition seemed slipping away. The burning of her eyes was in my brain which was as if laid open before her; as a hollow dish set open to the scorching sun. I was utterly at her mercy, without power of resistance; and as her breath grew yet more rapid and more heavy, I knew that she was in some way inhaling my very life.

Suddenly a flash of fear passed across her face – a spasm of agonised disappointment. For a moment it was as if she would, in one long, indrawn breath, draw the last of my strength from me; and then a man's voice sounded in my ear.

'I hope I am in time!'

She had fallen reclining against the cushions of the sofa. I looked up dazedly, and the cripple stood in the centre of the room, his hat in his hand.

'You had better let me take you away,' he said, and I heard it half consciously. Turning to look at her, I saw her lie panting and exhausted. I cannot tell the horror of her appearance. Her eyes still sought mine hungrily as before. Her hands, lying in her lap, fumbled each other, her fingers knotting and intertwining. Her lips moved, and all her body quivered with passion. It was a dreadful fancy, but I could liken her to nothing but some bloodsucking thing; some human leech or vampire, torn from its prey, quivering dumbly with its unsated appetite.

At the time I only half understood what passed around me. I knew that the danger was over and that escape lay before me. I saw the cripple waiting for me to rise and was conscious of the horror with which she inspired me. But I was bewildered. My brain seemed numb, and when I endeavoured to stand up my limbs refused their office. Seeing my powerlessness the cripple moved forward and with his healthy arm assisted me. It was with difficulty that I stood, for there was no sensation in my feet or legs and it was only by leaning on my companion that I made my way laboriously to the door.

No word had been spoken beyond the two sentences which the cripple had uttered. Reaching the door of the room I turned to look at her once more, supporting myself against the door post. She had not moved. Under the influence of the passion that was upon her she evidently had no other thought or emotion. There was no sign of shame or confusion on her face; nothing but the blind craving for the prey that was being taken from her. Even there, across the full width of the room, her eyes sought mine with the same despairing longing. But she only made me shudder now. The cripple still supporting me, we passed together from the house.

Of the remainder of that evening my memory is confused and faint. I know that I was helped to my chambers and that there, with the assistance of the cripple and some third person, though who, or whence or where he joined us, I know not, I was put to bed. That night was one long, half-waking swoon, and far into the next afternoon I lay motionless upon my back without speaking or wishing to speak, save only to tell the woman who took care of my rooms that I needed no help or food. As the twilight fell the same good woman came again, and yet again late at night. But I was scarcely conscious, and had no wishes. Even speech was an effort.

For seven days, all through the Christmas holidays, I lay in this state, taking little nourishment; hardly speaking, hardly thinking clearly. At last, on the day after Christmas, I found courage and strength to attack the mail which had been accumulating on my sick-room table. I had expected to find her handwriting on one at least of the envelopes. In this I was disappointed. But some instinct led me to open first one envelope the address of which was written in a hand that was strange to me. It contained nothing but a newspaper clipping:

'A sad accident occurred last night at 19 Grasmere Crescent, W. The house was inhabited by Mrs Walter Tierce, the widow of the late Walter Tierce, Esq. Last evening Mrs Tierce, who was twenty-six years of age, retired to rest as usual. This morning she failed to answer the knock of the servant at the door, and on the maid entering the room she noticed a strong and peculiar odour. She was frightened and went out and fetched another servant. The two entered the room and found Mrs Tierce dead, and an overturned bottle of chloroform by the pillow. It was evidently an accident, and no inquest will be held. A curious coincidence in connection with the sad affair is that this is the second death in the same house within a week. On Monday last, a maid in the service of Mrs Tierce died suddenly of heart disease. Her funeral occurred yesterday afternoon, when Mrs Tierce attended it.'

Attached to this clipping with a pin was the date line of the evening newspaper from which it was taken – 'Friday, December 19th'. That was the day after that terrible evening, and a week ago now. The funeral must have already taken place.

Though, as I have said, the handwriting on the envelope was unfamiliar to me, I had my conjecture as to whom the message was from, and after keeping the envelope for all these years, the clue has come which shows that the conjecture was correct. Six weeks ago I received information that I had been appointed executor of the estate of the late James Livingston, of Hereford. James Livingston? The name was unknown to me. Thinking that there might be some mistake, I called at the solicitor's office from which the intimation came. No, there was no mistake, the solicitor informed me; he had drawn up the will, and Mr Livingston had given him special instructions how to communicate with me.

'And you say you never knew him at all?' he asked musingly, 'that is certainly curious for he seemed to know you. But you could not well have forgotten him. He was a cripple – almost entirely paralysed in his right side.'

The Stone Chamber

HB Marriott Watson (1863–1921)

Born in Melbourne, Australia and brought up in New Zealand, Marriott Watson came to England as a young man to earn his living as a journalist. He came to know many of the major literary figures of his time, from George Bernard Shaw to Thomas Hardy, and he collaborated with Peter Pan-*author JM Barrie on a play about the eighteenth-century poet Richard Savage. The great scandal of Watson's life was his relationship with Rosamund Tomson, a fin-de-siècle poet who published her work under the name Graham R Tomson and who had already been twice married when she met him. She left her second husband for Watson and they lived together for many years without marrying. She died of cancer in 1911. Devastated by her death and by the later loss of their son who was killed in the First World War, Watson grew to depend on alcohol in his later years and died of cirrhosis of the liver at the age of fifty-seven. Best known for swashbuckling historical fiction (*The Adventures of Galloping Dick, Godfrey Merivale, Captain Fortune, *etc.), Watson also published many stories of the supernatural. Of these the best-known – and the only one to qualify as a vampire story – is 'The Stone Chamber' which appeared in a volume entitled* The Heart of Miranda and Other Stories, *published in 1898 and dedicated to Henry James.*

It was not until early summer that Warrington took possession of Marvyn Abbey. He had bought the property in the preceding autumn, but the place had so fallen into decay through the disorders of time that more than six months elapsed ere it was inhabitable. The delay, however, fell out conveniently for Warrington; for the Bosanquets spent the winter abroad, and nothing must suit but he must spend it with them. There was never a man who pursued his passion with such ardour. He was ever at Miss Bosanquet's skirts, and bade fair to make her as steadfast a husband as he was attached a lover. Thus it was not until after his return from that prolonged exile that he had the opportunity of inspecting the repairs discharged by his architect. He was nothing out of the common in character, but was full of kindly impulses and a fellow of impetuous blood. When he called upon me in my chambers he spoke with some excitement of his Abbey, as also of his approaching marriage; and finally, breaking into an exhibition of genuine affection, declared that we had been so long and so continuously intimate that I, and none other, must help him warm his house and marry his bride. It had indeed been always understood between us that I should serve him at the ceremony, but now it appeared that I must start my duties even earlier. The prospect of a summer holiday in Utterbourne pleased me. It was a charming village, set upon the slope of a wooded hill and within call of the sea. I had a slight knowledge of the district from a riding excursion taken through that part of Devonshire; and years before, and ere Warrington had come into his money, had viewed the Abbey ruins from a distance with the polite curiosity of a passing tourist.

I examined them now with new eyes as we drove up the avenue. The face which the ancient building presented to the valley was of magnificent design, but now much worn and battered.

Part of it, the right wing, I judged to be long past the uses of a dwelling, for the walls had crumbled away, huge gaps opened in the foundations, and the roof was quite dismantled.

Warrington had very wisely left this portion to its own sinister decay; it was the left wing which had been restored, and which we were to inhabit. The entrance, I will confess, was a little mean, for the large doorway had been bricked up and an ordinary modern door gave upon the spacious terrace and the winding gardens. But apart from this, the work of restoration had been undertaken with skill and piety, and the interior had retained its native dignity, while resuming an air of proper comfort. The old oak had been repaired congruous with the original designs, and the great rooms had been as little altered as was requisite to adapt them for daily use.

Warrington passed quickly from chamber to chamber in evident delight, directing my attention upon this and upon that, and eagerly requiring my congratulations and approval. My comments must have satisfied him, for the place attracted me vastly. The only criticism I ventured was to remark upon the size of the rooms and to question if they might dwarf the insignifcant human figures they were to entertain.

He laughed. 'Not a bit,' said he. 'Roaring fires in winter in those fine old fireplaces; and as for summer, the more space the better. We shall be jolly.'

I followed him along the noble hall, and we stopped before a small door of very black oak.

'The bedrooms,' he explained, as he turned the key, 'are all upstairs, but mine is not ready yet. And besides, I am reserving it; I won't sleep in it till – you understand,' he concluded, with a smiling suggestion of embarrassment.

I understood very well. He threw the door open.

'I am going to use this in the meantime,' he continued. 'Queer little room, isn't it? It used to be a sort of library. How do you think it looks?'

We had entered as he spoke, and stood, distributing our glances in that vague and general way in which a room is surveyed. It was a chamber of much smaller proportions than the rest, and was dimly lighted by two long narrow windows sunk in the great walls. The bed and the modern fittings looked strangely out of keeping with its ancient privacy. The walls were rudely distempered with barbaric frescos, dating, I conjectured, from the fourteenth century; and the floor was of stone, worn into grooves and hollows with the feet of many generations. As I was taking in these facts, there came over me a sudden curiosity as to those dead Marvyns who had held the Abbey for so long.

This silent chamber seemed to suggest questions of their history; it spoke eloquently of past ages and past deeds, fallen now into oblivion. Here, within these thick walls, no echo from the outer world might carry, no sound would ring within its solitary seclusion. Even the silence seemed to confer with one upon the ancient transactions of that extinct House.

Warrington stirred, and turned suddenly to me. 'I hope it's not damp,' said he, with a slight shiver. 'It looks rather solemn. I thought furniture would brighten it up.'

'I should think it would be very comfortable,' said I. 'You will never be disturbed by any sounds at any rate.'

'No,' he answered, hesitatingly; and then, quickly, on one of his impulses: 'Hang it, Heywood, there's too much silence here for me.' Then he laughed. 'Oh, I shall do very well for a month or two.' And with that appeared to return to his former placid cheerfulness.

The train of thought started in that sombre chamber served to entertain me several times that day. I questioned Warrington at dinner, which we took in one of the smaller rooms, commanding a lovely prospect of dale and sea. He shook his head. Archaeological lore, as indeed anything else out of the borders of actual life, held very little interest for him.

'The Marvyns died out in 1714, I believe,' he said, indifferently; 'someone told me that – the man I bought it from, I think. They might just as well have kept the place up since; but I think it has been only occupied twice between then and now, and the last time was forty years ago. It would have rotted to pieces if I hadn't taken it. Perhaps Mrs Batty could tell you. She's lived in these parts almost all her life.'

To humour me, and affected, I doubt not, by a certain pride in his new possession, he put the query to his housekeeper upon her appearance subsequently; but it seemed that her knowledge was little fuller than his own, though she had gathered some vague traditions of the countryside.

The Marvyns had not left a reputable name, if rumour spoke

truly; theirs was a family to which black deeds had been credited. They were ill-starred also in their fortunes, and had become extinct suddenly; but for the rest, the events had fallen too many generations ago to be current now between the memories of the village.

Warrington, who was more eager to discuss the future than to recall the past, was vastly excited by his anticipations. St Pharamond, Sir William Bosanquet's house, lay across the valley, barely five miles away; and as the family had now returned, it was easy to forgive Warrington's elation.

'What do you think?' he said, late that evening; and clapping me upon the shoulder, 'You have seen Marion; here is the house. Am I not lucky? Damn it, Heywood, I'm not pious, but I am disposed to thank God! I'm not a bad fellow, but I'm no saint; it's fortunate that it's not only the virtuous that are rewarded. In fact, it's usually contrariwise. I owe this to – Lord, I don't know what I owe it to. Is it my money? Of course, Marion doesn't care a rap for that; but then, you see, I mightn't have known her without it. Of course, there's the house, too. I'm thankful I have money. At any rate, here's my new life. Just look about and take it in, old fellow. If you knew how a man may be ashamed of himself! But there, I've done. You know I'm decent at heart – you must count my life from today.' And with this outbreak he lifted the glass between fingers that trembled with the warmth of his emotions, and tossed off his wine.

He did himself but justice when he claimed to be a good fellow; and, in truth, I was myself somewhat moved by his obvious feeling. I remember that we shook hands very affectionately, and my sympathy was the prelude to a long and confidential talk, which lasted until quite a late hour.

At the foot of the staircase, where we parted, he detained me. 'This is the last of my wayward days,' he said, with a smile. 'Late hours – liquor – all go. You shall see. Goodnight. You know your room. I shall be up long before you.' And with that he vanished briskly into the darkness that hung about the lower parts of the passage.

I watched him go, and it struck me quite vaguely what a slight impression his candle made upon that channel of opaque gloom. It seemed merely as a thread of light that illumined nothing. Warrington himself was rapt into the prevalent blackness; but long afterwards, and even when his footsteps had died away upon the heavy carpet, the tiny beam was visible, advancing and flickering in the distance.

My window, which was modern, opened upon a little balcony, where, as the night was warm and I was indisposed for sleep, I spent half an hour enjoying the air. I was in a sentimental mood, and my thoughts turned upon the suggestions which Warrington's conversation had induced. It was not until I was in bed, and had blown out the light, that they settled upon the square, dark chamber in which my host was to pass the night. As I have said, I was wakeful, owing, no doubt, to the high pitch of the emotions which we had encouraged; but presently my fancies became inarticulate and incoherent, and then I was overtaken by profound sleep.

Warrington was up before me, as he had predicted, and met me in the breakfast room.

'What a beggar you are to sleep!' he said, with a smile. 'I've hammered at your door for half an hour.'

I apologised for myself, alleging the rich country air in my defence, and mentioned that I had had some difficulty in getting to sleep.

'So had I,' he remarked, as we sat down to the table. 'We got very excited, I suppose. Just see what you have there, Heywood. Eggs? Oh, damn it, one can have too much of eggs!' He frowned, and lifted a third cover. 'Why in the name of common sense can't Mrs Batty give us more variety?' he asked, impatiently.

I deprecated his displeasure, suggesting that we should do very well; indeed, his discontent seemed to me quite unnecessary. But

I supposed Warrington had been rather spoiled by many years of club life.

He settled himself without replying, and began to pick over his plate in a gingerly manner.

'There's one thing I will have here, Heywood,' he observed. 'I will have things well appointed. I'm not going to let life in the country mean an uncomfortable life. A man can't change the habits of a lifetime.'

In contrast with his exhilarated professions of the previous evening, this struck me with a sense of amusement at the moment; and the incongruity may have occurred to him, for he went on: 'Marion's not over strong, you know, and must have things *comme il faut*. She shan't decline upon a lower level. The worst of these rustics is that they have no imagination.' He held up a piece of bacon on his fork, and surveyed it with disgust. 'Now, look at that! Why the devil don't they take tips from civilised people like the French?'

It was so unlike him to exhibit this petulance that I put it down to a bad night, and without discovering the connection of my thoughts, asked him how he liked his bedroom.

'Oh, pretty well, pretty well,' he said, indifferently. 'It's not so cold as I thought. But I slept badly. I always do in a strange bed'; and pushing aside his plate, he lit a cigarette. 'When you've finished that garbage, Heywood, we'll have a stroll round the Abbey,' he said.

His good temper returned during our walk, and he indicated to me various improvements which he contemplated, with something of his old ardour. The left wing of the house, as I have said, was entire, but a little apart were the ruins of a chapel. Surrounded by a low moss-grown wall, it was full of picturesque charm; the roofless chancel was spread with ivy, but the aisles were intact. Grass grew between the stones and the floor, and many creepers had strayed through chinks in the wall into those sacred precincts. The solemn quietude of the ruin, maintained under the spell of death, awed me a little, but upon Warrington apparently it made no impression. He was only zealous that I should properly appreciate the distinction of such a property. I stooped and drew the weeds away from one of the slabs in the aisle, and was able to trace upon it the relics of lettering, well-nigh obliterated under the corrosion of time.

'There are tombs,' said I.

'Oh, yes,' he answered, with a certain relish. 'I understand the Marvyns used it as a mausoleum. They are all buried here. Some good brasses, I am told.'

The associations of the place engaged me; the aspect of the Abbey faced the past; it seemed to refuse communion with the present; and somehow the thought of those two decent humdrum lives which should be spent within its shelter savoured of the incongruous. The white-capped maids and the emblazoned butlers that should tread these halls offered a ridiculous appearance beside my fancies of the ancient building. For all that, I envied Warrington his home, and so I told him, with a humorous hint that I was fitter to appreciate its glories than himself.

He laughed. 'Oh, I don't know,' said he. 'I like the old-world look as much as you do. I have always had a notion of something venerable. It seems to serve you for ancestors.' And he was undoubtedly delighted with my enthusiasm.

But at lunch again he chopped round to his previous irritation, only now quite another matter provoked his anger. He had received a letter by the second post from Miss Bosanquet, which, if I may judge from his perplexity, must have been unusually confused. He read and re-read it, his brow lowering.

'What the deuce does she mean?' he asked, testily. 'She first makes an arrangement for us to ride over today, and now I can't make out whether we are to go to St Pharamond, or they are coming to us. Just look at it, will you, Heywood?'

I glanced through the note, but could offer no final solution, whereupon he broke out again:

'That's just like women — they never can say anything

straightforwardly. Why, in the name of goodness, couldn't she leave things as they were? You see,' he observed, rather in answer, as I fancied, to my silence, 'we don't know what to do now; if we stay here they mayn't come, and if we go probably we shall cross them.' And he snapped his fingers in annoyance.

I was cheerful enough, perhaps because the responsibility was not mine, and ventured to suggest that we might ride over, and return if we missed them. But he dismissed the subject sharply by saying:

'No, I'll stay. I'm not going on a fool's errand,' and drew my attention to some point in the decoration of the room.

The Bosanquets did not arrive during the afternoon, and Warrington's ill-humour increased.

His love-sick state pleaded in excuse of him, but he was certainly not a pleasant companion. He was sour and snappish, and one could introduce no statement to which he would not find a contradiction. So unamiable did he grow that at last I discovered a pretext to leave him, and rambled to the back of the Abbey into the precincts of the old chapel. The day was falling, and the summer sun flared through the western windows upon the bare aisle. The creepers rustled upon the gaping walls, and the tall grasses waved in shadows over the bodies of the forgotten dead. As I stood contemplating the effect, and meditating greatly upon the anterior fortunes of the Abbey, my attention fell upon a huge slab of marble, upon which the yellow light struck sharply. The faded lettering rose into greater definition before my eyes and I read slowly:

'*Here lyeth the body of Sir Rupert Marvyn.*'

Beyond a date, very difficult to decipher, there was nothing more; of eulogy, of style, of record, of pious considerations such as were usual to the period, not a word. I read the numerals variously as 1723 and 1745; but however they ran it was probable that the stone covered the resting place of the last Marvyn.

The history of this futile house interested me not a little, partly for Warrington's sake, and in part from a natural bent towards ancient records; and I made a mental note of the name and date.

When I returned Warrington's surliness had entirely vanished, and had given place to an effusion of boisterous spirits. He apologised jovially for his bad temper.

'It was the disappointment of not seeing Marion,' he said. 'You will understand that some day, old fellow. But, anyhow, we'll go over tomorrow,' and forthwith proceeded to enliven the dinner with an ostentation of good-fellowship I had seldom witnessed in him. I began to suspect that he had heard again from St Pharamond, though he chose to conceal the fact from me. The wine was admirable; though Warrington himself was no great judge, he had entrusted the selection to a good palate. We had a merry meal, drank a little more than was prudent, and smoked our cigars upon the terrace in the fresh air. Warrington was restless. He pushed his glass from him. 'I'll tell you what, old chap,' he broke out, 'I'll give you a game of billiards. I've got a decent table.'

I demurred. The air was too delicious, and I was in no humour for a sharp use of my wits. He laughed, though he seemed rather disappointed.

'It's almost sacrilege to play billiards in an Abbey,' I said, whimsically. 'What would the ghosts of the old Marvyns think?'

'Oh, hang the Marvyns!' he rejoined, crossly. 'You're always talking of them.'

He rose and entered the house, returning presently with a flagon of whisky and some glasses.

'Try this,' he said. 'We've had no liqueurs,' and pouring out some spirit he swallowed it raw.

I stared, for Warrington rarely took spirits, being more of a wine drinker; moreover, he must have taken nearly the quarter of a tumbler. But he did not notice my surprise, and, seating himself, lit another cigar.

'I don't mean to have things quiet here,' he observed,

reflectively. 'I don't believe in your stagnant rustic life. What I intend to do is to keep the place warm – plenty of house parties, things going on all the year. I shall expect you down for the shooting, Ned. The coverts promise well this year.'

I assented willingly enough, and he rambled on again.

'I don't know that I shall use the Abbey so much. I think I'll live in town a good deal. It's brighter there. I don't know though. I like the place. Hang it, it's a rattling good shop, there's no mistake about it. Look here,' he broke off, abruptly, 'bring your glass in, and I'll show you something.'

I was little inclined to move, but he was so peremptory that I followed him with a sigh. We entered one of the smaller rooms which overlooked the terrace, and had been diverted into a comfortable library. He flung back the windows.

'There's air for you,' he cried. 'Now, sit down,' and walking to a cupboard produced a second flagon of whisky. 'Irish!' he ejaculated, clumping it on the table. 'Take your choice,' and turning again to the cupboard, presently sat down with his hands under the table. 'Now, then, Ned,' he said, with a short laugh. 'Fill up, and we'll have some fun,' with which he suddenly threw a pack of cards upon the board.

I opened my eyes, for I do not suppose Warrington had touched cards since his college days; but, interpreting my look in his own way, he cried:

'Oh, I'm not married yet. Warrington's his own man still. Poker? Eh?'

'Anything you like,' said I, with resignation.

A peculiar expression of delight gleamed in his eyes, and he shuffled the cards feverishly.

'Cut,' said he, and helped himself to more whisky.

It was shameful to be playing there with that beautiful night without, but there seemed no help for it. Warrington had a run of luck, though he played with little skill; and his excitement grew as he won.

'Let us make it ten shillings,' he suggested.

I shook my head. 'You forget I'm not a millionaire,' I replied. 'Bah!' he cried. 'I like a game worth the victory. Well, fire away.' His eyes gloated upon the cards, and he fingered them with unctuous affection. The behaviour of the man amazed me. I began to win.

Warrington's face slowly assumed a dull, lowering expression; he played eagerly, avariciously; he disputed my points, and was querulous.

'Oh, we've had enough!' I cried in distaste.

'By Jove, you don't!' he exclaimed, jumping to his feet. 'You're the winner, Heywood, and I'll see you damned before I let you off my revenge!'

The words startled me no less than the fury which rang in his accents. I gazed at him in stupefaction. The whites of his eyes showed wildly, and a sullen, angry look determined his face. Suddenly I was arrested by the suspicion of something upon his neck.

'What's that?' I asked. 'You've cut yourself.'

He put his hand to his face. 'Nonsense,' he replied, in a surly fashion.

I looked closer, and then I saw my mistake. It was a round, faint red mark, the size of a florin, upon the column of his throat, and I set it down to the accidental pressure of some button.

'Come on!' he insisted, impatiently.

'Bah! Warrington,' I said, for I imagined that he had been overexcited by the whisky he had taken. 'It's only a matter of a few pounds. Why make a fuss? Tomorrow will serve.'

After a moment his eyes fell, and he gave an awkward laugh. 'Oh, well, that'll do,' said he. 'But I got so infernally excited.'

'Whisky,' said I, sententiously.

He glanced at the bottle. 'How many glasses have I had?' and he whistled. 'By Jove, Ned, this won't do! I must turn over a new leaf. Come on; let's look at the night.'

I was only too glad to get away from the table, and we were soon upon the terrace again. Warrington was silent, and his gaze went constantly across the valley, where the moon was rising, and in the direction in which, as he had indicated to me, St Pharamond lay. When he said goodnight he was still preoccupied.

'I hope you will sleep better,' he said.

'And you, too,' I added.

He smiled. 'I don't suppose I shall wake the whole night through,' he said; and then, as I was turning to go, he caught me quickly by the arm.

'Ned,' he said, impulsively and very earnestly, 'don't let me make a fool of myself again. I know it's the excitement of everything. But I want to be as good as I can for her.'

I pressed his hand. 'All right, old fellow,' I said; and we parted.

I think I have never enjoyed sounder slumber than that night. The first thing I was aware of was the singing of thrushes outside my window. I rose and looked forth, and the sun was hanging high in the eastern sky, the grass and the young green of the trees were shining with dew. With an uncomfortable feeling that I was very late I hastily dressed and went downstairs. Warrington was waiting for me in the breakfast room, as upon the previous morning, and when he turned from the window at my approach, the sight of his face startled me. It was drawn and haggard, and his eyes were shot with blood; it was a face broken and savage with dissipation. He made no answer to my questioning, but seated himself with a morose air.

'Now you have come,' he said, sullenly, 'we may as well begin. But it's not my fault if the coffee's cold.'

I examined him critically, and passed some comment upon his appearance.

'You don't look up to much,' I said. 'Another bad night?'

'No; I slept well enough,' he responded, ungraciously; and then, after a pause: 'I'll tell you what, Heywood. You shall give me my revenge after breakfast.'

'Nonsense,' I said, after a momentary silence. 'You're going over to St Pharamond.'

'Hang it!' was his retort, 'one can't be always bothering about

262

women. You seem mightily indisposed to meet me again.'

'I certainly won't this morning,' I answered, rather sharply, for the man's manner grated upon me. 'This evening, if you like; and then the silly business shall end.'

He said something in an undertone of grumble, and the rest of the meal passed in silence. But I entertained an uneasy suspicion of him, and after all he was my friend, with whom I was under obligations not to quarrel; and so when we rose, I approached him.

'Look here, Warrington,' I said. 'What's the matter with you? Have you been drinking? Remember what you asked me last night.'

'Hold your damned row!' was all the answer he vouchsafed, as he whirled away from me, but with an embarrassed display of shame.

But I was not to be put off in that way, and I spoke somewhat more sharply.

'We're going to have this out, Warrington,' I said. 'If you are ill, let us understand that; but I'm not going to stay here with you in this cantankerous spirit.'

'I'm not ill,' he replied testily.

'Look at yourself,' I cried, and turned him about to the mirror over the mantelpiece.

He started a little, and a frown of perplexity gathered on his forehead.

'Good Lord! I'm not like that, Ned,' he said, in a different voice. 'I must have been drunk last night.' And with a sort of groan, he directed a piteous look at me.

'Come,' I was constrained to answer, 'pull yourself together. The ride will do you good. And no more whisky.'

'No, by Heaven, no!' he cried vehemently, and seemed to shiver; but then, suddenly taking my arm, he walked out of the room.

The morning lay still and golden. Warrington's eyes went forth across the valley.

'Come round to the stables, Ned,' he said, impulsively. 'You shall choose your own nag.'

I shook my head. 'I'll choose yours,' said I, 'but I am not going with you.' He looked surprised. 'No, ride by yourself. You don't want a companion on such an errand. I'll stay here, and pursue my investigations into the Marvyns.'

A scowl crossed his face, but only for an instant, and then he answered: 'All right, old chap; do as you like. Anyway, I'm off at once.' And presently, when his horse was brought, he was laughing merrily.

'You'll have a dull day, Ned; but it's your own fault, you duffer. You'll have to lunch by yourself, as I shan't be back till late.' And, gaily flourishing his whip, he trotted down the drive.

It was some relief to me to be rid of him, for, in truth, his moods had worn my nerves, and I had not looked for a holiday of this disquieting nature. When he returned, I had no doubt it would be with quite another face, and meanwhile I was excellent company for myself. After lunch I amused myself for half an hour with idle tricks upon the billiard table, and, tiring of my pastime, fell upon the housekeeper as I returned along the corridor. She was a woman nearer to sixty than fifty, with a comfortable, portly figure, and an amiable expression. Her eyes invited me ever so respectfully to conversation, and stopping, I entered into talk. She inquired if I liked my room and how I slept.

'Tis a nice lookout you have, sir,' said she. 'That was where old Lady Marvyn slept.'

It appeared that she had served as kitchen maid to the previous tenants of the Abbey, nearly fifty years before.

'Oh, I know the old house in and out,' she asserted; 'and I arranged the rooms with Mr Warrington.'

We were standing opposite the low doorway which gave entrance to Warrington's bedroom, and my eyes unconsciously shot in that direction. Mrs Batty followed my glance.

'I didn't want him to have that,' she said; 'but he was set upon it. It's smallish for a bedroom, and in my opinion isn't fit for more than a lumber room. That's what Sir William used it for.'

I pushed open the door and stepped over the threshold, and the housekeeper followed me.

'No,' she said, glancing round; 'and it's in my mind that it's damp, sir.'

Again I had a curious feeling that the silence was speaking in my ear; the atmosphere was thick and heavy, and a musty smell, as of faded draperies, penetrated my nostrils. The whole room looked indescribably dingy, despite the new hangings. I went over to the narrow window and peered through the diamond panes. Outside, but seen dimly through that ancient and discoloured glass, the ruins of the chapel confronted me, bare and stark, in the yellow sunlight. I turned.

'There are no ghosts in the Abbey, I suppose, Mrs Batty?' I asked, whimsically.

But she took my inquiry very gravely. 'I have never heard tell of one, sir,' she protested; 'and if there was such a thing I should have known it.'

As I was rejoining her a strange low whirring was audible, and looking up I saw in a corner of the high-arched roof a horrible face watching me out of black narrow eyes. I confess that I was very much startled at the apparition, but the next moment realised what it was. The creature hung with its ugly fleshy wings extended over a grotesque stone head that leered down upon me, its evil-looking snout projecting into the room; it lay perfectly still, returning me glance for glance, until moved by the repulsion of its presence I clapped my hands, and cried loudly; then, slowly flitting in a circle round the roof, it vanished with a flapping of wings into some darker corner of the rafters. Mrs Batty was astounded, and expressed surprise that it had managed to conceal itself for so long.

'Oh, bats live in holes,' I answered. 'Probably there is some small access through the masonry.' But the incident had sent an uncomfortable shiver through me all the same.

Later that day I began to recognise that, short of an abrupt return to town, my time was not likely to be spent very pleasantly. But it was the personal problem so far as it concerned Warrington himself that distressed me even more. He came back from St Pharamond in a morose and ugly temper, quite alien to his kindly nature. It seemed that he had quarrelled bitterly with Miss Bosanquet, but upon what I could not determine, nor did I press him for an explanation. But the fumes of his anger were still rising when we met, and our dinner was a most depressing meal.

He was in a degree of irritation which rendered it impossible to address him, and I soon withdrew into my thoughts. I saw, however, that he was drinking far too much, as, indeed, was plain subsequently when he invited me into the library. Once more he produced the hateful cards, and I was compelled to play, as he reminded me somewhat churlishly that I had promised him his revenge.

'Understand, Warrington,' I said, firmly, 'I play tonight, but never again, whatever the result. In fact, I am in half the mind to return to town tomorrow.'

He gave me a look as he sat down, but said nothing, and the game began. He lost heavily from the first, and as nothing would content him but we must constantly raise the stakes, in a short time I had won several hundred pounds. He bore the reverses very ill, breaking out from time to time into some angry exclamation, now petulantly questioning my playing, and muttering oaths under his breath. But I was resolved that he should have no cause of complaint against me for this one night, and disregarding his insane fits of temper, I played steadily and silently. As the tally of my gains mounted he changed colour slowly, his face assuming a ghastly expression, and his eyes suspiciously denoting my actions. At length he rose, and throwing himself quickly across the table, seized my hand ferociously as I dealt a couple of cards.

'Damn you! I see your tricks,' he cried, in frenzied passion. 'Drop that hand, do you hear? Drop that hand, or by...'

But he got no further, for, rising myself, I wrenched my hand from his grasp, and turned upon him, in almost as great a passion as himself. But suddenly, and even as I opened my mouth to speak, I stopped short with a cry of horror. His face was livid to the lips, his eyes were cast with blood, and upon the dirty white of his flesh, right in the centre of his throat, the round red scar, flaming and ugly as a wound, stared upon me.

'Warrington' I cried, 'what is this? What have you?...' And I pointed in alarm to the spot.

'Mind your own business,' he said, with a sneer. 'It is well to try and draw off attention from your knavery. But that trick won't answer with me.'

Without another word I flung the IOUs upon the table, and turning on my heel, left the room. I was furious with him, and fully resolved to leave the Abbey in the morning. I made my way upstairs to my room, and then, seating myself upon the balcony, endeavoured to recover my self-possession.

The more I considered, the more unaccountable was Warrington's behaviour. He had always been a perfectly courteous man, with a great lump of kindness in his nature; whereas these last few days he had been nothing other than a savage. It seemed certain that he must be ill or going mad; and as I reflected upon this the conjecture struck me with a sense of pity. If it was that he was losing his senses, how horrible was the tragedy in face of the new and lovely prospects opening in his life. Stimulated by this growing conviction, I resolved to go down and see him, more particularly as I now recalled his pleading voice that I should help him, on the previous evening. Was it not possible that this pathetic appeal derived from the instinct of the insane to protect themselves?

I found him still in the library; his head had fallen upon the table, and the state of the whisky bottle by his arm showed only too clearly his condition. I shook him vigorously, and he opened his eyes.

'Warrington, you must go to bed,' I said.

He smiled, and greeted me quite affectionately. Obviously he was not so drunk as I had supposed.

'What is the time, Ned?' he asked.

I told him it was one o'clock, at which he rose briskly.

'Lord, I've been asleep,' he said. 'Help me, Ned. I don't think I'm sober. Where have you been?'

I assisted him to his room, and he undressed slowly, and with an effort. Somehow, as I stood watching him, I yielded to an unknown impulse and said, suddenly:

'Warrington, don't sleep here. Come and share my room.'

'My dear fellow,' he replied, with a foolish laugh, 'yours is not the only room in the house. I can use half-a-dozen if I like.'

'Well, use one of them,' I answered.

He shook his head. 'I'm going to sleep here,' he returned, obstinately.

I made no further effort to influence him, for, after all, now that the words were out, I had absolutely no reason to give him or myself for my proposition. And so I left him. When I had closed the door, and was turning to go along the passage, I heard very clearly, as it seemed to me, a plaintive cry, muffled and faint, but very disturbing, which sounded from the room. Instantly I opened the door again. Warrington was in bed, and the heavy sound of his breathing told me that he was asleep. It was impossible that he could have uttered the cry. A night light was burning by his bedside, shedding a strong illumination over the immediate vicinity, and throwing antic shadows on the walls. As I turned to go, there was a whirring of wings, a brief flap behind me, and the room was plunged in darkness. The obscene creature that lived in the recesses of the roof must have knocked out the tiny light with its wings. Then Warrington's breathing ceased, and there was no sound at all. And then once more the silence seemed to gather round me slowly and heavily, and whisper to me. I had a vague sense of being prevailed upon, of being enticed and lured by something in the surrounding air; a sort of horror circumscribed me, and I broke from the invisible ring and rushed from the room. The door clanged behind me, and as I hastened along the hall, once more there seemed to ring in my ears the faint and melancholy cry.

I awoke, in the sombre twilight that precedes the dawn, from a sleep troubled and encumbered with evil dreams. The birds had not yet begun their day, and a vast silence brooded over the Abbey gardens. Looking out of my window, I caught sight of a dark figure stealing cautiously round the corner of the ruined chapel. The furtive gait, as well as the appearance of a man at that early hour, struck me with surprise; and hastily throwing on some clothes, I ran downstairs, and, opening the hall door, went out. When I reached the porch which gave entrance to the aisle I stopped suddenly, for there before me, with his head to the ground, and peering among the tall grasses, was the object of my pursuit. Then I stepped quickly forward and laid a hand upon his shoulder. It was Warrington.

'What are you doing here?' I asked.

He turned and looked at me in bewilderment. His eyes wore a dazed expression, and he blinked in perplexity before he replied.

'It's you, is it?' he said weakly. 'I thought...' and then paused. 'What is it?' he asked.

'I followed you here,' I explained. 'I only saw your figure, and thought it might be some intruder.'

He avoided my eyes. 'I thought I heard a cry out here,' he answered.

'Warrington,' I said, with some earnestness, 'come back to bed.'

He made no answer, and slipping my arm in his, I led him away. On the doorstep he stopped, and lifted his face to me.

'Do you think it's possible...' he began, as if to inquire of me, and then again paused. With a slight shiver he proceeded to his room, while I followed him. He sat down upon his bed, and his eyes strayed to the barred window absently. The black shadow of the chapel was visible through the panes.

'Don't say anything about this,' he said, suddenly. 'Don't let Marion know.'

I laughed, but it was an awkward laugh.

'Why, that you were alarmed by a cry for help, and went in search like a gentleman?' I asked, jestingly.

'You heard it, then?' he said, eagerly.

I shook my head, for I was not going to encourage his fancies. 'You had better go to sleep,' I replied, 'and get rid of these nightmares.'

He sighed and lay back upon his pillow, dressed as he was. Ere I left him he had fallen into a profound slumber.

If I had expected a surly mood in him at breakfast I was much mistaken. There was not a trace of his nocturnal dissipations; he did not seem even to remember them, and he made no allusion whatever to our adventure in the dawn. He perused a letter carefully, and threw it over to me with a grin.

'Lor, what queer sheep women are!' he exclaimed, with rather a coarse laugh.

I glanced at the letter without thinking, but ere I had read half of it I put it aside. It was certainly not meant for my eyes, and I marvelled at Warrington's indelicacy in making public, as it were, that very private matter. The note was from Miss Bosanquet, and was clearly designed for his own heart, couched as it was in the terms of warm and fond affection. No man should see such letters save he for whom they are written.

'You see, they're coming over to dine,' he remarked, carelessly. 'Trust a girl to make it up if you let her alone long enough.'

I made no answer; but though Warrington's grossness irritated me, I reflected with satisfaction upon his return to good humour, which I attributed to the reconciliation.

When I moved out upon the terrace the maid had entered to remove the breakfast things. I was conscious of a slight exclamation behind me, and Warrington joined me presently, with a loud guffaw.

'That's a damned pretty girl!' he said, with unction. 'I'm glad Mrs Batty got her. I like to have good-looking servants.'

I suddenly interpreted the incident, and shrugged my shoulders.

'You're a perfect boor this morning, Warrington,' I exclaimed, irritably.

He only laughed. 'You're a dull dog of a saint, Heywood,' he retorted. 'Come along,' and dragged me out in no amiable spirit.

I had forgotten how perfect a host Warrington could be, but that evening he was displayed at his best. The Bosanquets arrived early. Sir William was an easy-going man, fond of books and of wine, and I now guessed at the taste which had decided Warrington's cellar. Miss Bosanquet was as charming as I remembered her to be; and if any objection might be taken to Warrington himself by my anxious eyes it was merely that he seemed a trifle excited, a fault which, in the circumstances, I was able to condone. Sir William hung about the table, sipping his wine. Warrington, who had been very abstemious, grew restless, and, finally apologising in his graceful way, left me to keep the baronet company. I was the less disinclined to do so as I was anxious not to intrude upon the lovers, and Sir William was discussing the history of the Abbey. He had an old volume somewhere in his library which related to it, and, seeing that I was interested, invited me to look it up.

We sat long, and it was not until later that the horrible affair which I must narrate occurred. The evening was close and oppressive, owing to the thunder, which already rumbled far away in the south. When we rose we found that Warrington and Miss Bosanquet were in the garden, and thither we followed. As at first we did not find them, Sir William, who had noted the approaching storm with some uneasiness, left me to make arrangements for his return; and I strolled along the paths by myself, enjoying a cigarette. I had reached the shrubbery upon the further side of the chapel, when I heard the sound of voices – a man's rough and rasping, a woman's pleading and informed with fear. A sharp cry ensued, and without hesitation I plunged through the thicket in the direction of the speakers. The sight that met me appalled me for the moment. Darkness was falling, lit with ominous flashes; and the two figures stood out distinctly in the bushes, in an attitude of struggle. I could not mistake the voices now. I heard Warrington's, brusque with anger, and almost savage in its tones, crying, 'You shall!' and there followed a murmur from the girl, a little sob, and then a piercing cry. I sprang forward and seized Warrington by the arm; when, to my horror, I perceived that he had taken her wrist in both hands and was roughly twisting it, after the cruel habit of schoolboys. The malevolent cruelty of the action so astounded me that for an instant I remained motionless; I almost heard the bones in the frail wrist cracking; and then, in a second, I had seized Warrington's hands in a grip of iron, and flung him violently to the ground. The girl fell with him, and as I picked her up he rose too, and, clenching his fists, made as though to come at me, but instead turned and went sullenly, and with a ferocious look of hate upon his face, out of the thicket.

Miss Bosanquet came to very shortly, and though the agony of the pain must have been considerable to a delicate girl, I believe it was rather the incredible horror of the act under which she swooned. For my part I had nothing to say: not one word relative to the incident dared pass my lips. I inquired if she was better, and then, putting her arm in mine, led her gently towards the house. Her heart beat hard against me, and she breathed heavily, leaning on me for support. At the chapel I stopped, feeling suddenly that I dare not let her be seen in this condition, and bewildered greatly by the whole atrocious business.

'Come and rest in here,' I suggested, and we entered the chapel.

I set her on a slab of marble, and stood waiting by her side. I talked fluently about anything; for lack of a subject, upon the state of the chapel and the curious tomb I had discovered. Recovering a little, she joined presently in my remarks. It was plain that she was putting a severe restraint upon herself. I moved aside the grasses, and read aloud the inscription on Sir Rupert's grave piece, and turning to the next, which was rankly overgrown, feigned to search further. As I was bending there, suddenly, and by what thread of thought I know not, I identified the spot with that upon which I had found Warrington stooping that morning. With a sweep of my hand I brushed back the weeds, uprooting some with my fingers, and kneeling in the twilight, pored over the monument. Suddenly a wild flare of light streamed down the sky, and a great crash of thunder followed. Miss Bosanquet started to her feet and I to mine. The heaven was lit up, as it were, with sunlight, and, as I turned, my eyes fell upon the now uncovered stone. Plainly the lettering flashed in my eyes:

'*Priscilla, Lady Marvyn.*'

Then the clouds opened, and the rain fell in spouts, shouting and dancing upon the ancient roof overhead.

We were under a very precarious shelter, and I was uneasy that Miss Bosanquet should run the risk of that flimsy, ravaged edifice; and so in a momentary lull I managed to get her to the house. I found Sir William in a restless state of nerves. He was a timorous man, and the thunder had upset him, more particularly as he and his daughter were now storm-bound for some time. There was no possibility of venturing into those rude elements for an hour or more. Warrington was not inside, and no one had seen him. In the light Miss Bosanquet's face frightened me; her eyes were large and scared, and her colour very dead white. Clearly she was very near a breakdown. I found Mrs Batty, and told her that the young lady had been severely shaken by the storm, suggesting that she had better lie down for a little. Returning with me, the housekeeper led off the unfortunate girl, and Sir William and I were left together. He paced the room impatiently, and constantly inquired if there were any signs of improvement in the weather. He also asked for Warrington, irritably. The burden of the whole dreadful night seemed fallen upon me. Passing through the hall I met Mrs Batty again. Her usually placid features were disturbed and aghast.

'What is the matter?' I asked. 'Is Miss Bosanquet…'

'No, sir; I think she's sleeping,' she replied. 'She's in – she is in Mr Warrington's room.'

I started. 'Are there no other rooms?' I asked, abruptly.

'There are none ready, sir, except yours,' she answered, 'and I thought...'

'You should have taken her there,' I said, sharply. The woman looked at me and opened her mouth. 'Good heavens!' I said, irritably, 'what is the matter? Everyone is mad tonight.'

'Alice is gone, sir,' she blurted forth.

Alice, I remembered, was the name of one of her maids.

'What do you mean?' I asked, for her air of panic betokened something graver than her words. The thunder broke over the house and drowned her voice.

'She can't be out in this storm – she must have taken refuge somewhere,' I said.

At that the strings of her tongue loosened, and she burst forth with her tale. It was an abominable narrative.

'Where is Mr Warrington?' I asked; but she shook her head.

There was a moment's silence between us, and we eyed each other aghast. 'She will be all right,' I said at last, as if dismissing the subject.

The housekeeper wrung her hands. 'I never would have thought it!' she repeated, dismally. 'I never would have thought it!'

'There is some mistake,' I said; but, somehow, I knew better. Indeed, I felt now that I had almost been prepared for it.

'She ran towards the village,' whispered Mrs Batty. 'God knows where she was going! The river lies that way.'

'Pooh!' I exclaimed. 'Don't talk nonsense. It is all a mistake. Come, have you any brandy?'

Brought back to the material round of her duties she bustled away with a sort of briskness, and returned with a flagon and glasses. I took a strong nip, and went back to Sir William. He was feverish, and declaimed against the weather unceasingly. I had to listen to the string of misfortunes which he recounted in the season's crops. It seemed all so futile, with his daughter involved in her horrid tragedy in a neighbouring room. He was better after some brandy, and grew more cheerful, but assiduously wondered about Warrington.

'Oh, he's been caught in the storm and taken refuge somewhere,' I explained, vainly. I wondered if the next day would ever dawn.

By degrees that thunder rolled slowly into the northern parts of the sky, and only fitful flashes seamed the heavens. It had lasted now more than two hours. Sir William declared his intention of starting, and asked for his daughter. I rang for Mrs Batty, and sent her to rouse Miss Bosanquet. Almost immediately there was a knock upon the door, and the housekeeper was in the doorway, with an agitated expression, demanding to see me. Sir William was looking out of the window, and fortunately did not see her.

'Please come to Miss Bosanquet, sir,' she cried, very scared. 'Please come at once.'

In alarm I hastily ran down the corridor and entered Warrington's room. The girl was lying upon the bed, her hair flowing upon the pillow; her eyes, wide open and filled with terror, stared at the ceiling, and her hands clutched and twined in the coverlet as if in an agony of pain. A gasping sound issued from her, as though she were struggling for breath under suffocation. Her whole appearance was as of one in the murderous grasp of an assailant.

I bent over. 'Throw the light, quick,' I called to Mrs Batty; and as I put my hand on her shoulder to lift her, the creature that lived in the chamber rose suddenly from the shadow upon the further side of the bed, and sailed with a flapping noise up to the cornice. With an exclamation of horror I pulled the girl's head forward, and the candlelight glowed on her pallid face. Upon the soft flesh of the slender throat was a round red mark, the size of a florin.

At the sight I almost let her fall upon the pillow again; but, commanding my nerves, I put my arms round her, and, lifting her bodily from the bed, carried her from the room. Mrs Batty followed.

'What shall we do?' she asked, in a low voice.

'Take her away from this damned chamber!' I cried. 'Anywhere – the hall, the kitchen rather.'

I laid my burden upon a sofa in the dining room, and despatching Mrs Batty for the brandy, gave Miss Bosanquet a draught. Slowly the horror faded from her eyes; they closed, and then she looked at me.

'What have you?… Where am I?' she asked.

'You have been unwell,' I said. 'Pray don't disturb yourself yet.'

She shuddered, and closed her eyes again.

Very little more was said. Sir William pressed for his horses, and as the sky was clearing I made no attempt to detain him, more particularly as the sooner Miss Bosanquet left the Abbey the better for herself. In half an hour she recovered sufficiently to go, and I helped her into the carriage. She never referred to her seizure, but thanked me for my kindness. That was all. No one asked after Warrington – not even Sir William. He had forgotten everything, save his anxiety to get back. As the carriage turned from the steps I saw the mark upon the girl's throat, now grown fainter.

I waited up till late into the morning, but there was no sign of Warrington when I went to bed. Nor had he made his appearance when I descended to breakfast. A letter in his handwriting, however, and with the London postmark, awaited me. It was a pitiful scrawl, in the very penmanship of which one might trace the desperate emotions by which he was torn. He implored my forgiveness. *Am I a devil?*' he asked. *'Am I mad? It was not I! It was not I!'* he repeated, underlining the sentence with impetuous dashes. *'You know,'* he wrote; *'and you know, therefore, that everything is at an end for me. I am going abroad today. I shall never see the Abbey again.'*

It was well that he had gone, as I hardly think that I could have faced him; and yet I was loth myself to leave the matter in this horrible tangle. I felt that it was enjoined upon me to meet the problems, and I endeavoured to do so as best I might. Mrs Batty gave me news of the girl Alice. It was bad enough, though not so bad as both of us had feared. I was able to make arrangements on the instant, which I hoped might bury that lamentable affair for the time. There remained Miss Bosanquet; but that difficulty seemed beyond me. I could see no avenue out of the tragedy. I heard nothing save that she was ill − an illness attributed upon all hands to the shock of exposure to the thunderstorm. Only I knew better, and a vague disinclination to fly from the responsibilities of the position kept me hanging on at Utterbourne.

It was in those days before my visit to St Pharamond that I turned my attention more particularly to the thing which had forced itself relentlessly upon me. I was never a superstitious man; the gossip of old wives interested me merely as a curious and unsympathetic observer. And yet I was vaguely discomfited by the transaction in the Abbey, and it was with some reluctance that I decided to make a further test of Warrington's bedroom. Mrs Batty received my determination to change my room easily enough, but with a protest as to the dampness of the Stone Chamber. It was plain that her suspicions had not marched with mine. On the second night after Warrington's departure I occupied the room for the first time.

I lay awake for a couple of hours, with a reading lamp by my bed, and a volume of travels in my hand, and then, feeling very tired, put out the light and went to sleep. Nothing distracted me that night; indeed, I slept more soundly and peaceably than before in that house. I rose, too, experiencing quite an exhilaration, and it was not until I was dressing before the glass that I remembered the circumstances of my mission; but then I was at once pulled up, startled swiftly out of my cheerful temper. Faintly visible upon my throat was the same round mark which I had already seen stamped upon Warrington and Miss Bosanquet. With that, all my former doubts returned in force, augmented and militant. My mind recurred to the bat, and tales of bloodsucking by those evil creatures revived in my memory. But when I had remembered that these were of foreign beasts, and that I was in England, I dismissed them lightly enough. Still, the impress of that mark remained, and alarmed me. It could not come by accident; to suppose so manifold a coincidence was absurd. The puzzle dwelt with me, unsolved, and the fingers of dread slowly crept over me.

Yet I slept again in the room. Having but myself for company, and being somewhat bored and dull, I fear I took more spirit than was my custom, and the result was that I again slept profoundly. I awoke about three in the morning, and was surprised to find the lamp still burning. I had forgotten it in my stupid state of somnolence. As I turned to put it out, the bat swept by me and circled for an instant above my head. So overpowered with torpor was I that I scarcely noticed it, and my head was no sooner at rest than I was once more unconscious. The red mark was stronger next morning, though, as on the previous day, it wore off with the fall of evening. But I merely observed the fact without any concern; indeed, now the matter of my investigation seemed to have drawn very remote. I was growing indifferent, I supposed, through familiarity. But the solitude was palling upon me, and I spent a very restless day. A sharp ride I took in the afternoon was the one agreeable experience of the day. I reflected that if this burden were to continue I must hasten up to town. I had no desire to tie myself to Warrington's apron, in his interest. So dreary was the evening, that after I had strolled round the grounds and into the chapel by moonlight, I returned to the library and endeavoured to pass the time with Warrington's cards. But it was poor fun with no antagonist to pit myself against; and I was throwing down the pack in disgust when one of the manservants entered with the whisky.

It was not until long afterwards that I fully realised the course of my action; but even at the time I was aware of a curious sub-feeling of shamefacedness. I am sure that the thing fell naturally, and that there was no awkwardness in my approaching him.

Nor, after the first surprise, did he offer any objection. Later he was hardly expected to do so, seeing that he was winning very quickly. The reason of that I guessed afterwards, but during the play I was amazed to note at intervals how strangely my irritation was aroused. Finally, I swept the cards to the floor, and rose, the man, with a smile in which triumph blended with uneasiness, rose also.

'Damn you, get away!' I said, angrily.

True to his traditions to the close, he answered me with respect, and obeyed; and I sat staring at the table. With a sudden flush, the grotesque folly of the night's business came to me, and my eyes fell on the whisky bottle. It was nearly empty. Then I went to bed.

Voices cried all night in that chamber – soft, pleading voices. There was nothing to alarm in them; they seemed in a manner to coo me to sleep. But presently a sharper cry roused me from my semi-slumber; and getting up, I flung open the window. The wind rushed round the Abbey, sweeping with noises against the corners and gables. The black chapel lay still in the moonlight, and drew my eyes. But, resisting a strange, unaccountable impulse to go further, I went back to bed.

The events of the following day are better related without comment.

At breakfast I found a letter from Sir William Bosanquet, inviting me to come over to St Pharamond. I was at once conscious of an eager desire to do so: it seemed somehow as though I had been waiting for this. The visit assumed preposterous proportions, and I was impatient for the afternoon.

Sir William was polite, but not, as I thought, cordial. He never alluded to Warrington, from which I guessed that he had been informed of the breach, and I conjectured also that the invitation extended to me was rather an act of courtesy to a solitary stranger than due to a desire for my company. Nevertheless, when he presently suggested that I should stay to dinner, I accepted promptly. For, to say the truth, I had not yet

seen Miss Bosanquet, and I experienced a strange curiosity to do
so. When at last she made her appearance, I was struck, almost
for the first time, by her beauty. She was certainly a handsome
girl, though she had a delicate air of ill health.

After dinner Sir William remembered by accident the book on
the Abbey which he had promised to show me, and after a brief
hunt in the library we found it. Shortly afterwards he was called
away, and with an apology left me. With a curious eagerness I
turned the pages of the volume and settled down to read.

It was published early in the century, and purported to relate
the history of the Abbey and its owners. But it was one chapter
which specially drew my interest – that which recounted the
fate of the last Marvyn. The family had become extinct through
a bloody tragedy; that fact held me. The bare narrative, long
since passed from the memory of tradition, was here set forth
in the baldest statements. The names of Sir Rupert Marvyn and
Priscilla, Lady Marvyn, shook me strangely, but particularly the
latter. Some links of connection with those gravestones lying
in the Abbey chapel constrained me intimately. The history of
that evil race was stained and discoloured with blood, and the
end was in fitting harmony – a lurid holocaust of crime. There
had been two brothers, but it was hard to choose between the
foulness of their lives. If either, the younger, William, was the
worse; so at least the narrative would have it. The details of his
excesses had not survived, but it was abundantly plain that they
were both notorious gamblers. The story of their deaths was
wrapped in doubt, the theme of conjecture only, and probability;
for none was by to observe save the three veritable actors –
who were at once involved together in a bloody dissolution.
Priscilla, the wife of Sir Rupert, was suspected of an intrigue
with her brother-in-law. She would seem to have been tainted
with the corruption of the family into which she had married.
But according to a second rumour, chronicled by the author,
there was some doubt if the woman were not the worst of the
three. Nothing was known of her parentage; she had returned

with the passionate Sir Rupert to the Abbey after one of his prolonged absences, and was accepted as his legal wife. This was the woman whose infamous beauty had brought a terrible sin between the brothers.

Upon the night which witnessed the extinction of this miserable family, the two brothers had been gambling together. It was known from the high voices that they had quarrelled, and it is supposed that, heated with wine and with the lust of play, the younger had thrown some taunt at Sir Rupert in respect to his wife. Whereupon – but this is all conjecture – the elder stabbed him to death. At least, it was understood that at this point the sounds of a struggle were heard, and a bitter cry. The report of the servants ran that upon this noise Lady Marvyn rushed into the room and locked the door behind her. Fright was busy with those servants, long used to the savage manners of the house. According to witnesses, no further sound was heard subsequently to Lady Marvyn's entrance; yet when the doors were at last broken open by the authorities, the three bodies were discovered upon the floor.

How Sir Rupert and his wife met their deaths there was no record. 'This tragedy,' proceeded the scribe, 'took place in the Stone Chamber underneath the stairway.'

I had got so far when the entrance of Miss Bosanquet disturbed me. I remember rising in a dazed condition – the room swung about me. A conviction, hitherto resisted and stealthily entertained upon compulsion, now overpowered me.

'I thought my father was here,' explained Miss Bosanquet, with a quick glance round the room.

I explained the circumstances, and she hesitated in my neighbourhood with a slight air of embarrassment.

'I have not thanked you properly, Mr Heywood,' she said presently, in a low voice, scarcely articulate. 'You have been very considerate and kind. Let me thank you now.' And ended with a tiny spasmodic sob.

Somehow, an impulse overmastered my tongue. Fresh from

the perusal of that chapter, queer possibilities crowded in my mind, odd considerations urged me.

'Miss Bosanquet,' said I, abruptly, 'let me speak of that a little. I will not touch on details.'

'Please,' she cried, with a shrinking notion as of one that would retreat in very alarm.

'Nay,' said I, eagerly; 'hear me. It is no wantonness that would press the memory upon you. You have been a witness to distressful acts; you have seen a man under the influence of temporary madness. Nay, even yourself, you have been a victim to the same unaccountable phenomena.'

'What do you mean?' she cried, tensely.

'I will say no more,' said I. 'I should incur your laughter. No, you would not laugh, but my dim suspicions would leave you still incredulous. But if this were so, and if these were the phenomena of a brief madness, surely you would make your memory a grave to bury the past.'

'I cannot do that,' said she, in low tones.

'What!' I asked. 'Would you turn from your lover, aye, even from a friend, because he was smitten with disease? Consider; if your dearest upon earth tossed in a fever upon his bed, and denied you in his ravings, using you despitefully, it would not be he that entreated you so. When he was quit of his madness and returned to his proper person, would you not forget – would you not rather recall his insanity with the pity of affection?'

'I do not understand you,' she whispered.

'You read your Bible,' said I. 'You have wondered at the evil spirits that possessed poor victims. Why should you decide that these things have ceased? We are too dogmatic in our modern world. Who can say under what malign influence a soul may pass, and out of its own custody?'

She looked at me earnestly, searching my eyes.

'You hint at strange things,' said she, very low.

But somehow, even as I met her eyes, the spirit of my mission failed me. My gaze, I felt, devoured her ruthlessly. The light shone on her pale and comely features; they burned me with an irresistible attraction. I put forth my hand and took hers gently. It was passive to my touch, as though in acknowledgment of my kindly offices. All the while I experienced a sense of fierce elation. In my blood ran, as it had been fire, a horrible incentive, and I knew that I was holding her hand very tightly. She herself seemed to grow conscious of this, for she made an effort to withdraw her fingers, at which, the passion rushing through my body, I clutched them closer, laughing aloud. I saw a wondering look dawn in her eyes, and her bosom thinly veiled, heaved with a tiny tremor. I was aware that I was drawing her steadily to me. Suddenly her bewildered eyes, dropping from my face, lit with a flare of terror, and, wrenching her hand away, she fell back with a cry, her gaze riveted upon my throat.

'That accursed mark! What is it? What is it?...' she cried, shivering from head to foot.

In an instant, the wild blood singing in my head, I sprang towards her. What would have followed I know not, but at that moment the door opened and Sir William returned. He regarded us with consternation; but Miss Bosanquet had fainted, and the next moment he was at her side. I stood near, watching her come to with a certain nameless fury, as of a beast cheated of its prey. Sir William turned to me, and in his most courteous manner begged me to excuse the untoward scene. His daughter, he said, was not at all strong, and he ended by suggesting that I should leave them for a time.

Reluctantly I obeyed, but when I was out of the house, I took a sudden panic. The demoniac possession lifted, and in a craven state of trembling I saddled my horse, and rode for the Abbey as if my life depended upon my speed.

I arrived at about ten o'clock, and immediately gave orders to have my bed prepared in my old room. In my shaken condition the sinister influences of that stone chamber terrified me; and it was not until I had drunk deeply that I regained my composure.

But I was destined to get little sleep. I had steadily resolved to keep my thoughts off the matter until the morning, but the spell of the chamber was strong upon me. I awoke after midnight with an irresistible feeling drawing me to the room. I was conscious of the impulse, and combated it, but in the end succumbed; and throwing on my clothes, took a light and went downstairs. I flung wide the door of the room and peered in, listening, as though for some voice of welcome. It was as silent as a sepulchre; but directly I crossed the threshold voices seemed to surround and coax me. I stood wavering, with a curious fascination upon me. I knew I could not return to my own room, and I now had no desire to do so. As I stood, my candle flaring solemnly against the darkness, I noticed upon the floor in an alcove bare of carpet, a large black mark, which appeared to be a stain. Bending down, I examined it, passing my fingers over the stone. It moved to my touch. Setting the candle upon the floor, I put my fingertips to the edges, and pulled hard. As I did so the sounds that were ringing in my ears died instantaneously; the next moment the slab turned with a crash, and discovered a gaping hole of impenetrable blackness.

The patch of chasm thus opened to my eyes was near a yard square. The candle held to it shed a dim light upon a stone step a foot or two below, and it was clear to me that a stairway communicated with the depths. Whether it had been used as a cellar in times gone by I could not divine, but I was soon to determine this doubt; for, stirred by a strange eagerness, I slipped my legs through the hole, and let myself cautiously down with the light in my hand. There were a dozen steps to descend ere I reached the floor and what turned out to be a narrow passage. The vault ran forward straight as an arrow before my eyes, and slowly I moved on. Dank and chill was the air in those close confines, and the sound of my feet returned from those walls dull and sullen. But I kept on, and, with infinite care, must have penetrated quite a hundred yards along that musty corridor ere I came out upon an ampler chamber. Here the air was freer, and I could perceive with the aid of my light that the dimensions of the place were lofty. Above, a solitary ray of moonlight, sliding through a crack, informed me that I was not far from the level of the earth. It fell upon a block of stone, which rose in the middle of the vault, and which I now inspected with interest. As the candle threw its flickering beams upon this I realised where I was. I scarcely needed the rude lettering upon the coffins to acquaint me that here was the family vault of the Marvyns. And now I began to perceive upon all sides whereon my feeble light fell the crumbling relics of the forgotten dead – coffins fallen into decay, bones and grinning skulls resting in corners, disposed by the hand of chance and time. This formidable array of the mortal remains of that poor family moved me to a shudder. I turned from those ugly memorials once more to the central altar where the two coffins rested in this sombre silence. The lid had fallen from the one, disclosing to my sight the grisly skeleton of a man, that mocked and leered at me. It seemed in a manner to my fascinated eyes to challenge my mortality, inviting me too to the rude and grotesque sleep of death. I knew, as by an instinct, that I was standing by the bones of Sir Rupert Marvyn, the protagonist in that terrible crime which had locked three souls in eternal ruin. The consideration of this miserable spectacle held me motionless for some moments, and then I moved a step closer and cast my light upon the second coffin.

As I did so I was aware of a change within myself. The grave and melancholy thoughts which I had entertained, the sober bent of my solemn reflections, gave place instantly to a strange exultation, an unholy sense of elation. My pulse swung feverishly, and, while my eyes were riveted upon the tarnished silver of the plate, I stretched forth a tremulously eager hand and touched the lid. It rattled gently under my fingers. Disturbed by the noise, I hastily withdrew them; but whether it was the impetus offered by my touch, or through some horrible and nameless circumstance – God knows – slowly and softly a gap opened between the lid and the body of the coffin! Before my startled eyes the awful thing happened, and yet I was conscious of no terror, merely of surprise and – it seems terrible to admit – of a feeling of eager expectancy. The lid rose slowly on the one side, and as it lifted the dark space between it and the coffin grew gently charged with light. At that moment my feeble candle, which had been gradually diminishing, guttered and flickered. I seemed to catch a glimpse of something, as it were, of white and shining raiment inside the coffin; and then came a rush of wings and a whirring sound within the vault. I gave a cry, and stepping back missed my foothold; the guttering candle was jerked from my grasp, and I fell prone to the floor in darkness. The next moment a sheet of flame flashed in the chamber and lit up the grotesque skeletons about me; and at the same time a piercing cry rang forth. Jumping to my feet, I gave a dazed glance at the conflagration. The whole vault was in flames. Dazed and horror-struck, I rushed blindly to the entrance; but as I did so the horrible cry pierced my ears again, and I saw the bat swoop round and circle swiftly into the flames. Then, finding the exit, I dashed with all the speed of terror down the passage, groping my way along the walls, and striking myself a dozen times in my terrified flight.

Arrived in my room, I pushed over the stone and listened. Not a sound was audible. With a white face and a body torn and bleeding I rushed from the room, and locking the door behind me, made my way upstairs to my bedroom. Here I poured myself out a stiff glass of brandy.

★ ★ ★ ★ ★

It was six months later ere Warrington returned. In the meantime he had sold the Abbey. It was inevitable that he should do so; and yet the new owner, I believe, has found no drawback in his property, and the Stone Chamber is still used for a bedroom upon occasions, being considered very old-fashioned. But there are some facts against which no appeal is possible, and so it was in his case. In my relation of the tragedy I have made no attempt at explanation, hardly even to myself; and it appears now for the first time in print, of course with suppositious names.

About Us

In addition to No Exit Press, Oldcastle Books has a number
of other imprints, including Kamera Books, Creative Essentials,
Pulp! The Classics, Pocket Essentials and High Stakes Publishing
> oldcastlebooks.co.uk

For more information about Crime Books go to > crimetime.co.uk

Check out the kamera film salon for independent, arthouse and
world cinema > kamera.co.uk

For more information, media enquiries and review copies please
contact Harriet > Harriet@oldcastlebooks.com